Homecoming Chaos

Homecoming Chaos

A Model MD Novel

D. W. BROOKS

Homecoming Chaos: This is a work of fiction; therefore, the novel's story and characters are fictitious. Any public agencies, institutions, or historical figures mentioned in the story serve as a backdrop to the characters and their actions, which are wholly imaginary.

Cover design by 100covers.com

Publisher's Cataloging-in-Publication data

Names: Brooks, D. W., author.
Title: Homecoming chaos : a model MD novel / D. W. Brooks.
Description: Houston, TX: Life: The Reboot, LLC, 2023.
Identifiers: LCCN: 2023908328 | ISBN: 979-8-218-15050-1 (paperback) | 979-8-9890807-1-7 (Kindle) | 979-8-9890807-0-0 (ePUB)
Subjects: LCSH Physicians--Fiction. | Family--Fiction. |African-Americans--Fiction. | Atlanta (Ga.)--Fiction. | Mystery fiction. | Romance fiction. | Love stories. | BISAC FICTION /Romance / Suspense | FICTION / Mystery & Detective / African American & Black | FICTION / Romance / African American & Black
Classification: LCC PS3602 .R66 H6 2023 | DDC 813.6--dc23

Printed in Houston, TX, USA.

Dedication

To my husband, who has offered so much amazing support during this long journey.

To my parents, who knew I wanted to write since I was little but unfortunately didn't get to see that dream come to fruition.

To my family and friends, who kept telling me to get it done, even when it looked like there was no hope.

To Raymond Oglesby and Robert Bell, who both reviewed this manuscript. Thank you for your help.

To Liza, who helped me get this moving and for being an amazing source of support and friend. I owe you!

Homecoming Chaos

Prologue

"Can I buy you a drink?"

Rachel lifted her head to see who was intruding on her private funk. The man was reasonably attractive, with an eager expression on his face. After a quick visual scan, Rachel couldn't find anything wrong with him; his only flaw was that he was *there*. Perhaps a bar on a Friday night was the wrong place to indulge in a grump session; men and women were out *en masse* looking for a good time. Hell, five months ago, she would have been searching for a good time as well.

Before Ben.

Now, after Ben, she wasn't quite ready for the requisite small talk to determine if she wanted to see this smiling face in the morning.

"No? Well, it looks like you've had a long day. Me, too," he said, edging up to the bar next to her stool and attempting to get the busy bartender's attention. At least he didn't break out a lame pickup line. A sidelong glance showed a pleasant-looking man of average height with green eyes and blond curly hair. Just intriguing enough to warrant a quick chat. Rachel sipped her glass of red wine—she nursed one drink on days like this, she wanted to think—and tucked a strand of her bobbed shoulder-length blond hair behind her ear.

"Just trying to unwind after a long week. What's your damage?" she asked and flashed a quick smile. Her smile was her pull—it brightened her face and highlighted her hazel eyes.

He smiled at Rachel as the bartender made her way over. "Work sucks, but what's new?" he replied with a chuckle. After ordering his drink, he turned to face her. "I'm sorry your week was tough. A pretty girl like you should enjoy herself. Do you come here often?"

Inwardly cringing, Rachel maintained eye contact as she said, "I haven't been here in a while. But it's close to my job, and I needed a drink and a change of scenery." *Here comes the barrage of tired pickup lines,* she thought.

True to expectations, he said, "Change of scenery?" He winked at her and continued, "I can fix that. Let's get out of here and go somewhere more private so that we can *talk*."

Ugh! Rachel groaned and dropped her head. When would she ever learn? Looking him in the eyes, she asked, "That's your line? That's all I get? You didn't even show any imagination there, huh?" Picking up her glass, she stood to face him. At her full height of five foot one, she had to tilt her head back to see his eyes. "Work on your game and don't lead with the punchline. Have a wonderful evening," she said and inched through the crowd to another section of the bar, leaving the now embarrassed man to nurse his loss.

Shaking her head, Rachel eyed another potential spot to nurse her drink. Finding an empty stool close to the door, she made her way over and slid onto the seat. There were only couples around her, so she thought she might sit quietly and think. If this didn't work, she would just leave—this bar trip may not have been a good idea. Settling in, she retreated into her mind, considering her job and her past.

Rachel loved her job as a lab assistant and was excited about going to work every day. She majored in microbiology in college with a plan of attending medical school. Actual anatomy had stymied her, so she canceled that plan and earned her master's degree. Originally, she wasn't sure what to do with that degree, but a career fair introduced her to forensics. For three years, she worked at a successful lab and spent most of her time doing toxicology and different DNA tests. Not much microbiology. But helping to solve mysteries and figuring out who a hair or bodily fluid sample belonged to was fun. Rachel was efficient and tried to help other technicians out when she finished her tasks. She believed this would put her in a position to become a supervisor. She was close to a promotion—she could feel it. Yet, given her history in Wisconsin, it was amazing she made it this far.

"Excuse me. Do I know you?" Another male voice drifted into her consciousness. Glancing up, she saw an older man—rather out of place for this joint—neatly dressed but not dressed to impress. Definitely not someone she knew, and hopefully not someone who was trying to pick her up.

"Sorry, sir. I don't think so. I'm just leaving," she said. He looked disappointed.

Coming to this Happy Hour was obviously a bad idea. She needed to go home now. Since she was near the door, it took only moments to escape the confines of the bar. December in Atlanta was typically chilly. This afternoon had been a bit more temperate, and while she was wearing a dark-blue sleeveless sheath dress, she left her matching sweater at the office. Now it was cold and dark. Looking at her watch, she noticed it was a little after eight. Not too late to swing back by the lab and pick up her sweater before heading home for the weekend. She opened her bag to look for her valet ticket.

The older gentleman had followed her outside to the valet stand.

"I'm sure I know you," he said, touching her arm. "Didn't you attend college in Wisconsin?"

Rachel stopped, puzzled. "Yes, I did, in Madison. Did we have a class together?" She held up a finger to ask the valet to wait for a moment while she listened to the man, now curious.

"No, I'm older than you." He smiled, then plowed forward. "I used to work at a diner, Mickie's Dairy Bar, by the campus. I remember you used to come in with several friends to get breakfast once a week—I believe you had a name for it. It always stuck with me because you were all such cute girls who liked science. I can't believe I ran into you here. Small world, huh?"

Rachel remembered the Micro Breakfast Club and eating at Mickie's with her friends, but she didn't remember him. That wasn't a surprise. But how else would he know about something that happened several years ago and so many miles away? She smiled at him pleasantly while trying to place his face. He looked to be in his sixties, thin, short gray hair, medium build, about six feet tall, and glasses. Nothing sparked her memory.

"Well, that brings back memories. How long have you been down here?" she asked, trying not to freak out, the valet stub forgotten.

"I've been living in Atlanta for about a year and moved here mainly because of my daughter. I don't *love* this town, but what can I do?" He smiled back, noticing her discomfort. "I didn't mean to hold you up. It's so nice to meet someone from the past. Would you like to get a cup of coffee and reminisce about Wisconsin?"

Rachel shook her head. "I just came here for a drink to unwind. I need to get some sleep. It's been a really long week."

"Are you sure? I miss Wisconsin. Everyone seemed friendlier there, like they cared about each other. Maybe it's because I'm new here. It's not as cozy as my hometown." He paused. "I remember one time when this girl at the college had gotten into trouble on campus—something about a boy—her friends tried to help her out. Would that happen here? This city is enormous." He took a cigarette out of his pocket and lit it. "Hey, wasn't that girl one of your friends? Part of the Micro Club?"

Rachel momentarily narrowed her eyes, but maintained her composure as she grew more nervous. "No, I don't think so." She felt a flicker of recognition, but it faded. *Who is this?* she wondered.

"You know, I think she was. Bianca was her name, I think. What happened to her? Do you know?" He stood there puffing on his cigarette. A chill went down Rachel's spine. His eyes seemed cold, though his words were, supposedly, inoffensive. "I think she died. Didn't she?" he added, dropping his cigarette on the ground and stepping on it.

She was now officially unnerved. "Who the hell are you?" Rachel asked. "What do you want? Stay away from me, or I'll scream!" With pointed urgency, she resumed the search for her valet ticket and backed away from the stranger a few steps.

He laughed menacingly. "Oh, I'm sorry. I didn't mean to upset you. Seeing you brought back some memories, like when we first met. I guess you don't remember. I didn't mean to scare you. Maybe one day we could meet for a coffee?"

Something about his voice: Rachel had a quick flash of recognition—and of their first meeting. His appearance was different. He seemed different from before, more sinister. She had no intention of meeting him again, anywhere, but tried to be polite. "Oh yeah. Now I remember. Let me get your contact information—and your name…"

"Oh, that's right. You don't remember my name. I'm William. Here's my card." He handed his card to her. "I look forward to seeing you again." He pivoted and quickly strolled back into the bar.

Rachel watched him walk away, then started rifling through her purse with more urgency. *That was weird and scary*, she thought. She found her valet stub and handed it to the young parking attendant, who had tried to be discreet as he'd eavesdropped.

"Are you OK? Do you need me to call anyone?" The valet also was a touch shaken by the intensity of the encounter.

She shook her head and exhaled. She didn't realize that she had been holding her breath while William (if that was his name) walked away. Luckily, another person was waiting in line by then, and the valet retrieved her car in less than five minutes. She spent those minutes peering over her shoulder, hoping William wouldn't come back outside. She wasn't alone, but those moments with William had frightened her. While she hadn't finished her one drink at the bar, any slight buzz she might have had was completely gone at this point. She exhaled again when her car appeared.

Sliding into her vehicle, she drove off. The lab was three blocks away. While she drove, her mind drifted to William's words. She remembered Bianca. The situation was *way* more complicated than William knew. Rachel had tried not to think about those horrible events over the past six years. She hated getting sucked into a whirlwind of painful memories and the flood of renewed guilt over what went down.

I'm sorry, she thought, as she struggled not to cry. How did he find her? How did he find her *here*? As she drove, she became more and more unnerved. She grabbed her cell phone from her purse and called the one person who would understand.

No answer. *Damn it! Typical. Probably with some guy.* She left a frantic message, hoping her friend would pick it up soon.

There was no gate at the lab's parking lot entrance, but she had to use her entry card to gain access to the front door, elevator, and her office on the third floor. There were only a few cars in the lot. No one was at the security desk—probably time for rounds—so she skipped the sign-in sheet and entered the elevator.

The doors opened onto the third floor. It was almost completely dark. The third floor was usually empty by six on Fridays. As a cost-saving measure, only the first floor was open for any weekend or after-hours projects.

She hadn't been lying to the guy at the bar. Rachel was tired, and her conversation with William had further drained her. She had planned to grab her sweater and go home. Standing at her desk, she couldn't resist checking her work email one more time. She could use the mental diversion. Placing her key chain and entry card on her desk, she leaned over to log into her account—mostly routine work stuff. But the last email in her account grabbed her attention—in the wrong way.

Shit, she thought, as she printed it out. *This can't be happening.*

Rachel closed her eyes and sank into her desk chair. Bianca's face flashed in front of her, as did the events of that long-ago evening. She picked up her key chain and turned it over in her hands. On the chain itself, there was a flash drive that she removed from the ring. Holding it up, Rachel took a long, hard look at it.

Some people would be happy to get their hands on this, she thought. *I should turn it in*. But she didn't have the courage. With the William encounter and that email, she felt everything closing in. She slid the flash drive into her top drawer and locked it.

By the time Rachel reached the first floor with her sweater and email in hand, the security guard was still not at his post. She noted that because he was only supposed to be away for a maximum of five minutes. Rachel smiled to herself. She would have to mention this to the head of security on Monday. Getting additional points with the bosses would help her get that promotion. Shaking her head, she walked to her car, thinking ahead to the bottle of wine she had in the refrigerator in her apartment.

But once she reached her car, her stomach dropped. She saw a familiar face: one she recognized instantly—another blast from the past.

"What are *you* doing here? How did *you* find me?" she asked.

The man grinned. "It's fate." He stepped toward her as she nervously shifted her weight from side to side.

This can't be happening, she thought, as he reached her.

1
Return to Atlanta

The sound of the flight attendant on the loudspeaker startled Jamison Jones Scott out of her light sleep. Despite having traveled frequently in her lifetime, she still couldn't sleep comfortably on a plane. The seat location—first-class or economy—didn't make a difference. The plane was nearing its destination, so the passengers needed to finish filling out their declaration cards. Jamie was returning to Atlanta to stay at her parents' home with only the clothes on her back, a computer bag, the few items of clothing in her duffel, and a stethoscope. She had nothing to declare.

Her seatmate appeared to be sleeping through the announcements. Jamie was jealous. The four-year-old in front of her turned around and started babbling excitedly in French. She must have noticed that Jamie was finally awake. With her head still fuzzy from her nap, Jamie couldn't completely follow the child's rapid words, but the gist was that she wanted something from Jamie. Something about a playdate? Jamie smiled at the girl and hoped the girl's mother would intervene. No such luck; she was asleep as well. The child eyeballed Jamie expectantly. Jamie realized she and the seatmate had started this situation by playing with the dark-haired child while they were over the ocean. Now, when she didn't agree to the latest request, the little girl scrunched up her face to cry.

"Nous atterrissons bientôt. Elle ne peut pas aller avec vous," Jamie's seatmate answered, eyes still closed. "Mais vous pourriez être en mesure de visiter. Je suis sûr qu'elle tu aimerait garder les enfants." He grinned.

Jamie gasped while the young girl clapped. This guy had just volunteered her as a babysitter!

"Je suis désolé, mais il se trompe. Je ne serai pas disponible," Jamie stated. "Je parie qu'il a une surprise, pour toi." The child looked at Jamie's seatmate for her present and clapped again. This reply made him open his eyes.

"Qu'est-ce que c'est? Qu'est-ce que c'est?" the child asked. Startled, her pregnant mother woke up and turned around in her seat sheepishly.

I'm sorry, she mouthed. She made her eager daughter turn around in her seat and asked her to leave the other passengers alone. The girl was disappointed, but her mother handed her a shortbread, which made her forget the people behind her.

Her seatmate smiled, opened his eyes, and said, "I could have given her the stuffed bear I bought. I have a daughter the same age." He stretched gingerly. "I can't wait to get home. I've been traveling for too long. What about you? Looking forward to getting home?"

Jamie thought about her return to Atlanta. She hadn't been home in a while, so she wasn't sure how she felt.

Revel in the chaos.

Revel in the chaos.
Revel in the chaos.

Jamie tried to live by this motto for most of her life because her life seemed to invite chaos. She learned to expect—and sometimes encourage—complications. As the plane taxied to a halt, she repeated her motto to herself. This phrase, tattooed on her right hip, particularly applied now.

The international terminal of Hartsfield-Jackson Airport had changed since she was last there. Her brother, Jonathan, would pick her up at the baggage claim—alone, she hoped, and not sporting a clingy girlfriend. Time to re-acclimate and re-establish family bonds. Dealing with an unknown woman in her face when she wanted to spend time quietly with her brother wasn't at the top of her to-do list.

As she waited in line to get through passport control, she thought about how she got to this point—back in Atlanta after several years abroad. She had spent two of those years working with the non-profit organization Doctors Overseas. Jamie worked in several locations, including the Central African Republic. She had her reasons for joining the charitable organization; not all were altruistic, and she kept those to herself during her entrance interview. The horrors she witnessed overseas helped her put her personal chaos into perspective. She realized her issues were nothing compared to what people endured in other parts of the world. This realization allowed her to embrace her job and enjoy what she was doing, despite the frequent threats of bodily harm. To help maintain her sanity while overseas, she traveled a lot and spent six months in Italy working with a designer friend.

The agent summoning her snapped her out of her reverie. Handing over her passport, she said, "Nothing to declare. Coming back home for my mother's birthday and Christmas."

At the check-in counter, the inspector carefully examined her and her passport photo. Jamison understood the scrutiny. At the time of that picture, she had been at the height of her glamor phase with a history of modeling and a resulting, above-average concern about how she looked. In medical school, she often showed up at rounds with perfectly coiffed hair and more than a swipe of mascara and lip gloss.

But in Africa, those concerns fell away. Right now, Jamie was makeup-free, and a baseball cap covered her hair. She was still beautiful, but now it was a girl-next-door beauty. Jamie had high cheekbones, almond-shaped dark brown eyes, a straight nose, a square jawline, and her golden-brown skin was still smooth. She wasn't stomping down runways anymore, as in her past life, because she had shifted her priorities.

Her mother would hate it.

"Welcome to Atlanta," the inspector said as she stamped her passport. "Have a pleasant stay."

Jamie breezed through customs after obtaining her two bags. As she neared the baggage claim area, she glanced around for her baby brother. "Baby" didn't apply anymore—he was only one year younger, at 33, and an unmarried architect. He was four inches taller than her and, at six-foot-three, should have been easy to spot. Their last conversation, almost two weeks ago, led to a discussion of his attempts to extricate himself from his latest three-month stand. Typically, he met a beautiful woman, declared himself "in love" after a week, and then bent himself into a pretzel to get free. Her years away hadn't changed this pattern. Jamie didn't see her brother at the luggage carousel they had selected. Impatiently, she reached into her pocket for her cell phone.

"Jamie Jay! Are you lost?" a husky voice whispered in her ear. Using his childhood nickname for her, Jamie whirled around to see her brother.

Jonathan stood before her, as handsome as ever and *alone*. Wearing a pair of pressed khakis and a light blue oxford shirt, he looked like he could have been a model himself. His skin was a shade darker than Jamie's, and he had high cheekbones, a square jawline, and long eyelashes! No wonder the girls fell hard!

"Jon-Jon! It's great to see you!" Jamie excitedly threw herself into his arms. She suddenly remembered the safe feeling of getting a hug from her younger brother. Tears pricked at the back of her eyes. Maybe coming home wouldn't be so tough. She had missed this guy.

Jonathan stepped back for a second. "Wow, you look amazing, but you've *changed*! I've never seen you in public without makeup," he noted, tilting her face from side to side. "Why were you wearing all that stuff before? You look so much younger now," he teased and hugged her again. "Are these your bags? Is this it?"

"One small black laptop bag and a green duffel bag. My entire life fits into two pieces of luggage and a fanny pack these days, and that includes medical gear." She smiled at him. "Younger, huh? I *feel* older. Things I witnessed in Africa put years on you."

"I'll give you that. But I *know* you had some fun, too. You can tell me all about it." He turned to observe the flow of the moving crowd to the automatic doors. "I paid to park today, so let's grab your gear fast and get back to the car. Mother and Dad are eager to see you. They're both at the house waiting for us."

Jamie bit her lip in confusion. "Waiting for me *now*? Won't I get to freshen up first? At least wash my hair? Oh God, she's going to freak out, isn't she?" she asked with concern.

"Eh, she knows you said you're different. I suspect she believes you got fat or something." As Jamie opened her mouth in protest, he added, "Don't shoot the messenger. I know you were working in war-torn countries and likely wouldn't get fat. You know Mother. She has certain expectations, and logic doesn't always play into them. When she goes off on these tangents, Dad just shakes his head."

It sounded like some things hadn't changed. Jonathan led her toward the exit, holding her bags. Once outside, Jon resumed his comments.

"Besides, Mother's busy trying to work her magic on her grandbabies since they may be the only ones she ever has," he continued. "Jillian's grateful for the help, so she doesn't care if Mother gets too pushy. You know Jillian has four kids now? She told me she has been feeling tired lately. I bet she's going to have another baby."

At the mention of children, Jamie stopped short for a moment—a fellow traveler almost bumped into her and brushed by her angrily. After mumbling an apology, Jamie continued, this time walking and talking. "You're kidding. Not number five? How does she manage the four? I knew Richard wanted a lot of kids, but didn't he already have two before marrying her? Isn't a small army enough?" Jamie said, as they crossed the street to the parking deck.

"He wants a girl. He had two sons with his first wife, and now he and Jillian have four more boys."

"Really? What are the odds of that after six boys? Anyway, I don't remember Jillian wanting a lot of kids. I guess it works for them," Jamie said. "What level?" she asked when they reached the elevator.

"Three. I got lucky." He pressed the elevator button. "What about you, Jamie Jay? Have you changed your stance on children? I know you didn't want any when you left. Wasn't that one reason you called off your wedding? Broke Mother's heart?" he smirked as they exited the elevator. "I kid about the breaking of Mother's heart. Kind of. Here's my car."

He stopped in front of a gray convertible Mercedes and put her bags down. Jamie's heart sank. "You didn't bring my car?"

"That car is a gas-guzzling contraption. It's at my house taking up space. I had hoped you had wised up while you were away." Jamie's vehicle was a black 1969 Chevy Camaro. Jon hated it. Everyone in the family hated it. "Toss your gear in the trunk. I've done my job." He laughed as he got in the driver's seat and popped the trunk.

Jamie tossed her luggage in the open trunk. She had been carrying her luggage here and there for several years now and had been uncomfortable when Jonathan first grabbed it. Eh, she was back in America and needed to readjust to some displays of chivalry.

She slid into the passenger's side and continued their conversation. "I don't think I broke Mother's heart. She *was* angry with me. Do you think she was 'heartbroken'?" Jamie quizzed.

Jonathan drove to the tollgate and paid the fee. As he pulled into the street, he glanced at Jamie. "Really? Do you think breaking off your engagement to a surgeon and canceling the wedding, declining a job with a prominent medical clinic, declaring that you don't want children, and making plans to move to Africa, all within three days, didn't upset Mother? *And* Dad? Hell, I was upset, too!" He shook his head. "We thought you were happy, and then to find that nothing was right with you was hard to hear. And then you were gone…"

"I didn't plan it that way. I just couldn't pretend anymore. There was just so much going on in my head."

"Like what? I know you weren't in love with some of the wedding plans. You never told us about anything else, including me. You just *left*. Holidays, birthdays, you were just gone. It's been hard on the parents."

"And you?" Jamie asked.

"You know me. I missed you, but I don't get all sensitive. I leave all the hurt feelings to my sisters."

"Oh, I don't know what to say." She paused for a moment. "I spent a lot of time thinking and dealing with some of my demons, and I'm in a much better place now. I can handle my issues instead of just running." She tipped her chin up resolutely.

"Demons? You said nothing about that. You know I would have listened."

"I left because there were some things that I wasn't ready to deal with. Did you know my going to college was a brokered deal with Mother and Dad? I agreed to go under some duress." Jamie paused and took a breath, unsure if she wanted to continue. Talking about that painful situation always brought back all the feelings. Could she get through the details without crying? Would Jon even understand? She had only been back in the country for an hour, and the chaos had already begun. *Geez!*

"Did you know I lived with a photographer in New York while I was modeling when I was sixteen?" Jamie asked Jonathan,

Jonathan snickered. "How did you get away with that?"

"Emancipation." Jonathan gasped as Jamie continued. "No, I told Mother I was renting an apartment with three other models. Whenever Mother came to town, I met her at that apartment, but I had moved in with my boyfriend. I was so in love with Zach that I didn't care about lying to her. I was making *great* money, especially for a teenager." She fiddled with the zipper on her fanny pack. "I had no intention of *ever* going to college. All that mattered was my soul mate," she said, making air quotes. "I had no long-term plans."

He gave her an incredulous side-eye. "I'm surprised. Before the engagement fiasco, you always seemed to be the most agreeable of us all." Jonathan considered her previous statement. "So, how did Mom and Dad get you to attend college?"

Another deep breath. "I got pregnant," Jamie whispered.

"What?" Jonathan turned in his seat to stare at her. "I never knew about that."

"Keep your eyes on the road." She called his shocked attention back before continuing. "I'm very good at secrets. I got it honestly," she said. "Remember, I rarely came home while I was in NYC, so no one knew what I was doing. As a model, I had to stay skinny." She paused again, a wave of relief flooding over her. Finally, the secret was out—partially. "I started rationing my food, but that didn't work for me. Instead, I began throwing up my food. Thus, I was half-assedly taking the pill, and ta-da, I was pregnant."

"Did Mother know you were on birth control? I remember Mother telling you and Jillian that only loose women needed birth control if they weren't married," Jonathan asked.

"Didn't tell her." Jamie mimicked the old-fashioned lectures that Margaret repeatedly gave her and her sister. "Only women who weren't raised right needed birth control. Keep your legs closed, and there will be no need. Don't want to ruin my chances of marrying a suitable man, you know," she said. "It's what her mother told her, so she told us."

"So, you had an abortion?"

She gazed out the window as they sped down Interstate 75/85. This was when talking got hard. But she had promised herself she wouldn't start this visit by holding back—that always led to big ugly explosions. No more of those… "I gave her up for adoption," she whispered.

It was all Jonathan could do not to swerve off the road. *Did Jamie have a baby*? "How did I not know this? Why didn't you say anything?" He gaped at the news and tried to remember if he had missed any signs back then. Probably, but he had only been 15.

"It was a tough time. Really tough." She shot him a glance with tear-rimmed eyes. Everything was coming back, and her heart broke a little all over again. *Damn—here come the tears*. "Mother took over and set up the adoption. I had no say. I didn't even tell her I was pregnant until I was six months along. It's a miracle the baby survived. I wasn't taking care of myself or her. Mother admitted me to an exclusive clinic in New York, where I stayed until I gave birth. Part of the deal was that I would enroll in school afterward."

"That sounds like a deal Mother would make. Appearances and all." Regaining his composure, Jonathan asked quietly, "Do you know where your daughter is?"

"Nope. I didn't want to know then. She can find me now if she wants because I'm OK with her searching for me. For a long time, I tried to pretend it never happened."

"Was med school part of the deal, too?"

"No, I needed to improve my standing in Mother's eyes. I couldn't believe I made such a mess on my own. Med school was respectable. I considered OB/GYN but ended up in dermatology." She took a deep breath and exhaled, as if releasing pent-up stress. "Respectability and perfection. They're huge expectations to live up to."

"Man, that sounds heavy, and I wish you had told me. I know I was only in high school, but maybe I could have helped. I know I don't get the same pressure from Mother as you and Jillian, but I could've been there for you."

Jamie nodded, not trusting her voice. It was still painful, but she had kept the tears at bay. *Baby steps.*

Jon exhaled slowly while stealing another side glance at his sister. A lot was going on there—he could see it on her face. He wanted more information—she seemed willing to talk, and he wanted to listen. Before she left town, he had considered her his best friend. "So, why did you call off the wedding?"

Good question—Jamie had searched for this answer over the past four years. "Even though no one knew about New York, I knew. *The* entire situation embarrassed me. I started dating Eddie during my residency. He was lovely and on track to be prestigious and *respectable*! *And* he was handsome." More fiddling with the zipper. "Want to know a secret?" she asked Jon but continued immediately without waiting for his answer. "I almost said no when he proposed."

"As you know, I've avoided marriage, too." He laughed for a moment, then shifted uncomfortably in his seat. “It’s upsetting that you kept all of this to yourself. I feel like I missed a big part of your life.”

“I’m not very good at expressing feelings, which Eddie constantly mentioned while we were engaged. I thought I could get better, so I said yes. But a huge wedding? The thought of having more children and working part-time forever? Being only with Eddie forever? It just seemed *boring*.” She studied the roof of the car. “I started having eating issues again and hanging out in Buckhead. I woke up in some places with some people I didn’t know and who weren’t *Eddie*. It was out of character for me.”

Jonathan cocked his head. “I thought that was my domain. I have been in compromising positions a few times myself,” he said, interrupting her, trying to lighten the mood a bit.

“But you weren’t engaged. I needed to straighten myself out before I could move forward.” She licked her lips. “I couldn’t keep lying to Eddie like that. But I couldn’t pretend that I was happy, either. Mother didn’t understand how I could leave everything on the table like that. That was the original cause of our last fight. Of course, *everything* came up, every mistake I had ever made. It was ugly.”

Jon let out a sigh. He hoped that this reunion would be joyful. This news made him suspect Jamie’s return might lead to a nasty confrontation.

Jamie continued, “Mother got married for potential. Not that she doesn’t love Dad, but she went against all conventions to hang on to what he was going to accomplish. It worked well for her—a massive house in Fulton County, part-owner of a forensics and research lab, member of Atlanta’s upper echelon. That strategy wasn’t for me.”

“Don’t be too hard on yourself. According to Mother, I should be married with kids, too, although she doesn’t lean on me as hard. A little more than before, but not as hard. Anyway, I can't seem to find the right girl," Jon comfortingly chipped in.

"That phrase, 'right girl', may be part of your problem," Jamie responded with a smile. Her younger brother was *SO* gorgeous and so wrong about so many ladies. "Look for a *woman*, one that has more on her mind than what she's wearing and what you're driving." She scanned the inside of the car as they rode. "I see your leather is still smooth, and your car's in one piece. So, Rena didn't destroy your car when you broke it off. I thought she was going to be attached to you when you picked me up."

He smiled at his big sister. "No, I'm trying a different approach. I spoke to her and broke it off nicely. Typically, I would have ignored her until she went away. That hasn't worked out so well." He gave Jamie a good-natured wink. "We'll see if she cuts up my clothes when I go pick up my stuff. Do you want to come with me? It might give you a reprieve before entering the lion's den." He hoped she would say yes. He had missed their talks and shenanigans, as Jamie had been present for many a breakup in the past. Reluctantly *and* with sarcasm, of course.

Gads. Walking into an angry ex's place with her brother wasn't on her list of things to do today, but the catharsis of telling most of what had happened had made her tired. Dealing with her brother's drama might be a welcome break. She would even be nice about her brother's situation. "Sure, let's go for it," Jamie replied. Maybe it would be an oddly fun reminder of past days.

"Rena's a nice girl, a student-teacher."

"Still twenty-one, right?" *That didn't last long...*

"Yeah, but she's an adult," he replied in his defense.

"Barely, man." *Oops…* Jamie couldn't resist the opportunity to poke at her baby brother's relationship follies. *He might regret the invite after this…* "You keep finding these girls who don't know the game. You tell them you love them, move 'em in, take 'em everywhere as if they're the next greatest thing, and then dump 'em. I bet she either bleached or destroyed your belongings. This may be worth the price of admission," she teased.

Jonathan had to acknowledge that Jamie was right. He dated girls in their early twenties. Immature girls with magnetism. Wonderful, sexy, freaky girls. But inevitably, he would figure out that he didn't have as much in common with them as he'd thought. He only saw the exterior of these women and spent *very* little time getting to know them. Jon realized this was a problem. He had certainly received his fair share of critique and questioning from his parents, sisters, and even the girls themselves. If he got out of this one without too much drama, perhaps he would take those comments to heart.

After navigating some Atlanta traffic on 400 and a quick phone call to Rena, they pulled into an apartment complex in Sandy Springs. Rena's apartment was in the last building of a nice, modestly appointed group of buildings. The Mercedes slid into a space in front of the building, but before either could exit the vehicle, a pile of clothes came flying over a second-story balcony.

"Is that your stuff?" Jamie leaned back in her seat in surprise. "I hope there wasn't anything of value here."

The pair walked to the pile of shredded and bleached material.

"Not a surprise." Jamie nudged the pile with her toe.

Both cautiously peered up at the balcony. A young, pretty woman with a short burgundy bob stuck her head over the railing.

"Jonathan, I can't believe you brought your new girl over here," Rena yelled down. "I don't believe your story. You never mentioned a sister!"

Jamie closed her eyes and shook her head incredulously. "What did you two do with your time? Wait, please don't answer that." To Rena, she said, "Hello. I'm his older sister, Jamison. He just picked me up from the airport. It's nice to meet you, even under these circumstances. You *seem* nice."

"I *am* nice. And even if *you* are his sister, I know he's dating someone else. He just disappeared one night. Didn't even let me know he was going." Her eyes welled with tears as she leaned over the balcony. "You said you loved me!"

Jamie rolled her eyes and turned back to her brother. Maybe this wasn't worth the price of admission, after all. "This is sad. Say *something*." This *was* bringing back memories—pitiful ones. *Jon owes me for this…*

Jonathan frowned at her and then turned to Rena. "I did love you. I still do. But not how you need to be loved." This was the standard statement Jonathan issued to all former girlfriends—his signature break-up line. It even sounded hollow to him this time. He hoped it didn't sound as bad to Rena. "You are a wonderful woman and will be a wonderful mate for someone ready for that kind of commitment. I'm not right now."

"You could've talked to me about it."

"You're right. I'm sorry. Let's get coffee and talk it out. Would that work?"

"When?" she asked, wringing her hands.

"My sister just got back to town after four years. So, I'm going to be busy for a while. I'll call you next week, I promise."

With that, Jonathan picked up his pile of ruined clothes and walked back to his car. Fortunately, they were dry. Unfortunately, they smelled strongly of bleach.

"This is the outcome I expected. Please, make sure you call her," Jamie told him as he passed her to put the ruined clothing in the trunk.

When they got into the car, Jonathan's cell phone rang. Looking at the display, he cautioned, "It's Mother."

"Damn, I guess I can't put it off any longer. Let's head to the house," Jamie said.

2
Home Sweet Home

"Here we are," Jonathan unnecessarily announced as they pulled up to the gate of their parents' neighborhood. He let down the car window and entered the code to open the gate. Their parents lived in a large mansion in an exclusive gated Buckhead neighborhood. As the car cruised past several equally impressive homes, Jamie appraised her surroundings and had a rush of memories from her last time on the Scott property.

That was the day she had canceled everything in her life and, after a fight with her mother, left the country. Looking back, Jamie knew she had handled everything horribly, even if her reasoning had been sound. She was a better, smarter person now. The past four years exposed Jamie to the most miserable circumstances, which changed her somewhat. She hoped she could show her newfound maturity to her family.

Jamie snapped back to the present when Jon reached their destination. In their parents' circular driveway,

Jonathan pulled up behind a white Land Rover and a black 7-Series BMW. There was a panel truck and a catering van further around the driveway.

"Lucky you—both Mother and Dad are home." Jonathan turned the car off. "Have you figured out how to start your first meeting with Mother in four years?"

"Nope. I'm going to wing it," she said and hopped out of the car. "I'll get my stuff after seeing Mother because I may have to go stay at a hotel." She smiled.

You might be right, Jonathan thought as he got out of the car.

Standing in the middle of the driveway, Jamie further surveyed her surroundings. "Why is there a van and a caterer here?" Jamie asked Jonathan. He regarded her strangely. He didn't have time to respond because a stately man appeared in the front doorway.

"Dad!" Jamie made her way to him. He was older, grayer, but still trim. Jamie and Jonathan got their height from Gregory, who was over six feet tall.

"Jamison! It is good to see you!" Dr. Gregory Scott said, opening his arms. She folded herself into her father's embrace. Oddly, she felt a few prickles of tears. She had missed him and his insistence on calling her by her given name. "I wasn't sure you were ever going to return," her father revealed.

Now she felt like shit. Her beef hadn't been with him, but she had punished him, too. *I have to make this up to him,* she thought.

"It's good to be home. It's been a long, exciting, and scary four years," she disclosed to him.

"I want you to tell me all about it. When I was younger, I thought about doing some work in third-world countries, but there was never time," Gregory said, ushering her into the foyer. "I admire you for doing that."

Jonathan followed them in.

A small, busy-looking woman approached Gregory and said, "I've made a couple of menu revisions based on the space and the number of expected people. Would you like to look, or should I show your wife?" She pushed up her glasses.

"Definitely show my wife. She's in the study just down that hall." He pointed to a corridor to the right.

"Thank you," the planner said as she trotted away. Jamie watched her disappear down the hall. Two men walked by from the backyard to the front door.

"What's going on here?" Jamie asked, this time to her father.

"Your mother's sixtieth birthday party. I thought that's why you came home."

"Uh, no. I didn't know there was a party. Jon, you didn't tell me that." She whirled around to look at him.

Jon assumed an innocent expression. "I thought you would figure that something was going on. It's her sixtieth birthday. Did you believe that there would be no celebration?" He smirked and headed to the kitchen. "You *have* been away a long time."

Jamie eyed her father helplessly. "I'm not prepared for the full-court press here. What am I going to wear? My hair? Oh, my God!" She then yelled at Jon's retreating form, "I'll get you for this. You did this on purpose!"

Gregory patted her on the back. "I'm sure you and your mother will work out your attire. You have two days. It won't require a miracle," he said, smiling, and kissed her on the cheek. "I want you to tell me about your travels after you settle into your old room. Where's your luggage?"

"It's in the car. I'll get it," she said, turning around.

"Get your brother to get it. He owes you, I guess. Let me have another hug." Jamie obliged. "It's so nice to see my eldest again. A lot has happened since you've been away." Gregory's voice was so soothing that Jamie's irritation with her current situation went down. *Oh, she missed her dad…*

The planner came out of the study looking flustered. She bumped into Gregory, dropped her papers, and gasped. "I'm so sorry. Your wife just made some requests that will be difficult to complete in *two* days." She and Gregory bent down to gather up the scattered documents. The planner thanked him, still flustered, and pulled out her phone to call her supplier and the caterer. "Excuse me, I have to deal with this," she said and ran off.

"I take it Mother hasn't changed these days," Jamie remarked.

"Your mother is who she is. That'll never change. But I know she missed you."

Jamie tried not to roll her eyes. "We'll see, Dad. I'll play it by ear." She was leery of that first meeting. She wasn't looking forward to having her heart ripped out and stomped on.

"Do you want to go freshen up, dear? You remember your room, right?" Gregory walked into the kitchen to send Jon out to get her luggage.

Jamie strolled to the wide and stately staircase that led upstairs. The glossy wooden banister had always been a temptation to the teenaged Scott siblings. During Jamie's holiday visits home, there had been several banister races—

one ending with Jillian needing stitches. The three swore to take the reason to the grave. Their mother would have killed them herself!

The house itself had changed little. Her mom had done some minimal redecorating, but the basic décor—classic contemporary—remained the same. As she reached the top step, she could see her brother heading out the front door to gather her bags. To her left was the "girls" wing, and to her right was Jon's room and the guest rooms. Her parents bought this house while she was in New York, so she had never lived here full time, only during the holidays. Still, she had some fabulous memories from those times. It was nice to be home again.

The first door to the left was the room assigned to her. Jamie entered the simply appointed room decorated in blue, white, and seafoam green. The attached bathroom incorporated blue and white colors. Jamie sat on the edge of the bed and looked around the room. Since she never lived here, the room didn't hold many personal touches, as did Jon's and Jillian's rooms. There were plenty of pillows, a complete set of cherry wood bedroom furniture, and a mid-sized flat-screen TV above the chest of drawers. It represented a fitting guest room since she was now a guest—a nervous guest at that. What if her mother verbally eviscerated her again? Could she deal? Jamie realized she was delaying her meeting with her mom for as long as possible. What else could she do to kill time?

She peeked in the closet to see if she had left any clothes behind from four years ago. Unfortunately, she found nothing that would be appropriate for what would be a formal event on Sunday night.

She went into the bathroom and removed her baseball cap to inspect the state of her hair in the mirror. It was fine for a quiet home visit, but not for a dressy affair. Jamie had let her relaxer grow out while she was out of the country. She typically flat-twisted her natural hair to emphasize the wave pattern. Before this trip, she had only washed, conditioned, and air-dried her hair, thinking that she would have some time after her arrival to moisturize and comb it. Now, it was just squashed down by her hat. *Ugh.* Since she wouldn't be able to prep before talking to her mother, she would have to atone by looking her best for the party. For such a formal affair, she would have to visit a salon for a trim and style.

There was a knock on the bedroom door. "Come in!" Jamie yelled as she tucked her cap back onto her head and came out of the bathroom. Jon placed her bags inside her door. "Mother is waiting for you downstairs. I'm going to my room to avoid the tearful reunion." He didn't live there anymore but still called his childhood room "his room".

Jamie sighed. Time to woman up. "OK. Let me wash my face, and I'll be down. Where is she, exactly?" she inquired.

"Still in the study. Good luck." He went down the hall.

Jamie dug around in her duffel bag and found her makeup bag. It contained the bare minimum of cosmetics. She returned to her bathroom, washed her face, and added mascara and a touch of mauve lip gloss. Jamie checked herself. Not too bad for a woman that had spent the last 24 hours on a plane or in an airport. Before she lost her nerve, she pushed herself out of the room and down the stairs, where she came face-to-face with her younger sister, Jillian, with two of her sons. Jillian was shorter than Jamie but had the same facial shape and skin color. You could tell they were sisters. Jillian stopped short.

"PJ! I didn't know you were here. Give me a hug!" she joyously stretched out her arms. Quickly, she embraced Jamie while the 3-year-old and 1-year-old boys clung to her legs. The boys had never seen Jamie before because they were born while she was away. "You look sensational. Africa was good for you!" Jillian complimented.

"You look magnificent as well. I see you're still calling me PJ."

Perfect Jamie. Jillian smirked. "Well, it still fits, huh?"

Jamie ignored the snide comment and turned to her nephews. "Who are these little men? And where are the others?" Jamie stooped to their eye level.

Jillian stooped as well and disengaged the arms of the smallest boy. "This is Aaron." Aaron hid his head on his mother's shoulder. The other boy had moved behind his mother and peeked out from around her back. "This one behind me is Jacob. He's three. Jacob, this is your Aunt Jamie. Go on, hug her."

Jacob obediently came out and walked up to his aunt. "Hello," he started. "Do you want to play with me?"

"Sure, Jacob. What do you want to play?" Jamie asked, smiling.

"Gamma plays Candy Land with me on the computer. Do you want to play, too?"

"I would love to, Jacob. You're such a handsome and sweet young man. Do you help your momma take care of your brothers?"

"I help with Aaron. Ricky and Anthony don't need help. They're bigger than me," he snickered. "You're funny, Aunt 'Amie. Where's Gamma Scott? Let me get the game." Jacob took off running, yelling, "Gamma! Gamma!"

Both Jamie and Jillian stood up, Jillian lifting Aaron onto her hip. Jamie marveled at how fit her younger sister was after giving birth to four children--she hoped to have gotten that gene. "Rick and Anthony are at music lessons, so I dropped in with the boys to see Mother and Dad. Richard has been out of town for a case, but he's returning today. I wish you had told me you were coming. We could have planned a dinner or something."

"Jonathan knew. I'm surprised he didn't tell you. I don't need a fancy dinner because I'm coming home. Besides, there will be an epic to-do soon enough. How long has this been in the works?"

"Actually, not very long. We were going to take her out for dinner, but about ten days ago, she decided she wanted a large party. So, it's been hectic." She moved to the side to avoid two workers carrying a table. "It's a cool coincidence that you will be here for it."

"I don't know if it was a coincidence." Jamie winked at her sister and touched her nephew's nose. Jamie had spoken to Jonathan almost two weeks ago and told him she was coming home. *Coincidence, my ass*. Jon had a lot to answer for. He must have blabbed to their mother that she was coming, and Margaret turned this into a gathering, a celebration of sorts. Perhaps this reunion would not be as miserable as she expected.

Jillian frowned. "So, Jon knew you were coming? And Mother did, too? So that's what caused the change in plans." No one had told her, and after four years away, Jamie still had a party. *Perfect Jamie*, indeed.

Oblivious to her sister's change in mood, Jamie considered her options. "I guess I need to find Mother. By the way, Jon's upstairs in his room."

"You haven't seen her yet? Oh, my. That should be interesting." Jillian gave Jamie a sidelong glance. "I think I'll take Aaron to see Jon. Good luck!" She and her son went up the stairs.

Jamie took a deep breath and headed toward the study. *Damn, everyone keeps wishing me luck. I hope it's not a bad sign.*

As she headed toward the study, Jamie could see Gregory in the backyard supervising the set-up for the birthday festivities. After speaking to her mother, she would go see what the fuss was about and perhaps offer her dad a hand. She apprehensively placed her hand on the knob of the study door.

The door opened, startling her, and Jamison—with an "i"—was suddenly standing face-to-face with her mother, Margaret Jameson--with an "e"—Scott, the matriarch of the Scott family. The change in spelling was to enforce that Jamie was a girl. With a masculine unisex name, Margaret wanted no confusion there. Jon's refusal to call her anything other than Jamie J once he learned to speak led to the shortened name—much to Margaret's chagrin.

Jacob was sitting on the study couch, playing with a tablet.

"Jamison, oh my, you're here! Come on in, give me a hug, let me look at you!" Margaret folded her eldest child into her arms, moved her to arm's length to give her a critical once-over, and pulled her into the study. "You seem healthy, but you will need a bit of polish before the soiree. I will call Althea right now for a hair appointment and time at the spa." She examined Jamie's hands. "And a manicure, and probably a pedicure." She took Jamie's ball cap off. "Well, my Lord. What is going on with your hair? You have no relaxer. Your hair is… Althea has her work cut out for her if you are to be presentable at the party. Isn't it exciting? You've come home; we're having a party; we can open a whole new chapter in our family." Margaret reeled this off without a breath as she led Jamie over to the desk.

Jamie appraised her mother as they walked. Margaret was a little grayer than before and now wore her hair in a short, layered cut. Her appearance hadn't changed much otherwise in the intervening years. Jamie hoped she had inherited that gene as well. Six inches shorter than Jamie, Margaret had always been very curvy and had maintained her shape as she aged. Jamie redirected her attention to what her mother was saying.

"Here are the plans for Sunday. It will be a lovely function, with a few dignitaries sprinkled in and some people from some important families as well. The RSVP rate has been quite impressive, given the short notice. Some upstanding single men, too. Wait, you didn't get married in Africa, did you? That wouldn't surprise me. I haven't understood you over the past four years. But you are home again. We can get you back on track. It's not too late to get you a position at a hospital or clinic, married to a nice man, and you can still have a couple of children." Jamie stood there, stunned.

This sounded like the conversation they had four years ago.

Before she left, Jamie told her mother that she broke it off with her fiancé and turned down the dermatology position because she was unhappy, stressed, and ill. Margaret berated her and, ignoring all that Jamie had just said, began planning the next steps in Jamie's life. While Margaret made plans to phone Jamie's ex-fiancé to arrange some sort of conciliatory meeting, Jamie walked out of the house. She hadn't returned until today.

Mother hasn't changed, Jamie thought, *but I have.* She would not let her mother take over this time.

Margaret was a steamroller. She was from an esteemed, wealthy, black family in Alabama. Her father was a doctor who owned multiple properties, and she grew up as a member of various elite groups in black society. Margaret attended Spelman College and, while there, met Gregory, who was attending Morehouse. He hadn't been wealthy; instead, he attended college on a scholarship. Margaret fell in love with a man with a lot of potential over her family's objections. They married when she graduated, and Gregory was still working on his doctorate. Margaret earned her Master's in business while he completed an internship at a university forensic lab. She was the one who convinced Gregory to open his lab before many other private labs opened. Margaret helped negotiate contracts with police departments, hospitals, and courts and handled most of the hiring. Typically, she was quite exacting with the requirements for employment. Gregory was fine with that; he mostly let Margaret handle those details, although he did have veto power. The lab had been incredibly successful over the years, and there was a plan to open another location soon.

Margaret took the lead for her family on most issues. She had decided when it was time to start a family and chosen the children's names. Jamie was the oldest surviving child, as there had been another son who had died before Jamie was born. His death had intensified Margaret's helicopter tendencies. She handled most of the discipline for the children and selected their social and extracurricular activities. Margaret also approved Jamie's move to New

York City to model—too monumental an opportunity to miss. She eventually accepted Jillian's marriage at twenty-one to a man twice her age, although well-positioned and wealthy. Margaret hadn't pushed Jonathan about marriage as much, although Jon had mentioned earlier that was changing. Now that Jamie was back, the pressure on both siblings was going to be intense.

When Margaret paused, Jamie finally got a word in edgewise. "Hello, Mother. It's good to see you, too. No, I'm not married. No, I'm not looking to get married or have kids right now, and I would welcome some time at a spa." She gave the study a once-over and turned back to her mother, defiant.

"That's good to hear," Margaret started, but Jamie held up her hand.

"I'm happy to be home. I know you didn't plan this party until Jon told you I was coming back." She took a moment to allow Margaret to respond. When she impatiently crossed her arms as she continued to assess Jamie's hair, Jamie spoke again.

"However, you need to understand that I'm not looking to be fixed up. If I meet someone, great; if not, fine. I just want us to get along this time around." Jamie took a deep breath and continued. "I've had a lot of time to think, and I'm in a good place. I want us to talk, to repair our relationship, but I'm too grown to be bullied. OK?" She locked eyes with her mother.

Margaret was shocked, furrowed her brow in response, and opened her mouth to retort. But she stopped herself. It was rare for anyone to speak to her with such sass, and Jamie had spent a lot of time trying to please her parents, particularly after her huge mistake in New York. Margaret was glad to have Jamie home, but this new attitude would take some getting used to. It probably wasn't permanent, so Margaret held her tongue. In a flash, she quickly rearranged her face to hide her consternation. No reason to start a fight right now. She had some plans for her daughter and only needed to bide her time. She smiled pleasantly at her eldest as she turned to go back to her grandson.

"That's fine, dear. It's just marvelous to have you home. We can talk more later." Margaret sat down on the couch next to Jacob. Jamie was immediately leery about this response. A mother who backs off was up to something. Jamie felt herself sinking into a bad space—a flashback to their last argument in this house. All those feelings of fear, confusion, and anger washed over her again. Trying to maintain her composure, Jamie closed her eyes and reminded herself of her mantra—*revel in the chaos*. She had to take advantage of her mother's attitude. She was sure this reprieve was temporary, so she planned to enjoy it.

3
First Night

Jonathan stuck his head in the study door. "Since we have a quorum, I was going to order some food and go pick it up. Are you two interested?"

"I'll call something in, Jon. Let's order some burgers from Lucky's. It's something that the children will like. Check with Jillian to see if she wants me to order for Ricky and Anthony. She's still here, or did she go pick up the boys from their music lessons?" Margaret walked over to the wooden desk and logged on to the laptop to find the restaurant menu on the web. Jamie and Jon relayed their orders quickly—they both ordered the same thing each time. Fortunately, a burger place would always have burgers! "Jamie, go find your sister and father so they can place orders, too," she said.

Jamie was glad to escape the study after the intensity of the previous conversation and dutifully went on the requested mission.

Jillian was in the kitchen searching through the refrigerator for drinks for herself and her son. Aaron was in his grandfather's arms at the kitchen table. The pair was playing peek-a-boo, with the little boy giggling loudly at the silly faces that his grandpa made with each peek-a-boo revelation. That was something that Jamie had never expected. During her childhood, Gregory spent a lot of time working, so there were few moments like this with her father outside of holidays. *Maybe things have changed more than I thought.*

"Mother wants to order some dinner. She wants you guys to place your orders in the study. Jillian, you can order for your boys if they are coming over here," Jamie instructed, sliding onto a stool at the bar.

"Where does she want to go?" Jillian asked, sipping from a bottle of sparkling water she got from the refrigerator. She handed a sippy cup of juice to Aaron.

"Lucky's. Does that work?"

"That sounds good. Dad, what do you want? I'll tell Mother. Aaron, stay with Grandpa for a few minutes," Jillian said. Since the family visited Lucky's frequently over the years, Gregory told his daughter his choices as she headed out of the room. Jamie and Gregory remained in the kitchen with Aaron, who grinned at his grandpa as he slurped from his cup.

"So, how are you, Dad?"

"I'm doing OK. Busy. Business is good."

"You're OK health-wise?"

"Nothing too bad. Mild high blood pressure, managed with medicine. Watching my weight. I've started exercising. I don't know if you saw the exercise equipment upstairs?" Gregory smiled. "Just trying to stay around for my grandkids—present and future." He winked.

Jamie blushed. It didn't upset her when her father commented about marriage and children. Maybe it was because there was no judgment? "I'm sorry I didn't contact anyone while I was away," she said. "That was selfish of me." A wave of shame washed over her. She was very ashamed of her callousness—especially toward her father. Trying to atone for that would be a challenge.

Gregory bobbed his head. "That hurt. But I'm your father. I can forgive you if you don't let it happen again."

"I promise." She grew animated as she changed the subject. "I can't wait to tell you about Africa. You know what? The coolest part was that I had to become a family practitioner. I even had to do emergency procedures in some desperate situations." She gleefully revealed.

"Weren't you nervous? You trained to be a dermatologist," Gregory asked, leaning forward intently. Aaron didn't appreciate the loss of his grandpa's undivided attention and banged his almost empty cup on the table. Jamie followed her father's lead and covered and uncovered her eyes in a quick game of peek-a-boo, except she stuck out her tongue. Aaron was so distracted that he stopped banging and started watching her intently. Amused, Gregory nodded to her, pleased with her quick thinking. Jamie laughed to herself before she responded to her father.

"I remembered a lot of what I might have forgotten otherwise. The patients didn't have a bunch of specialists around. Often, you did what was necessary. I believe all doctors should spend time with an organization like Doctors Overseas. It could make a difference when they go into practice."

"That's not a bad idea, Jamison. Maybe you can spend some time trying to start that at a local medical school like Morehouse." He changed the topic and shifted Aaron's position on his lap. “What do you plan to do now that you’re back?”

“I don’t know. It seemed like a good time to come back. But I do not know what my next step is. I guess I should ask—can I stay here for a while?” She smiled.

“Silly. I won’t dignify that with an answer. As for your next step, take some time to figure it out. You’re young and have lots of options. You could even come to work at the lab.”

“Thanks, Dad,” Jamie went over to her father and nephew. Her tone and mood shifted. “You haven’t asked me anything about why I left. I know Mother told you some details.”

“She told me. I also figured it out when there was no wedding. You must have been in an awful place to leave and stay away for so long.” Gregory swallowed and grabbed his daughter’s hands. Aaron frowned as these adults squished him a bit, but he still had a little juice. “I also know about New York.”

Jamie gasped.

“I’m sorry that I didn’t intervene then. You were drowning, and I was too busy to provide much help. I left dealing with you to your mother, which may not have been the right thing.” He paused, searching for the right words. “I love your mother deeply, and she’s a wonderful woman and mother. However, she can be controlling. I didn’t step in when you needed me. It’s a great regret of mine.” He put his arm around his daughter. “It sounds like you were struggling again before you left. I know what your mother told me, but I would like to hear it from you one day, whenever you’re truly ready. Now, I want to talk more about Africa.” He touched her shoulder as tears welled up in her eyes.

"Thank you," she whispered. "It wasn't your fault, wasn't anyone's fault. I made some stupid choices." She took a deep breath. "That's why Africa was good for me. It was unofficial therapy! I had some official therapy, too. I had to figure out what I wanted. I also needed to forgive myself for New York, so I could move on because I hadn't done that before. It would have been a terrible mess if I had gotten married then."

"Understood," he said. Aaron had finished his juice and started banging his cup on the table again. "Ma-ma! Ma-ma!" he chanted, whimpering. As if she had radar, Jillian appeared in the kitchen with Jacob and Margaret in tow.

"Richard just called. He already landed and will pick the boys up from music lessons and head over here," Jillian said, sitting down on the other side of their father.

She seemed content. *Is she that happy?* Jamie wondered.

Jillian then announced, "I told him you were home, Jamie, and that we're all here at an impromptu gathering to celebrate the prodigal daughter/sister returning." Jillian scooped Aaron up from her father's lap. "Jon should be back in a few with dinner for everybody. Perhaps we should set the table and prepare some drinks. Juice and milk for the kids and something stronger for the adults. Sound good? There's a highchair in the breakfast room. Can you grab it, Dad?"

He did as she asked. Jillian plopped Aaron in the chair, dumped a few animal crackers on the tray, and went behind the bar to start the beverage service.

Jamie watched in awe. Her sister was so different, so efficient. Jillian had two kids when she left and was pregnant with the third. She was tired. This Jillian appeared organized, prepared, and had some new skills. She was taking drink orders and mixing cocktails like a bartender. *I guess she had to learn that for Richard and some of his clients,* Jamie thought.

Jillian had to grow up quickly after marrying Richard. He was much older than her and was a partner at a successful law firm with clients around the country. When they met, Jillian was an intern at his law firm. According to Richard, for the marriage to work, Jillian had to postpone her plans for law school. He was busy, and Jillian would have to manage his household and raise a family. His wishes were a little old-fashioned, but Jillian was in love. Margaret and Gregory were originally against the union because of the age difference, his marital status (he was separated), and the postponement of law school—although they had nothing against Richard himself. But Jillian overrode their objections by eloping in Hawaii as soon as she graduated from college.

While Jillian never said it, Jamie was pretty sure that Jillian had wanted a divorce six months after the wedding. Marriage wasn't what she thought it would be. But she found out she was pregnant with Rick, and their mother got in her ear. *No further disgracing of the family name. Work it out.* Jillian threw herself into her relationship and was now the perfect wife and mother. At least, by appearances. Now, she seemed happy, so everything appeared to be working out. Jamie wasn't doing what she'd thought she would be, so who was she to judge?

While they waited for Richard and the boys and Jon and the food, the family settled into the kitchen and drank a few cocktails. Margaret retrieved the tablet from the study and started playing with Jacob again. Jillian, Gregory, and Jamie chatted about the boys and their activities. Jillian was trying to convince Jamie to attend a few as a "good aunt." Gregory and his youngest daughter had spent much of their time discussing the grandchildren and their antics. The warmth of the martini and the change in time zones had made Jamie sleepy. She was barely keeping up with the conversation. Jillian noticed her drooping eyelids and deftly swapped her martini for a cup of coffee.

She was good at this, Jamie thought gratefully, taking a sip. It woke her up enough to listen to her family, but she still couldn't contribute many coherent thoughts.

Time passed, and there was a commotion in the front foyer. Richard, Rick, and Anthony noisily entered the house. "Boys, it's your aunt, Jamie, back from Africa!" Richard said. Her brother-in-law came into the kitchen and hugged Jamie. He was now bald but still in good shape. It was impressive that everyone in the family remained fit while she was away. Anthony didn't remember Jamie since he was only a year old when she left the country. He said hello and went over to his grandmother.

Rick did vaguely remember her and came over to hug her. "Hi, Aunt Jamie. How long are you here?"

"I believe I'm back for good."

"Cool." Rick turned to his mother. "Where's dinner, Mom? I'm hungry." He swiped an animal cracker from Aaron's tray table, and Aaron let out a wail.

"Boys! Rick, don't take his food. If you want something, ask, but dinner will be here any minute." Rick stuck out his tongue at his baby brother and went to rifle in his mother's purse for the remaining crackers. Anthony crawled into his grandfather's lap.

"Where is Jon?" Margaret asked. "Everyone's hungry, and the children need to eat." She pulled out her phone to call her son but stopped when the front door opened.

"Dinner's here!" Jon burst in, hauling several bags of food. "I've done my part. Someone else will have to divvy up the goods. My food is in a separate bag, so I don't have to wrestle with you all." He grinned as he handed the bags over to Margaret, who kissed him on the cheek and started passing out food.

The older boys tried to peer into the bags to see what Jon had brought them, while their grandmother tried to nudge them and their questions out of her way. Richard scooped up his youngest son from the highchair and greeted his wife with a kiss. Within a matter of minutes, everyone had dinner. The adults sat around the kitchen table, and the three older boys sat on barstools. Even Jacob—he wanted to be like his big brothers. There were several pairs of eyes making sure he was safe.

Everyone was boisterous and happy. Jillian, Jon, and Jamie shared memories of their childhood. One story about Jon climbing through a window on the second floor after missing curfew shocked both parents, who wondered why they hadn't heard this tale before. Jon claimed innocence until Jillian connected the event to a ripped new winter coat and a loud, vivacious girlfriend that Margaret had not approved of. Amid the laughter, Margaret mildly scolded her son for his shenanigans, but in the end, even she had to laugh. Rick and Anthony appeared to be listening intently—Jillian told them not to take any notes. Jon told the boys they would talk later, leading to more laughter and Jillian chiding her brother for trying to corrupt young minds.

As she ate, Jamie realized she had missed these times. It was weird—the family continued while she was away and seemed to be in a good place. It was a good time to be home.

By the time everyone finished eating, Aaron had fallen asleep in his mother's arms, and Jacob was curled up on the kitchen floor by Jillian's chair. Jamie eyed the boys wistfully and wished she could curl up on the floor as well. She had monster jet lag and was almost asleep in her seat.

Jillian started packing up gear and children for the trip home. She and Richard lived in the Decatur area, about a twenty-five-minute drive from the Scott house. Margaret suggested they stay in Jillian's old room, but Richard wanted to get home since he had been out of town for a few days. The family of six wandered out the front door around ten p.m., with Jon not too far behind them.

Jamie helped her mother load the dishes into the dishwasher. Their housekeeper only worked half-days on Fridays. Her mother kept moving each dish Jamie placed in the dishwasher to a different location in the machine. For a moment, Jamie wished she had walked out the door with one of her siblings. She reminded herself to remain calm, since there would often be no buffer between her and her mother. To keep from butting heads, she focused on cleaning off counters and putting condiments back into the refrigerator. Her efficiency was almost nonexistent because she was so tired, but she was trying to help.

Seeing Jamie's failing efforts, her mother gave her a break. "Thanks for your help, Jamison. I'll finish up here. Go to bed since you're dead on your feet. We'll be up early in the morning because we have a lot to do," Margaret said.

Jamie was too tired to argue. She headed up to her room while her mother finished putting things away. Jamie made it up the stairs, went into her room, and stripped down to her bra and panties. Too tired to sift through her bag for a t-shirt, she crawled under the seafoam and white duvet. To her surprise, she didn't fall asleep immediately. Her mind worked through the entire day and her return home. So far, so good. She would need to work each day to maintain her current state of mind—this calmness. After about ten minutes, she sank into a dreamless slumber.

4
Midnight Mystery

Instead of waking eight hours later to a bright sunrise, her mother awakened Jamie around midnight by turning on an overhead light. As Jamie tried to focus, she realized that her mother was talking. It took a moment to comprehend what Margaret was saying. *The police? Something about the lab?*

Margaret shook her once. “Jamison, get up. The police are here. Someone has found a dead body outside the lab.”

“What? Someone’s dead at the lab?” She tried to sit up. Her brain was full of cotton. Jet lag was a beast.

“Murdered. Get up. Your father needs you.” Margaret hurried out of the room.

Jamie swung her legs over the side of the bed and tried to figure out where her clothing had fallen on her stumble to the bed. *Murder? What the hell is going on?* she thought as she dressed.

Jamie found the elder Scotts, still in their robes, and two police officers and two detectives in the living room.

"Dr. Scott, what can you tell us about Miss Thorne? Why was she at the lab after hours on a Friday night?" a tall, handsome Caucasian detective named Nicholas Marshall was asking the questions. The other detective, a shorter, older African American man named Ronald Dixon, was taking notes. Her parents sat on the couch. The inquiring detective sat in an upholstered chair across from them, and the other detective leaned against the doorjamb.

Everyone's head snapped towards the doorway when Jamie entered.

She was glad she had stopped to put her hat back on before entering the room. Margaret jumped up to introduce her daughter to the officers and detectives, and Jamie then plopped down next to her father on the sofa. "What's going on?" she whispered to her father.

The interruption annoyed Nick, but he returned to his line of questioning. "Dr. Scott? Is there some reason she was at the lab so late?"

Gregory shook his head with a stricken expression on his face. "I do not know, Detective Marshall. I left the lab early today; I was only there for a couple of hours. My wife is having a party on Sunday, so I came home. Also, my daughter Jamison was coming home after four years. So, I don't know why Rachel would return to the building after work. She wasn't on the schedule. Margaret, do you know?" He turned to his wife.

Margaret had regained her composure and faced the detective calmly. "I didn't go in at all today. However, Rachel was in the habit of going out after work to Happy Hour." Margaret emphasized her words with air quotes.

"Perhaps she met someone unsavory while she was out. You said someone found her in a car in the parking lot, correct?"

The detective responded in the affirmative. "We need to see your security feeds. The security guard on duty had gone home by the time the good Samaritan found the body. We sent officers to locate him. I need you to come with me and let us into the lab. Perhaps she went inside after hours and left some clues about what she was doing."

Gregory and Margaret both stood up. "Let us get dressed. We will follow you down there and give you whatever you need," Gregory said.

"Wait, wait. Hold on. Do you have a warrant? Do we need an attorney?" Jamison stood up, too. She was almost as tall as the detective and incredibly pretty up close, which caught him off guard. "Aren't there proprietary issues at the lab?"

Nick paused and deferred to Ronald. Ronald chimed in. "We're just trying to get information about this woman's death. You can call a lawyer if you wish, but retaining one may slow things down."

"Hmmm." Jamie stared at both detectives. She couldn't read either of them, but the situation gave her pause. She recognized the importance of finding out what had happened to their employee. However, the family business needed to be shielded as much as possible. Jamie hadn't been back long, and her brain was still cloudy and jet-lagged, but she recognized the potential perils in just letting the police roam free in the lab. "Dad, Mother, someone should call Richard," she said, scrutinizing both parents.

Margaret said, "Good idea. I'll call while I change. He can meet us there." She gave the detective and the other officers a superior glance. "Richard Bradshaw, he's a partner at Bradshaw, Taylor, and Kline, and he is our son-in-law."

She turned to walk into the master suite, with Gregory following.

Nick shook his head, and Ronald was less subtle with a steady scowl. Both had heard about Richard's firm and peripherally knew Richard. This situation just got a lot more difficult. Nick didn't suspect the family, but involving a lawyer usually complicated their police work. He turned back to Jamie, who was studying his reaction. He adjusted his face so she couldn't sense his annoyance.

Jamie noted the subtle change and smiled to herself. She could tell she had annoyed him. *Even annoyed, he's pretty cute*. "I need to get my coat. If you will excuse me," she said, heading back to her bedroom.

Upstairs, Jamie changed clothes, retrieving a pair of skinny black jeans from her bag. As she slid into her jeans, her mind wandered to the detective. She typically dated guys that were taller than her—with her ex-fiancé being the lone exception—Eddie had been the same height. A strong jaw, wavy-ish hair, nice lips, and a commanding presence—which Jamie suspected the detective had in spades—didn't hurt either. Just the type of guy she would typically go for if the circumstances were different. Rifling through the dresser, she found a white Henley shirt she'd left on a previous visit. She had gained almost fifteen pounds since then, and the shirt fit snugly. She now had boobs! Placing the hat back on her head, she was glad she had an appointment at the hair salon later in the day.

Yikes, she thought after catching herself primping in the mirror. *Am I trying to impress the detective who's investigating us? Girl, it has been a long time. Although he is hot*. She shook her head exasperatedly. As she headed out, she remembered to grab her coat.

Downstairs, Jamie's parents were waiting for her. The two officers were already ready for the brief trip to the lab; Detective Dixon had gone to the car, and Detective Marshall was standing beside the front door. He eyed Jamie appreciatively and quickly averted his eyes when she caught him staring at her. *Investigating a murder here,* he told himself, *not picking up a date.*

"Richard will meet us there," Margaret murmured to Jamie as she walked up. "Gregory, Jamison, and I will take our car and meet you there," she said to the detective.

The detectives assented and headed out to Ronald's sedan.

Jamie walked behind her parents as they went to the garage to get into Gregory's sedan. She slid into the back seat. To her surprise, Margaret glided behind the steering wheel, and her father got in on the passenger's side. She would ask about that later, but other matters were more pressing.

"Dad, do you know why she, what was her name, Rachel, was there? Is something going on at the office?" Jamie asked as they drove off the property.

"Of course not," Gregory said. "Like your mother said, Rachel was a solid employee—very bright. I was planning to promote her soon. The lab has been busy, and most of the workers seem to be happy. No drama."

Margaret didn't wholly agree and was glad to share what she knew. "She was a smart young lady. This is absolutely horrible." She paused for effect. "I know she broke up with her boyfriend a few months ago. Since then, she had been more social and had gone to bars and clubs, hoping to find another young man. I told her that the bars weren't the best place to search for a companion, but she was determined, I guess. Young people often look for the wrong thing in a mate. And…," she paused to lock eyes with Jamie through the rear-view mirror, "sometimes the right man is just tossed away without a second thought. Regret's a tough emotion."

"Here we go, Mother. Please, don't start now. There are other issues to deal with, such as a dead body. It's not the time to talk about my supposed relationship failings." She sat back in her seat. "Anyway, I know my ex is happily married now and has a kid. I talked to him while I was in Africa."

Margaret looked surprised.

"You didn't think I knew about that, did you? Everyone is where they should be now. Let's give it a rest," Jamie said wearily.

"Margaret, let's focus here," Gregory said. "I really can't listen to you two bicker over old history. I hope nothing associated with the lab caused this young woman's death."

"Just say nothing, Dad. Let Richard handle it. At least, until we figure out the detective's angle," Jamie said, closing her eyes.

The car ride lulled Jamie to sleep. After twenty minutes, Margaret maneuvered the car into the lab parking lot after being waved in by a police officer. There were several police cars, forensic vehicles, and a coroner's van with yellow police tape blocking off a section of the parking lot. A couple of news stations had vans parked on the street with reporters milling around outside the yellow tape. When the car stopped, Jamie woke up with a start.

Richard, whose home was closer to the lab, was standing on the sidewalk near the front door. Nick was standing a few feet away from Richard, awaiting their arrival.

Richard came over to update the Scotts on the situation.

"Here's what I know. A passerby pulled into the lot to turn around and noticed the victim sitting in her car. Something seemed odd, so the good Samaritan got out, saw something was wrong, and called 911. The woman had a broken neck. No evidence now that she was in the building, but she may have been leaving the lab when she died," he said. "Also, her skirt was around her waist. The medical examiner will let us know if any sexual activity or assault was involved."

"Unfortunate circumstances, but what is our liability here? Should we let them in the building?" Margaret asked.

"Two workable options: Make the surveillance tapes available, and if there is something on them, let them in to check the involved areas only. Or fight it and wait until evidence shows she was in the office after hours. My suggestion is to release the surveillance tapes now and limit their entry. This limits your liability and protects any trade secrets and test results in the labs," Richard turned to Jamie. "What a welcome home, huh?"

"It wouldn't be home if it weren't wild," Jamie said, glancing toward the milling crowd. "Can we find out what else is happening there? They know more than they're telling us." The elder Scotts waited expectantly for Richard to respond.

"I'll tell the detectives that we'll make the surveillance tapes of the parking lot available. Jamie, do you want to come with me? You might glean some medical information that they don't want to tell us."

She agreed, and he and Jamie walked over to the detective.

Detective Marshall was speaking to the medical examiner when they reached him. He held up his finger to Richard and Jamie. They kept their distance.

The medical examiner glanced at the newcomers but continued his comments. Parts of the conversation drifted toward them through the overall din of the scene.

"The victim suffered a C2 fracture…"

"… can't determine if it was accidental or intentional."

"Death was essentially instantaneous."

Not enough information to answer any of their questions.

The detective noticed that Richard and Jamie had inched a little closer to his conversation with the medical examiner. While monitoring their (mainly Jamie's) movements, Detective Marshall asked the medical examiner about sexual assault. The older gentleman shrugged, adding that he would have to do more examinations and testing to be sure.

"Do you think she died in the car or the building? Any blood or fluids? The Crime Scene Unit techs are going over the car with a fine-tooth comb, but I'm just trying to get a sense of what we're looking at." The detective narrowed his eyes. "Give me something to work with."

"Gave you all I got. We'll take the body now so your guys can finish your work. Your techs can have the car and the building," the medical examiner said as he turned to leave.

Detective Nick sighed quietly. This case already felt like it was going to be a beast. He had already sent several officers to canvass the immediate area for witnesses, but that had turned up nothing so far. The man who discovered the body had nothing else useful to add; however, they would continue questioning him to rule out his involvement. He turned back to Jamie and her unknown companion.

Richard chimed in. "Detective, I'm Richard Bradshaw, the Scotts' attorney. We'll give you the surveillance tapes for the outside of the building, and if there is evidence on the interior tapes, we'll also hand those over. We want to cooperate fully with the investigation. However, there are trade secrets and work products to protect as well as privacy concerns. We won't open the building unless there's evidence or a subpoena."

The detective audibly groaned, and his two companions gave him a side-eye. *Lawyers*. Perhaps he would have had better luck talking with Jamie alone. That might have been more enjoyable. He mentally slapped himself. This wasn't the time to entertain those types of thoughts—especially for someone involved in the case, no matter how pretty she might be. He was a sucker for tall women; they were always his kryptonite. With effort, he turned his attention back to the case.

"Will you answer some questions about the victim and her job here? It's still unclear why she was here on a Friday night." Nick tried to get the conversation back on track.

"You can ask about basic information. Nothing about her specific job in the lab or any work product. The Scotts will be glad to give you her personal information so you can interview her friends and family." Richard motioned for the elder Scotts to come over and took a few steps toward them. "Remember, basic information only," he said over his shoulder.

"What do you know about the victim?" Nick asked Jamie under his breath as her parents neared. "Have you met her before?"

"Sorry. I don't know many people who currently work here, Detective." She gazed at him. Jamie could sense the interest—both in her and what she might know. *He is very cute*, she thought again. Playing along for a few minutes could be fun.

"Do you have any idea what she was working on? I'm checking for anything to go on. Lawyers make everything so difficult. As a doctor, you know this."

Jamie grinned at him. "I got nothing. And you won't be able to get any extra information out of me without our attorney present. Thanks for playing, though." Before he could reply, her family had reached them.

Under Richard's watchful eyes, the elder Scotts gave the detective very basic information about the victim. Margaret had contact information for the employees on her phone. She also noted that Rachel had worked for them for approximately three years and took the job shortly after she had earned her master's degree. No, she was not married, and they didn't know if she was currently in a relationship.

"I try not to get into other people's business," Margaret added, to a barely concealed eye roll from her daughter and a grin hidden by a quick head duck from Gregory.

Unfortunately, Nick caught this and filed it away. *Margaret Scott may be an excellent resource.*

Margaret repeated that she and Dr. Scott had not been in the office much on Friday because of the planning of a function on Sunday. They didn't see Rachel and didn't know about her schedule that Friday. Yes, they would make the names of the employees that worked with her available so that the police could interview them.

The family remained in the parking lot for almost two hours. After their initial encounter, Jamie hadn't talked to the handsome detective again. She watched him surreptitiously from across the parking lot as he worked until she couldn't keep her eyes open any longer. The family wasn't questioned again, but Richard wanted to remain at the lab until the place cleared out. He also wanted to listen to any interviews that the police gave the press. Finally, Richard gave the OK for the family to go home around two-thirty a.m.

After her eventful day and night, Jamie had hoped to get some sleep, but the police visit and midnight trip intervened. And in a few hours, it would be clear that Margaret had other ideas about what time Jamie would get up.

Margaret wanted her daughter to be her version of presentable for her sixtieth birthday party, even after a late night at the lab. That meant time at the salon. Althea, the beautician, often made emergency appointments for Margaret as a sign of respect. While Margaret had been ordering the evening meals, she had also made an urgent call for one on Saturday. On such short notice, Althea could only attend to Jamie early in the day. Saturdays were so busy.

Margaret cheerfully relayed this information during the return trip home, but Jamie didn't hear her. When they pulled into the driveway, Gregory had to shake her awake. Once again, Jamie trudged up the stairs to her bed. She put forth even less effort into getting ready this time than she did before. She crawled into bed, fully dressed, except for her shoes and hat.

5

The Day After

He skulked around quietly in the dark in his small RV, trying to stave off the nightmares that visited him whenever he went to sleep. Last night did not make it any easier to rest. The memories still haunted him—prison, dead Bianca, nighttime visitors in his cell. After his release from prison, he had to confront the women who'd contributed to the end of his life as he knew it.

It didn't go well. The first woman he'd confronted in that parking lot ended up dead.

As a result, he couldn't sleep.

He got up and grabbed a beer out of the small refrigerator in the back. He hadn't spoken to Bianca's father since arriving in Atlanta. The old man didn't know that he had seen Rachel last night. The plan had been for the father to make the initial contact. But the young man hadn't followed the plan.

Now he had ruined it all, and that would piss off Bianca's father.

Early that Saturday morning, one lab employee, Tatiana Daniels, paced back and forth in the bedroom of her small apartment. She had just heard about Rachel's death on the news, and it unleashed a variety of emotions. The first was sadness at the death of a friend. The second was fear. Never one to believe in coincidences, she noticed a missed call from Rachel last night–one hour after she left the message. The third was regret. Perhaps if she had answered, things would have gone down differently.

She had been busy with the lab security guard, Marcus Robinson, at the time of the call. It was slow at the lab, with most lab technicians already gone for the weekend. Only a few remained on the first floor to cover late deliveries or emergencies. Tatiana and Marcus entered the first-floor lounge closet and had sex, which was why the guard wasn't at the desk when Rachel returned to the building. Their affair had been going on for a few weeks, and the pair used a variety of places both in and out of the lab building for their trysts.

She knew he was married, but he was nice-looking, and she was bored.

Besides, she always found her sex partners by proximity—be it at high school in the heart of Chicago, at the College of Lake County, or at the University of Wisconsin at Madison for the two minutes she was there. She fell in lust quickly and burned out fast. The man's relationship status was hardly a consideration. Marcus was married with children but was a bit of a horndog. She was a pretty girl with few scruples and a high sex drive. Nothing good could come of them thrown together during slow shifts.

Tatiana first met Rachel in Madison. The love of science connected them. Tatiana had always loved science, but she didn't get any support in that area during childhood. In college, it was different. The trio—Rachel, Bianca, and Tatiana—were like the science Three Musketeers.

But shit had gone wrong, and everyone tried to cover their tracks. She dropped out of school and tried to put the situation behind her by living under the radar. Without completing her degree, however, minimum wage jobs were all she could swing. A chance contact, through social media, reconnected Rachel with Tatiana. Tatiana used a threat of exposure to convince Rachel to help her get a job at the lab. Rachel fudged her friend's background to make it look like Tatiana had been closer to a degree than she truly was. Dr. Scott took Rachel's word about her qualifications, and there had been no need to investigate any further since Tatiana was a good employee. It had been easy to rekindle their friendship where they had left off after that.

Three weeks ago, however, Tatiana received a phone call from a man asking questions about the events in Madison. She fired off an email to Rachel to arrange an emergency lunch date, but Rachel refused to worry. She said that no one knew anything. If they didn't panic and fly off the handle, there would be no problems. Rachel had been *so* calm. Tatiana's idea of calm involved sex with Marcus in various forbidden locations. It was ironic because sex had started this entire crisis six years ago.

Now, Rachel was dead, and Tatiana felt in her bones that her death and that call were just the beginning of something bad. She just couldn't prove it yet.

Tatiana also knew that Rachel had a flash drive with pictures from the night in question. They had fought about destroying it. The police would be all over Rachel's office, computer, and house. That flash drive could raise questions if they knew where to look, but Tatiana had no way of retrieving it. Reluctantly, she realized she might have to attend the Christmas party at the Scotts' home to see what was going on. She hated that type of affair, but she might have to make that sacrifice. She tapped her foot nervously, and her already short nails were in her mouth as she wracked her brain, trying to figure out how to save her ass.

At 6:30 a.m., a bright and refreshed Margaret appeared at Jamie's bedroom door.

"Get up, dear. We've things to do today," she said, coming in and opening the blinds. The sun was just coming up. "Your father has to make other arrangements for any lab work that might need to be completed over the weekend before the police release the scene."

Jamie did not move. Her mother leaned over and shook her shoulders. No response. Margaret then pulled the covers back and saw that Jamie was still in her clothes. Margaret shook her again.

"Get up so we won't be late," she said.

Jamie opened one eye with difficulty and scowled at her mother. "You can't be serious. I feel like someone's standing on my head. I need a few more hours."

"Althea expects to see us in forty-five minutes. Judging by the mop on your head, she'll need all available time to make you presentable again. Good Lord, I know you were in Africa, but was there no hair care there? I never thought you would just let yourself go like this." A typical Margaret comment. The sentiment was one that Jamie expected, but it was too early, and she wasn't in the mood.

"Of course, there was hair care in Africa. I let my relaxer grow out, and I have no intention of having Althea or anyone else put another one in today." Jamie rolled over. "If it's that important to you, I'll get it flat-ironed." Before her mother could speak again, Jamie eased out of bed. "If I have to get up now, I need to jump in the shower. Is there coffee ready? What kind of coffee do you have?"

"I have several. A lovely one hundred percent Kona coffee and a one hundred percent Jamaican Blue Mountain. Which would you like?" Margaret asked.

"Surprise me," Jamie replied.

"I'll go put a pot on if it'll help you get moving." Margaret left the room to get the coffee started. Jamie searched in her duffel for clean underwear, a clean shirt, and jeans.

The shower helped a little. She didn't feel like death warmed over, just like she was on death's doorstep. But, at least, that was functional. The travel mug of Kona coffee her mother placed in her hand also helped as Margaret ushered her out the front door and into the car. The aroma sparked memories of leisurely mornings at brunch while she lived in Italy, and the first sip was barely sweet and black. Margaret had remembered how she liked her coffee. Yum! She would have to get the brand name when they returned to the house.

At the salon, Althea settled Jamie into her chair. Despite Margaret's belief, Jamie's hair was in good condition and only needed deep conditioning and a trim. Jamie had thick brownish-black hair that she could wear in a big afro or have a decent curl pattern with the right products and processes. Althea talked to Jamie about her hair regimen and gave her some additional natural-hairstyle options. Both women knew these options were for future use because the drama that would ensue if Jamie wore her hair naturally at the party was not worth it. Jamie agreed to let Althea show her some different styles at a later appointment.

It was nice to have someone else wash her hair. The gentle scalp massage put her to sleep again. The flat-ironing process was time-consuming and uncomfortable—it reminded her why she didn't do it often—but she was happy with the results. Althea placed some curls in her now shoulder-length hair and gave her tips for up-dos for the party.

Jamie asked the stylist about strategies to maintain this hairstyle and ended up buying some hair products, including a hair wrap and bonnet. After allowing her relaxer to grow out, she used name-brand products to manage her hair when she could find them. But in most cases, Jamie had to improvise and use everyday items such as coconut and olive oils. Managing natural hair differed from flat-ironed or relaxed hair. It took more effort. Either way, she knew she would never hear the end of it if she couldn't maintain her hair until Sunday night.

Her mother, who had moved to another part of the salon, was happy that Jamie was showing some interest in her appearance. She had one of Althea's assistants superficially work on her short hair so she could monitor her daughter. Both women then spent the next forty-five minutes getting manicures and pedicures in the spa section of the salon.

"I must congratulate Althea on her fabulous work. You look lovely, my dear—like you did before you left," her mother said as they left the salon. Jamie tried not to roll her eyes again. At this rate, her eyes would be on the ground behind her after they rolled out of her head. She couldn't allow every comment her mother made to annoy her.

Deep breaths might help. Maybe I should take up yoga?

It was only 11 a.m. The makeover day had just begun.

Once they left the salon and got into the car, Margaret described the next steps in the plan. "We need to visit a boutique because I know you had no need for formal wear in Africa. Just a simple dress, a bit of jewelry, and some nice shoes—nothing too flashy."

"That sounds reasonable, Mother. Where's a good place to go shopping these days? I would have shopped in Europe if I had known about the party. There were some fabulous shops in Paris which I just flew through. I could have done some damage." Jamie's eyes crinkled as she spoke.

"It's been a long time since you and I have had a day together of shopping and girl time," Margaret said, smiling. "Phipps Plaza is a good place to start. I missed shopping with you. You're my eldest girl. Even if I seem harsh, I'm really glad you're back."

Jamie resisted the urge to snort at her mother. "That's very nice. I missed you, too," she said.

"You spent time in Paris?" That topic had always interested Margaret. She and Gregory had gone there for their twentieth wedding anniversary, and she wanted to return. It was her ideal retirement location.

"I didn't spend all four years in one place. Let's see, I also visited different cities: Nairobi, Mombasa, Johannesburg, and Kribi. I also visited several beaches and spent some time in Paris, Berlin, and London. There was a little time in India and six months in Italy working with a designer friend." Jamie's voice became wistful. "I loved being able to travel so much. That's one thing that I'm going to miss."

"That part does sound lovely. But to get to that, you had to spend time in some dangerous places. I don't know if I could do it." Margaret shook her head as she drove.

"Dad wanted to do something like that at one point," Jamie said.

"He's said that before," Margaret agreed, staring ahead intently as she drove. "But your father's too busy with the lab and the potential expansion to do something like that. It's just a dream. Besides, he would have to go alone." She exchanged a glance with Jamie as they neared the mall. "I couldn't go myself. What would I do?"

"You'd surprise yourself with what you can do, Mother."

As they pulled into Phipps Plaza, Margaret said, "It looks like you gained some weight while you were away. You used to be so worried about that. Never mind, you're still thin, so size shouldn't be a problem. What are you, a ten or a twelve? What *were* you eating in Africa?"

That merited an eye roll. "Size six, up from a two. Remember when I left, I was throwing up? I'm tall; I should never be that thin." *Deep breathing.* "Now, I keep my food down, and I'm healthier than I was before. I think it's an improvement." She replied, justifying herself to her mother. Improvement indeed! With the modest weight gain, Jamie now wore a B-cup and had developed a few curves. She was not voluptuous by any means–still tall and thin—but she thought it worked for her. Luckily, her mother hadn't seen the tattoo on her hip yet!

"Eh, well, I guess that's true. Maybe some exercise would be good." Jamie noticed Margaret had managed not to acknowledge Jamie's comment about her issues before she left town.

A silence fell between them as they walked into the mall and visited various stores. Luckily, they found a simple, knee-length, sleeveless black sheath dress with a low-cut back and shoulder wrap in one of the first stores they entered. After putting it on, Jamie took a moment to pose in the full-length mirror. This dress was something she would have selected before she left. It was uncomfortable simply because she had been living in jeans and t-shirts for several years, but it was nice to dress up. Margaret loved the dress on her and volunteered to buy it. Jamie had planned to purchase her clothes, but her mother insisted she would foot the bill for this shopping trip. After a short debate, Jamie let it go.

Shopping for shoes was more challenging. Jamie had a penchant for high, strappy sandals and always gravitated toward them when wearing heels. Margaret liked lower heels for her daughter because she didn't want her to tower over men and potentially limit her marriage prospects. Gregory was more supportive. But because he had been hands off, the key message received had been Margaret's. As she got older, Jamie ignored her mother on this topic, which caused strife.

This set the scene for the shoe shopping portion of the trip. With the help of the perky redheaded sales associate, Margaret identified a pair of kitten heels she thought would be perfect. Jamie refused even to try them on. She picked up some five-inch black platform sandals. Margaret shook her head. This went on for a few minutes and then moved to other stores; the pair left a trail of frustrated salespeople in their wake. Jamie resisted all efforts to put her in low-heeled shoes and finally convinced Margaret to return to the first store. The original saleswoman saw them coming and made a beeline for the pair. It was slow in the store, and she could sense that Jamie and Margaret would be a good sale–with the right type of help. And she was right, as she directed them to the dressy high-heeled sandal section with which Margaret accepted defeat. There, they settled on a pair of four-and-half-inch strappy black sandals. The salesperson earned her commission!

While Jamie thought they were done, Margaret had other ideas for her daughter's makeover. They purchased some makeup at the cosmetics counter, courtesy of Margaret's insistence.

As they walked through the mall carrying her bags, Jamie asked her mother, "Are you buying anything for yourself? I figured you'd be searching for a fabulous dress. Or are you already set?" She again thought they were leaving, but she was still wrong. Few people were in the mall, but she and her mother seemed to be the only people going away from the doors. Jamie was still tired, so she was jealous of those who were going home.

"I have my dress and accessories already. Now that I have you situated, I can go home and put the finishing touches on the decor and food," Margaret replied. "I would like to stop in the Louis Vuitton store to see if they have a rolling bag in stock. I need a new business bag. Hey, would you like some new luggage?"

"Where are you going to need a fresh bag? And that's too pricey for me," Jamie said, frowning.

"Dear, I know you arrived with a duffel bag, but since you are home, you need to upgrade your image. You left your nice luggage for your sister four years ago. You need to rebuild. I would love to buy you a piece or two, initially," Margaret said as they headed into the store.

Jamie was touched and frightened at the same time. "Mother, I currently don't have a job or a place of my own. Maybe I shouldn't spend thousands of dollars on luggage that I can't even fill because I only own five pairs of pants and five shirts." Jamie protested.

"You aren't. I am. Besides, I have no doubt you can get a job and your own home whenever you're ready." Margaret walked into the store.

Jamie watched as her mother shopped for luggage without finding the piece she wanted. After a thorough search of the store and several intense conversations with the salesperson, Margaret decided not to buy anything. The process was slow and irritating, and by the end, Jamie had almost dozed off in a chair.

Exasperated, her mother hustled her out of the store and glared at her as they made their way to the parking garage.

"Stop looking at me like that. You haven't let me sleep since I got here," Jamie said. She would have rolled her eyes again, but her mother wasn't looking at her, and she was dozing off as she spoke. *I will give her a good eye roll later,* she thought as she drifted off.

6
Nick Marshall, Detective

For his Saturday morning, Nick Marshall got up early to chase down leads on the murder of Rachel Thorne. The Scotts agreed to give him a copy of the outside video feeds. He knew he didn't have to wait for them to hand them over, but in the name of cooperation, he wanted to give them some time to follow through on their promise. Besides, staying cooperative with the family gave him cover to spend time with their daughter, Jamie. That was the pleasant thought that drove him out of his bed to get to work.

While in the shower, Nick thought about the captivating woman he had just met. *Jamie, Jamison, Dr. Scott.* He hadn't been able to get her out of his mind. She was tall, beautiful, intelligent, and quick on her feet. Even in their limited interactions, he could sense that. And since he was wildly attracted to her—he had to admit that to himself—she had to be a bit high maintenance. His friends said he had a type after all, so it stood to reason. He shook his head. He had a job to do… no distractions.

Unlike the Scotts, he remained at the lab building until around 4:30 a.m. He also arranged for the local police in Kentucky to contact the dead woman's parents. It was now 8 a.m., but as a detective, he learned to function well on a few hours of sleep. He enjoyed the hunt for clues and was also a fan of the adrenaline rush. Since childhood, he had been called "The Bulldog" because he wouldn't let things go. It served him well in his line of work.

This same doggedness also helped destroy his marriage. He and his girlfriend dated throughout college and got married right after he graduated from the police academy. An unplanned pregnancy, one month into their marriage, led to a daughter, Gabriella. Even with the new addition, Nick was still very aggressive in his career plans. He wanted to be a detective, so he did what he needed to do to get there. His ex-wife, Daniela, who had plans of her own as a news reporter, felt trapped as the primary caregiver for the baby, since she had minimal support from Nick. She thought she was missing out on choice assignments. Nick suggested a swap, with a focus on his career first and then hers, but this was not an acceptable plan for her.

First, Daniela nagged Nick about his lack of support, pushing him further away. Then, she found that support elsewhere, at the TV station. The day Daniela told him about her affair with the evening news producer, Nick was closing a narcotics case that got him his shield. Her leaving barely disturbed him because the marriage was already dead. They hadn't had sex or slept in the same bed for several months. To make things worse, Nick had wished the news producer luck. However, he *was* upset about Gabby leaving and made his feelings about that known—that he was willing to fight for Gabby, but not Daniela. That didn't go down well with his wife, and that was that.

As he pulled on his clothes, he evaluated his small apartment. After his family left, he bought a small one-bedroom condo with a pull-out sofa for his daughter's visits. Daniela got an anchor job in another city on the opposite coast, and she, Gabby, and the producer moved there. Gabby spent her summers with Nick in Atlanta until she got busy with extracurricular activities. She was a soccer player, and Nick didn't want to interfere with her athletic opportunity—she had serious potential. Gabby also really loved the game, so Nick thought flying across the country and missing tournaments wouldn't be the best thing for her. As she got older, he considered moving to be near her, but Daniela and the producer were always looking for other opportunities in the news business; he didn't want to set up a scenario where he followed them everywhere. So, he and Gabby talked and used FaceTime at least once a week, and he flew out there every summer and every other holiday. The previous Thanksgiving had been in Oregon. He planned for Gabby to spend Christmas with him this year, but Daniela and her husband went to Europe to cover a meeting. How could he compete with Christmas in Europe? The trio agreed to rework the schedule, but they had not finalized the details yet.

Nick entertained few guests. His apartment was a typical bachelor pad, with scattered photos of his daughter and a collection of valuable sports memorabilia on display. Gabby resembled him, with dark brown, curly hair, a square jawline, gray-green eyes (Nick's were blue-gray), and a café au lait complexion from her mother's Puerto Rican ancestry. He had installed an alarm and motion detection camera to protect his small investments. Neither his decor nor his lack of urgency impressed the women he'd entered tentative relationships with after his divorce. This suited him fine.

To speed the start of his day, he picked up coffee at a drive-through coffeehouse. After placing his order, he pulled up to the shop's window, where the barista tried to strike up a conversation.

"Sorry, it'll be a few moments," the red-headed woman said, batting her eyelashes. "I can't believe it's almost Christmas! Have you finished your shopping yet?"

Nick smiled at her but wasn't interested in talking, although she was attractive. It couldn't hurt to be polite. "Not at all," he said, handing over his debit card.

She took his card and tried again. "Did you pick out something for your girlfriend yet? That's usually the hardest gift to buy." Before Nick could reply, a colleague handed her two coffees to give to Nick. She returned his card and passed over the beverages with a hopeful grin.

"Thank you. I would love to stay and chat, but I should get to work. Have a good one." He tipped his head and headed to the precinct in his black Chevy SUV. Suspecting his partner, Ronald, would be grumpy after his brief night's rest, Nick had ordered a coffee for him, too. He parked in his precinct's parking lot and paused to gather up his briefcase and make sure he didn't forget anything. Once he stepped outside the car, the precinct loomed in front of him—a multi-story, nondescript brick building. He couldn't wait to start his day—he loved his job.

Nick hurried to the door, balancing the steaming cups. It was a little colder today than it had been last week.

Although it was a Saturday morning, the precinct was busy. Crime never sleeps. Nick spotted his partner at the assignment desk on the first floor, flirting with the sergeant behind the desk. Ronald was a flirt, but never stepped across the line. His wife, Estelle, a patrol officer, would kill him. She had a gun and knew how to use it. No one believed she would, but there was just enough doubt to keep Ronald honest.

"Ron, good morning! I got you some coffee."

Ron stepped back from the assignment desk and accepted the cup from his partner. "Thanks, man. On days like this, I think about retiring. Estelle's at home in bed where I should be." Ron was about a decade older than Nick and had already put in the prerequisite years for retirement. It was a common conversation between the two men. He took a sip of his beverage. "Caramel. I appreciate your attention to detail."

"I do what I can for my partner."

The men walked side by side to the elevator and rode up to the second floor. They greeted the front desk officer, asked about messages, then made their way to their adjacent desks in the middle of the patrol room.

"Dead women depress me, Nick. I may joke about retiring, but every dead woman pushes me closer to moving to Florida. Go to the Keys, relax on the dock, and stop chasing after the soul-sucking killers of the world." Ron sat down and leaned back, placing his feet on his desk.

Nick sat on the edge of Ron's desk and drank his coffee, causing his partner to clench his jaw. He hated people's butts on his desk. Everyone was aware of the pet peeve; they did it to annoy him. "I hear you. But there has been some movement on the home invasion murder in Decatur," Nick said, picking up a folder and flipping through it.

The case was a sensitive one. Masked criminals killed a single mother in front of her children during a home invasion. The children went to live with a grandmother in

Peachtree City. The electronics that were stolen had disappeared, but they found the stolen jewelry at a seedy pawnshop that Ron dealt with in a previous case. Community leaders were angry and had led several well-publicized neighborhood protests in response. Public frustration was rising, and there was some concern about widespread unrest. There had been several burglaries before the murder, and the neighborhood perceived the police as less than responsive. City Hall had stressed the importance of solving this case to the detectives and their direct superiors. It was getting tense.

"Since we caught the case at the lab, the lieutenant is going to hand the home invasion case over to Marco and Allen to follow up." Nick shifted on Ron's desk. "Today, let's interview the people that worked with the victim and try to retrace her steps last night to see where she went and who she saw."

"And who saw her?" Ron added. "This could be a pickup gone wrong. Single woman, pretty girl out on a Friday night. She might have run into the wrong guy or girl."

"It could be that simple. I just can't shake the feeling that there's something more." Nick went to sit at his desk and took a swig of his beverage. It was almost lukewarm, but he still welcomed the caffeine kick. "Have you seen the lieutenant this morning?" Nick inquired. Their lieutenant had entered the police academy with Ron. While their career paths had diverged, there was still a more personal relationship between them. Thus, Ron was the liaison to the man.

"I saw him when I first walked in. I briefed him on the Thorne details, on where we are, nowhere, and our likely next steps. He said, 'Go with God.'" Ron checked his cell phone and shook his head. "Even he knows this case is a dog.

I've already put in for a cell phone dump to see who the victim had been talking to. We'll hopefully get it in a few hours. We also need to go to her apartment. They sealed it off early this morning." Ron submitted.

"At least, he's not on our asses," Nick said, firing up his computer. His phone and computer were linked, so all the information he had gathered at the scene was also on his laptop.

"That reminds me. The computer guys already have their hands on her home computer. Does she have one at work?" Ron asked.

"I'm sure she does, but you know getting that one will be more challenging. The Scotts are not just going to hand it over. Let's start with our notes from last night. Rachel Arielle Thorne was originally from Versailles, Kentucky, which is just outside of Lexington. Master's degree in microbiology from the University of Wisconsin in Madison. Here are some co-workers to speak with: David Yego, a technician in what appears to be the same department, and the manager of the lab, Joan Abbott. Tatiana Daniels, same department. Chris McIntosh and Abel Beaumont are in different departments so maybe? The security guard who was on duty last night was Marcus Robinson. Didn't you speak with him already?"

Ronald confirmed. He had volunteered to make that call last night. "I talked to him briefly this morning as I drove in. He said he saw nothing and made up an excuse to get off the phone before I could schedule a meeting. I could tell he was afraid he would lose his job, as he should be. There was a dead body on the premises during his watch. Let's set up a time to chat face-to-face." Ron started to re-enter the number into his phone.

Before he could complete the call, detective Marco Alvarez, wearing a leather jacket and cowboy boots, walked up to his desk. The tall man was originally from Texas and brought his specific sensibilities to Atlanta. He was also fluent in Spanish and Portuguese and had spent some time working undercover in Latino gangs while living in Texas. He moved to Atlanta with his new wife less than one year ago and had steadily integrated himself into the precinct. Marco gave Ron a quick handshake and Nick a chin tilt.

"I heard you had something for me," he said, sitting on the corner of Ron's desk. Ron swatted at him to get his butt up. Marco laughed and stood up.

"Here's the address for the pawnshop where the stolen items appeared. I've been there before. The owner's a bit squirrelly about police. Enter as a customer and then flip the script on him. Try scary. He responds to strength." Ron texted him the address.

"I can do scary," Marco said in his deepest scary voice. "Also, did you talk to the neighbor who just returned to town?"

"No, he just came back yesterday. I think he was visiting his daughter in Tennessee for Thanksgiving. He didn't leave until the morning after the robbery. He claims to know nothing. Lean into him," Nick said. "The case file with his contact information's in your email."

"Got it. I'll let you know what we find." Marco headed out of the room to find his partner.

Ron then called the security guard again, who answered on the first ring—and was a little more cooperative this time. Sure, he was at home. He hadn't been able to sleep since he heard about everything that had happened, and he expected they would want to see him. He would do whatever was necessary to help. Ron told him they would be at his home in a few minutes.

Ron hung up. “It’s a go. The security guard’s shaking in his shoes. Let’s head to Thorne’s apartment first and let him sweat,” he said to Nick.

7
In the Light of Day

Jamie dozed in her seat for a few minutes as they drove out of the shopping center's parking lot. The ride home would have been an appropriate time to nap, but her mind kept returning to the previous night's events although she was drowsy; her mother hadn't also mentioned the midnight trip all day. Today, Margaret seemed unfazed by the horrors of last night. Jamie was confident that her mother knew more about her employee than she was willing to tell the police.

She finally gave up on her nap and took the plunge. "Mother, what do you know about the dead woman? Do you know why she would have been at the lab last night?"

"Why would I know anything? I don't get into other people's affairs. Don't give me that look." Margaret didn't even have to look to know that Jamie was giving her that look. "I don't have time to keep up with everyone's drama. I have my own life to manage, and I have to keep up with my children and husband."

"Well, this is a death—likely murder—outside your business, and you don't seem interested. Aren't you curious? I am. I would like to know why she was there. She had to be coming from the lab. All the bars and restaurants aren't that close, not to walk at night," Jamie persisted.

Her mother stared at her for a moment. "Must you try to involve us in this mess? You just returned to town. Do you want the first news anyone hears about you to be associated with a murder?"

"No one cares about me coming back to town aside from my family, so I doubt they're breathlessly awaiting updates on my status. However, this woman's death may interfere with business. Perhaps we should get ahead of it before it costs you money." Jamie knew *that* would tweak her mother's interest. Since the lab had been her idea, she considered its success her fourth child. Anything that might destroy it required swift and strong action.

"Well, since you put it that way." Margaret navigated toward the highway to return home. "I know that sometimes, the employees in the lab carpool to a bar in Little Five Points after work and leave their cars in the lab lot until later in the evening. She might have gone down there and picked up the wrong guy." Margaret suggested.

"That's possible. Has it gotten that dangerous at the bar scene there?" Jamie peeked at her mother. "What department was she working in at the lab? Perhaps she was running a test that she wanted to check on before she went home."

"You would have to ask your father about that. Oh, hang on. Rachel mostly worked in the toxicology section. The lab manager, Joan, can tell you the details. She'll be at the party tomorrow. Greg's very impressed with her. I think your father relates to her 'coming from nothing and making something of herself' story." Margaret kept her eyes straight ahead. "There is also another lab technician and researcher that Rachel often worked with—David Yego. He's difficult. He's from some African country. I don't remember which one off the top of my head. Kenya, I think. He seems very smart, but he's an odd one." Margaret switched topics quickly. "Are you going to wear your hair up tomorrow night?"

"Don't know yet. Back to the lab. Is the other lab technician—what's his name, David—is he going to be there tomorrow?"

Margaret recognized the tone. "Jamison, this is my birthday celebration. Please do not go around interrogating the guests. I don't think I invited him, but I'm pretty sure your father did—against my explicit request, I might add. Gregory wanted to reward the managers and people with potential. Several people from work will be there to mingle. As I said, David's a weird one. I don't think he's a manager material, but Greg thinks he's a talented researcher." Margaret pursed her lips. "Let's talk about something more pleasant. When are my two oldest children going to settle down? No one's getting any younger."

Jamie pretended to doze off. Both she and Jon had never enjoyed having this conversation with Margaret. Jamie had avoided it for four years. Now she was sure her mother would make up for the lost time. Margaret took the hint, and they rode in silence until they arrived back at the house.

Jamie hopped out as if she were on a spring as soon as Margaret stopped behind Jon's car. The older woman knew Jamie had been pretending to sleep, but she got out of the car without comment and brought Jamie's packages in.

Jon and Gregory were in the kitchen, sitting on barstools debating their choice of beverage. They were both dressed in athletic gear, having just finished a workout session—Jon running and Gregory walking on the treadmill. From the sheepish looks on their faces, Jamie suspected they had been talking about a woman. Gregory wouldn't want to discuss that topic in front of his wife and daughter. He failed to realize they were all aware of Jon's issues with women.

"Hi, Dad. Hi, Jon." Jamie kissed her father on the cheek. "I know you're discussing women. Who's the lucky girl now?" She walked over to the refrigerator; she hadn't eaten since the previous night. Margaret entered the kitchen.

Jon smirked. "Even after all this time, you still know me. Tomorrow, my date will be a lovely young accountant. She's done some business with Dad. He introduced us."

Jamie shook her head as she grabbed a lemon yogurt and poured a glass of juice. Too many food choices! Sitting down at the table, Jamie studied her father. Since when did he take part in fixups and blind dates? Jon had just officially ended one relationship yesterday. So much for wanting to settle down.

"Margaret, the planner will be here first thing in the morning, as will the crew that'll finish the set-up. She called while you were out," Gregory said. Margaret came over to kiss him as he gave Jamie a brief appraisal from his seat. "Jamison, your hair looks lovely. I'm sure you found something to wear for the festivities. You two left so early this morning that I figured you'd be asleep by now."

"I'm exhausted. And after I eat, I'm going to take a nap. I wanted to ask you a couple of questions about last night, though."

Margaret shook her head and asked if her husband or son had made anything for lunch. Both men looked bewildered, which led to another head shake. "Oh well, you'll have to fend for yourselves for lunch. It's late, anyway. I took some frozen soup out this morning, so we'll have minestrone, a kale salad, and French bread for a light dinner. I assume you're staying, Jon?"

Like Jon would ever turn this offer down? Jamie thought humorously.

Jon winked and smiled at Jamie, then turned an innocent face to his mother. After Margaret pursed her lips in response to her son's mischievous grin, she turned back to her husband. "Jamie is going to grill you about last night's events and the people who work at the lab. Please dissuade her. This death's already a problem and none of our business," she noted as she attempted to persuade Gregory.

Jamie spooned some creamy yogurt into her mouth. "I'm sure being dead is a problem for Rachel, Mother. She worked for you and may have died either in your parking lot or in your building. Hey, have you looked at the surveillance videos yet? Was she in the building?" she asked her father.

"I haven't watched them yet. Richard is going to come by and examine the feed with me so we can pass it on to the police," Gregory said warily, sipping his drink. He could see the clouds gathering in the room between Jamie and Margaret. He had to tread lightly.

Jon chimed in. "I knew Rachel a little. I met her at one of the office holiday parties and saw her out a few times. I think she was dating a high-school football coach at one point. His name was Ben. I met him once, too."

"I didn't know you knew her so well. Did you date her?" Margaret stopped what she was doing at the stove and glared at her son. "That would have been inappropriate."

"No, Mother. I knew that would offend your sense of decorum. It was as I said. I talked to her. We hung out in

Buckhead. Single people who see each other out can have conversations." He cast a sneaky look at his mother and smirked. "She was pretty though—she had pretty eyes, great lips, and other nice assets as well."

Margaret threw up her hands. Jamie ignored his joke and plowed forward. "Was she the type to pick up someone at a bar? And leave with him?" she asked the room. "Or was she dedicated enough to her job to work on a Friday night?"

"Well, she shouldn't have been in the lab. If any urgent lab work comes in, the on-call technician should handle it. There's a process. She wasn't on call. I believe Chris, Abel, and Tatiana were," Gregory said.

"Dad, can I be there when you watch the video feed?" Jamie said. "And Mother says the lab manager will be here tomorrow, too? Could you introduce me?"

On seeing his wife's plaintive expression, Gregory tried to split the difference. "Of course, I'll introduce you. But you have to respect your mother's wishes and avoid grilling the guests."

"OK." Jamie got up and stood next to her mother and the soup pot. "That smells divine," she stated. The aromas of the tomatoes, the garlic, and the oregano made her mouth water. She tried to get a taste, but Margaret slapped her hand away. "OK, OK. Please don't let my greedy brother eat it all," Jamie pleaded jokingly and started to walk out of the room but paused at the doorway.

"Dad don't forget. Let me know when Richard comes," Jamie repeated, and her father agreed again.

Satisfied for the time being, she went upstairs and fell onto her bed. This was her third attempt at sleep since she arrived. *Maybe I can get a few hours this time,* she thought, drifting off.

8
Liars and Cheats

Detectives Ron and Nick left the precinct and got into Nick's SUV. Rachel's apartment was in a quiet, upscale apartment complex in North Druid Hills. It wasn't a gated community, so they didn't have to check-in at a guardhouse. Ron read the posted addresses and directed Nick to the block of units they wanted.

Nick pulled into a parking space in front of Rachel's building. She lived in a first-floor unit, now sealed with police tape. To their surprise, a security guard for the apartment complex stood outside her door. They displayed their badges, and the guard made a call on his cell before allowing them to enter.

"Good morning, detectives," the uniformed man said. He was a stout, short, older man and was sweating even in the cold. There were traces of a deep southern accent in certain words, which suggested a childhood in a more rural area of the South than Atlanta. "My manager asked me to stand guard after the police put the police tape up because lookie lous were hanging around even at three in the mornin'. I just let her know you were here. She'll probably come by to ask a few questions. We both knew Rachel, and it's hard to believe she's gone."

"Thanks," Nick said. "Since she knows we're here, you can let us take a quick look around, right?" The guard was uncomfortable but decided not to press the issue. Both detectives put on latex gloves, and Ron pulled the tape from around the door.

Before the security guard left, Ron asked, "How well did you know her?" Nick and Ron walked into the apartment's vestibule, leaving the guard outside.

"Not that well. Just to say hello." He took a package of cigarettes out of his pocket and lit one. "I've been working here for two years. She lived here for about one and a half years. I remember because she locked herself out on the first day. I let her in." He took a puff from his cigarette. "She kept to herself mostly, but she had a boyfriend for a while. He came around a while, then suddenly stopped." He snapped his fingers. "Didn't know what happened. He just disappeared."

"Did she have other visitors?" Nick asked.

"None that I noticed. Oh, here comes my manager," the guard added.

An obese, stern-appearing woman arrived in a golf cart. She wore a large gray puffy coat, which added to her girth. A red stretchy beanie covered her salt and pepper hair, and the chill in the air made her pale cheeks bright red. The woman was panting as she got out of the cart and ambled toward them.

"I'm so glad this is on the first floor." She wheezed as she spoke. "Let me see your badges. I need to put your information in my records," she said to the two men.

Nick and Ron pulled their badges out again. The manager continued, “Thanks. I rented this unit to Rachel. She shared an apartment in a different complex when she first moved to Atlanta. Then she moved in here by herself.”

“Do you know who she roomed with when she first moved to Atlanta?” Nick asked as the manager struggled to follow them into the apartment. The guard remained outside smoking but watched the interaction with interest.

“I think it was someone she worked with at her job. I don’t remember the name.” The manager stopped in the vestibule. “How long before you get everything out of here? You handle that, don’t you?”

“No, sorry. Her parents will have to arrange that. She paid rent for the month, correct? I’m sure her parents will come soon to pack up her things,” Ron replied and tilted his head toward the door. “We’ll take over from here. Thanks.”

She got the hint. She and the security guard backed away. They didn’t go far because those lookie lous the guard had mentioned were gathering around the apartment again. Ron closed the door, and he and Nick split up. The patrol officers who secured her apartment had logged and tagged her laptop, and CSU printed the place and collected samples. Still, Nick and Ron wanted to get a sense of who Rachel was with their own eyes.

Rachel’s two-bedroom apartment was tidy even after all the police traffic; it was full of high-end products. The décor in the living and dining rooms was tasteful—the walls were white, and all the furnishings were black or gray. The black leather sectional couch with recliner filled most of the modestly sized living room. There was no art on the walls, but there were hanging framed photos—one an older portrait of Rachel with her parents and another more recent one of Rachel in a cap and gown with her proud family. All three people were grinning in both, and you could feel the love radiating from both photos. *She really was a pretty, happy girl*, Nick thought. A fifty-five-inch flat-screen TV lived in a large black entertainment center that also held a Blu-ray player and several game consoles. There weren't any magazines at all in the living room. The dining room contained a square black table with seating for six. Again, the set filled most of the room; it was immaculate. Her kitchen contained many expensive stainless-steel, almost new gadgets: a coffee maker, juicer, blender, pressure cooker, air fryer, toaster, slow cooker, and mixer. It seemed she only used the coffee maker regularly. The kitchen cabinets contained a nice set of cookware with All-Clad stamped on it. Again, not frequently used. The fridge and pantry were almost empty—a half-filled bottle of Cranberry juice, a bottle of wine, a carton of milk, A box of Cinnamon Toast Crunch—that threw the detectives off for a moment. But when Nick found a half-empty package of Oreos tucked behind everything in the freezer, an image of a woman with a sweet tooth that she indulged in secret appeared in his mind. The kitchen itself was tidy, with only one coffee cup in the sink. The washer and dryer sat in an alcove next to the kitchen. Both appliances were empty.

Her bedroom was less restrained, with solid, if boring, wood furniture and another large, flat-screen TV with a Blu-ray player. But here, Rachel had allowed her imagination to run free more. The walls were a deep purple—that would cost her family her security deposit. The duvet cover had swirls of lavender and purple, with some matching shams and a pile of decorative pillows on the bed. Rachel had made the bed up before she left on the day she died. The walls held several concert posters—one of Prince, The Time, and Vanity 6, one of Queen, and one of the Foo

Fighters. The diversity of musical interests intrigued the detectives; Rachel might have been interesting to know. The closet was so full that there were clothes sticking out of the door. Many still had expensive tags on them. There was also a jewelry box in the closet with some delicate pieces—good quality gold, a nice diamond tennis bracelet, and a few gemstones.

Back in the bedroom, the detectives searched everywhere to get a better sense of the victim. There was only one nightstand in the room. Ron frowned as he leaned to open a drawer. “Isn’t it usually a bad idea to open someone else’s goodie drawer?” Nick snickered. His partner proceeded with his task.

In one nightstand drawer, there was an unopened iPad. In another, two paperbacks with bookmarks. Finally, in the top drawer, Nick and Ron found boxes of condoms and a strawberry-flavored lubricant—all unopened.

“Either she regularly filled this drawer, or she was between men,” Nick said. “I would hate to die suspiciously. Would you want someone looking through all your stuff and making assumptions about your sex life?”

“It wouldn’t be so bad. I would be a legend,” Ron said, laughing for a moment and then becoming solemn. He glanced around the bedroom. “She didn’t have a landline, so no answering machine.”

He walked into her bathroom and opened the medicine cabinet. “Hey, here’s a prescription for Prozac. She was on the pill as well. Nothing else of interest.” He paused at the bottles of makeup and facial cleanser—some unused. Ron was not an expert in this area, but he recognized they were not drugstore brands. He glanced around the bathroom. The tub was reasonably clean, with a few blond hairs caught in the drain. The shower curtain matched the duvet, and the towels were purple. One towel was on the floor—one of the few things that were out of place in the entire apartment. The hamper, also purple, was half full of towels, underwear, and bras.

Ron then ventured into the guest bedroom, which was also tastefully decorated in purple tones with a flat screen TV above the chest of drawers. The walls were lavender, and the comforter was purple. The closet contained a couple of men's shirts and a pair of jeans, which all likely belonged to the former boyfriend. A set of nice hardside suitcases sat in the corner of the closet. There was nothing else in the room or closet.

She stuffed everything into one closet, with this entire space unused. Still hoping he might come back, I guess, Ron thought.

Nick rifled through her desk, also in the main bedroom, and flipped through some bank and credit card statements. "Ron, she had a deposit of around eighteen hundred dollars every two weeks. She paid her bills regularly. She had high credit card balances paying only the minimums. How did she buy all this stuff?" He flipped through a few more. Interestingly, the last paper statement was from October. Checking the dates, a new statement was out already, but there was no copy in the pile. That situation struck Nick as odd—that as a millennial, she had received paper statements at all. *Yet another question to answer about this young woman,* Nick thought as he relayed that info to Ron.

His partner nodded. "Interesting point about the statements. Maybe she likes having things on paper. Maybe her parents have an idea about that part." Ron tilted his head and motioned toward Rachel's closet. "Her paycheck could not cover all this stuff. There's another TV in the guest bedroom. She has more electronics than I do," Ron said.

"Man, you still have a console TV from the eighties. Your wife won't let you upgrade," Nick said jokingly.

"Hey, Estelle wants to retire on the beach. We're saving our money. The console plays: we watch it." Ron grinned. "If I want to see a game in high def, you have a large flat screen I can use."

Nick grew serious. "Hang on here. She had twenty-five thousand dollars in her savings account. Where did that come from? Given her salary, she couldn't have saved this much money. Maybe from her parents?" Nick asked, quite puzzled.

Ron did not know. He came to read over Nick's shoulder.

"Do you think she would have been ripe for some quick way to make money?" Looking further back at her banking statements, Nick paused. "It looks like her balance was higher over the past couple of years. Wait, the latest shopping spree was around four months ago. I guess that's how she was financing a lot of that shopping. She used little of what she bought, though. Maybe she needed to join Shoppers Anonymous," Nick said.

"Wasn't that when the boyfriend disappeared? Wonder if he was the source of the money?" Ron asked.

"Didn't someone say he was a coach? Unless he was a coach for the Falcons, he didn't have this kind of money." Nick placed the statements back on the desk. "My gut says that there's more to this woman. Based on what we know about her so far, it doesn't seem like she brought random guys home with her. Everyone seemed to know that she had a boyfriend. Obviously, I could be wrong, but that's what I am going with right now," Nick stated.

"Maybe she was waiting for that boyfriend to come back to her. Let's go talk to the runaway boyfriend."

When the detectives left Rachel's apartment, the manager and security guard were still lurking around—the manager was back on her golf cart. Ron asked the manager to lock the door to the unit.

"Please make sure no one enters the property until the police release the scene," he said. "Ms. Thorne's family will contact you to pick up her things."

The manager agreed and then tried to shoo the onlookers away without leaving her cart.

While Ron spoke with the manager, Nick received a phone call. The person on the other end of the line said a few things, and Ron could see Nick's frown.

"That was CSU. The only prints in Rachel's car were hers and one other set, which was identified as Ben Hargrove. His employer printed him for his job. No blood or biologicals. No stray hairs. The steering wheel and the driver's door handles were wiped clean. Her purse contained a driver's license and credit cards. No work ID," Nick relayed to Ron in a low voice. Switching back to the call, Nick replied, "Keep looking and let us know if anything else turns up. Thanks."

Nick turned to Ron as they got to the truck. "The boyfriend. Of course. He needs to answer a few questions. What's his address?" Ron had downloaded the coach's phone number and address to his phone before they left the station, so he pulled out his phone to retrieve it. Nick tapped his foot to hurry his partner's search along—he was in a hurry, but he was partly trying to annoy his partner. He turned his head to mask a smile.

Ron dismissed his partner's impatience as he worked to locate the address quickly. His younger partner enjoyed pushing his buttons—a mini-battle of the generations if you will. When the address popped up, Ron recognized the location and relayed it to Nick. Ben's home was only a few miles from Rachel's, which had to have been convenient while they were dating. After a call to confirm he was home, the detectives headed over. The security guard would have to stew for a while longer.

Ben Hargrove's home was on a street of wooden duplexes with small, wooded yards. As they pulled up to his house, a short, pretty, dark-skinned African American woman opened one door of the duplex warily. She was eight or nine months pregnant.

"Yes?" she said as they traveled up the walk.

"Good morning, ma'am. We're here to speak with Ben Hargrove about a case we're working on," Ron said, pulling out his badge.

A taller, fit, light-skinned African American man with a shaved head came up behind her. "I got this, babe," he said, edging by her, stepping out onto the front porch, and closing the door behind him. *Protective or hiding something?* Nick thought to himself.

"Sorry about that, but I knew you would come to talk to me. I'm Ben." He looked sheepish and started shifting his feet back and forth. "My wife doesn't know about my time with Rachel because I was seeing 'em both at the same time."

"I understand, man," Ron said. "But I must ask, how did you find out about Rachel so quickly?"

"One of my friends texted me about it. When I heard the details, I figured I would be high on your list of people to interview," Ben said.

"You were going out with Rachel until a few months ago? It looks like you cut it close," Nick said.

"Anna getting pregnant is why I broke it off with Rachel." Ben dropped his head, then lifted it again to take stock of the two men. "I hate that this happened to her."

"I take it she didn't know about Anna. When was the last time you talked to her? She probably wouldn't have taken the news of your impending parenthood too well, would she?" Nick said.

Ben focused on Nick. "I didn't tell her. I haven't seen or talked to her since our breakup five months ago."

Ron got more aggressive. "If Anna found out about Rachel, that would cause some problems in your happy home, right? You realize you have an excellent motive to be angry at Rachel." Ben's eyes widened, a touch of panic setting in. "You're sure she didn't know about your other life?" Ron asked, leaning in.

"No, no, she didn't know! You think I could have had something to do with this?" He paced on his porch and continued in a furious whisper, waving his hands at his waist. "I wouldn't have done anything like that to Rachel. I'm upset about what happened to her. But beyond that, I haven't seen her in months. I swear."

"Where were you last night?"

"I was with Anna. We went to a baby shower dinner that some of her friends had planned. It lasted until about ten, and then we went with a couple of friends to listen to music. The baby's due soon, so we want to enjoy our last few nights out without a kid." He glanced at the front door, where the three men could see Anna scoping out the scene through the window. Ben waved and turned back to the detectives. “Please, don’t mention my history with Rachel. Anna threatened to leave if she ever found out I had cheated on her. If she found out about Rachel, she would leave and take my baby. I’ll tell you where we were so you can check, but please don’t tell her.” *Definitely panicky now.*

The detectives agreed not to give him away if his story checked out and took the information. As Nick and Ron walked back to their vehicle, Nick said, “Anna probably needs to know what kind of man she’s hitched her star to.”

Ron said, “I’m sure she’s aware. Do you see how she stayed by that window? She’s probably giving him the business now that he’s back in the house. Women have a radar like that.”

Starting the car, Nick shook his head. “Don’t be all righteous about this. There’re no women present. You should be glad Estelle’s not here, or you would be single again, looking for a place to bunk,” he said.

Ron smiled.

“Anyway, let’s check his alibi, but my gut says he’s not the guy. Let’s talk to the security guard next—he’s expecting us, correct? We can also go to the restaurant and bar area near the lab, flash her picture around, and see if anyone saw her last night. Get some patrol to check around, too. After that, though, we should get the video feeds from the Scott family. If we have time, we can speak with people that work at the lab.”

Ron exhaled. “That’s a tall order for one day. Can we get some lunch? I didn’t eat anything, given my late night and very early morning. A young boy has to keep up his strength.” Ron checked his watch.

“Estelle sent you out without anything this morning?” Nick teased.

"I didn't say that. What she sent me out with was a lovely parting gift. Part of the reason I'm tired," Ron said defensively.

Nick grinned but didn't provide a comeback.

Within twenty minutes, they were in front of Marcus Robinson's residence, a small, brick-and-white, one-level home with a well-kept yard on a quiet street. Marcus answered the door before the detectives knocked. The young man had been awaiting their arrival.

"Mr. Robinson, I'm Detective Ronald Dixon, and this is my partner, Detective Nick Marshall. We would like to ask you some questions about Rachel Thorne and the events at the lab."

The young man backed up as he allowed the detectives into his home. Marcus was not very tall—around five foot seven, average weight, dark-skinned, with a baby face. That face was struggling to maintain its composure. He invited them to have a seat as he moved a toy truck and other items from two chairs in the living room. There were a few pieces of furniture in the room, but there were many toys and clothes on most of the flat surfaces. "Sorry about the mess. Kids," he said. "My wife has the kids corralled in our bedroom until you leave." He offered them something to drink, which they refused, and parked herself on the couch across from them. "What can I tell ya?"

"How long have you worked as a lab guard?"

"Only six months. I was a guard at a storage place before. I enjoy workin' at the lab—it's quiet, I get some weekends off, and Dr. Scott, Rachel, Joan, and everyone else are good people. I mean, Rachel was… this is…" He trailed off.

"You left out Mrs. Scott."

"I mean, she seems nice, but she doesn't talk to—I dunno— folks who are below her, I guess. I'm just the security guard, and I don't think she sees me on most days."

Nick filed that away. It fits with what he noticed last night. "How many security guards are there, and when did your shift start last night?"

"There're several guards that work shifts, and the security head, Kevin. We also have several part-time guards who work staggered hours or fill in for sick folk. Yesterday, one part-timer worked from six a.m. to twelve noon. I came on at eleven a.m. and was supposed to get off at eight p.m. A part-timer was supposed to work last night. But he called in sick, so I covered his shift."

"So, you were working when Rachel left for the day for the first time. Did you see her?"

"I saw her leave around six. I was sitting at the front desk when she left. She said goodbye. I didn't see her come back, though." He lowered his gaze, shifting in his seat. "I didn't see no one coming or going after that."

"Are you sure Rachel didn't come back to the office? Is there some other entrance?"

"Didn't see her or no one else. There's a back entrance, but you need a badge to open it, and it sets off a buzzer at the security desk. Anyone who uses the back entrance must check-in and enter their badge code at the front desk to turn it off. We've had people forget, and the entire lab goes on lockdown until someone comes forward," he explained.

Ronald and Nick glanced at each other. Neither believed his story but didn't want to accuse him until they had more information. "Just a few more questions. How well did you know Ms. Thorne? Did she say anything when she left?" Nick inquired.

"She spoke to me every morning when I was on duty—just to say hi, you know? I know she was dating some guy named Ben a while back." The young man blushed.

"How do you know that? I thought you only spoke to say hi," Ron said.

"You know what I mean. We'd talk for a few minutes if I saw her in the break room. I can't hang around for long, or I will lose my job. She must have mentioned her boyfriend at some point." He glared at both detectives as frustration set in. "It was common knowledge at the lab."

"Was it common knowledge when they broke up?" Nick asked.

Marcus thought for a minute. "Yeah. It was rather messy how it went down. I think she had gone away with him for the weekend, and when they returned to Atlanta, they both went to their own places. The next day, she comes home from work and finds all his stuff gone, man. From what I heard, he never said anything or called her again."

"How do you know this?" Ron asked.

"Folks at the lab talk. That was the main talk for a few days. I believe she took off work and tried to visit him at his apartment. But he had moved without telling her." Marcus was enjoying the gossip portion of the conversation.

Nick and Ron exchanged glances.

"Anna really needs to know about her man," Nick said to Ron, low enough that Marcus couldn't hear.

"Anyway, it took her a while to get happy again," Marcus said. "You know, on some Thursdays and Fridays, several people would sometimes go out for a happy hour down the street. I assumed that was where she was going based on when she left. She had on lipstick and high heels—

she usually wore flat shoes at work. That I remember. She had nice legs. Not that I was looking, but you know how it is."

The detectives circled back around what Nick said, "So you didn't see her return to the lab? What would you say if I told you she came back into the building, but the video didn't show you there?" Nick was lying, but he and Ron thought there was more to Marcus's discomfort.

"I would say you were mistaken. You couldn't have seen that," Marcus said definitively. He set his jaw, and with his baby face, he resembled a determined child.

"How do you know?" Ron asked.

"I just know that's not true, that's all. I do my job like I'm supposed to," Marcus said, without making eye contact.

They knew then he was lying. "I think you took a break from your post and don't know if she came in or not," Nick said, taking a stab at what probably happened. He got up and walked around the living room.

Marcus turned his head to watch Nick pace. "I don't know what…" he started.

"Stop," Ron said. "My guess is you have a girlfriend in the building that you were spending some time with. Am I right?"

"We need to know what happened. Right now, we're wondering if there was some collusion between the killer and you," Nick said.

Marcus glanced back and forth between the two detectives. "Heh, heh," he babbled, fidgeting in his chair. His forehead glistened with sweat.

"Heh, heh," Ron mimicked as Nick walked over to Marcus and stood directly in front of him. "Want to change your story?"

Marcus motioned for Nick and Ron to lean closer. "OK, you got me. I was otherwise occupied. I paused the video feed," he said softly. "Please, don't tell my wife or my boss."

Nick threw a disgusted look at Marcus. *Are there no more faithful men today?* he thought.

"It's just a thing. My friend and I get together when things are slow. No one gets hurt," Marcus said.

"Well, no. Somebody got hurt." Ron pursed his lips at the young man's statement. "So, obviously, you weren't with Rachel. Who is it?"

"I don't think it matters," Marcus said.

"We need to check your story, or we could just question everyone about who you hang out with—including your wife," Nick said.

"OK, OK. Tatiana Daniels. Just don't tell her I sent you her way. She's a private person," Marcus said.

Nick doubted she was all that private if she was hooking up in coat closets, bathrooms, or anywhere at all at work, but figured that they would get nothing else out of him now.

"Thank you for your time. We may be back to speak with you again as the investigation proceeds," Nick said as he and Ron prepared to leave.

"OK, but I don't know what else I can tell you," Marcus said, walking them out.

Nick and Ronald settled in the SUV for a moment after the encounter, feeling a tad discouraged. "There's probably something more there. Once we see the feeds, we can jack him up, if necessary," Ron said. One of his favorite parts of being a police officer.

“Everyone involved with this case so far is a liar and a cheat,” Nick said. “This is destroying my faith in humanity today.”

9
Five Points of Investigation

The pair of detectives drove down to Little Five Points, a funky cool neighborhood in East Atlanta. Home to several distinctive restaurants and bars, record stores, coffee shops, a radio station, theaters, and other types of businesses. It was also a great place to see street art. It has a Bohemian vibe and has been compared to Haight Ashbury in San Francisco. While Little Five Points is eclectic, there are standard big box stores just south of the area. Plenty to do and see.

Perfect neighborhood for a woman who was trying to forget her problems to visit on a Friday night, thought Nick.

Several bars were likely culprits for Friday night happy hours and hookups. While the neighborhood was a great walking neighborhood, it would take a bit of legwork to hit each bar that Rachel might have visited without guidance. They hoped there would be some beat officers in the area who could lend a hand if they needed it. Ron was also on the lookout for lunch.

After finding a parking spot, which wasn't an easy feat so close to lunchtime on a Saturday, the pair started at the closest bar, the Vortex Bar and Grill.

Nick had always liked the look of the place, as the doorway of the establishment was a skull with large, dramatic red eyes. Once inside, the décor was a bit more vintage. The scent of burgers—a specialty of the joint—made Nick's mouth water, but they couldn't stop for lunch yet. The detectives asked the on-duty manager about the previous night's patrons. Nick had a picture of Rachel on his phone and showed it to any workers who were on last night. After striking out there, they visited two other establishments before lunch: Little 5 Corner Tavern and the Porter Beer Bar. In each case, the on-duty manager had not been there the previous night but could direct them to someone who had been. The story was the same at each place: *Hey, she looks dead. Is she dead? No, I haven't seen her before. How did she die?*

Neither man was pleased with their results, and the displeasure was palpable. "This has been fruitful," Ron snarled. "Can we eat now? I'm starving and can't ask any more questions until I eat." He was tense and cranky as he scanned the throng of holiday shoppers and visitors leisurely strolling in nearby establishments. Ron had always found Little Five Points fascinating from a distance. As he got older, the noisy, vibrant crowd made him tired. Days like this made retirement seem like a good idea.

During their investigation, they had passed a pizza joint, Little Five Points Pizza, and to appease Ron quickly,

Nick asked, "Pizza—would pizza do? Let's grab a slice there."

As Ron rubbed his chin and contemplated this choice, Nick turned and walked toward the pizza joint. Ron was an excellent partner, but he had a one-track mind, often helpful when solving cases, but lately, his mind was elsewhere. He made several comments about leaving the job behind over the past few weeks, and comments about his marriage had shown signs of strain. Nick asked a few questions about how things were going, but Ron stonewalled him each time. They had only been partners for just over a year, so Nick didn't feel comfortable pushing the issue. Ron tucked his hands in his pockets and followed him into the restaurant.

It took a little time and physical wrangling for Nick and Ron to walk their way up to the counter through the Saturday holiday crowd. Fortunately, most customers were in the holiday spirit, so no one responded angrily to any stubbed toes and the physical jostling required to place an order. The odor of oven-baked dough and fresh tomato sauce with garlic wafted through the air. The atmosphere was friendly, with strangers starting conversations with strangers. Once they arrived at the counter, the detectives ordered two slices of pepperoni pizza and a Coke each. After they were served and had paid for their orders, they walked out of the small, crowded space. It was sunny, and the temperature had increased, so they wolfed down their slices outside. While they ate, both men watched the crowds of people milling around. Even in December, there were significant numbers of tourists at Little Five Points. This made it more challenging to find people who may have seen the victim on the previous night and identify anyone she might have left with—if that was what she had done.

As Ron ate, he lost his edge. "I'm sorry I was so testy." He took another sip from his beverage. "There are some other places that we should hit. I know how to figure out the likely spots a young woman might visit on a Friday night." He threw away the remains of his drink in a nearby garbage can and pulled out his phone. "Which tech worked the car last night?" He called the CSU lab without waiting for a reply and asked for the tech from last night. After asking a few questions, he turned back to Nick, who had continued eating.

"Let's check out the Wrecking Bar Brewpub."

"Why?"

"There was a valet stub in her car. It was between the seat and the console. It may not be from last night, but it might be a favorite destination. It's a couple of blocks away from here, so we can walk it or try to drive it." Ron explained.

"Let's walk. It's Saturday during the holidays. We'll never find another parking space. There might be some other places to check on the way." Nick fell in step with Ron. "That was a good idea to check for valet stubs. I can't believe we didn't think of it before."

"That's why we're partners, man. We work together. I think she came here, had a few drinks, met somebody more aggressive than she expected, and here we are. Perhaps this joint has cameras, either inside or out."

To get to the Wrecking Ball Brewpub, they followed Moreland Avenue for a little more than a quarter of a mile and passed the Bass recreation center. Moreland was busy, so the two men stopped talking since they couldn't hear each other over the car noise from the road. Once they arrived at the establishment, Ron was winded. And there was parking available onsite.

"I underestimated the distance and overestimated my stamina. Exercising right after I eat is not a good idea. Let me catch my breath," Ron said, pausing and sweating. "And we could have driven. I wouldn't have to walk back."

His partner laughed and took stock of the brewpub's front— a historic Victorian mansion—home to The Wrecking Ball. The building had white ionic columns and a semicircular portico entrance with slate/terracotta detailing. There was a white wooden fence around the front. The historical aspect had been well preserved. The building had been a home, a church, and a dance studio in the past—Nick remembered the history because one of his ill-fated dates had taken place there. The restaurant and bar were great, but his date enjoyed the various beers a little too much and got sick in his car on the way home. There was no second date.

Nick spotted a small camera almost hidden on one column aimed at a temporary valet stand set up in front of the building. He pointed it out to Ron. "They don't trust their valets. That should give us something to look at since we know she often used the valet service. Hopefully, we could see if she left the bar alone."

They headed into the building. The lighting was dim, and the bar area was mostly wood with a high gloss—the bar itself, the shelves where the different spirits were located, the walls, and the floor. Few patrons sat at the bar since the doors had opened at noon. A dining area was out on a patio with a few leisurely customers. Ron and Nick stopped in the bar area and looked around. A bartender saw them and walked over. "What can I do for you?" he asked.

Nick pulled out his badge. "Good afternoon. We would like to ask you some questions about a woman who may have been in your establishment last night." He pulled out his phone and found the picture of Rachel Thorne. “Were you working last night?”

The bartender shook his head. “I just got back to town this morning. Kaitlyn worked last night if I’m not mistaken. She’s around here somewhere; you would think she lives here.” He grinned and scanned the entire establishment. A young server walked by, and the bartender stopped him. “Have you seen Kaitlyn? Could you have her come up here? It’s the police.” The server got wide-eyed and scurried off to find her.

Ron asked the bartender about video feeds in the bar and outside at the valet stand. “We have surveillance. Let me get the manager for you. Hey, here comes Kaitlyn. Kaitlyn, these are the police asking about last night.” He headed to the back office. Kaitlyn walked up to the officers and pushed her straight shoulder-length hair behind her ears. “I hear you’re looking for me. What’s the problem?” she asked. Her voice was initially a little husky, but by the end of her comment, her words came out in a squeak.

Nick studied the young blond woman standing before him—average height and build, with a young-looking face with no makeup and wide gray eyes. She smoothed her clothing and furtively glanced back toward the rear of the pub. “Were you working at the bar last night?” Ron asked her.

“Yes, I was. Is there a problem?” Better control of the squeaking this time.

“Not with you. We just wanted to ask you about a customer last night.” He showed her the picture.

Her eyes got wider. “I remember her. Why are you asking? Is she dead? What happened to her?” She began gnawing on her index finger.

Both detectives were a little surprised by her response. "Why do you remember her? Was there something about her that caught your attention?" Nick noticed that the young woman was drawing blood.

Kaitlyn appeared lost in thought for a moment. "I remember her because she was standing next to this curly-headed guy who tried to pick her up. He reminded me of my brother. She was somewhat rude to him and shot him down quick. I remember she moved to another part of the bar. I watched because I thought the guy would follow her and cause a problem, but he went on about his business. I lost track of her then." She peeked again at the back of the pub. "Can I go?" She was so anxious at this point that she was almost dancing on the spot.

Nick and Ron also looked at the back of the pub. "Is something going on back there that you're trying to hide?"

"No-ooo-thing, really." That squeak was back. "Please, don't tell my boss. I moved out of my boyfriend's place and couldn't afford to move into an apartment on my own." Kaitlyn took a deep breath, composed herself, and lowered her voice to a whisper. "I've been staying in the storeroom. Please. That server caught me putting my gear away. I haven't saved up enough money to get a place yet."

"Hey, not my business," Nick whispered back. He turned to the manager as he came from the back office.

"Detectives, I'm Alan, the manager on duty. I found the surveillance video from last night and the video from outside at the valet station. You can come back here to look." He gestured toward the office. His fingers were tobacco-stained, and the detectives could smell a whiff of smoke trailing him as he walked.

Unfortunately, the office was just large enough for a desk, a table, a computer screen, and *one* person.

The three wedged into the small space in front of the computer screen, with the manager taking a seat and the detectives standing on either side. Despite the cloying smell of tobacco in the office, Ron had leaned over and was breathing on the manager's neck. The manager was uncomfortable but didn't want to antagonize the police. "I paused the feed at around seven last night. Do you know what time the young woman came in?" the manager asked, his voice crackly like he'd smoked cigarettes his entire life.

"Not completely sure. She left the lab around six-thirty, so she should have been here by then. Roll back to about six-thirty, and let's go from there." Ron answered.

The manager rewound to the requested time and pressed play. He got out of the chair to allow one detective to take a seat. Nick took it, and Ron leaned over his shoulder. Nick tried to shoulder him back and little and asked jokingly, "Do you need to see the eye doctor?" Ron ignored him and remained trained on the video.

They peered at the video and identified Rachel and her dark-colored dress when she entered the bar around 7:05 p.m. They followed her to the bar, where she ordered a drink from the woman they had just spoken to. They saw the curly-headed man speak to her, then a brief conversation, and then Rachel stood up and gathered her drink. Then the abrupt ending of their contact. *Ouch, she did shoot him down abruptly*, Nick thought.

They then watched the blond-headed Rachel move away from the would-be suitor down the bar. He went in the opposite direction and connected with a dark-haired woman. The pair left together not long after. Rachel remained at the bar for a while longer. A man with gray hair and glasses spoke to her briefly, and when Rachel left around 8:10, he followed her out.

Alan leaned over to switch the feed to the valet stand view. Another blast of a second (third?)-hand smoke hit Nick in the face. It took focus to get his eyes back on the screen. At the valet stand, Rachel stood alone, waiting for her car. The last man who had spoken to her came up behind her and engaged her in conversation. He was older—gray hair, his gait, the neat clothing that looked dated. It was difficult to read her facial expression, but the detectives could see the gradual change in body language. At first, she appeared relaxed, but as the conversation continued, the young woman visibly recoiled from the man. He seemed to lean in as she backed away. After the conversation was over, she retrieved her car from the valet and left. The older man went back inside. Ron asked the manager for a copy of the feed and handed him a thumb drive.

"OK, so I guess it is possible she picked up someone on the way back," Ron said to Nick, who shook his head.

"It seems unlikely timing-wise. Who was that older guy she was talking to? Maybe the bartender remembers him. He seemed older than the usual Friday night crowd," Nick said.

"He was older, wasn't he? What were they talking about? He seemed to know her." Ron switched tracks. "Where's the valet from last night? Maybe he heard something?"

After handing over the copied thumb drive, the manager scratched his head at the question and redirected them sheepishly back to the on-duty bartender. "He manages the valet schedule," Alan added as he walked them back to the bar area. Both detectives were grateful to be out of the smoky room, but they thanked him for his help.

The bartender was behind the bar pouring a drink for a customer when Nick and Ron reentered. They relayed the manager's comments, to which the bartender raised an eyebrow. "I am surprised Alan told you that. He likes to act like he does more than smoke, as I am sure you noticed. Let me check the schedule for last night to see who was working." Pulling out his smartphone, the bartender tapped his phone screen to pull up the information. "Oh, the valet last night was Manuel. He doesn't come in until six. Kaitlyn lives with him. She should know where he is." After making sure his customers at the bar were set for the moment, he rushed off to search for Kaitlyn again.

Ron and Nick rolled their eyes. With Kaitlyn's previous admission, it was unlikely that she would know where he was, but they didn't want to blow her cover, so neither said anything. The young woman came to the bar with the bartender.

"Kaitlyn, is Manuel at your apartment? The police would like to speak to him," the bartender inquired, staring directly at her.

"Uh. I'm not sure." Her face reddened. "He works construction during the week. This job is his second job on the weekends. On Saturdays, he could be anywhere. You would have to call to track him down."

"You don't know what his plans are for today?" the bartender asked pointedly as Kaitlyn almost hyperventilated. Nick thought she was going to pass out.

"That's OK. We can find him. Just give us an address and a number. We can do the work." What a relief that was for the young lady. Nick entered the information that Kaitlyn relayed into his phone. The young woman was grateful for the shift in questioning. The detectives thanked the bartender for his help, and he returned to his post behind the bar. Kaitlyn had stepped back.

"Thank you for not telling him. He's a tattletale. I'd be on the street in a minute," she said.

"I don't think this situation will work for you if you can't answer questions without freaking out. Just my two cents," Nick said.

Ron added, "There are hotels and apartments with move-in specials that you should consider. Also, if there was some abuse in your relationship—not saying that there was—but if there was, there're also other resources that can help you." He scribbled a number on one of his business cards and handed it to her.

"I don't want to get Manuel in trouble or for him to lose his job. Don't tell him I gave you his information," Kaitlyn said, accepting the card. "Thanks for the advice. I will check out some of those specials," she agreed, finally smiling, showing teeth so perfectly straight and white they looked like dentures or veneers.

The detectives left the building but stopped to review what they had just learned and to bounce ideas off each other.

"Another day of protecting and serving," Ron said, grinning. "Now, we need to find this Manuel guy to see if he noticed anything when our victim came out. Were they any other interactions with anyone before she left. Then there's also the lab video."

"The feed from the lab should give us an exact time that she arrived and let us see if she was alone when she got there." Nick cleared his throat and shook his head at Ron's expression. "Please, don't say it. You think the lab's involved?"

"Not necessarily the lab itself. But there is something wonky about this entire case. There has to be more going on. I now agree with you," Ron said as he clicked through his smartphone. "We just received the data dump for Rachel's phone. A cursory scan shows the victim didn't speak to many people over the last couple of days of her life. Just her mother and quick phone calls to her former boyfriend's cell phone. He said he hadn't spoken to her."

Nick cracked a smile and leaned over Ron's shoulder to read the phone screen. "He purposely left the calls out. But looking at the length of the calls, it seems he didn't speak to her. She probably called and hung up when he didn't answer. Anyway, I didn't get the vibe that he was a killer. Mostly a guy hoping that his two women never meet."

Ron put his phone back in his pocket. "Agreed, but it merits some follow-up."

Nick added, "Did you notice that she also called her co-worker, Tatiana, at what looks like right after she left the bar last night?" He let his mind work for a minute. "I wonder if something specific made her call Tatiana right then. The guy in the bar? Someone else? There's something there." He shook his head. "As for the Scotts, we'll have to dig into their business a bit more. I suspect there're some skeletons."

"There are skeletons everywhere. I'm getting too old for this," Ron replied. Then he groaned as he realized they would have to make the return journey to the car on foot. "*I am too old for this*!"

After making the trek back to the SUV, Ron was still a little out of breath, but he was in better shape this time as he settled into the passenger seat. Less sweaty, which meant Nick was less worried. *Ron can't have a heart attack, right? I need to get him back to the gym.*

Before Nick pulled out of the parking space, they wanted to establish their next interview. Ron called the precinct and ran Manuel's name and address to determine if he had an arrest record. Of course, he did: a couple of arrests for assault and one misdemeanor for domestic violence, with several short stints in the county jail.

"Kaitlyn needs to be more selective about who she moves in with," Ron told Nick while relaying this information.

Nick doubted it would be that simple; relationships were often messy. "I hope she stays away. But there's no guarantee she won't go back."

They called Manuel's cell phone on speaker. He answered on the first ring. "Hey, baby. When are you coming over?" Manuel answered.

Ron made a face and replied in a deep bass voice, "As soon as you tell me where you are."

"Who the hell is this? ¿Estás jodiendo con mi chica? Voy a patear tu culo." Manuel said.

"Hola, Manuel. Este es el detective Nick Marshall y el detective Ron Dixon. No sabemos su chica, pero me gustaría ver que patear mi culo," Nick replied with a grin. He was fluent in Spanish because of his Puerto Rican ex-wife—they had been together a long time—and his daughter often spoke to him in Spanish so her stepfather wouldn't understand what she was saying. Daniela had asked Nick not to go along with that because it made her husband feel bad. But Nick figured the guy could learn Spanish himself and nip the problem in the bud, right? Bad parenting.

Silence on the other end. "Hey Manuel, are you still there?" Ron asked.

A voice with a different tone came over the phone. "Hello, detectives. I'm sorry about the misunderstanding. I obviously thought you were someone else. What can I do for you today?" Manuel sounded like a reasonable and respectable young man. Nick and Ron could see how a reasonable-appearing woman might find this version of Manuel enticing.

Ron relayed their interest in questioning him for a few minutes about his shift/time/experience at the bar last night. He politely told them he was at his apartment and hoped they would not judge him by the mess because he had worked a few hours at a construction site earlier this morning. Ron said they would arrive at his apartment shortly and asked him not to leave, which Manuel quickly agreed to.

By the time the detectives got to the construction worker's door, Manuel had likely straightened his apartment somewhat—it wasn't that messy. The light-brown-skinned young man wore tortoise-shell glasses and pressed khaki pants; he looked more like an accountant than a construction worker. He offered beverages, snacks, and the best seats in the apartment and asked if the temperature and lighting were OK. Perhaps he thought they were there for some previously undiscovered crime.

"You were working as a valet last night, correct? Did you see this woman?" Nick asked, showing him Rachel's picture on his phone. The detective assessed the young Hispanic man. He was attractive, tall, and a shade thin—definitely the type of guy that could pull a girl based on looks alone.

Manuel inspected Rachel's picture on Nick's phone. "Yeah, I remember her. She was cute. Some guy came up to her and started talking before I even went to get her car. She seemed freaked out by whatever he was saying."

Nick connected the thumb drive to his phone and found the images of the two men speaking with Rachel in the bar. "Do you recognize the man that came up to her outside?"

Manuel studied the images carefully. "That older guy. That's him. He was creepy. I was even a little scared, so you know he must have been weird."

"Did you hear their conversation?" Nick asked.

"Some of it." Manuel leaned back in his chair. "He seemed to be from the same place she was. Madison, I think. He mentioned someone who died, which made her jumpy. The girl who died was a friend or in her class or something."

"Did you catch his name?"

He thought for a moment. "William? Will—no, it was William. He gave her his card before she got in her car."

Finally! This was the first solid evidence that this might be related to someone that Rachel knew or had tried to escape from in her past. That was helpful to know.

"Oh, yeah. He said he had just moved down here. I don't know if it was true, but that's what he said."

"Thank you for your help." Nick and Ron stood up to leave. "We will need you to come down to the station and make an official statement about what you saw, and we may need to speak with you again." Ron handed Manuel a card. "You need to stay out of trouble."

"OK. I guess you looked me up. I've been trying to stay out of trouble, man. I turned over a new leaf." Manuel studied the card. "Sorry about before. I thought you were this guy who has been hitting on my girl. He has been calling her regularly, and I could not let that pass."

"Well, threatening to beat someone up wouldn't be turning over a new leaf."

"True, true. I've had some anger issues in the past, but I'm in anger management classes now." He smiled sheepishly. "I guess I need more classes."

"How long have you been with your girl?"

“Not long—a few weeks. My old girlfriend and I disagreed, and she left. She was a great girl. I probably should have been nicer to her. But what’s done is done.” He seemed reasonable at that point. Then, “But my new girl is fine and great with her mouth, if you know what I mean.”

“OK,” Nick started back toward the door. “That’s something I didn’t need to know.” He shuddered.

“Keep those details to yourself,” Ron agreed.

Manuel did a facepalm. “Oh. Sorry. Maybe I’m still a work in progress.”

10
Pride and Misdemeanors

Two small bodies leaped onto Jamie's bed. Her little nephews were happy to have an excuse to jump on a bed even if there was a groggy aunt in it. As Jamie rolled over, Ricky squealed happily, "Grandpa says he and Dad want you downstairs! And Grandma has pie!"

"Pie! Pie! Pie!" echoed little Anthony.

Jamie's head felt stuffed with cotton, and her mouth was dry. A wave of regret washed over her. She was the one who asked to be there when they watched the video feeds. While she was eager to see them, more sleep might have been a better choice.

The boys, however, once tasked with their mission, would not let it go. Jamie needed to eat, too—no need to restart bad habits now that she was home. The boys successfully tugged her out of bed, babbling the entire time.

After splashing some water on her face, she slowly went down the stairs, with the happy boys tailing her. Jamie looked into the kitchen, where her mother, siblings, and nephews grabbed seats around the kitchen table, eating the soup that Margaret had prepared earlier. The smaller boys were eating grilled chicken nuggets and mixed fruit, along with their bread. Richard and Gregory weren't at the table but probably had already finished their meal before going into the study. Jamie detected a whiff of apples laced with cinnamon, ginger, and nutmeg in the air, which smelled delicious. She acknowledged everyone at the table and grabbed a piece of bread as she made it over to the kitchen stove.

"The soup smells good," Jamie repeated, peering into the stockpot.

"Thank Olivia." Margaret got up from the table to get a bowl and fill it for Jamie. "I wasn't sure you would get up to eat—you seemed so tired."

"I feel better, thanks. I didn't think the entire family would be here." She looked at Jon. "Shouldn't you be out finding new women to add to your harem?" she asked him sarcastically. Accepting the bowl from her mother, she fell into a place at the table. Margaret tsk-tsked her comment.

Jon snorted. "Funny. I may have to remove myself from the dating scene for a while. Rena has been blowing up my phone all day to get me to set up our closure date," he said. "It has been less than a day since I said I would call her. She's called me almost two dozen times—leaving messages or just hanging up."

Jamie dug into her meal. "You sure can pick 'em!" she said, trying not to laugh.

Jon shrugged and slid a set of car keys across the table to her. "You should be nicer to me. I brought your miserable hunk of a car over here. Will I get any credit for keeping it registered, insured, and running while you were away?"

Jamie jumped up, leaned over, and kissed his cheek. "My car's outside? I missed my baby! Excuse me." Jamie darted out of the kitchen.

There was an air of exasperation throughout the kitchen. Several family members gritted their teeth. No one liked her car. It was too old, too loud, unattractive, and demanding on gas. As she rushed outside to steal a quick glimpse, Jamie recalled the first time she laid eyes on the vintage Camaro. A guy she went out with a few times in New York took her to a car auction in New Jersey—a day trip. She mentioned once that she thought muscle cars from the sixties were very sexy. He wanted her to think he was very sexy, too. He spent a lot of time pretending that he knew what he was shopping for and placed bids on a few beaters—he was going to "fix them up." Once the Camaro appeared, she tuned out her date completely. She bid on it—and won—and he realized she was better at auctions than him. That was the end of their relationship. But she held on to the car and fixed it up. Four years ago, Jamie left it with her brother to manage while she was gone. She gave him access to an account with money for registration and repairs if needed.

I owe Jon more than a drink, Jamie thought as she stood in front of her vehicle. Three thousand pounds of black muscle car shone back at her. She couldn't wait to drive her but realized she would have to. Mother would not tolerate her tearing out of the driveway during dinner. Besides, she still wanted to watch the video footage.

Jamie returned to the table with a huge smile on her face and resumed eating. After another bite of soup, she exhaled happily. "Mother, I'm going to steal Olivia away when I get a place. This is fabulous!"

Jillian shook her head as she tried to keep Aaron's and Jacob's meals in front of them and off the floor. "She won't go," Jillian said. "I have tried to get her to come to my house—and I've offered to increase her salary."

"Well, duh—that's not a surprise. She may not want to deal with your small army," Jamie said with a smile. Jillian stuck out her tongue at her older sister. Aaron and Jacob copied her and burst out giggling. Laughing, Jillian tried to shush them.

"Oh, but she'll come to my place. I have no army and will have no army for the foreseeable future. My place will also be smaller," Jamie joked.

"You're hilarious. However, you don't have time to joke right now—Richard and Dad are waiting for you in the study," Jillian said, hooking her thumb in that direction. Jamie hurriedly took one more bite of soup and left her bowl on the table. "Don't touch it—I'll be right back." As Jamie entered the study, she found both Richard and Gregory looking perplexed. They were both sitting at the mahogany desk in front of a 32-inch monitor, and both looked up when she entered the room.

"What's up?" Jamie asked.

"We might have a problem," Richard said, turning back to the computer screen. "We can see Rachel walking up to the front door. However, the front cameras inside the door are blank for twenty-eight minutes."

"What do you mean?" Jamie asked, leaning over their shoulders, and examining the screen.

"The signals for the inside cameras are… We can see the security guard go on rounds, then the signals disappear. Nothing but static," Richard added.

"We see her walk up to the front door. Then, nothing from the inside front camera aimed at the security desk or the third-floor cameras for the office area or cafeteria," Gregory said.

"We didn't see her again for eight minutes, after which she reappeared, carrying her sweater and some paper, walking out of the building. She parked her car just outside the camera range," Richard added.

"We don't know what happened in front of the building. She may have left right then. She may have hung around for a while. It's a mystery," Gregory said, leaning back in his chair.

Richard asked, "Are there any other cameras in the area?"

Gregory thought for a moment. "I don't know. Nothing is facing the parking lot. The police can find out if any of the businesses around there have security cameras aimed in the right direction."

They all turned back to the screen. Jamie pointed at the image of the frozen woman on the screen. "Was that paper in her car?" Jamie asked. She backed up from the screen. "I wonder what was on it. She didn't have it when she went into the building."

"It could be some test results, which would be against lab policy, or an email, an interoffice memo. It could be any variety of things. It may not have anything to do with what happened to her," Gregory said.

"True. As for the police, I don't see any reason we shouldn't turn this over. There's nothing sensitive evident on the video." Richard leaned back in his chair. "There'll be some questions about the missing video. It could be as simple as your security guard turning off the feed so that he could take a long break. We need to get into the security system to see if someone turned it off from inside the building or from the outside."

"Who was the security guard on duty last night?" Jamie asked.

"I don't remember now. Hold on," Gregory shifted the keyboard to log into his personal account. "Marcus was," he said, searching for the man's contact information.

"When are we going to turn this over to the detectives?" Jamie couldn't help but think about the tall, handsome detective she'd met the previous night. Even under the present circumstances, she wouldn't mind seeing him again. *Broad shoulders, blue eyes, curly hair, tall enough that she could wear her highest heels and still steal a kiss, big hands. Yeah, big hands…* Jamie got lost in her imagination for a moment.

"I'll call Detective Marshall now. Maybe he'll come by tonight or in the morning." Richard said, pulling out his phone.

Margaret had come into the room as Richard started the call. "Oh no! My party's tomorrow. Can we not ruin everything by having police roaming around? It wouldn't be appropriate." Her mother's somewhat agitated voice snapped Jamie's lovely daydream. *Typical,* she thought bemusedly and tried to catch up with the surrounding conversations.

"Understood, Margaret," Richard replied and left a message on Nick's cell.

Married to Margaret's youngest child for ten years, he had never called Margaret "Mother" because of their closeness in age. Richard had been married previously and had two older children with his first wife. They went through a somewhat acrimonious separation, and in response, he became a man-about-town until Jillian started interning at his office. Margaret and Gregory knew him previously from charity events. That their youngest daughter fell in love with a much older man was a subject of contention. Richard thought back to when Margaret showed up at his office to convince him to leave Jillian alone. Everyone in the office knew about Jillian and Richard—the world's worst kept secret—so Margaret Scott sweeping in led to a lot of gossip and law clerks finding reasons to hang around his office door to see what was happening. Margaret had been polite but made it clear she would not make his life easy if he continued to sneak around with Jillian. There was also some concern about appearances—the young woman with the older, not-so-divorced man. To appease them, Richard probably gave up more than he had to in the divorce to speed it along. It didn't appease the family much, though. Once the couple eloped in Hawaii and returned to Atlanta to inform everyone, Margaret cried. That's a honeymoon killer, indeed. Jillian skipping law school was another issue. Since Jillian was an adult, her parents had to accept the situation. Nonetheless, there was often an undercurrent of tension in his interactions with Margaret.

"I'll hold you to that, Richard," Margaret replied. Richard gave her a smile that could have been considered insincere.

Jamie interjected before Margaret and Richard got into a pissing match. "Excuse me. Is my soup still around?" She darted out, not missing those crazy family dynamics.

Escaping the tension in the study was a relief, but the kitchen was no calmer.

Jon and his two older nephews had finished most of the soup, bread, and salad and were circling the apple pie like locusts. Jillian gave up trying to maintain some measure of decorum and just let it go. Ricky and Anthony also found a half-gallon of ice cream in the house freezer.

Entering the kitchen, Jamie had to dive to protect her bowl from a scavenging three-year-old. Jacob smiled mischievously at her as he stealthily reached for her bread.

"Hey! That's still mine, young man. I plan to eat that," Jamie said as she slid into her chair and observed the scene around the room. Caught, he gave her a slobbery kiss on the cheek and turned toward the melee around the pie.

"Momma, Momma, can we have some ice cream with our pie?" Anthony asked, holding the tub over his head.

"Sure, why not? You're already hyper, so more sugar can only help, right?" Jillian stood up for a moment. "Bring the ice cream here. I'll scoop some on your pie, and you both need to sit down and eat. Quietly."

Aaron whispered, "Ice cream, Mommy."

Jillian kissed Aaron on top of his head. "I will give you a bit with your pie." Aaron smiled. While she loved all her boys, she was most worried about Aaron. He was born at 29 weeks after she developed appendicitis and had to have emergency surgery. He struggled in the NICU for a while and was still working to catch up on his developmental markers. She found she had a soft spot for him.

Jon wedged himself between his nephews after transferring the pie to the table. Anthony brought over the ice cream. As Jillian doled out the dessert—even for her grown brother—Jon asked about the conversation in the study. "What was on the video?"

"Jillian, can you give me a slice, too?" Jamie asked. To Jon, she replied, "There's some missing video."

Jon stopped what he was doing. "Really? That makes this situation more concerning."

"Not that someone dying wasn't bad enough," Jillian said. "And that's all we will say about that with the boys in the room. So, Jamie, tell me more about your last four years."

"I worked in several places in Africa." Jamie offered some details about the work she'd done while she was away, but after a minute or two, she could see her sister's eyes glazing over. "Is that not what you wanted to know?" Jamie asked, eating some of the pie, which diverted her attention. "Did our mother bake this? Or was it Miss Olivia? Delicious!"

Jon rolled his eyes. "You know better. Definitely not Mother. And surprisingly, not Miss Olivia," he said between bites. He tilted his head toward Jillian, who had the good grace to blush.

"Yes, I baked it. What?" Jillian dared her sister to say anything. "Anyway, I know you were single when you left here. We won't discuss that fiasco right now. But what I want to know—did you date anyone interesting while you were away? Any cool foreign men with sexy accents?"

Jon scoffed but continued to eat.

"Stop it. I live vicariously through the exploits of my single siblings. Besides, it wouldn't have surprised me if you had gotten married and had a kid while you were away—just to piss off Mother. Of course, she would have forgiven you," Jillian added.

Out of the corner of her eye, Jamie glanced at Jon, who probably was going to say something uncomfortable. "Language," she warned, half-joking. "You thought I would risk Mother's wrath that way? I can't even imagine that conversation. And who says she has forgiven me for anything?"

"Don't be ridiculous, PJ. You're the golden daughter," Jillian said as she gave Jacob a small spoonful of ice cream. "Anyway, I heard you spent time in Europe. I want to hear the gory details."

Jamie frowned in irritation but left it alone. "I was working! And when I left here, I had just broken off an engagement, so I wasn't looking for anything serious. I went out with some nice men. No one that you need to know about." Jamie licked her spoon. "What about you? When I left, you had two children, and now you have four. Are there any more on the horizon? Any plans to try for a girl?"

Jamie caught a flash of something—anger? Annoyance? —in Jillian's eyes before she answered. "That's private!" her sister growled, then paused and dropped her head. Jamie wondered if something was behind the attitude, but Jillian turned on a dime before she could get into it.

"Nope. The shop is closed," Jillian said, putting a spoonful of ice cream in her mouth. "Richard shouldn't want to try again. He's fifty-five now and is too old for any new babies. So, no girl." She smiled at Jamie. "Therefore, it's up to you to provide me with a niece to spoil."

Jamie swallowed hard and tried to laugh it off. *You have one, but I didn't tell you about it*, she thought, remaining silent. One day, she would have to have that conversation with her sister, but not tonight. "Maybe one day," she said. It was odd how, since returning home, the daughter she gave up for adoption occupied her mind more than she had in a long time. That would take some unpacking as well.

Ricky chimed in. "Girls suck, Momma." Anthony agreed. Jillian shushed them. "Language," she admonished gently.

Jon added, "Nah, man. Girls are exceptional—your momma, aunt, and grandmother were all girls. They don't suck, do they?"

While both boys considered this astonishing fact, Jon remembered something. "Jamie, did Mother tell you about the guest list?"

"No. I thought it was going to include the genteel people of Atlanta and surrounding areas."

"Of course. But I believe she invited your friend, Felice. I think she also invited your ex." Jon disclosed.

Jamie's mouth dropped open. *What the hell? Was this some sinister plan to set them back up?* Thoughts raced through her head. "Jon, he's married now. He won't come, will he? Why would she do that?" Words flew out of her mouth.

Just then, Richard and Margaret returned to the kitchen. Gregory had gone straight to the master suite to rest. Richard picked up Jacob and suggested that they go home. Ricky and Anthony stood up and tried to get their dishes into the sink, but got sidetracked, wrestling with each other and Jon. After a frown from Jillian, Jon tried to be the mature uncle and get the boys on track.

Jillian stood up and gave Richard a quick kiss on the cheek. "I'm so tired; let's sleep in late tomorrow. You hear that, Jake? You'll need to make your breakfast in the morning." The boy giggled. When Jillian and Jacob's faces were next to each other, you could see the resemblance. The other boys resembled their father.

After getting the dishes into the sink, Jon assessed the atmosphere in the room. The Bradshaw family was packing up to go, and he could see that Jamie was ready to pounce on their mother. He didn't need to be there for that.

"Going to sleep in my room tonight, Mother," he said, preparing for his escape.

Margaret hugged her only son, and he went upstairs. Margaret then said goodnight to her daughter, son-in-law, and four grandbabies by giving each adult a hug—the one for Richard was VERY perfunctory—and stooping down to eye level for the boys. As usual, they swamped their grandmother with kisses as she giggled with joy. Margaret had an amazing relationship with her grandkids. Her behavior around them would surprise most people because it wasn't in character. Jillian and Richard took advantage of that moment to make final preparations to leave. After disentangling herself from the mass of boys, the older woman walked back toward the master suite, and their parents ushered the boys out. Jamie jumped up and followed her mother—loaded for bear.

"Mother, did you invite Edward to your party?" she asked accusingly as her mother reached the doorway of the elder Scotts' suite.

"Yes, dear. I know he's married now, but he is a leading doctor in town. I thought it would be good to have someone here that you know. Same with Felice." She kissed Jamie on the cheek. "The goal of everything I do isn't to ruin your life. I consider your well-being first—on most occasions. Goodnight." She entered the room and closed the door.

Jamie couldn't help but be afraid, even with her mother's reassurances. She had spoken to Eddie since she left—he called her when he got married and was going to have a baby. They may not have gotten married themselves, but they had tried to remain friendly. She hadn't seen him since that last conversation, after which she packed her belongings and left his heirloom engagement ring on the foyer table. Having their first reunion at a party wasn't a good idea.

Having Felice there was a different matter. Felice was her best friend from medical school. They had intermittently exchanged generic emails during the first year she was away. But everyone had gotten busy, and their connections became more tenuous. *It would be nice to catch up*, Jamie thought. *This could be good if I avoid an embarrassing scene with Eddie.*

Once she reached her room, she heard her sister and family finally trudge out of the door. Jamie quickly prepared for sleep, including wrapping her hair in a scarf. Using a wide-toothed comb, she created a beehive with her hair, combing the thick dark brown tresses from left to right. She had to secure a few of the recalcitrant strands with bobby pins. Wrapping her creation with the silk scarf she had purchased earlier, Jamie made a face at her reflection in the mirror. She looked like the mother from the Simpsons. *Not sexy…* As she headed toward her bed, she thought regretfully about her natural style, which she missed.

She had a full belly and should have fallen asleep quickly, but her mind refused to rest. Jamie was now worried about the potentially messy reunion with her ex. Running different scenarios in her head didn't help.

Exhausted, she gave up. *I'll worry about this in the morning*. She drifted off to sleep.

Leaving the construction worker's apartment, the detectives walked back to the SUV. Nick's phone rang.

"Marshall, here."

"Xavier and I went to speak with the pawnshop owner. It didn't go so well," Alvarez said. Xavier Davis had been his partner since he transferred in; they were similar in their law-enforcement philosophies. Both were big, brash guys and had worked gang cases. It was no real surprise that the partners visited the pawnshop owner without backup.

"You didn't kill him, did you?" Nick asked.

"No, but you probably need to get over here. I had to detain him, and he's demanding that he speak with you or Ron."

"Detain? What the hell?" Nick slid into his SUV. Ron eyed him and followed his lead. Nick put his phone on speaker. "Are you at the pawnshop? We're on our way."

Ron chimed in, "What's up?"

Alvarez took a deep breath. "We started to question him…"

"Straight up?" The men exchanged glances and shook their heads.

"Yeah, I know what you said. We just stopped by to ask a few questions. But before I could say much or identify myself…" The detectives could hear Alvarez speaking to someone else. "Sorry about that. It's insane over here. Some neighborhood bangers tried to rob the place with a nine-millimeter." He paused. "There was a shootout. It's a mess. Pawnbroker's alive but frightened and will only speak with you now. He trusts you. The gang unit believes that this was a hit."

"Oh, shit! A hit?" Nick repeated.

"Does it seem likely?" Ron asked. "Did you get to question the bangers?"

"That's a no. Folks in body bags can't answer."

"You realize that you, Xavier, and the pawnbroker will need to watch your backs now. If these were hitters, there might be contracts on all of you as we speak. We'll be there soon," Nick said and hung up. "God, that sounds like a clusterfuck of epic proportions!"

"If these guys did the home-invasion murderers, this might be a more complex situation than we originally thought," Ron said.

For the duration of the ride to the scene, the detectives reviewed the facts they knew about the previous home invasions. "We're going to have to reassess everything completely," Nick said as they pulled in front of the pawnshop.

It *was* a shit show. Police officers and SWAT officers dressed in body armor, steel-toed boots, bulletproof helmets with face shields, with assault rifles streamed in and around the small, stand-alone building. The windows of the building and the cars parked out front were all shot at, with the shards of glass scattered all around the sidewalk and inside the building; the gunfire had also extended to the strip mall next door. Yellow tape surrounded the entire parking lot and part of the lot for the neighboring building—a bright reminder of the carnage that had just occurred in the area. There were two ambulances and two coroner vans parked inside the yellow cordon; the EMTs and the coroners were tending to both the living and the dead. Two fire trucks outside the cordon offered additional first aid to victims caught in the crossfire. And finally, in the strip mall parking lot, a throng of reporters and camera persons streamed outside the yellow tape and mingled with the neighborhood residents who had come out to see what had happened. The journalists yelled questions at anyone who was in the vicinity. The detectives showed their badges to gain access to the scene.

Both scanned the scene in awe. It looked like a war zone.

How is anyone still alive? Nick thought.

Nick spotted Alvarez standing in front of one of the coroner's vans, speaking with Internal Affairs. Nick and Ron walked up to him as the IA officer walked away.

"You need to go to a casino tonight or buy a Powerball ticket because you, Xavier, and the pawnbroker are the luckiest men alive," Ron said, saluting Alvarez.

"Man!" Alvarez gave Ron a dap handshake, and Nick patted his back. "That was close! My wife's going to be upset." Alvarez took a deep breath. While he talked a good game, Alvarez recognized he came close to death today. He looked calm on the outside but felt like jelly inside—partly from the fear of having to tell his wife about this. "There's the pawnbroker. You should talk to him now before he goes to the hospital to get checked out."

The detectives followed his suggestion to speak with the pawnbroker, who, seated in the back of an ambulance, was finally willing to talk about the stolen jewelry. The middle-aged white man who had talked such a big game to Nick and Ron in the past was a shell of his former self. He kept tucking an unlit cigarette between his lips. Despite the outside temperature, sweat was still rolling off his forehead. When he spoke, his voice was tremulous and faint—like his spirit. Fear will do that to you.

Nick shook his hand and inquired about his health. The frightened man narrowed his eyes at the detective and took another pretend drag on his cig, hand shaking.

Ron went to chat with the CSU techs inside what remained of the pawnshop, and the pawnbroker got out of the ambulance so he could light that cigarette. Nick had to wait for the pawnbroker to regroup, so he discussed the pawnbroker's status with the EMT, a very attractive young African American woman named Ashley. She had cornrows that were ombre—they went from black to blond at the tips—and a big smile.

"He's fine physically. Mentally, I think it is going to take a while," Ashley stated as she packed up spare supplies. "I would go easy on him."

Nick laughed. "I have never gone easy on this guy, ever. This will be a novel experience." He turned and searched for the man who had settled about 15 feet away from the ambulance and was sitting on the concrete. Nick squatted down next to him and looked him in the eye.

"I am glad you are ok, man. I hear you are ready to talk?"

The pawnbroker frowned and took a drag on the now-lit cig. "I will talk—tell you everything I know. But you have to protect me, detective. Someone tried to kill me today!" his voice rose with each word.

Nick nodded, trying to maintain control, and could see Ron heading in their direction. "I know. We will make sure you are. We have safe houses available. I will have to discuss this with my lieutenant and the DA. You also have to have something good for us. Something that we can use."

The pawnbroker's eyes widened, and he stood up. "SOMEONE TRIED TO KILL ME TODAY!" He was shouting at this point. "If you folks had left me alone, this wouldn't have happened!" Ron reached them and looked at the agitated smoker. Before he could say anything, the man went on.

"IF I HAVE SOMETHING GOOD FOR YOU? People coming into my shop—my respectable shop that I have been running for TWENTY YEARS. SHOOTING AT ME! I had a good relationship with all the neighborhood until you all started coming around." By now, he was walking toward the ambulance again, with Ron and Nick trailing him.

When he reached the ambulance, Ashley reminded him he needed to put out his cigarette before getting back in the vehicle.

"WHAT? SOMEONE TRIED TO KILL ME TODAY! I SHOULD BE ABLE TO SMOKE WHEREVER I NEED TO." He was almost hysterical and crying. "WHERE IS MY PROTECTION? SOMEONE TRIED TO KILL ME TODAY!" His plaintive wails attracted the attention of all the first responders in the area.

Ron and Nick looked at each other. *How was this guy the tough guy they had been dealing with?*

With this unfolding situation, it was unlikely that Nick and Ron would get to the Scott home tonight.

11
Trouble

Early Sunday morning, William knocked on the door of the RV that was conspicuously parked in the Walmart parking lot. He tried to maintain his composure after hearing about Rachel's death on the news.

Damn fool! he thought. *That was not the plan.*

His Friday meeting with Rachel would have had much more resonance if it had an opportunity to fester in her head.

William suspected Rachel wouldn't recognize him—he appeared different, older now. His daughter had been a member of the Micro Club, the group of science-loving girls that Rachel had created along with his daughter that regularly met at Mickie's restaurant in Madison. He had gambled that Rachel would have no recollection of the actual people who worked at Mickie's, and just providing some pertinent data would give the illusion of familiarity. And it may have—until the crazy man ruined it by killing her.

Now, the question was, what should he do about it? It was unlikely that the police would find the distraught young man and trace him back to Rachel, not without help. But there was a possibility of exposure for him. He would have to think about this.

The young man opened the RV door but wouldn't let William in.

"What do you want? I'm busy," he mumbled, squinting at William.

"Not quite. What the fuck did you do?" William hissed at him. "And how long do you plan to stay in this parking lot? I'm sure the police will be called about your RV." He evaluated the disheveled man who looked to be on his last leg. Hair uncombed, what was once a white sleeveless t-shirt, now stained gray, wrinkled, baggy blue jeans. Bare feet. He didn't smell like he had showered in a couple of days. William couldn't help but notice how much the young man had changed. When he was the star running back of the Wisconsin football team, he had been muscular and fit, six foot one with an unlined baby face. Full of life. Not so anymore… "Not sleeping again?" William questioned.

"Not really, but I would like to get to it. I have one other thing to do. You don't have to be involved. Besides, Walmart doesn't care how long I stay here—I wish you didn't," the young man retorted.

"That wasn't the plan. I didn't want Rachel dead—not that I'm crying about it—but I can't get my money out of her if she's dead. Same for the other one. No more killing," William said.

"They ain't got your money no more. They spent that shit a long time ago. You're wasting your time. Payback—that's my way."

"No, no, no. If the other one doesn't have it, she needs to figure out how to get it. I need the money. I don't care how she gets it. She doesn't want to go to jail and end up like you."

The man in the trailer grunted. "You do things your way—if I see her first, it might not go down the way you want." He closed the door in William's face.

William stood for a moment. *Well, I guess I need to get to her first*, he thought.

For the first time since Jamie returned home, Gregory insisted Margaret let her sleep late on Sunday. By mid-morning, however, the rumble of people coming in and out and the constant hum of voices rousted her out of her peaceful sleep. She rolled around for a few minutes to see if she could doze off again but had no luck. Sitting up on the bed's edge, she glimpsed the newly purchased party dress. Her mother had placed the shoe box on the chair in the room and the bag with the new cosmetics on the small end table. There appeared to be something shiny hanging from the dress's hanger.

Yawning, Jamie got up to investigate. It was a spectacular 25-carat diamond and platinum eternity choker. The colorless diamonds were square-cut and graduated in size with a center diamond of two carats. She recognized it as her mother's, the one Margaret's father (Jamie's grandfather) gave her at her presentation to society in Alabama at age 16. Jamie's grandfather purchased it at an estate auction, and it was probably over ninety years old. Margaret had insured the necklace for over $200,000 and typically kept it in a safe deposit box. Jamie and Jillian coveted the necklace as young girls and had both worn it at different times for formal events. Jillian even wore it at her wedding reception.

It looks like it's my turn to wear it, Jamie thought. Jamie picked the delicate piece up and held it to the light—the diamonds shimmered in the sunlight. She then noticed a pair of diamond studs next to the makeup. She would have to remember to thank her mother for the loan.

Since she wanted to take a nice, luxurious bath before the party, she skipped showering for now. Jamie tossed on a t-shirt and jeans and was almost out of the door before she remembered her hair. She exhaled in frustration and started trying to unwrap the scarf as she entered her bathroom. After removing the bobby pins, Jamie shook the beehive down. She grabbed the wide-toothed comb and ran it easily through her hair. *This was easier than twisting and untwisting my hair*, Jamie thought as she admired how the thick tresses framed her face. She spent a few moments posing in the mirror, reliving her modeling days. *Not bad…*

With the addition of the choker necklace, she would have to wear her hair up tonight.

After further inspection, Jamie added a bit of lip gloss and mascara to round out her morning look. She felt more human after getting some sleep, and there would be many people around today. She also didn't want to antagonize her mother. She wanted to ask a few more questions about the deceased employee, and an irritated Margaret would make that much more difficult.

Jamie walked down the staircase into a whirlwind of activity throughout the house. Margaret had gambled that the weather would be temperate enough in early December to host part of the function outside. The organizers were putting up two white tents in the backyard to cover a large bar, several buffet stations, and multiple tall tables. There was also a small dance area next to the stage for the band. Inside, other workers were reconfiguring the living room, music room, and dining room into spaces better for mingling, with indoor bars, serving areas, and a table for the deejay in the music room.

In the kitchen, the food prep workers had taken over. Jamie was greeted with the aroma of blueberries, cinnamon, and rich coffee, which reminded her of a small coffee shop she had frequented in Italy. There was a pot of coffee, a basket of muffins and bagels, and a bowl of fruit set out for the residents of the house on the bar. Aluminum foil-covered trays filled with goodies for tonight's festivities filled the rest of the counter space in the kitchen. Grateful for someone's consideration, Jamie got a cup of coffee and put a blueberry muffin, a banana, an apple, and a container of yogurt from the fridge on a plate. She ate while standing in the corner, watching the food attendants finish their work. No one in her family ventured into the kitchen during her meal, so after refilling her coffee, she walked to the study, which was probably where everyone was.

On her way to the study, Jamie ran directly into the gorgeous detective from the investigation. *Those eyes…* Fortunately, she didn't shower him with coffee. He reached out to steady her from falling. *And the big hands…*

"Sorry, Detective…, I forgot your last name. I hope I didn't spill anything on you," Jamie apologized, a bit flustered. His piercing eyes scanned her face, and she was breathless, standing that close to him as she looked up into his chiseled face.

It's not the time for this. But he has such pretty eyes and eyelashes! she thought to herself. *Stop it!*

"It's Marshall. No worries, you didn't get me. Although, if my sources are correct, you would know how to treat a burn. Dermatologist, right?" As he hadn't released her arm yet, their proximity allowed him to get an up-close-and-personal view. A natural beauty—almost no makeup, almond-shaped eyes, high cheekbones, square jawline. He had looked the Scott family up on the web and found some photos from Jamie's modeling days. Stunning then and stunning now… And tall. He rarely dated anyone under five foot ten, and she was about five foot eleven. *Kryptonite indeed.* He lingered a bit longer, and she gave him a small smile.

"Yeah. Glad not to make a mess of things," she said. He slowly smiled back, and she could see a hint of perfectly straight white teeth between his perfectly kissable lips. For a moment, she thought about kissing those lips with those hands gliding down her back. Her brain short-circuited. *Uh-oh.*

"Jamison, good morning!" Jillian strolled through the front door, alone, and broke the palpable attraction. Jillian was wearing a pair of jeans that emphasized all her curves and a blue cashmere turtleneck. She looked radiant this morning like she had gotten some sleep last night. She made a beeline for the pair. Nick dropped his hand that had been on Jamie's arm; she felt the loss of connection.

"You're the detective working the case, right? It's nice to meet you—I'm the other daughter, Jillian." She shook the detective's hand.

Jamie stepped back and took a deep breath. *Got to keep a clear head here.* "Jillian, where are the kids?" she asked.

"I hired a sitter for the day and night, and the nanny's there, too. I'm here to help Mother. It's a chance for me to be without children for a day. What's not to love?" she smiled, scanning the room. "Where is she? Where's Mother?"

"I have no idea. I just came downstairs, got breakfast, and ran into the detective here."

Jillian eyed both and smirked. "Well, all right then. Richard's already here. Let me find Mother. As you were!" she walked off.

Jamie could feel herself blushing. She read her sister's expression and dreaded the gossip that would be forthcoming. Focusing on the man in front of her, Jamie asked Nick, "How long have you been here? Have you spoken to my father or Richard yet?"

"That's why I'm here. I called your brother-in-law last night to schedule this meeting. I planned to come last night but had to deal with a crisis." He smiled again, which she returned with a tilt of her head, exposing the curve of her neck. Nick could see her pulse point and the delicate slope from her jaw to her shoulder. He had the sudden urge to kiss her right there.

Focus… Nick tried to get his mind back on the reason for his visit. "Attorney Bradshaw said to come in the front door since there would be people coming in and out all day. Could you direct me to the study?" the enchanted detective asked.

"I can do better; I'll walk with you. This way," Jamie offered, turned, and started toward the study. As a gentleman, he tried not to stare at her retreating form. But… she had a nice ass—*not too big, not too small.* Probably perfect for his hands… Before he could get too far down that rabbit hole, Jamie turned and motioned to him. "Are you coming?"

Nick fell in step next to her. *Perhaps once the case is over…*, he thought while observing her from the corner of his eye. *Great profile, erect posture—must be the modeling. Many tall women don't have the confidence to walk with their shoulders back and neck up.* He liked that. She could feel his eyes on her but led him to the study door without comment. Richard and Gregory stood up as they walked in.

"Thank you for coming, Detective Marshall. Here are copies of the video feeds from the labs on Friday night," Richard said, handing him a flash drive.

"I take it you already looked at them?"

The three members of the Scott family exchanged glances. "We reviewed them. Unfortunately, they won't be as helpful as you might expect. I think there was a glitch in the system, so some data was lost," Richard said. "Perhaps it rebooted before Rachel got to the lab. You can look for yourself later."

"Thanks. Our forensics team will examine this. We might need to get into the system with our agents—just to look. Would that be possible?" Nick asked. Gregory shot a glance at Richard, who then agreed.

Nick continued, "Thanks. We'll let you know if we have questions about the feeds." Nick didn't let on that their security guard had turned off the feed to have a tryst, but it was nice to have that permission for the system, anyway.

There was an expectant pause in the room—three pairs of inquiring eyes—all waiting for more details from the detective. Nick scanned the room and chose his words carefully when they continued to stare.

"This is an ongoing investigation—I can't tell you much," he said. "We've interviewed a few key people but need to speak with more. This includes your lab manager and some of the victim's co-workers. We haven't been able to set up those interviews yet."

"Well, Joan and David should both be here tonight at the party," Gregory said. Jamie and Richard glared at him.

"Hey, we want this dealt with quickly, and all the interested parties will be on the premises. Perhaps they'll be more forthcoming in an atmosphere that is less like an interrogation?" At their continued silence, Gregory grew indignant. "What? I have nothing to hide!" which wasn't true, given the video feed issue. "Would you like to come tonight?" he asked the detective.

Nick shook his head. "It's a party and not the best place to ask questions."

"Hell, most of the lab workers that Rachel interacted with will be here. I don't know—perhaps interviewing several at once will allow you to clear my lab of any irregularities. We received a few calls this morning and comments on our website. I don't want this hanging around for too long." He straightened up. "I'm very sorry for what happened to Rachel, but the faster you find the animal that did this, the better."

Margaret came in at the tail end of the conversation.

Nick hadn't yet replied to Gregory's inquiry. Unexpectedly, she said, "Both the Chief of Detectives and the Police Commissioner will also be in attendance. I'm sure they would appreciate that their detectives fully take advantage of all available opportunities to solve murders?"

Nick grimaced. The other three people in the room dropped their heads. He concurred, not willing to start a verbal battle that he would likely not win. "Yes, ma'am, it sounds like a good idea. My partner and I will plan to attend." Placing the flash drive in an evidence bag he pulled from his jacket pocket, he headed toward the study door. "Thanks again. Oh, yeah, what time is this party, and what is the attire? I don't want to stand out."

Margaret said, "Oh, dear. Where are my manners? The soiree starts at five, and the attire is formal. Since it may be too late to rent a tuxedo, a nice dark suit would be acceptable." Margaret caught him eying Jamie surreptitiously. She added, "You can bring a date."

"Ma'am, I own a tux. It's been a while since I've attended any event that required one, but I can manage. Thank you," Nick said. "But since my presence is for work, I think a date would be inappropriate," he added.

"Very well, we'll see you then," Margaret said calmly.

Sensing that he had been dismissed, Nick again turned to leave. Richard, Margaret, and Gregory returned their attention to the computer. Jamie exhaled silently and trailed him out of the study. She realized she had been holding her breath when her mother suggested that Nick bring a date. Not sure why she would care about him having a date—*he's probably married, or in a long-term relationship*, she told herself.

Nick made it into the hall but paused once he realized Jamie was behind him.

"I just wanted to make sure you got out of here OK. There are many halls that you could get lost down. You could wander around for a while," she said, smiling. "Besides, it gets a bit thick with them, even for me. I'm out of practice."

His heart rate increased as he locked eyes with her. They were deep, dark brown inviting pools--he could feel himself getting pulled in, and warning bells went off in his head as he forced himself to pull back. "Thanks for the concern. This is nothing." He returned her smile but thought it prudent to get out of the house before he fell on his face, or some other mortifying event occurred. To be hospitable, she walked to the door with him.

Jamie stood at the door, watching him as he strolled to his car. It took willpower not to glance back with a goofy grin on his face. He waved as he drove off.

As Nick drove out of the subdivision, he tried to make a list of all the reasons he should stay away from Jamison Scott. That list was short: the case. He kept coming back to all the positives: gorgeous, tall, hot, smart, hot, gorgeous. *Not good, Marshall.* He warned himself. This woman was going to be trouble.

12
Condolences

Although it was a Sunday, Nick took the surveillance flash drives directly to the police computer lab to see if they could retrieve the missing data. As he suspected, it didn't look like anyone had wiped the data; it appeared someone had turned off the system completely. The computer experts had nothing else to offer there. There was also little information about the victim's activities outside the building. The security videos were a wash.

After receiving that disappointing news, he met Ron at the lab. He had called him as he left the Scott house. After the video findings, the Scotts and their attorney granted the police and CSU techs entry into the lab. Richard met Nick and Ron there and gave them access to the pertinent areas.

Since it was difficult to assess where the victim went once she entered the building, the CSU techs had a lot of areas to cover. They tested the lobby, stairwells, elevators, and the third-floor hall and office for fingerprints, biological fluids, and visible clues. The lab fingerprinted every company employee when hired, which meant they could easily eliminate many prints. Nick and Ron believed that the evidence collected at the lab would be confusing without the missing segment of the surveillance video. The mass of data would take forever to sort out.

On the third floor, the large office space that housed the technicians' cubicles was the next stop for the detectives and CSU. One-half of the room contained an array of medium-sized cubicles. The other half contained multiple printers and other office supplies. The walls of each desk area were high for privacy. Most of the desks and dividers were minimally decorated, which seemed to surprise the detectives. Richard commented that the research staff also had additional desk space where they managed their research projects. This didn't apply to Rachel specifically, but it explained why many of the desks were almost bare, except for computers.

Ron and Nick examined Rachel's space, which was in the back corner of the cubicle area. Richard watched from the doorway. Her desk was neat, with only a closed laptop and a pencil cup on it. In one drawer were two pictures with images of the victim and a man whom Ron and Nick recognized as the erstwhile coach boyfriend. The pictures were candid, and the couple looked thrilled to be together. Given what Nick and Ron knew now, the pictures invoked some sadness—Rachel had unknowingly been living a lie with Ben. They couldn't open the top drawer—Nick made a mental note to grab a CSU tech to get that open if they couldn't find a key. In the other drawers, there were no papers with potential passwords, nor were there any key rings or loose keys. When Ron tried to give the laptop to the CSU technicians, Richard stopped him, citing "work product." He also would not allow them to dump the work phone number without him screening the information first.

"We can get a subpoena," Ron said.

"You can do that," Richard said. "How about we give you access to her email account and calendar after eliminating any work-product-related items?"

The detectives didn't see any reason to argue the point. If needed, they could get the subpoena quickly. Richard walked away to contact the Scotts.

"Oh yeah. Margaret Scott invited us to her birthday party this evening. We can conduct informal interviews with the employees in attendance," he said to his partner as they waited for Richard to get back to them.

"Oh really? Did you wrangle us this invite?"

"Not intentionally. But it could make our jobs easier," Nick said, peering out the window at the parking lot. Rachel had an ideally located cubicle. She would have been able to see outside—albeit into the parking lot—while sitting at her desk. That was much better than many other cubicles.

The lead CSU tech came into the office area. "This is going to take days to sort out," she said, taking her gloves off and running her fingers through her hair. "It may be near impossible from an evidence standpoint until we have more information. We'll let you know what we find."

"Thanks," Nick replied. "While you are here, could you open that drawer?"

She nodded and sat at the desk to work on it.

The detectives stepped away from the dead woman's cubicle to give her room.

"The lack of video is a problem because we can't make heads or tails out of her last steps in this building," Ron said.

"Maybe what's in this drawer will help. No one locks a drawer in their office unless there is something of interest in it, right? Are any of your drawers locked?" Nick asked Ron.

"Only the one with my gun. Otherwise, I'm an open book. Besides, all my important information is in my head. I can't let you find out about all my secret crime-solving tools."

Nick shook his head. "I think her emails may give us some idea of what's been going on in her life over the past few days. Phone calls, too." He checked his watch. "Let's get ready for this evening. Mrs. Scott requested we wear a dark suit or a tux," Nick informed Ron.

"What? Specifically, a dark suit? I don't even know if my black suit's back from the cleaners," Ron said. "You may have to go alone."

Before Nick could reply, the tech returned. "The drawer's open. Don't you guys know how to pick locks? Come look."

Nick nudged Ron. Sure, they could pick locks. Funny that she had called them out. She rolled her eyes at their expressions. The pair followed her back to the cubicle.

The drawer held a few pencils, pens, various clips and pins, several flash drives, and a small container of hand sanitizer.

"Got to keep those cubicle mates from stealing her hand sanitizer. Why was this locked?" Ron asked.

"Are these flash drives old or new? Maybe that's why?" Nick said. He placed them in evidence bags and handed them to the CSU tech. Richard came over quickly and took them from the technician with a shake of his head. "Work product," he said. "Let me look at them first to ensure there's no proprietary information here."

The CSU tech scratched her head and backed away; this time, both detectives glared at the attorney in frustration. Having nothing useful to the case in their hands, Nick and Ron turned to leave. Richard was on their heels.

While waiting for the elevator, Nick and Ron tried to piece together what they knew. "OK, let's try to set up a scenario. She comes through the front door, and no one is at the front desk. So, she doesn't sign in. Goes up to the third floor into her office. Was there someone in there that shouldn't have been?" Nick said.

"That seems odd, though. If someone was in the office area, there's no real reason to be upset with her for being there, is there? And how would they have gotten in?" Ron said.

Nick shook his head in response and quickly assessed their surroundings. The office area was on the right side of the hall. On the left side of the hall was a locked wooden door.

The elevator opened, and the three men stepped in. As the elevator doors closed, Nick asked Richard, "What's on the other side of the hall?"

"One of the research labs," Richard replied. "And no, you can't go in there without a warrant. There was no evidence of her entering that area that night, and since she wasn't a researcher herself, there was no reason for her to be there. So, we won't be extending your access without one."

When they reached the first floor, Nick called the lead CSU tech on his cell phone to ask if anyone had examined the door across the hall from the third-floor office. She said no and promised to include that evaluation. The three men parted ways.

Watching Richard's retreating figure, Ron asked Nick, "What are you thinking?"

"I'd like to get inside that lab. It may be difficult, though," he disclosed.

"I doubt that'll happen. Trade secrets and all. Without a reason to go in, we're still nowhere," Ron said.

Nick's phone rang. "Maybe this'll help."

The call was from the precinct switchboard. The operator had their lieutenant on the line. Ms. Thorne's parents had arrived at the county coroner's office to see their daughter, but they also wanted to speak with the detectives working on the case.

Nick replied they would meet them at the coroner's office. Ron eyed him questioningly.

"The parents are here," Nick said and slid into the SUV. Ron followed.

Mr. and Mrs. Thorne were lively, energetic people, but the news of the death of their only child drained most of the life out of them. They were in their late 60s and had been married for over 40 years. The birth of Rachel resulted from many years of trying and multiple miscarriages. They lavished love and attention on their precious daughter. The Thornes were both retired—he from a factory supervisor position and she from an office administrator position. Still active in church and civic activities, they volunteered at the children's ward at the hospital and at the local soup kitchen. There was dancing at the local Arthur Murray Dance studio every week. They both played golf and tried to fit in 18 holes before Bible study on Wednesdays. For a while, Rachel had hinted about the seriousness of her latest relationship, so her parents awaited a future wedding and grandchildren. Now, all of that was gone.

When Ron and Nick arrived at the coroner's office, they could sense the despair in the parents, despite never having met them before. The Thornes were sitting quietly on the couch outside the viewing room, waiting for the detectives. They had driven down from Kentucky as soon as they received the call and came directly to the coroners. The pair quickly stood up when Ron and Nick walked in. Seeing Rachel's parents made Nick's heart drop.

The Thornes were neatly dressed and barely holding on to their composure. Tears rolled down Mrs. Thorne's face, and her red-rimmed eyes were swollen from crying. She was very pale, but her cheeks and nose were all red and chapped from frequent tissue wipes. Mr. Thorne's eyes were red as well, but he wasn't currently crying as he quickly tucked a white handkerchief in his pocket and straightened his jacket. His wife grabbed his hand, and he placed his other hand around her shoulders as they waited for the men to speak.

"Mr. and Mrs. Thorne, I'm Detective Nick Marshall, and this is Detective Ron Dixon. We're working on your daughter's case," Nick stated quietly. Everyone shook hands, and the Thornes sank back onto the small couch, waiting expectantly for the two younger men to give them information.

I hate these conversations, Nick thought. Speaking with bereaved family members required tact and compassion while still attempting to elicit information.

"First, we just want to express our condolences. We're going to do everything we can to find out what happened to your daughter," Ron said.

Mr. Thorne attempted to speak first, but his voice wavered. He cleared his throat and continued. "I just looked at the dead face of my only baby, young man. She didn't deserve this. Do you know anything? What do you need from us?"

"We have some leads that we're looking into. We are also examining her computers and phones to see who she had been communicating with." Nick glanced at Ron, who nodded back. "We've already spoken to Rachel's ex-boyfriend, Ben."

"Ex? She didn't tell us that. When did that happen?" This news further upset Mrs. Thorne. She swung her eyes wildly between the detectives. Her shoulders sagged as the implications sank in. She pulled out a Kleenex from her purse as more tears flowed. Mr. Thorne gathered her weeping form into his arms as tears began streaming from his eyes, as well.

Oh, dear, Nick and Ron both thought. Rachel wasn't one who shared information with her parents, meaning they might not have much to share with them. The conversation paused for a few moments to allow the couple to regain their composure. As the tears subsided, Nick gingerly broached the subject again.

"I'm sorry. I thought you knew. From what we've learned, the relationship ended five months ago. We spoke to him and are going to speak with her co-workers and friends to dig deeper. How long will you be in town, and where will you be staying?" Nick quickly continued.

Ron added, "As we progress in the investigation, we may have other questions for you."

"Yes, of course. The coroner said that we can't take Rachel home yet," Mr. Thorne said softly, while his wife released a hiccupping sob. "We'll be at the La Quinta Inn in Midtown. But we'll be spending some time in her apartment when we're allowed to go in." Mr. Thorne wearily shook his head. "I never expected to bury my daughter. My wife and I are getting up there in age. We just wanted Rachel to find someone and start a family so she wouldn't be alone." The last word trailed into a sob.

"I can't believe she and Ben broke up, and she didn't tell us. Was there something else she was keeping from us? Did she think she couldn't talk to us?" Mrs. Thorne choked up again. Mr. Thorne put his arms around her again.

"Please, let us know if we can do anything," he said and turned to tend to his wife.

Once outside, Nick checked his watch. "That never gets easier."

"Nope," Ron said.

Nick tried to change the subject to a lighter one. "Let's get moving if we want to get to the shindig."

"You stupid," Ron said, still thinking about the Thornes. His phone chimed with a text message. "Shit. Estelle's at the ER. Looks like you're on your own tonight."

"Really? Is she OK?"

A second message came in. "Estelle says she's been throwing up non-stop for a couple of hours. She's been complaining about her stomach for a few days. She's still in the waiting room. I'm heading over there." He paused as another message came in. "Please, tell the Scotts I'm sorry about missing their soiree. And I *am* sorry. You in a monkey suit is always a funny sight and…" He paused for effect. "There will be some lovely ladies there. I love to live vicariously through you. Hey, what about the Scotts' daughter? She's tall like you like 'em and pretty," he teased.

A flash of uncertainty crossed his face, but then Nick adopted an innocent expression. "I don't know who or what you're talking about. I'm going to ask a few questions, look around, and partake of the excellent liquor and delectable food that I'm sure will be there," he said in a serious tone. *Hopefully, Ron will back off.*

His partner raised an eyebrow—he didn't buy it. "Wait. Your face tells me you have already thought about the pretty doctor. Unfortunately, I don't have time to get into this more right now, but don't worry, I will." Ron got into the SUV. "Take me to my car, Nick, so I can go check on my wife."

"I was going to say that you were stupid, but you pulled out the sick wife card. That's not fair." Nick got in the SUV and drove them back to the precinct.

13
Soiree Shenanigans

The party planner almost lost her composure in the run-up to the event. Margaret was very exacting about the decor, the food, and the music. She requested they incorporate Casablanca lilies into the floral arrangements. When the original samples included Stargazer lilies, it did not go over well. The planner learned a hard lesson.

Typically, hosts did not expect last-minute functions to be so precisely orchestrated, but this was a big-ticket event. Looking around at the start of the festivities, the young planner was pleased with the outcome. The food arrangements were heavenly, there were twinkling lights both inside and in and around the tents outside, and festive holiday music wafted in from a string quartet in the backyard. There was a small, lighted dance floor in front of the string quartet. There were also decorative flood lights lining the pathways throughout the backyard. The planner was pleased that she had located enough vintage incandescent bulbs for the floodlights and twinkling lights.

They added a warm glow to the festivities and visual interest—those bulbs were beautiful! She hoped the lady of the house would be as pleased.

By four forty-five p.m., guests started to arrive. By five-thirty, the house and backyard were filled with select members of the upwardly mobile and powerful in Atlanta—the women in chic dresses and the men in swanky suits and tuxedos.

Margaret flowed among her guests like water. She was in her element. As she scanned the scene, she was quietly pleased with the outcome, despite the rapid planning. She hadn't held any large events since her oldest daughter had canceled her wedding about four years ago. It had been awkward. And Margaret still did not wholly understand why Jamison called it off. She knew her child had been angry about the adoption, but that was long ago. Oh, well, there was nothing she could do about that now. She could, however, work to find her daughter an appropriate match. Tonight would be the first step.

She gingerly patted her short, perfectly feathered hair and smoothed her dress nervously as she greeted another guest. Her dark-green, floor-length gown was form-fitting and glittery with sequins and stones; she knew she looked amazing. But she didn't feel as comfortable as she did during previous gatherings of this magnitude. Maybe she was out of practice. Gregory—dressed in a black tuxedo—was entertaining a city official. Margaret watched with interest from across the room. When she'd met him, Gregory wasn't much of a schmoozer. She taught him how to work the room. And her three children were successful and doing important things. No one could deny her success, even if they thought she was interfering and overbearing. Taking a deep breath and giving her already-neat hair another pat, Margaret vowed that this party would just be another example.

From her bedroom window, Jamie could see the cars pull into the circular drive. All the stylishly dressed people handed their keys to the valets, who were parking vehicles down the street in a church parking lot. She could hear the quartet playing outside. Taking a deep breath, Jamie realized she was nervous. It had been a long time since she lived in this world. She was out of practice.

Also, she couldn't get the murder out of her mind. She planned to shadow that lead detective all night. He might not be too happy with that, but she was quite resourceful. Of course, getting closer to him was only about protecting her parents' business and learning about the murder—*right?* It had nothing to do with the detective being tall, handsome, blue-eyed, and kind of hot—who was she kidding? Extremely hot—*not at all. That smile.* She shook her head. It was just a coincidence that the lead detective was just her type. With one notable exception, she had only dated tall, well-built men of all ethnicities all her life. It wasn't her fault the detective was *that guy.*

Jamie peeked out the window again, took another deep breath, and inspected herself in the full-length mirror on the back of the closet door.

She had to admit that she looked good tonight. The black dress with the plunging back was a good choice. The strappy sandals called back to her younger days and even her time on the runway. Her hairstyle would please her mother. To better show off the choker, she put her hair up as Althea suggested. In all honesty, Jamie missed her natural twist-out, but this hairstyle worked, too. With one final twirl, she left the room and went down the stairs.

Margaret saw her as soon as she hit the bottom step. "Jamison, dear! Come meet Dr. William Milton from the CDC. Bill, this is my other daughter, Dr. Jamison Scott. She just returned from several years with Doctors Overseas. You should make a point of chatting this evening—there may be some collaboration opportunities that may benefit both of you," she said.

Jamie and Dr. Milton shook hands and exchanged pleasantries. Almost seamlessly, Margaret identified another person to introduce to Jamie. She politely pulled over Gregory to speak with Dr. Milton and ushered Jamie over to the next person.

After several instances of this, Jamie felt overwhelmed. Her mother was trying to introduce her to every important and self-professed important person in attendance. It hadn't escaped her notice that some introductions were business, and some were personal. Margaret had a plan—to marry off and employ Jamison. Jamie found her mother's actions both obvious and annoying—a throwback to how things were before she left. But given that she had promised herself that she wouldn't allow her mother to goad her during this visit, she let it go as she smiled through the meet-and-greets.

Jillian and Richard approached them between two of these engineered one-on-ones. Jillian was glowing in a deep-red, ethereal gown. Although she was shorter than Jamie, her towering platform heels made Jillian significantly taller than usual. She clutched her striking husband and gave Jamie a knowing look.

Jamie could tell Jillian was already tipsy.

Jillian acknowledged her mother and said to her sister, "Is Mother rounding up the eligible bachelors for you? Of course she is. She will not let you escape this time without sealing the marriage deal."

Margaret shook her head. "Richard, please keep your wife out of the cocktails. I will *not* have her causing a scene at this party!" Although Jillian's words frustrated Margaret, she turned and glided off to chat with another very important person. She nodded at her only son, Jonathan, and his date, who had just walked up to the group.

Jonathan gave both Jillian and Jamie a kiss and greeted Richard. He cut a dashing figure in his black tuxedo—the Scott children were all feeling glamorous tonight. "This is Isabella Saldana," he said, introducing his date. The petite woman smiled at everyone in greeting.

"I bet I know what that exchange was about, Jamie?" he guffawed.

Jamie felt herself flush and changed the subject. "Richard, could you introduce me to the lab manager or some of Rachel Thorne's co-workers? Have you seen them here yet?"

Jonathan and Richard quickly scanned the crowd while Jillian searched for the nearest bar. "While you two do that, I'll get myself another cranberry martini. It's a party, ya'll! So, tonight, gotta leave that nine to five on the shelf and just enjoy yourself," she sang to herself. Jillian grabbed three antipasto pizzas from the tray of a passing server and asked about the location of the blinis with caviar. When the young woman pointed out a male server across the room, Jillian waved her arm to get his attention. Richard seemed to ignore her behavior.

"What's going on here?" Jamie asked Jillian, gently touching her arm.

"Nothing, PJ. I'm out with my husband and no kids. I'm never without kids. Don't get me wrong, I love my boys, but tonight, I'm free!" She twirled a bit and struck a pose. "I plan to eat, drink, be merry, and schmooze all night. Again, it's a party; lighten up. I'll be back." Jillian kissed Richard and trotted off.

Jamie watched her go. She hadn't seen her sister in years. But there seemed to be some underlying resentment toward Jamie and the general situation she hadn't been fully aware of. Jillian had never been much of a drinker and had a more reserved personality. Here she was, almost completely in her cups already and more snide than usual. *What was going on?* She would have to make time to talk with Jillian about it.

Richard's voice pulled her back to the conversation. He said, "I don't know any of them very well. I have met them both in passing and haven't seen them here yet. You, Jonathan?" He seemed unconcerned about his tipsy wife.

"I know Joan, but I haven't seen her yet. Maybe she's in the backyard." Jon exchanged glances with Jamison. "Speaking of seeing people, have you seen Felice or Eddie yet?"

Jamie shook her head. She was looking forward to seeing Felice, but not Eddie. Felice would have been her maid of honor. A tall, elegant, gay Jewish woman, Felice was one of the few people who knew about her pregnancy and the child she had given up. During residency, both were busy—Jamie had met Eddie by then—and their lives diverged. It didn't help that Felice was not fond of Eddie. She thought he was wrong for her friend. *Turns out she was right.* As Jamie's life spiraled out of control toward the end of the engagement, she considered reaching out to Felice but just never found the time. Part of it may have been a reluctance to admit that Felice had been right.

It wouldn't have been the first time Felice was correct about something affecting Jamie. Perhaps she should heed more of her advice.

As for Eddie, Jamie wasn't sure what to expect. She knew he married a bank teller within a year after she'd broken things off, which didn't bother her *much.* A nagging voice would occasionally nudge her with *how did he find someone to marry quite so fast?* They had dated for two years before becoming engaged. He was a surgical resident at the same hospital and was marriage-approved by Margaret because Eddie came from an excellent family. But he was conservative, both politically and in his attitude toward relationships. He appreciated she was a doctor but thought she *had* to stop working or perhaps work part time after they had children. Since he wanted four kids (or more), her career would have been truly damaged. Jamie wasn't even sure she wanted children and was even less keen about halting her career (at the time).

At the time of the engagement, it seemed a reasonable concession. But as the wedding date neared, the entire relationship felt like a noose. She started rebelling—first in small ways, then in more obvious ones. All she knew was that she didn't want a cookie-cutter life *with him.* No matter how it went down, she left him. He owed her nothing. Eddie and his wife had just welcomed a baby, and his wife quit her job to be a stay-at-home mom. He was getting what he wanted, and she wanted to be happy for him. But did she have to see him while she was just getting her bearings? At least she looked good.

Jon said, "Let's walk outside, and I'll point Joan out if she's here. Dad will have to point out the other people."

He smiled at his date. "Besides, I have to introduce this lovely lady to more people." Isabella returned the smile and linked her arm to his.

The group traveled through the crowd and entered the backyard through the sliding glass door in the salon. The weather had held up, and it was very mild for December. There were heaters under the tents that Jamie had not noticed before. The musicians played holiday tunes and pleasant standards, but few people were on the dance floor.

There were quite a few people in the backyard, but the dessert table with a large, elaborate cake centerpiece caught Jamie's attention first. The 3-foot-tall cake was shaped like her parents' lab building, with icing and fondant work that looked like bricks and windows. Jamie had to admit it was quite stunning. There were also mini-cheesecake, mini-Tres Leches cakes, red velvet cake squares, pecan squares, and a variety of cookies. Jamie reminded herself that she needed to get some food. She couldn't remember if she had eaten anything since breakfast. With her complicated history of rationing and bulimia, she had to remain vigilant.

Jonathan pointed out a slightly overweight woman standing over the dessert tray with an expression of longing. Her yellow dress hung off her like a shawl, and her makeup was way overdone. Her auburn hair made her easy to identify from a distance. It was the lab manager. "That's Joan. Jamie, you want me to introduce you?" he asked. But before they could make their way over, a hand landed on Jamie's shoulder. She turned to find herself staring into a pair of dark blue-gray eyes.

"Oh, h-hi! You made it," she stammered. She hated she was stammering and sounding like anything but the grown, sophisticated woman she tried to be. She needed to get a grip.

Nick quickly appraised her expression, among other things. She looked guilty—sexy guilt—but guilty all the same. Given the lustful glances between the two, Jonathan and Richard quietly turned away but secretly monitored the situation. Isabella turned, following her date's lead, but in response to her questioning glance, Jon whispered into her ear that he would fill her in later.

Nick leaned in and whispered in her ear, "You aren't trying to interfere with my investigation, are you?"

Jamie shuddered; the feel of his breath on her neck and ear caused electric impulses to travel across her skin. She closed her eyes to regain composure. *Damn*, she thought to herself. *Why is this guy getting to me like this?* It made her angry.

"What do you mean? I'm simply attending a family party." She paused and took a deep breath. "It's nice that you made it. You clean up nicely." Jamie opened her eyes and looked directly at him.

"Avoiding the question? Well, your father already described his lab manager. Your brother offered to introduce you to her. You strike me as the type who would get in the middle of my murder investigation. Were you going to question my witnesses?" Nick asked.

Oops. She decided to make nice. "Well, if you plan to speak with her at this function, you can't stop me from standing nearby and asking a few questions myself. I don't think you would want to try, anyway." She smirked. "You're spending way too much time interrogating me instead of getting information about our employee's death." She turned to where she last saw Joan, but Nick tapped her shoulder.

"I have another question," he stated. Jamie turned back to face him as he continued. "Why do you care? You seem pretty invested in your family, but you stayed away for years. I suspect avoiding your family was part of it. Now you are back and sliding right back in. Why?"

She tried to deflect. "It's the family lab. Shouldn't I care?" But really, his question made her think. *Was she trying to prove something to her folks?* This guy was touching all her familial weak spots so fast—*something to consider.*

"Are you coming?" she asked.

Nick set his jaw. He was already dancing around the accepted norms for investigative activities—hopefully, it wouldn't bite him in the butt. "Sure. Where's the manager now?"

Joan had moved from the dessert tray to a portable bar. She had decided that a cocktail would distract her from the tasty desserts.

As the pair turned toward Joan, Jamie saw Margaret heading in their direction, with Eddie in tow.

"Oh, no!" Jamie murmured.

Nick heard her comment, but Margaret was upon them before he could ask what she meant.

"Detective." She acknowledged him, then positioned herself to box him out of the conversation.

"Jamison, dear. Here's Edward. He made it to the party. Isn't that lovely?" she said, smiling. "I'm sure you two need to catch up." Margaret gently put her hand on Nick's arm and said, "I believe I see the police commissioner over there. Let's go say hello!"

Nick looked back at Jamie as Margaret whisked him away to speak with the commissioner. He wasn't even sure if the man would know who he was. Moving up in the ranks had not been a priority for Nick, but he played along for the time being.

14
Once Engaged

Jamie watched them walk away and tried to use that moment to settle her nerves. She hadn't seen Eddie in four years. She had even gotten her belongings out of his condo without running into him. This was an uncomfortable moment—which she was sure her mother engineered—but it was bound to happen at some point.

Eddie sensed her discomfort and tried to take the edge off. "Hi, Jamison." He gave her a crooked smile—one feature she found irresistible once upon a time. "I see your mother continues her trend of making everyone around her as uncomfortable as ever."

Jamie flashed a quick smile. He was being gracious. "True. She has elevated it to an art form," Jamie replied in agreement. They were the same height when she did not have on heels, so she was currently several inches taller. That never bothered him, and he had always encouraged her to wear high heels because he liked her shapely legs. He was very cute, with a boyish face. The years had added a goatee and ten additional pounds of muscle. “You look good. Have you started working out?” she said.

He had been exercise-averse when they were together.

“Yeah. I’m getting older, and everything goes to my gut if I don’t do something about it.” He stepped back to see her better. “You look good, too. Africa must have been good for you.” He scanned her up and down appreciatively. “You’re not as thin as you were. I always liked when you weren’t trying to maintain your model weight.”

“Really? You never mentioned that. I thought you were into the glamor,” she said.

“I always thought I had outkicked my coverage with you. When you left, I wasn’t surprised. Hurt, but not surprised.” Eddie smiled. “That’s water under the bridge now for both of us. Are you back in town for good?”

“I think so. I have to figure out what I’ll do with the rest of my life, but for now, this is my next stop.” She closed her eyes and swallowed hard. “Where’s your wife? Did she come tonight?”

Eddie’s eyebrows went up. “I didn’t think you would mention her.”

“Why? We almost got married. I care about what happens to you.”

“Maybe. The way you disappeared without looking back? You seemed to be glad to be rid of me.” The hurt came rushing back—she could see it in his face. “Maybe my coming tonight wasn’t such a good idea,” he said, trying to regain his cool.

Her eyes glistened with tears. She didn’t mean to hurt him and hated seeing the effect her exit had on him.

“I just want to say I’m sorry I didn’t handle our breakup well. I hope we can be friends one day.” Jamie realized how lame that sounded, but Eddie didn't appear to mind. "I'm sorry for all the pain I caused," she continued, then hesitated. "It wasn't about you. It was me and my fucked-up-ness. If we had gotten married, we would be miserable. Besides, you found someone who was ready for you. You have a kid. Again, I ask, is she here? I would like to meet her."

He shook his head. "Arnelle and I thought it would be best she stayed home with the baby—he's only four weeks old. She wants a bit more time to get her body back," he said, making air quotes at the word body. "I told her she's beautiful, but she didn't think she was ready for a formal event. Your mother also recommended that she stay home. Besides, Arnelle knew you would be here."

Jamie smiled weakly. "And that bothered her?" She compulsively put her hand to her hair but remembered her neatly pinned hair and put her hand back down. "I guess I could see how that could be uncomfortable, based on our former situation. But she has nothing to worry about because we've both moved on. You're married with a baby. Wow!" Jamie realized she had subconsciously reached out and touched his arm during that statement. She removed her hand quickly and changed the subject. "So, where are you working now?"

He seemed relieved to be moving to another topic. "I have surgical privileges at several hospitals and am an adjunct professor at Emory. So, it's all good," he answered. Shifting the conversation away from himself, Eddie asked, "What did you do while you were in Africa? You trained as a dermatologist—I can't see that there would be an urgent need for someone who was strictly a dermatologist over there."

"I actually worked mainly as a general practitioner over there. When things were calmer, I had a dermatology clinic every so often to deal with skin issues that may not have been life-threatening." Jamison was warming up to her topic. "I believe all medical students need to complete a rotation there or in some underserved area. It's life-altering," she stated.

"Yeah, you were always more adventurous than I was. I'm perfectly happy staying in my lane. All of us may not have survived that experience. I don't think I was built for that. But I knew you were."

Before Jamie could respond, Margaret made her way back over. "Oh my, even now, you two are such a striking couple," she said, putting her hand on Eddie's shoulder. "Oh, well—missed opportunities. Edward, I thank you for coming tonight, and I will call you to plan a nice brunch with you and your wife. Although you and my daughter did not get married, there's no reason we should be strangers, is there?" she rhetorically asked, kissing him on the cheek. "If you'll excuse me, I need to steal Jamison away. Please, have some food and grab a drink. The chairman of the surgical department at Emory is here, and I mentioned you were here. He may have some ideas for you at the hospital."

Eddie obediently walked in the direction that Margaret pointed. That action reminded Jamie why she and Eddie hadn't been right for each other. She did, however, marvel at how this party doubled as a networking opportunity for everyone Margaret had invited. It's why everyone would deal with the crap her mother dished out—she repaid loyalty well.

I need to learn that skill, Jamie thought.

"Where are we going now, Mother?" she asked.

"Dear, I have several other people to introduce you to. The head of the largest health care system in Atlanta is here tonight, and I would like you to have a quick chat with him. Feel out if there may be someplace for you there. I also invited a handsome single lawyer I want you to meet." She evaluated Jamie's empty hands. "Have you had anything to eat? You need to keep up your strength."

"I will eat after you've finished all your introductions. No need to interrupt my enjoyment of the desserts with a conversation," Jamie said.

Margaret set her jaw but squired Jamie with laser focus to the executive vice president. He and Jamie had a pleasant conversation and established that there were probably ways in which the clinic could use her skills and talents. As she still wasn't sure about her career plans, however, the conversation just laid some groundwork. They exchanged numbers and scheduled a phone call after the holidays to further discuss her options.

Like a hawk, Margaret swooped down at the right time, offered a few platitudes, and directed him to a real estate developer who was waiting by the band. There was a quick introduction to a lab employee named Tatiana Daniels, whom Jamie remembered being mentioned as a friend of Rachel's. The technician was a pretty girl who appeared younger than her probable years but had an air of world-weariness. She and Jamie exchanged a few pleasantries. Tatiana grew uneasy when Jamie expressed sympathy over her friend's death and asked about her education, but her mood improved when Jamie talked about her modeling career in New York. The young woman seemed interested in hearing more about her exploits.

As if on a timer, Margaret reappeared to move things along. As Tatiana retreated, Jamie remembered that her mother only invited employees destined for more to this party. So why was Tatiana here? She didn't have a graduate degree and wasn't planning to get one, which typically meant no additional promotions. It seemed odd. But Margaret had another person for her to meet. In her wake was Jamie's friend, Felice, whom she hadn't spoken to in four years.

"Hi, Jamie!" Felice greeted her cheerfully while flashing a knowing look at Margaret. She leaned in for a hug from Jamie. Jamie obliged and then held her friend at arm's length. Felice looked striking in her blue pants dress, her silky blonde hair in an asymmetrical bob. Her olive skin was still smooth. Felice was still as fabulous as she had been when Jamie last saw her.

Jamie replied in kind. "How are you? It's been a long time!"

"Too many years, right?" With the connection successfully established, Margaret melted back into the crowd. Once she'd left, both women took a deep breath.

"Hey, girl! You look good. Africa was good for you. You seem healthy for once," Felice said, twirling Jamie around.

Blunt, as always. "Yeah, it was a good time—dodging bullets and mosquitoes. You look great, too. Are you here alone?"

"Yeah. I'm a single woman again; I just kicked my cheating ex out of the house." Felice took a sip from her martini. "But don't feel bad for me. I'm ripe for a rebound, and Atlanta's filled with possibilities," she noted.

"And I would expect nothing less." Jamie paused. "I'm sorry that I didn't keep in touch."

"Well, I wasn't surprised. I was hurt but not surprised." That was the second time in thirty minutes that

Jamie had heard this sentiment. *I need to work on my relationship skills,* she thought. Felice patted Jamie on the shoulder. "I don't want to get into this here. It's a party!" She did a little twirl of her own while carefully balancing her drink. "My rebound may be around here somewhere."

"I'll leave you to your search. But can we have dinner sometime this week? Talk it out?" Jamie asked.

"Sure, if you pay." Felice smiled as she finished her drink. "I'm not sure you really *want* to talk it out, but I'm game for free food. I would like to repair things, Trey," Felice added. The use of her old nickname threw Jamie and gave her hope that she could fix things between them. Trey was shorthand for Three Last Names. Several people in med school—led by Felice—frequently joked with Jamie about her having three last names. Jamison was her mother's maiden name, Jones was her grandmother's maiden name, and Scott was her father's last name. No name of her own.

A woman walked by and smiled at Felice. "Call me," Felice said, shifting her focus to the woman. When the lady cast her eyes back over her shoulder at Felice, Felice trailed after her as Jamie watched. Felice hadn't changed much, but there was an understandable coldness between them. Jamie could feel it, although the words they'd exchanged had been pleasant enough.

Like clockwork, Margaret reappeared at Jamie's side. "Come on, Jamison. I want to introduce you to Sam Ikande—an attorney who just moved to Atlanta from DC. He works for the State Department. He's single."

"How did you meet him?" the startled Jamie questioned her mother.

"Don't worry about that. I know you just got back, but you need to get out and meet some eligible men. I plan to help you. Sam's only the first."

"Mother, I'm not looking for a relationship right now."

"Jamison, you're almost thirty-five years old. If you want to get married and have children, there's no time to waste." Margaret smiled at Sam, who was walking over. "You wasted four years, and now your life is at a crossroads. I refuse to allow you to waste any more time."

This statement touched a nerve, but Sam reached them before Jamie could respond.

"Hello, Mrs. Scott. It is so lovely to see you again. My mother sends her regards. She had to fly back to London but would love to have dinner with you when she returns." His British accent caught Jamie by surprise.

"Thank you, Sam. You and your mother are very sweet. This," she pushed Jamie ahead a bit, "is my daughter, Jamison." Once she introduced them, Margaret effortlessly took up a conversation with a passerby, one of Jon's partners at his architecture firm.

Jamie put a smile on her face, although she was still upset with her mother. Sam seemed nice enough as he explained his background. His mother was an American journalist who met and married a British business executive of Nigerian descent. His father's business took them around Europe and the Middle East during his childhood. Thus, Sam was fluent in several languages and found a job at State using his skills. He was in Atlanta for a contract job but would go back to DC when the job ended. Margaret met his mother through his sister, who was married to one of Richard's colleagues.

Again, Jamie marveled at her mother's social circle. After a few minutes of conversation, she and Sam exchanged numbers and stood there uncomfortably as Margaret watched over them. "I feel like a teenager," Jamie mumbled.

Sam grinned and agreed with Jamie. “We can’t escape yet. She’ll tell my mother that I wasn’t exactly ‘a proper gentleman’. I must make it look good.” They both cracked up at the absurdity of the situation.

“You can’t stop me!” A female voice rang out above the noise. A young woman Jamie didn’t recognize was furiously yelling at a young man, presumably her date. The crowd silenced as she unleashed a list of his supposed crimes. “You were flirting with her in front of my face! I’m not staying here for you to embarrass me!”

The young man tried to grab her hand while mumbling apologies for his alleged transgressions. She snatched it back and stomped away. The young man watched her retreating figure and headed off in the other direction toward a bar.

Sam and Jamie used that opportunity to escape Margaret’s eagle eye.

15
The Office After Hours

After the brief disruption, the crowd returned to their conversations. Jamie stopped at the main dessert table and scanned the crowd for Nick and/or Joan while trying to avoid Margaret. Nick was easy to spot because he towered over most of the guests. He had retreated into the house—probably to avoid Margaret as well.

"I thought you would try to escape once I lost track of you," Jamie said after she'd reached his side. "Have you spoken to everyone that you needed to?"

"No, I haven't. After your mother set me up with the commissioner, we ended up talking about the police department and crime in Atlanta until now. It was interesting, but the commissioner was tipsy." He grinned. "But drunk or not, I'm now on his radar. I need to solve this case."

Jamie said, "I knew where Joan was a while ago. I don't think she's left yet. There's no way she would leave before the cake cutting—that wouldn't make a good impression on my parents." She quickly scanned the crowd for Joan.

"There she is, beyond the dessert table. I take it you plan to join me?"

Jamie smirked, and Nick resigned himself to the not-unpleasant situation. The pair made it through the crowd to stand next to Joan. Jamie said, "Joan Abbott? I'm --."

Joan jumped and swallowed quickly. "Oh, I know who you are. Dr. Jamison Scott. Dr. Scott, your father—oh, but you know that—talks about you all the time and the good work you were doing. It's an honor to meet you!" She stuck out her hand for a handshake but quickly withdrew it on noticing the icing on her fingers. "Sorry, I indulged in dessert. I shouldn't have—I'm on a diet—but everything looks so delicious." She wiped her hand on a cocktail napkin and re-extended it. "This is such a lovely party, Dr. Scott. Your mother always does such a wonderful job with the decorations, food, and music. Not that I get invited to these types of things all the time or anything like that, but when I have, it's been impressive."

As she paused to take a breath, Jamie interjected, "Please, call me Jamie. This is Nick."

Nick, feeling left out, nudged her, but she continued, "I, too, am impressed with her party planning. It's been a while since I've attended one of these soirees, but it appears she hasn't lost her touch. My father told me a lot about you and the lab. It has changed *so* much." Joan placed her hand behind her ear to better hear Jamie, so Jamie motioned for Joan to follow her to a quieter spot away from the band. "My father's trying to get me to work at the lab, so…"

"I understand. What can I tell you?" For a couple of minutes, Joan went through all the official procedures at the lab. Jamie maintained a pleasant expression, waiting. Nick felt himself zoning out—the lab talk was boring and far from what he needed to know. He stared at Jamie's completely exposed back. There were no tattoos, and Nick wondered if she had tattoos in places he couldn't see.

When Joan paused again for breath, Jamie changed the subject. "You heard about your co-worker, Rachel, right? That seems so frightening. Picking up a random guy."

Joan took a sip from her drink and stated in a conspiratorial tone, "I don't think she picked up a guy that night. She was still upset about that young coach breaking up with her a few months back. If she were true to form, she would go out, have a drink, and go home alone. I am surprised that she came back to the lab. She often goes to Buckhead on the nights she goes to Happy Hour. She likes—liked—comedy clubs. To be honest, she always hoped she would run into that Ben guy. Although he had a new girlfriend and a baby on the way, she still hoped she could get him back. It's sad. She wasted too much time on that low-down dog of a man."

Joan took another sip, warming to her subject. "She was such a nice woman. Everyone liked her."

Something she said caught Nick's attention. "She knew he had another girlfriend?" Jamie nudged him for interrupting her flow, but Nick ignored her.

"Oh yes. I don't think he wanted her to know, but she trailed him from his job for one or two days after they broke up. Not to imply anything bad or anything, but she needed to know what'd happened. I went with her one day." She realized what she had said and hurried to add, "That's not what we were about at all. It was just that one time. She saw him with his pregnant girlfriend at his new place. It was obvious what happened."

"Who else did she hang out with besides you?" Jamie asked, reasserting control.

"She has—had—a small group of friends. Some from the lab and some from her gym. Most of her friends were getting married and having kids. She wanted that, too. She told some of us about her weekends on Mondays. A group of us used to eat lunch together once a week: me, Rachel, David, Bethany—she doesn't work there anymore, she just got married and moved to Nashville—Charles, who quit and went back to school, and Elizabeth, who has been out on maternity leave for a couple of weeks. I introduced Elizabeth to her husband, so she has me to thank for that. Chris, Abel, and Tatiana also hung out with us sometimes, but they're only technicians; they don't have advanced degrees." She paused for a moment. "I believe Tatiana had a previous relationship of some type with Rachel. Or am I confusing things?"

"So, only David and you are still working there out of this group with advanced degrees?" Jamie continued.

"Yes. I saw David here earlier. I was surprised. He's not very social, so I didn't expect him to come tonight." She scoped out the crowd. "I don't see him now, but I just saw him a minute ago."

"Are the other people you mentioned here?" Jamie asked. Joan raised her eyebrow conspiratorially.

"Yes, Tatiana's here somewhere. I didn't know she had an invitation, but it wouldn't surprise me.".

"Why?" Jamie asked.

"She's sneaky, that one. Of course, she got herself an invitation." Joan was enjoying herself. "There's more. I think she has a boyfriend at the lab. I've no proof, but I'm sure there's some hanky-panky going on there." Joan quipped slyly, using air quotes for the word boyfriend. Jamie nodded her head approvingly at this tidbit and filed it away. She slipped a sidelong glance at Nick, who already knew this and maintained a pleasantly interested expression. His mind was elsewhere. *Things were progressing nicely*, he thought. He was standing next to a beautiful, intriguing woman and working on a case. It could be worse.

Joan interrupted his train of thought. "Oh, there he is. There's David." She pointed at a tall, thin, studious-looking, dark-skinned man standing in the doorway that led into the house. Joan waved at him, but he ignored her signals and turned to leave. "That's odd. I'm sure he sees me," she said.

David *had* noticed his co-worker, Joan, and several other people standing by one bar in the backyard.

Inwardly, he winced. *Of all people to see right now?* She was a busybody and would harass him about everything. Since she was steadfastly single, Joan spent too much time trying to get her co-workers to their happily-ever-afters. One success—their former colleague, Elizabeth—and Joan fancied herself a matchmaker. Joan once tried to match David with someone, but he resisted, saying that he was otherwise engaged. She persisted. She continued to wave. It would be impossible to ignore her—he would never live it down.

He finally turned, smiled, and waved back.

"Now he sees me." Joan gestured to him. "He's an odd man, you know. He's from someplace in Africa."

Jamie bristled a bit. "Does that make him odd?" she asked.

"No, of course not—although they do have different ways over there. I'm not sure how he got so much education—it's not typical," Joan said, successfully lumping the entire continent of Africa into one tidy pile. "He's polite enough, but there's always something on his mind. He doesn't like to just sit down and chat. During our lunches, he sits with us, but he isn't with us, you know?" she continued.

Again, Jamie stiffened. "Really?" she asked.

If Joan was any indication, this lunch group might not be her cup of tea, either. Before she could say anything else, she felt Nick's hand on her back. He meant it as a warning to watch her temper, but it instantly pulled her out of the moment. His touch on her bare back sent small tingling sensations down her spine. All irritation at Joan disappeared as she gave herself another mental head slap.

I'm a grown woman, not a naïve waif, she thought. She glanced over at Nick—did he feel the same thing? *Take a chance,* a small, devilish voice whispered in her head. Before she could contemplate what that might be like, David made his way over.

"Good evening, David! I'm glad to see you here!" Joan said and attempted to give him an awkward hug. "David, I want you to meet Dr. Jamison Scott, Dr. Scott's doctor daughter. She just returned to town from working with…Doctors Overseas, is it? And this is her friend, Nick, is it?" She took another sip from her drink. "I was just telling them about the procedures at the lab, since Dr. Scott may take a job there. I also told them about Rachel—bless her soul."

David smiled and acknowledged Jamie and Nick. His ears perked up with the news that this woman may come to work at the lab. *In what capacity?* There were no position vacancies. So, Dr. Scott would likely create a new position for the younger Dr. Scott, which could create problems. He tried to learn more.

"It is very nice to meet you, Dr. Scott. Where were you located with Doctors Overseas?" he asked.

"I spent some time in several locations, like the Central African Republic, the Democratic Republic of Congo, and South Sudan. I wouldn't trade my experiences for anything in the world. Where are you from originally?" Jamie responded and then added her own question.

"Ma'am, I am Kenyan but was born in Somalia. They then forced us into a camp back in Kenya. I got a visa to go to college, but my family could not get out of the country. So, I send money back to help."

"I've heard about the tent cities there." Jamie knew that this occasion wasn't the best time for that discussion. "I would like to talk to you at some point. I have friends—perhaps there's something they can do to help your family."

That was unexpected. "Ma'am, thank you for the offer. Perhaps we can meet one day when you come to the lab." David sensed that more questions were coming. He could also tell that the tall gentleman with Dr. Scott was a police officer—not a police officer like the ones he encountered at home, but an officer all the same.

Nick recognized that David accurately identified him, and before he could ask questions, David gave a quick excuse and left. As David walked away, he admitted to himself that keeping his job could become more complicated. He needed to ensure he didn't lose his freedom at the lab with the addition of the very inquisitive doctor.

Inside the house, David searched for the older Scotts to complete his party appearance. His boss and wife invited him to this function, which he had accepted for political reasons. The elder Scotts had to see him. He stopped to pick up a bottle of sparkling water with lime from the bar closest to the DJ area. Appearances were key.

Taking a sip, he spotted Dr. Scott speaking to an older gentleman in the salon and headed in that direction. When his boss made a move to disengage himself, David tapped him on the shoulder.

"Good evening, Dr. Scott," he said.

"Good evening, David. So glad you could make it. Are you finding everything OK?"

"Yes, sir. Everything is exceptional. Thank you for inviting me, sir. Your home is lovely, sir."

Gregory chuckled at his employee's formality. "It's a party. You don't have to be so formal tonight. I will inform Mrs. Scott of your compliments. Relax a bit and enjoy yourself. Have you had any food? There are some wonderful hors d'oeuvres and lovely desserts. Make sure you try some different things."

"I will, sir."

Gregory shook his hand. David was always extremely respectful. He addressed most people as ma'am or sir. It was disconcerting for people who were younger or had less seniority. The man was notoriously tight-lipped beyond his education and work references. There was some chatter about his family in Africa, and Gregory knew he had spent some time in Russia as a student. His credentials were better than his current position. One day, he would get the details.

"Have you mingled any? You already know my wife. My son, Jonathan, daughter, Jillian, and son-in-law, Richard, are all here, somewhere—you've met them before. Have you met my oldest daughter? I am trying to convince her to come work at the lab."

Margaret walked up at that moment with a city council member.

"Excuse me, Gregory. I just wanted to discuss the zoning for the potential expansion with Mr. Armstrong if we decide to build an annex." To Mr. Armstrong, she said, "We haven't made any decisions but are considering building a new location. Could we talk about zoning issues?"

She continued to talk, and David gracefully backed away and headed toward the front door. He would grab one dessert—no need to let all this food go to waste—and then leave. He paused at the exit and scanned the scene in the backyard. Time to go before anyone else tried to talk to him.

16
Against Protocol

Joan drained the remains of her drink and turned to the bar to get another. She was going to need an Uber tonight. Jamie and Nick watched David walk away from them. Nick internally acknowledged that by remaining quiet, he learned a few facts for his investigation. Tomorrow would be a busy day, and he wouldn't get any more useful information tonight without pulling out his badge, which Mrs. Scott would frown upon.

"I think it's time for me to leave," Nick said to Jamie. "I have an early day tomorrow. Thanks for your hospitality." When she gave him a questioning look, he added, "I guess I should thank your mother and father."

"Are you sure you don't want anything to eat?" Jamie asked. "I feel bad. I didn't let you ask questions. Was this trip even worthwhile for you?"

"Oh, it was worth it," he responded, a touch too quickly. She blushed. He hadn't felt this kind of pull toward anyone in a long time, and suddenly he wanted to know more about her. Maybe the night didn't have to end just yet.

"Walk with me," he requested, holding out his arm. Without thinking, Jamie accepted the invitation.

In the far-left corner of the yard, there was a small gazebo and a fountain. Several trees, including a large Crepe Myrtle and a Southern Magnolia tree, secluded the area from the main yard. During the spring and summer, both trees often had many fragrant blooms, which made the area an ideal place to bring a book or someone special. Even without the flowers, the area was beautiful and offered a sense of regal solitude. A few of the partygoers had explored the area, but by the time Jamie and Nick walked to the gazebo, there was no one around. The music was still audible but was soft enough to allow for simple conversation. Nick took a seat on the small bench while Jamie walked over to the fountain.

"I've always liked this spot. It's quiet—at least on most days." She smiled, gesturing toward the sounds of the musical accompaniment. "I didn't grow up in this house, but when I came to visit, I would always come out here to read or think," she continued.

"It *is* nice out here. My parents' backyard was full of balls and bikes. I'm one of six kids—four boys and two girls. There was no place that was quiet anywhere in that house, ever." He stood up. "It's not too different now whenever I go back to my parents' place," Nick revealed.

"Where did you grow up?" Jamie asked her companion.

"I was born in New York State, but my father moved the family down here for a job when I was three. I went to Georgia State and then to the police academy. My folks moved to a cottage in Florida—my dad's retired now—and they putter and do what retired folks do while waiting for their grandchildren to visit."

"That sounds like fun. My sister has four kids; I only know two of them; the other two were born while I was gone. When I was a kid, I wanted a noisy house, but my mother wasn't down for the wild fireworks. She was prim, I guess," Jamie recalled, as Nick moved over by her side. "My childhood was full of things that prepared me for polite society. My mother felt we were meant for great things," she added, using air quotes on the last two words. "I'm not sure she got what she hoped for with me."

"It sounds like you've done plenty of great things," he responded, repeating her air quotes. "Didn't you do some modeling as a teen? Then medical school and relief work in Africa? I think that's impressive. There's still time for more impressive things."

Gathering up his courage, Nick reached out and gently turned her to face him. The tension between the two was thick. "You're mesmerizing. I'm not sure what's happening here. I don't want to step over the line or offend you, but…" Jamie held her breath as he reached down and brought her hand up to his lips.

Jamie closed her eyes and exhaled. "I won't be offended," she whispered.

He leaned in and kissed her. She wrapped her arms around his neck, and he enfolded her in his. The skin of her back was softer than he imagined, and he took the kiss deeper, engaging her tongue with his.

It had been a while since Jamie had been kissed like that. She had had some brief entanglements and relationships while in Africa and Europe, but most of them were based on proximity. Sex was involved, but it often felt perfunctory, as if the need for the release was more important than the specific person involved. But this—this felt different. She reveled in that feeling and matched his ardor step for step.

It took quite a bit of self-control for Nick not to let his hands roam further than the exposed skin of her back. After a moment, he groaned and stepped back. "Sorry," he said, searching her face for reassurance. "I lost myself for a few minutes," he said.

Jamie was unhappy that he'd broken the connection. She steeled herself and focused on his mouth. "Me, too," she purred and went back in for another kiss, which was just as intense, and he was just as involved.

When she broke away, Nick appeared sorry. While maintaining eye contact, Jamie gently wiped her lipstick off his face, smoothed her hair, and smiled. "I'm not sure what came over me there." She backed away a step—although she hoped he would reach out for her again.

"Yeah, that might be a good idea," he replied. It took a considerable amount of willpower to remain where he was.

"So, that..." Jamie said. "That was a pleasant surprise, but definitely unexpected."

Nick chuckled. "Yeah, this isn't how I usually meet women. I have known you for two days, and I can't quite get you out of my head. I will admit I'm a sucker for tall women." He smiled. "But I haven't been this awkward around a woman since I was a teenager."

"It's been a while for me, too," she admitted. The sound of an upbeat tune drifted over to them. She fiddled with her hands as she smoothed her dress and longed for a nice martini. She needed to calm her nerves. This was complicated ground they were treading. Her life was unsettled, and people were being murdered in the family business. Tossing in an entanglement with the lead detective on the case could make her life difficult. *But kind of sexy at the same time. Definite chaos.* As part of her new life strategy, she decided she couldn't let the uncertainty lie.

"OK. I have a new philosophy in life, and that is not to avoid questions. We seem to be interested in each other, right?" She slipped off her shoes as she moved back to face him. Months of not wearing heels had turned her into a lightweight. "Is this going to be a problem? I plan to ask questions, and I'm sure I'm going to step on your toes."

Nick placed a finger under her chin. "I can handle that. You won't get the best of me—I'm very good at my job," he assured her.

"You may be, but I'm very persistent—I don't think you can shake me."

"Don't think I want to…" And they were kissing again. This time, Nick let his hands wander as she pressed herself against him. His lips traveled down her neck to her shoulder, and he slid her shoulder strap over to get better access. Jamie nibbled his earlobe and tried to remember if she was even prepared for where this seemed to be headed.

A rational thought surfaced—*shave game*? A quick mental inventory—*acceptable.* Underwear—a delicate thong—*appropriate*. Birth control—*not handled.*

Wait, what? Was she really contemplating sleeping with this guy already? His hand was currently on her butt. Yeah, she would have to be honest: If she could figure out a place—*bedroom*—she would be naked in minutes. But birth control…

Before she could even further ponder the birth control situation, someone cleared her throat behind her. Nick and Jamie froze. He lifted his head, and Jamie slowly turned sheepishly to see her sister and brother standing there.

Jonathan turned away, but the still-tipsy Jillian was smirking.

"I knew it!" Jillian cheered gleefully. "Africa *has* livened you up a bit."

Jamie was relieved that she still had on all her clothes, but had they had a couple more minutes, she might have been naked on the bench. Not a good look, to be sure. She stood up straight, and Nick helpfully placed her shoulder strap back in place. She whispered her thanks and turned her attention to her giggling sister and uncomfortable brother.

"Why are you two out here?" Jamie tried unsuccessfully to sound indignant.

Jon said, "You should be glad that it was us and not Mother. I feel like I should shower now. Porn is cool," both sisters groaned at his words, "but not with my sister as the star. I left my date at the house for this." The siblings continued to stare at the embarrassed pair.

"Nothing happened. We just came out here to talk," Nick stammered as he straightened his tux.

"Don't hide it. I heard that you've been eyeing my sister since you first met. Just admit it and move on," Jon stated bluntly.

Jillian ignored that exchange and directed her comments to Jamie. "Mother's looking for you. She has a toast planned and a ceremonial cutting of the cake. Everyone's gathering for the toast. Be front and center with us. However, I believe she plans to celebrate your return, so straighten yourself up," Jillian noted, snickering. "I have some lipstick in my bag. Luckily, he didn't rip your dress off. That would have been difficult to explain." She turned to Nick. "You have lipstick on your face, too. We have to get Jamie back to our mother before she blows up the party, searching for her."

After a quick makeup repair job and making sure everything—including shoes—was in its original position and/or condition, the quartet started back to the party. Nick and Jamie walked behind Jillian and Jon. Every few steps, one would look over at the other and smile. Jon saw this out of the corner of his eye and said, "Ugh. Stop the googly eyes, or our mother will have you both for dessert."

The thought of that made all four walk faster.

17
A Toast with the Host

Margaret was impatiently waiting for her children to resurface. When she saw the quartet approaching, she immediately went to the stage microphone next to the band. As the queen of social event timing, she had already sent the wait staff around with trays filled with champagne flutes. She motioned for the musicians to lower the volume. They continued to play softly as background accompaniment.

"Good evening, everyone! I hope you are having a good time. It's been a wonderful evening, and I'm so grateful to have my entire family here to celebrate with so many of my dear friends and colleagues." She paused while everyone clapped and raised their glasses in salute. "You all know my wonderful husband, Dr. Gregory Scott, a brilliant researcher and an established business owner. We have been married for over thirty-five years, and I wouldn't trade one second of that time." She trailed off with a catch in her voice. Gregory stepped up next to her and kissed her on the cheek. The crowd clapped again.

The three Scott children recognized this strategy. Margaret had perfected the art of public speaking and the facade of shyness and humility. It was amusing how well it worked.

"I've been blessed with sixty years of good health," she said. "Yes, I'm glad to reveal my age. I'm thankful for everything I have." More applause. "I have also been blessed with three brilliant children. My youngest, Jillian—come here, dear." She led her daughter onto the small stage and continued her toast. "She graduated from Spelman summa cum laude but decided that she wanted to put her career on hold to raise her family. Jillian and her husband, Richard, have four charming sons, and I love my grandbabies very much. My only son, Jonathan," she said, gesturing to him as he came onstage. "He's an architect, and I'm still waiting for him to provide some grandchildren. Get married, Son!"

Laughter from the crowd. Jonathan dropped his head in mock shame. Margaret paused for effect as the laughter died down. "And my oldest, Dr. Jamison Scott, who many of you might not know well because she has spent the last four years working with Doctors Overseas in Africa. She's finally back home. We missed her so much." Another pause for effect. "So, this is a celebration—of my birthday, of my wonderful family, and to welcome home my daughter, Jamison!" Margaret lifted her glass, and everyone else followed suit. Nick caught Jamie's eye during the toast and winked.

As the cheers and applause continued, Margaret held her hand up. "While this is a joyous occasion, we would be remiss if we did not acknowledge the sense of tragedy that is also present at this gathering. One of our employees, Rachel Thorne, was senselessly killed this weekend. She was a lovely young woman with many hopes and dreams for the future—a future that was tragically taken away. We know the police will find the awful person who committed this horrible act. We also want to celebrate Rachel's life and pray that the police quickly find the perpetrator. To Rachel!" she finished as she held up her glass again.

"To Rachel!" and "Hear, hear!" echoed through the crowd.

"While that was a sobering note, it is important that we remember the message of the season and embrace our family and friends. Love is the key. Thank you and enjoy!" she ended with a flourish.

Amid the cheers and applause, Gregory stepped down from the stage and helped Margaret, Jamison, and Jillian down. Jon scrambled down on his own. The crowd parted to allow the family to reach the dessert table. A chant of "Cut the Cake" wafted through the crowd.

"Wait!" Gregory demanded, holding up his hand. "We have to sing Happy Birthday."

Everyone heartily obliged. As the song's last notes faded, Margaret made a delicate cut into the show cake. On cue, the wait staff appeared, distributing slices of the decadent red velvet cake.

Jamie hung back from her siblings a bit to wait for Nick to make his way through the crowd.

Richard, who'd been schmoozing with clients, both real and potential, found his way back to his wife's side and kissed her on the cheek. Jillian was grumbling about her mother. "At least she acknowledged I went to college. Usually, that fact gets brushed under the rug," she said to the crowd as she finished her glass of champagne. She scanned the mass of people, looking for another drink.

"She's very proud of you, dear," Richard said as he tried to shield her from a server with additional champagne glasses. He was unsuccessful. "Perhaps you should slow down some. Or at least eat some cake." He snagged a piece as a different server went by. "I'm not trying to tell you what to do—you've told me I do that too much—but I know how you hate hangovers. Just keep that in mind."

Jillian opened her mouth for Richard to feed her a bite of cake. She slowly chewed the tasty morsel and seductively licked her lips. "I'm only tipsy, baby. Take advantage of that while you can. Jamie had the right idea but the wrong location." She leaned in and whispered, "I have a bedroom upstairs in case you've forgotten. Meet me in five." She sauntered off.

Jon had gone to retrieve his date, Isabella, after he left the stage, and the pair arrived as Jillian made her sexual suggestion. Jon groaned at the look on Richard's face. "I'm learning too much about my sisters' sex lives tonight. I feel dirty." Jon shuddered, but gave Richard an obvious wink.

Richard cracked a mischievous grin and stared after his wife's retreating figure.

"Go on, man. You know you want to, and with four kids, you probably don't get much at home. Just be discreet. Mother will kill you two for having sex at her party—even if you are married." He gave Richard an imagined hat tip. "Go with God."

Richard acknowledged the group and quickly followed his wife.

Jon turned to Isabella. "I guess you've seen the weirdness that is my family. Today I have caught both of my sisters in compromising positions."

"Didn't you have times where you caught one or the other—or they caught you—when you were teenagers?" Isabella asked jokingly.

"This never happened when we were younger. Jamie was in New York modeling. I didn't know *what* she was doing there. Jillian didn't date anyone for long until she met Richard. That was a scandal. You know the drill from there."

Jillian and Richard *had* been a scandal. Margaret was horrified when Jillian said she was going to postpone law school because she wanted to get married to her boss. Her older boss, who was in the midst of a divorce. Since all Jillian ever talked about was becoming a judge, this threw her parents. Many conversations and arguments ensued, with Jillian eventually threatening to run off and elope as soon as the divorce was final. Cooler heads prevailed.

By February of Jillian's senior year, Richard and his wife were already working on dissolving their union. This hadn't been Richard's first affair, but it was the last one since his wife refused to overlook it. His wife was a doctor. She worked and put him through law school; after graduating, he returned the favor and put her through med school. But because they had two sons, she always put her career on the back burner by working part-time while he became a partner at a prestigious law firm. To expedite the divorce, Richard was more than generous and accepted joint custody of their teenage sons. Considering the amount of money involved in the settlement, it was a rapid process. Jillian stealthily planned their wedding during the settlement sessions. In June, once it was official, she and Richard flew to Hawaii to get married.

Afterwards, Jillian learned that breaking up a marriage—even one that may already have been on the rocks—didn't endear you to proper society. As an olive branch and to start the rehab process, Margaret threw a large reception about six months after the ceremony to introduce the new couple to society. Jillian and Richard had been married for ten years now. For Jillian, law school was still off in the distance. As far as anyone outside the marriage knew, she had accepted the direction her life had taken.

"Well, what about you? Any drama I should know about?" Isabella asked Jon.

"Nothing compared to my sisters. I'm just looking for a nice girl to settle down with. I'm rather boring," he said as Nick and Jamie walked up.

"Don't believe that. He's the sanest one of the three of us." Jamie winked at her brother and draped her arm over his shoulders. "I need to eat. I've had two glasses of champagne on an empty stomach. Where are Jillian and Richard?"

"Upstairs, I would guess, picking up where you two left off," Jon said.

"Wouldn't this be a good story for Mother? Jillian conceives Margaret's long-awaited granddaughter at her 60th birthday party?" Jamie whispered, and then she felt a tap on her shoulder. It was Margaret and Gregory. Jamie closed her eyes.

Perfect, she thought.

"I hope you are exaggerating about Jillian," Margaret said.

"I need some food, because I'm kind of giddy." She grabbed Nick's hand and rushed off.

"It's important that you eat, Jamison, with your history," Margaret called after her. Turning to Jon, she asked, "Why is Jamison holding the detective's hand? What's happening there?"

"Oh, Mother, you don't want to know. There's never a dull moment with your girls."

18
Just Like Old Times

Once inside the house, Jamison led Nick into the kitchen. She had always appreciated her mother's innovative design ideas. In the kitchen, this included the combination of maple and cherry woods, a large, angled island, a separate bar area, and a stove alcove with a hood. Very efficient use of space. But today, with the overhead lights down low and the holiday music drifting throughout, the room was giving off an enchanting ambiance.

The two catering staff members in the area gave her sidelong glances as they entered, but they recognized her and didn't say anything. One worker handed her a plate and made a sweeping gesture toward the many warming dishes lined up on half of the counter of the angled island. Jamie smiled at the woman and headed over, with Nick trailing behind. He wasn't as interested in the food as she was, but wasn't willing to say goodbye to Jamie yet. The shiny silver serving dishes contained antipasto pizzas, caviar blinis, stuffed mushrooms, lobster sliders, spring rolls, and more.

When she lifted the lid from each dish, they were both hit with tantalizing aromas that made Jamie's mouth water. She grabbed a mini pizza, a stuffed mushroom, and a spring roll and placed them on the plate.

"Nick, do you want anything while I'm raiding the stash? Please, don't make me eat alone."

Nick hesitated for a moment. *Anything to spend more time with her*, he thought. He turned to grab a plate and almost ran over the same staffer who had come up behind him with another plate. Accepting it, he selected a few items to eat—he hadn't eaten much since he arrived, either. He had to acknowledge that the food choices were quite tempting and not his typical fare.

"So, will you be eating the leftovers for the next week?" he asked, leaning against the angled island at the section without the serving containers. "There's so much food here. Did your mother assume that half of Atlanta was coming?"

"No, this is standard for her party planning; you can't ever run out during a party! Some will end up at the office, she will donate some to shelters, neighbors might get some, and we will eat the rest. Nothing goes to waste. With my mother, that concept's very important." She bit into the spring roll. "Oh, my God! This is fantastic! It's got shrimp in it. I'm going to have to get a few more of these." She took another bite. "This may be one of the best things I have ever had in my mouth. Want a taste?" she offered and instantly blushed. "I meant of the spring roll."

"I know what you meant." He leaned over and took a bite. "That *is* good. I haven't had quite that flavor combination in a spring roll before." He got one of his own and went to stand by her in front of the serving dishes. "You don't have to worry about me kissing you in here. I don't want to sully your reputation and all."

Jamie smiled. A couple of wait staff walked by, and Jamie was pretty sure she saw, in the distance, Richard and Jillian coming down the main staircase. *I guess they got it on upstairs*, she thought. "I think my reputation's not as stellar as my mother would like to pretend. Remember, I was a model. I'm surprised you haven't made any cracks about eating, food, or dieting."

"How old were you when you started modeling? How did that even happen?" he inquired, selecting another spring roll to eat.

"As you may have noticed, I'm very tall. At thirteen, a photographer gave my mother his card, saying I could be a model. She scoffed at first, but then she checked the guy out. She thought it would be a useful learning experience—some local shows and photo shoots. Maybe I could make a bit of money and save some for college." She took another bite. "Ironic, because my mother's family's wealthy. But when she married my father, she refused any money from my grandparents beyond the wedding and, as far as I know, hasn't taken any since."

"Interesting. But your modeling, it was bigger than that, huh?"

"A little. I took some test shots with the photographer, and he showed them to a local agent who signed me. I did a couple of local campaigns and was eventually sent to do some go-sees for Fashion Week."

Nick shook his head in confusion.

Jamie smiled and explained, "When you go and show your portfolio to various clients to get hired for jobs and shows. I got signed up for a few fashion shows that year. By the time I was fifteen, I was doing major shows and print ads. It was a heady time—parties, traveling."

"Well, at some point, you went to medical school. Why? It sounds like modeling was fun," Nick asked.

"Oh, it *was* fun. I made some money and thought I was grown. However, it didn't take long to determine that I'm not naturally a size zero, so eating became an issue. Oh, I had moved in with my boyfriend, too." She paused. "I can't believe I'm telling you this," she said, blushing.

"You don't have to. But I would like to know what makes you *you*. So, it's up to you. And unless you killed someone, the statute of limitations has likely expired." He grinned at her, and his eyes twinkled.

Jamie took a deep breath and stopped over-sharing. "I can't tell you all my secrets up front, can I? Where's the mystery in that?" She finished the spring roll. "Tell me something about you. How did you decide to become a detective?"

"Not much to it. I've always wanted to be one. My grandfather, uncle, and father were all police officers, and I wanted to be just like them. Two of my brothers entered law enforcement, too. Nothing amazing or weird at all." He popped a stuffed mushroom into his mouth.

Those lips… she remembered the feel of those lips on her skin. *God!* Jamie's eyes widened for a second, but she quickly ducked her head and took a bite of her mini pizza. She didn't want him to see the effect of his simple action on her.

"I was very dedicated to earning my shield and destroyed my relationship—I should say my marriage. My ex-wife didn't take my neglect lying down, so to speak. She found someone else." He paused and continued to look straight ahead as he waited for a response from Jamie.

Married? That was a surprise. Jamie stopped chewing but maintained a calm expression. "That sounds tough," she murmured.

"Don't feel bad for me. I gave as good as I got. Daniella was my college sweetheart, and we got pregnant immediately after the wedding. I didn't spend much time with my new wife or baby, and she found someone who would."

"So, you have a child?" Another surprise that diverted her attention from her food. That he had a daughter reminded her of her child again—a quick flash of a pale, tiny, screaming infant with reddish-brown hair. She had to bring herself back to the current conversation.

"A daughter, twelve years old. Before you think that I'm a total loser, she's an amazing young lady, and we spend time together during the summers and holidays." He chuckled to himself. "That probably scared you off."

"Nah, I like a challenge. Besides, we aren't trying to marry each other, right?"

"Who's talking about marriage?" Margaret and Gregory came into the kitchen behind several staffers trying to get some last-minute trays of food out. Jamie cringed. Again, her mother had walked in on the tail end of an awkward comment. She was going to have to pay more attention.

"Is there something going on that I don't know about here?" Margaret had noticed Nick eyeing her daughter since they met. Social status was important to her, and a police detective, as important as the job was, didn't have enough. "I hope you didn't get the wrong idea, Detective. My daughter likes to flirt. She will travel on the wild side, but she always returns home after a while," Margaret cautioned.

Jamie opened her mouth to speak, but nothing would come out. She was mortified.

Margaret continued to the refrigerator for a drink, oblivious to the sudden tension in the room.

Gregory eyed Jamison and subtly shook his head. He knew that Jamison and Margaret's reunion had been tenuous so far. This last comment could further strain the relationship. Jamison flushed bright red before all the color had drained from her face. This could lead to a repeat of the scene that led to Jamison leaving. He would not let that happen again. The family couldn't take another fracture like that one.

"Don't worry, dear. I'm sure Jamison doesn't want to deny us the chance to spend all our money on her wedding. I'm sure you will be the first to know if such an event were in the offing." Gregory said, trying to allay the tense atmosphere. To Jamison, he added, "We're going to pass out the party favors. We could use some help. Detective Marshall, I hope you've enjoyed yourself. I'm sure we'll be speaking with each other soon."

Nick saw that as his cue to leave. Turning to his hosts, he said, "Good night, everyone. Thank you for allowing me to come at the last minute. I enjoyed myself."

As he passed Jamie on his way out of the room, he whispered in her ear, "I like a challenge as well!" she smiled and blushed, thinking back to their make-out session.

Nick headed toward the front door. He saw Jon and his date milling around in the crowd and bobbed his head in acknowledgment when Jon locked eyes with him. There was a line for the valet. When he got to the front of the line, he handed the young man his check-in stub for his car. While he waited, he noticed the variety of expensive cars being brought to their owners. His vehicle, while respectable, did not quite match up.

As a police detective, it was unlikely he would ever drive one of those expensive cars. And with Margaret's pointed comment about his prospects, he had a rare moment of envy. He loved his job. He couldn't think of anything else he would rather do—and he had opportunities to join the FBI or even private security. But sometimes, he had to remind himself that he was doing OK, even if he wasn't ever going to be rich. In the past, he had dated both rich and poor women. For most of them, his lack of wealth didn't seem to matter much. But there was one or two who'd tried to convince him to upgrade his job or to hook him up with higher-paying consulting gigs or persuade him to move into management. That typically led to Nick quickly ending the relationship. Jamie didn't seem like that type of woman, but what did he know about her? While she had a definite physical pull on him, he should be more cautious. Feeling a nudge on his arm, he noticed Jillian next to him.

"I just wanted to say goodbye," she said.

"Really? Only goodbye?" he asked, knowing well that couldn't be all.

"I know. You don't know me. But I overheard what happened in the kitchen with my mother." Before he could open his mouth, Jillian lifted her hand. "I had just come downstairs, and I saw you and Jamie in the kitchen. I spent my teen years in this house. And I know the best places to stand to hear all conversations. So, I was being nosy; sue me," she joked. "When Mother came in, there was no way in hell I was going to brave that room."

"I wish I had missed that myself," Nick noted.

"Don't let my mother scare you. She has spent a lot of time trying to micromanage everyone's dating lives—

without success. I married a respectable attorney, but he wasn't who she wanted me with—since he was married when we met."

"Oh."

"I'm not ashamed, and it's not a secret. We fell madly in love. But as I was saying, I'm her only married child, and she doesn't consider it a success based on how we got together. Jon only dates cute bubbleheads, so Mother has given up on him for now. Jamie would be her crowning achievement. She was proud when Jamie made it big as a model, but then Jamie quit. Then she became a doctor and got engaged to a big-shot physician. But Jamie ended that. So, Mother sees Jamie's life and marriage prospects as something she needs to manage because she thinks Jamie makes poor decisions. Not that you're trying to marry my sister. However, even my mother can see that there's some chemistry between you two." Jillian moved her hands for emphasis as Nick listened intently.

She paused and whispered conspiratorially. "Mother's going to work hard to put a stop to it—whatever it is." She stood on her tiptoes and kissed Nick on the cheek. "Forewarned is forearmed. I typically wouldn't be so blunt, but I have been drinking a lot tonight." She put her fingers to her lips in a shushing motion. "Now, where's my husband?" she giggled and skipped off, the tipsy version shining through.

Watching her leave, he wondered if she would even remember speaking to him. His SUV pulled up in front of him, and after tipping the valet, he got in and waited in line to leave the property. It gave him time to think about the case and the girl. He believed that both went deeper than they originally appeared.

He turned on his radio and tried to lose himself in the music as he drove home.

19
Watch Your Keys

He stood outside the gate of the Scott property. The young man had been there for a while, but with people streaming in and out of the gates, he didn't attract attention. He was not quite brave enough to walk into the party, but he knew she would need to come out. He had come prepared.

There were several valets working at this party. Earlier, he bribed one of them with five hundred dollars to give him his vest and jacket and disappear. With the vest and jacket over his white shirt and black pants, no one was the wiser. He had only moved a few vehicles, conscientiously parking and retrieving cars. He'd even received a few tips. All the while, he was searching.

After Rachel's death, he spent some time on Saturday and early hours of Sunday hanging outside the lab—trying to get a glimpse of her, Tatiana. He learned about this party while striking up conversations outside the lab with workers who had come to the office out of curiosity. There were also journalists hoping for a scoop. It's amazing what tidbits you can learn from people. So, here he was, trying to find her. The situation with Rachel got out of control—he hadn't intended for her to die—and the same was true for Tatiana. He just wanted to speak with her. But if his temper took over, what could he do?

After the party, Tatiana walked out with a male friend and got in line for her car. He assessed her position so he could be in the right place to retrieve Tatiana's car. Once she got to the front of the line, he had slipped a little money to the valet in front of him to make sure he could assist her.

Unaware, Tatiana handed her ticket to the lead valet. Who then found her keys and summoned him to retrieve her car. *Perfect.* He could take a moment to search her car. Her address should be on the registration in the glove box. If he couldn't talk to her tonight, he could go to her home. He took the keys and tipped his head to Tatiana without exposing his face before running to the lot where most of the cars were parked.

After locating her Honda and gaining entry, he quickly hunted through her glove compartment for her car registration or a piece of mail with an address. Her registration address was a location in Illinois. *Interesting.* He took a picture of that document with his cell phone and quickly scanned the car for any other mail. There was a flyer with an Atlanta address under the passenger's seat. He took a picture of it and shoved everything else back into the glove compartment. Luckily for him, other cars were waiting in line. The extra time spent searching was minimal. By the time he pulled up to Tatiana, she was dancing from foot to foot, and her male companion had already left. He got out of the car and held the door open for her as she came around.

"Here's your car, ma'am. I hope you had a pleasant time," he said, tipping his head again.

She thanked him as she settled into the driver's seat. As he closed the door, he said, "Have a wonderful evening, Tatiana. Rachel sends her best."

Tatiana was smiling at the exchange of pleasantries and considering whether to give him a tip, but the mention of Rachel made her head snap up in shock. She peered at the valet through the driver's window. He was smiling at her panic. She forgot about a tip. As she drove away, she could see him in the rear-view mirror, waving at her. What had receded to a minor drumbeat of fear came roaring back. His face flashed back to her, and she felt a glimmer of recognition. *Oh, God, he was in her car!* How did he know where she was? There was no one alive that she could turn to, and she was terrified. Was she next?

20
Monday Morning Quarterbacking

Jamie woke up before her alarm on Monday morning. After checking her watch, she lay in bed for a few minutes, enjoying the quiet. While in Africa, she had a few quiet mornings. The doctors and nurses were always in the center of a village or town, so there was outside noise from people, animals, and sometimes cars. Here in this enclave, it was silent—almost lifeless. After savoring the few moments of this early morning quietness, she slid out of bed and pulled on a pair of jeans. Jamie had no robe; she really needed to reassess her wardrobe, especially if she planned to get a job. She splashed some water on her face and went downstairs, carrying her laptop. After a cup of coffee, she would take a shower.

The house looked like a couple hundred people had wandered through it, enjoying food and drink. *Is Olivia supposed to clean this up?* Jamie thought.

She was the first person out of bed for the first time on this trip. She had beaten Olivia into the kitchen—she wasn't even here yet—nothing was ready. Cooking wasn't Jamie's forte, but she remembered the conversation with her mother about coffee. She put on a pot of Kona and searched in the refrigerator for some milk or cream. She saw the container of spring rolls and took a couple.

After pouring her coffee, she sat at the kitchen table and fired up her laptop. Some of her former coworkers had emailed greetings and updates from Doctors Overseas. One learned online about Rachel's death at the lab and wrote to make sure Jamie was all right. Jamie found and read an article about the murder on a local news site. The media took a more sensationalistic view: a madman was killing women who visited nightclubs. Jamie believed the motive was personal. Regardless, she was going to the lab with her father this morning to learn more about the workings of the business—and to snoop. Based on what she had heard so far, her father might have been oblivious to what went on between his employees.

"Good morning!" Gregory came into the kitchen fully dressed in khakis, a blue chambray shirt, a blue tie, and a blue patterned sweater vest. He was carrying a sheath of papers. "I see you made some coffee. Thank you." He stopped to evaluate what she was wearing. "You're not wearing that to the office, are you? While we are on the casual side, jeans aren't acceptable."

"No, Dad. I'll take a quick shower before we leave and put on something more appropriate." As Gregory poured himself a cup of coffee, Jamie continued, "I have a lot to learn, so I'll be asking a lot of questions. Is that OK? I don't want to step on your toes."

"That's fine, dear. How else will you learn? I think you could help run the place. I'm getting old, and we could get you in a position to take over one day. You're smart and ambitious. I could see you as a CEO." Gregory sipped his coffee and smiled.

Jamie's eyelids fluttered rapidly in disbelief. She had never considered that role. Running the place? Not on her radar. Caring for patients had been her primary interest, but with the changes in her situation, that might not be the case anymore. "We'll see, Dad. Is Mother awake? Is she coming into the office as well?"

"No, she's awake, but I think she's going to work from home today. A cleaning service is coming to get the house back into shape, and she wants to oversee their work." He sat down across from Jamie. "However, she smelled your coffee and would like a cup."

"Cool. Give me 15 minutes, and I'll be ready to go. I take it you want to drive?" Jamie inquired.

"Yes, I do. We can talk during the ride. Besides, you might get in that death trap car and kill both of us. That car makes you crazy," Gregory said, smiling. Jamie exhaled in fake annoyance and left Gregory pouring a cup of coffee for his wife. As she went up the stairs, Olivia entered through the front door.

Jamie took a quick shower, then pulled on a pair of camel-colored, ankle-length trousers (her only non-denim pants) and a black, mock-turtleneck shirt. She fished her black ballet flats out of her duffel bag, slapped on some eyeliner and lip gloss, took her satin scarf off her head, ran a comb through her hair, and pulled it into a ponytail. She grabbed her small crossbody bag, laptop, cell phone, and coat and bounded back down the stairs. Gregory had been talking to Olivia but ended the conversation when Jamie appeared. He quickly ushered Jamie out the door.

The drive to the office was uneventful, and the Scotts arrived before anyone else. Gregory had diverted any weekend lab work to another facility. The police had not released the site until Sunday evening. The building would reopen for business that afternoon, and a cleaning service was coming at 8:30 to erase all evidence of a police presence. There was only one other car in the lot, and Jamie did not recognize it. CSU had already removed Rachel's car from its parking space.

Jamie remembered when her parents developed the plans for this building while she was in college. It had aged well.

Gregory swiped his keycard, punched his code into the keypad, and let them into the building. As they walked to the elevator, Jamie noticed remnants of fingerprint powder and crime-scene tape and slowed her pace to look around.

"Dad, does your security guard on duty that night still have a job?" Jamie asked, pausing by the security desk.

Gregory exhaled impatiently but tried to answer in an even tone as there was currently no security guard in sight. Not a good look for the guards after such a significant security breach. "That remains to be seen. He says he was not at his post when Rachel returned, which is a no-no. But as you saw, something or someone happened to the video feed. We have analytic technology that assists the security team when viewing the monitors at the security desk. But if someone hacked in, I can't hold the guard completely responsible, can I?"

"I don't know, Dad. It seems suspect to me. Are you sure he didn't turn it off himself? But then, you know him, and I don't. Maybe it depends on his previous work habits."

"I feel responsible. I know I wasn't here, but I feel like I should have been able to prevent this," the older man said in a downcast tone. Gregory pressed the elevator button and motioned for Jamie to hurry. "Let's go to my office on the fourth floor. I have some meetings scheduled today, and I'd like you to be there—just to get a feel for things," he stated.

"I don't know if that's a good idea, Dad… maybe I should spend some time looking around the lab. It's been so long since I have been here. I don't know how I could help." Jamie didn't want to attend any meetings. "Maybe I should review some of the information about the company first." He rebuffed her objections—he wanted her to be there.

On the fourth floor, Gregory used his keycard and opened the door into his spacious office area. Jamie noticed he had done some redecorating since she was last there. There was a large cherry desk in one corner and a mid-sized round table with four chairs. The suite also contained a washroom and a small room with a miniature lab set-up for downtime brainstorming. The office was in a corner of the building and had windows that faced both the parking lot and a small courtyard on the side of the building. There were chairs and a picnic table; if the weather was nice, the workers could take their lunches outside to get some sun. Margaret's suite, through a connecting door, was similar, but on a smaller scale and with no lab set-up. She only had one window facing the parking lot. Gregory planted himself behind his desk and gestured for Jamie to sit in a chair facing him.

"We have a large lab area on the first floor where the technicians run forensic tests, such as drug chemistries, forensic genetics, forensic toxicology, and trace evidence. There's a lab in the basement where we do firearm identification and reenactment and some other forensic tests. The second floor has several smaller labs and office areas for my team of five research associates. They apply for grants and complete research projects with me; however, they don't do forensics. The third floor has another large lab and the office area for my forensic technicians. There's also a small cafeteria area, and the lab manager has an office there. The fourth floor has your mother's office, my office, the billing department, and a conference room. Storage is on the fifth floor," he carefully explained.

"This is impressive. Mother said that you were considering expanding," Jamie said.

"Before all of this, we wanted to open another location in another part of the city so we could increase our forensic lab work. I also want to increase our associations with local universities for research grants and opportunities. But now, I'm worried about how this will play out on our expansion—hell, even on the contracts that we currently have."

"Solve the case and make sure there's nothing involving your lab in the murders," Jamie said. "If there is, find it and root it out." She paused. "Hey, I can help with that part, at least." She thought of something. "Dad. Did Rachel have an office?"

He lifted his gaze from a file he'd been examining. "Yes, she has a cubicle on the third floor. Do you want to have a look? The police had already examined the area. Richard didn't allow them to open her computer or dump her phones yet. I have to go through her files and check for work product."

"Sure. I need a keycard," Jamie said, standing up.

Gregory grabbed one out of a drawer and handed it over. "Don't take long. We have some people coming in a few minutes," he reminded her.

"OK," Jamie called over her shoulder as she left the room. Standing by the elevator, she realized she didn't know exactly where Rachel's office was. Not wanting to return to her father's office, she went to the third floor and began a quick search. She followed the signs to the office area.

Jamie could see additional evidence that the police had been present. The door was still ajar. She poked her head in and immediately knew which cubicle belonged to Rachel. The police had left the laptop, but Jamie wasn't going to try to hack into the device. The drawers of the desk were also empty.

This was useless, she thought. But she was curious about what the police might have found.

A bit frustrated, Jamie returned to her father's office a few minutes before the scheduled meeting. At 8:30 a.m., Gregory went to the first floor to admit the cleaning service.

Jamie remained in his office but had an idea while he was gone. She called him, too impatient to wait.

He answered on the first ring. "I'm coming right back…"

"I know. But I have an idea—each employee gets an entry card, right?"

"Yes, I believe so. The cards have no identifying characteristics. So, people often switch them out, borrow each other's, and get new ones with no real accountability for where the other ones were. Each employee has a code, too—you would have to ask your mother."

"Dad! Really?" Jamie's spirit dropped a bit. "That will make it harder to trace the ins and outs on that Friday. Where would that information be, or do I have to wait to ask Mother?"

Gregory paused. He hadn't been involved in the efforts to track the movements of his employees. Again, this was Margaret's area. Most employees didn't go to floors outside their purview, and none were interested in hanging around after their shifts ended. Researchers came into the building at odd hours to work on various research projects, which was never an issue before; however, now, it felt short-sighted. Margaret had decided that they should upgrade the current facility and that they should change the system when they expanded. Too late to affect the current situation. "If there is any information, it is on the security system. During the meeting, ask the security guard on duty—who is it? Zach?—to let you look at the computer in the security office."

"Thanks, Dad. I'll check it then." Jamie hung up. She didn't think the entry card and code search would tell her anything, but she would check.

Gregory returned to his office five minutes later. "Impatient, aren't we?" he winked at Jamie. "The cleaning crew's inside and has a lot to do." He settled at his desk and resumed gathering files.

"Dad, I have another question."

"Yes?"

"Since I can't get into her computer, is there any way to see any emails she received at work?"

"Sure, you can look," Gregory said, without stopping what he was doing. "All emails that come into a company email account have a copy saved on the mainframe."

Jamie frowned. "Is that legal?"

"Company policy says there should be no personal emails in company accounts. There may be sensitive information. It's mainly to protect the lab," he said.

"Can I see hers? Or is that improper?"

"It probably is. But you're going to work here, right? Management can check the intranet server on an as-needed basis." He opened an app connected to the intranet on his computer and logged in, entering Rachel's name. Jamie asked for the password and wrote it on a slip of paper—she would have to connect her computer to the company's network to use it herself. A long list of email correspondence popped up on Gregory's screen. He turned his computer around to face Jamie. "We have a few minutes before our security meeting. I will give you five minutes to poke around. Any email from a dot gov or dot edu address you can't open. I'm serious, Jamison. Don't open those. Otherwise, see what you can find. Excuse me for one moment, and then we can review some information about the lab." He walked into the attached washroom.

Jamie went around the desk and planted herself in her father's chair, turning the screen to face her. Most of Rachel's emails weren't marked confidential, so that was good. The system pulled all the emails over the last four weeks. The older emails came up first. Jamie exhaled after reading a few innocent emails between coworkers, happy hour plans, etc. She scrolled down to the last day of emails. Jamie's eyes began to cross.

Does everyone who works here get this many emails? Definitely a strike against this job, she thought, with a bit of humor.

Then one email from Friday caught her attention—the return email address was not internal, and the subject line was ominous: "I KNOW."

Jamie opened it quickly because she could hear her father coming out of the washroom. The email only contained one sentence: "I know where you are, and you will pay." She checked the time stamp and saw that it was 6:45 p.m. There was a column in this app that showed when an email was first opened. This one was opened at 8:30 p.m.

Oh my god, she thought, gasping.

Gregory stood in front of his desk. "Dear, your time's up. Please, get out of my chair."

"Dad, there's an email threat here to Rachel," she said, writing the sender's address and IP address on a Post-It note.

"Really? On the company server? We need to let the police know."

Jamie stood up and turned the monitor to face him. "I agree. But we can find out now where this email came from." Gregory opened his mouth to protest, but Jamie kept going. "We'll tell them—just give me a few minutes. Who operates your network here? Do you have someone who runs things?" She turned the monitor back around and started typing on the keyboard.

"Not specifically. What are you doing?"

"I'm searching for an online program that can help trace an email address. I'm not an expert by any means, but the clinics I worked in sometimes got threats, and the local police officers weren't much help. We tried to trace some of those threatening emails." Her father nodded grudgingly. She added, "It didn't matter much because most emails came from cafes or other open places. So, we never caught anyone. Here, since more people have their own Internet service, I might get lucky. Unless the sender's using a proxy server."

The previous statements confused Gregory, but he waited for Jamie to complete her task.

"Hey. Here's an address from the website. Into Google Maps." Jamie tapped a few more keys. "It's not too far from here." She plugged it into the Maps app on her phone.

"What are you doing now? Tell the police. You can't go over there by yourself."

"I won't. In fact, after our meeting, I'll contact the detectives in person. Does that work for you?"

Gregory wasn't sure he believed her, but it seemed like a reasonable plan. Besides, it was time for some difficult meetings to assess the security breakdowns of the past weekend.

The security team was first. While there might be a rationale for the guard on duty missing Rachel's entrance, there was no good reason he also missed her exit. He also wanted the security guards' thoughts about the camera issues. Marcus Robinson, the guard on duty; William Hutchinson—a part-time security guard; Zach—the guard working today; and the security head, Kevin Kane, came upstairs to Gregory's office at 8:45 a.m. and stationed themselves at the round table. Marcus shifted in his seat uncomfortably—he'd already spent the previous thirty minutes in a meeting with the security head threatening to "fire his ass." His goal for this meeting was to keep his job. Gregory pulled an additional chair over to the table and asked Jamison to join them. She diverted her attention from the computer and stayed in her father's desk chair, rolling it closer but remaining behind the desk. There was no room for the large chair at the table, and she was close enough.

As they got situated, the lab manager, Joan, rushed in, apologizing profusely.

"I'm sorry I'm late. Traffic was disastrous this morning. Did I miss anything?" When she noticed Jamison, she stopped rambling. “Hello, Dr. Scott,” she said, greeting Jamison. “I didn’t know you would be here.” Gregory brought a chair from Margaret’s office into the room for Joan.

“I just found out about this meeting this morning,” Jamie said, smiling. “I don’t plan to say much—I’m just listening. Pretend I’m not here.”

Gregory started the meeting. “Last weekend was a horrible one for this company. We need to reassess the security protocols.” A couple of heads dropped in discomfort.

Thus, began a meeting that Jamie would remember as one of the most painful she’d ever been involved in. Gregory wasn’t a forceful person, so his anger was painful to watch and not clearly expressed.

Perhaps Mother should have handled this one, Jamie considered.

Joan tried to be nice to everyone and come up with reasons for the lapses. Kevin wanted to keep his job, so he pushed Marcus under the bus and made it his mission to keep him there while he drove the bus back and forth over him. Marcus tried to protect himself from the shade that Kevin threw at him and threw some back his way. William and Zach tried to disappear. It was loud—louder than any other meeting ever held in that office. In the end, no one decided anything, and no one fired anyone. Everyone, however, had a headache.

21
Discomfort Everywhere

Forty-five minutes into the security meeting, Jamison took advantage of a break in the arguments to excuse herself. Gregory acknowledged her escape but remained focused on his staff and their excuses.

She retrieved the entry card and went down to the third-floor break room for more coffee. It was a modest area with two microwaves, a commercial single-cup coffee maker, an automatic coffee maker, a toaster oven, and a full-size refrigerator. There were also two vending machines—one for beverages and one for snacks. The snack machine was a hybrid of junk food options and healthier choices. Jamie noticed that her mother had stocked the shelves with several types of coffee, tea, and cocoa in K-cups, as well as moderately priced ground beans. Since there weren't many people in the office today, she opted for a single cup of hazelnut-flavored coffee and a granola bar from the snack machine. She positioned herself to wait, anything to avoid returning to that horror show of a meeting.

Within five minutes, researcher David Yego came into the room. Her presence surprised him.

"Excuse me. Good morning, Dr. Scott," he said. "I did not mean to bother you. I expected to be alone here since the building was closed this morning," he hastily explained.

"I'm here for a meeting. What brings you in?"

"I came to complete some paperwork. I am working on a research grant with your father's help. There are many things I could develop that could help my homeland," David said, choosing a drink from the vending machine.

"How long have you been working here?" Jamie asked. She picked up her brewed cup and took a sip. "Do you want any coffee? I could make you a cup."

David shook his head and took a sip of his soda. "I have been here for three years. Your father has been very generous. One day, though, I would like to go back to Kenya."

"What are you researching?" Jamie found David interesting. Talking with him brought back memories of her time in Africa.

"Looking for a vaccine right now." David reeled off the details of a future study, rattling off minutiae he hoped would soon overwhelm her. Jamison made him uncomfortable. She was too inquisitive. Besides, her father would probably want her to do her own research. That might compromise his freedom in the lab.

His plan was successful; he lost Jamie in the whirlwind of details. "Well, that sounds interesting," she said, struggling to keep her eyes from crossing again. "Would you mind taking me on a tour around your lab area? I want to see where the magic happens," Jamie asked, shifting the subject.

"Excuse me?"

"Sorry, that's a slang phrase. I would like to see where you work."

David panicked but maintained his dispassionate demeanor. "Oh, I am at a delicate point in my research. It would not be workable right now. I can take you around what would have been Rachel's bench. She had planned to work on something for your father; it would have been the first time she completed any research projects here. Now that I think about it, someone will have to take over her research project. Have you spoken to your father about who will take the lead there?"

Jamie shook her head vigorously. "No, I didn't know about that project; I thought she wasn't a researcher. Besides, there hasn't been time for that. I don't want to see anything sensitive. I know there are confidentiality agreements and patents and so on. Could you spare a few moments to show me around?"

David considered his options. He could take her down there, but… no. The older Scotts were easier to manage. Dr. Scott didn't check orders himself for the lab's research section, and David could funnel smaller, inexpensive things through Joan. Things he had not cleared for his research through the lab. Expensive items would raise flags. This new Scott seemed to want to get into everything. She could be a problem. He feigned propriety.

"I would do that, but I need to check with your father and Joan about what is allowable and what you have clearance to see. You understand, right?"

"My father and Joan are both here now. We can go upstairs," Jamie pressed. She sensed he wanted to escape and wasn't quite ready to let him off the hook.

Checking the time, he shook his head and concocted a lie. "I have to check my timer because I started an experiment when I first came in. I don't have time to meet with them right now. Perhaps, if I finish quickly, I will find your father to follow up on that." He held out his hand to shake hers and gave her a generous smile. His mind was racing. *She isn't going to let up.*

"How about I call my father? I'm sure..." Jamie tried one more time.

"If I don't get to the lab, my run will be unusable, and I will have to repeat some steps. I am sorry about that. I look forward to taking you on tour soon." He almost ran out of the break room.

Weird, Jamie thought, as she sipped her now-tepid coffee. She pulled the Post-It with the IP information from her pocket, which now had more information on it. During the security meeting, she had asked Kevin to write the log in info (again) and specific app she could use to access the company intranet on the slip of paper. Finding a little blank space, she scribbled notes about the conversation with David. As she thought about David's odd behavior, she noticed the location of the IP address. *Where is this?* Stranded without her own car, she enlisted her sister's help.

Jamie pulled out her cell phone and checked the time. It was 10 a.m.; the older boys would be at school for the day, and the younger ones would be there until after lunch. She dialed Jillian's number. It rang five times before she picked it up.

"Good morning," Jillian whispered into the phone. She was in bed in a darkened room. "Please, keep your voice down. My head's close to exploding."

"Good morning to you, as well. What are you doing?"

"I'm regretting my 'freedom' last night. I'm on my third cup of coffee and my first dose of ibuprofen. Where are you?"

"I'm at the lab with Dad, but I want you to come to pick me up. I have an errand to run, and then I need you to drop me back home so I can get my car."

"Jamie, I'm really exhausted. Richard was right—I hate hangovers. What exactly are you up to?" Jillian rolled over in her bed. "I don't plan on leaving this house today."

"Too much fun last night, huh? I heard you and Richard had a close encounter."

"Did I? I don't remember. I hope I used birth control."

"Too much information!" Jamie rolled her eyes. "Come get me. I have some information from Rachel's email account. I want to check it out before I pass it on to the police."

Jillian propelled herself up and moaned when her head throbbed. "To the tall, handsome police detective? That I could be down for," she noted as she reached for her coffee.

"You have a one-track mind. Are you coming? I'll tell you more when you get here."

"OK, if you insist. Give me thirty minutes. Do I need to dress in black, wear my ass-kicking heels?" Jamie could hear Jillian struggling to drag herself out of bed. "You owe me."

22
Sibling Rivalry

Jamie camped out in the break room, downloading and setting up the company email/security app on her laptop for the next thirty minutes. It was a perfect excuse to avoid her father and any subsequent meetings. If she came on board at the company, she would make some changes—meetings couldn't be so ineffective.

When Jillian pulled up around ten forty-five, she sent Jamie a text. On the first floor, William, the security guard, and Kevin, the head of security, were sitting behind the front desk. *I guess the security meeting is over*, Jamie thought, hurrying out the front door and sliding into Jillian's white Range Rover. As she closed the car door, their father texted: *Where are you? Another meeting is starting.* Jamie replied: *Jillian called. Going to spend a few minutes with her. Will be back after lunch.*

A small fib.

"Why are you putting this on me?" Jillian had on a baseball cap, a puffy black coat, and black sunglasses. She shook her head as she drove across the parking lot. "Where am I taking you? And please tell my family that I love them once I die from this hangover."

"Dramatic! Rachel received an email right before her death. I pulled the address associated with the email's IP address. We're going by." Jillian opened her mouth to complain, but Jamie held up her hand. "Then I'll pass what we find on to the police."

Jillian harrumphed. "As if that's likely."

"Hey, I *am* going to tell the police if we find anything. You don't sound like you believe me," Jamie said, surprised.

"Girl, I'm not fifteen years old, sneaking into college parties with you in New York. This is real talk. Sliding out of windows to avoid being caught was fun then, but I have four children and a husband. And I would like to go back to law school someday. I will not be following you into any dark buildings uninvited," she stated clearly, and gave Jamie a sidelong glance. "But I'll drive *you* there. Directions?"

Jamie replied by plugging the address into the Google Maps app on her phone. "Follow the disembodied voice—*please*."

Without further comment, Jillian dutifully followed the voice coming from the phone. But Jamie could sense some budding tension. "What's on your mind?" she asked.

"Why did you order me to come to get you?"

"I thought it would be kind of fun. You make it sound sinister," Jamie said.

"So now you call." Jillian's annoyance with Jamie started with her big sister waking her up today, but there was a lot of underlying resentment there. "But while you were gone? You never called me."

Jamie was silent but felt herself flush.

Jillian continued, "Before you left, we were planning your wedding. I was looking forward to having our kids grow up together. Then you just up and left." Jillian paused for a moment as the GPS gave her another direction, which she followed. She resumed her rant quietly. "You talked to Jonathan, but not me. I know why you didn't call Mother—but me?"

Jamie was at a loss for words and ashamed. It was selfish not to stay in contact with the people who loved her, but there was nothing she could do about that now. There was no excuse.

Jillian had just warmed up. "I'm glad to see you; really, I am. But it's been four years. I'm grown, but you didn't *ask* me to come now—you told me, as usual. Four years ago, you weren't happy, so you tossed everyone aside. Now you come back—you want everyone to forget how you ignored most of us for years. And let's not forget how you wanted to model in New York, and everyone had to adapt."

Every word was like a slap to the face. Years of resentment for her big sister. "What? I'm sorry that I didn't call, but I was in a terrible place," Jamie tried to explain.

Jillian exhaled loudly. The GPS directed her to "turn left at the next intersection". "Everyone gets in a bad place sometimes. But everyone else figures out how to deal without crapping all over everyone else." She stopped the car and leaned over to check the actual number of the address on the building on their right.

Jamie gulped.

"You're not the only one with issues. Some days, I would love to disappear to a foreign country. But I can't, so I deal—or go to therapy."

This had been simmering under the surface for years. "I'm sorry I didn't ask you if you wanted to come along today. I thought it would be exciting. I'm sorry."

Jillian paused for a moment. The anger passed just as quickly as it appeared. "Look, I'm hungover. I shouldn't have said anything."

"Hey, don't do that. If you said it, you were thinking about it. I should have called or kept in touch when I left. I was just so buried in my drama that I honestly didn't think about anyone else." She glanced at her sister. "I suck."

Jillian snickered. "True."

Jamie continued. "And for the modeling, I didn't consider that. I guess it must have been pretty disruptive to you and Jon when Mother went to New York so much to be with me."

"Yeah, it was upsetting. While Mother may be a pain, it was tough not having her around. I started my period while she was in New York and was too embarrassed to tell Dad. I just went into Mother's bathroom and used some of her feminine hygiene products." Jillian got out of the car. "Jon didn't care, though. He could stay out playing basketball or hanging out with his friends—or with his 'girlfriend'. Dad didn't notice that kind of stuff. It was a fun time for him!" she revealed.

"I never really thought about that. Oh, God, I really suck!" Jamie said as she got out of the car.

"Well, the situation wasn't the best. I understand Mother handled about sixty percent of the modeling deal, but I still get mad at you. Even after ten years, Mother is still touchy about Richard. Since I didn't go to law school and broke up a marriage, I'm a disappointment. I'm talking it out with my psychiatrist," Jillian said. "Is this the right place?"

They stopped their discussion and examined their surroundings. They were barely in Tucker, Georgia, and standing in front of a small strip mall.

Jillian counted the stores. "Where are we going here? There are several stores."

"I don't know," Jamie said. "Which of these places has Wi-Fi?" They studied the storefronts. There were several clothing shops, a coffee shop, and a restaurant. "Let's check the coffee shop first—they usually have Wi-Fi," she said.

"Check for what? You don't even know who you're looking for."

"True," Jamie said, walking toward the coffee shop. "Which is why I'll involve the police after I look around. Come on!"

Jillian followed her sister into the independently owned coffee shop. The sign on the glass front door proclaimed, "Free Wi-Fi". Inside, a few people were sitting at small tables using their computers or tablets. Jamie walked up to the counter, keeping an eye out for security cameras, and placed an order for a chai latte to go. Jillian ordered a large black coffee and paid for both drinks with cash. Two female employees were working behind the counter. While one crafted their beverages, Jamie asked the one at the register about security cameras.

"I have never been out here before. You're open until ten at night—are there always only two people working? Do you have CCTV or security cameras?" Jillian hid a smile. It was weird watching Jamie work these young women to get information. It wasn't a side that Jillian had seen often and might explain why Jamie typically got what she wanted from people.

"We have 'em." The young girl pointed to a small camera in the corner by the door. "The owner keeps a copy of each day's video on his computer. It's aimed at the register. We've had some problems with money walking out of the store."

The other young woman bobbed her head in affirmation and said, "Too bad for our boss that the thief was his daughter!" she laughed as she brought one beverage over and walked back to pour the second.

"We shouldn't say that. Lucky for us, there's no sound on that camera," the first young woman said.

Jamie took a sip of the latte. "Wow, this is good!" She took another sip. "Were either of you working on Friday night?"

The second girl brought the coffee. "I was. It was dead in here. Usually is on Friday nights. Why?" she asked.

Jamie leaned forward conspiratorially and whispered loudly, "Well. Don't tell anyone, but my sister's fiancé was late for a date on Friday night. He said he stopped here for coffee and to check his email and lost track of time. *I* think he was with someone else."

Catching on, Jillian chimed in. "I think he said that because he knew I wouldn't have any way to check and see if he was here." She faked exasperation. "I love him, but I'm so tired of his list of lies to me."

The counter workers glanced at each other. "Well, you can check. I hate lying men—my ex lied all the time. I had to break into his phone to find out what he was hiding." The register girl replied and motioned them closer. "I can log into the computer in the back through my tablet," she whispered.

The other worker was shocked. The register worker continued. "I installed a mirroring app. Let me grab my tablet." She went into the back and returned with her device. The barista led the Scott sisters to an unoccupied table out of range of the camera. "I can't afford to lose this job," she said. After typing in her boss's computer password, she pulled up the program. "What day are you looking for?"

"Friday night around six-thirty or seven," Jamie said. The young woman maneuvered to the file, opened it, and found the timeframe.

Jillian whispered to Jamie, "How'll you know who emailed?" She took a sip of her coffee; her head was still throbbing.

Jamie whispered back, "Look around; there's not a lot of traffic. It's a long shot."

"Here we go." Jamie and Jillian leaned forward to examine the tablet screen. There were only a few customers during those thirty minutes. Most were pairs or groups of young women who came in as a first stop during their Friday night out. But right around six forty, a man in his twenties came in and ordered a cup of coffee. He was alone and didn't turn to face the camera until he stopped for sugar and cream. For most of the time, he was almost out of camera range, but the camera clearly caught his face once. He appeared to be tall and may have once been attractive, but times were tough right now. His facial expressions and movements were manic.

Jamie yelled, "Stop there!"

The barista paused the security video. The drink maker slid out from behind the counter and joined them at the table when she heard Jamie shout.

"Do you remember him?" Jillian asked, slipping into the role of the spurned girlfriend. "What was he doing? Was he alone?" She kept her ring finger with her wedding set out of sight. She couldn't get the rings off without help, so she kept her left hand hidden.

The drink maker peered at the screen and replied, "I remember him. There were no other guys that came in during that time. He was alone and stayed in the corner looking at his phone." She raised an eyebrow at Jillian. "That's your man? You could do better."

"I know I could, couldn't I?" Jillian replied sheepishly.

Jamie pulled out her phone and took a picture of the screen. Looking at it, she thought it wouldn't be as helpful for identification as the videotape, but it was a start.

The woman with the tablet said, "I can enlarge the image if you want to take another pic." The second photo was much better.

Jamie thanked the employees. "Can we watch a few more minutes to make sure he didn't meet anyone?" she asked.

The barista obliged. The man went out of frame for most of the next ten minutes of the video, only surfacing to get more sugar. More importantly, there were no other customers—male or female—during that time.

At that moment, a group of older women came into the shop and stood patiently at the counter. The drink maker nodded at Jamie and Jillian and rushed back to the counter to take their orders. The remaining barista turned off her tablet and stood up.

Jamie shook her hand eagerly—still in character. "Thanks for your help. Now maybe I can get my sister to break up with this loser. Y'all have a nice day." Jamie and Jillian thanked both women and walked out the door. The other barista headed to the register to assist her coworker.

"You're quite shady, girl," Jillian said. "I should break up with the lying boyfriend, huh?"

"Yeah, he probably was emailing while he was out of view of the camera," Jamie noted as she checked to see how much time had passed. It was lunchtime, and she needed to get back to the lab before their father sent a search party out for her. "Do you want to grab some lunch and drop me off at home, so I can get back to the lab before Dad gets too annoyed?" she politely asked, bearing in mind Jillian's earlier rant on issuing commands.

"When are you going to call Detective Marshall? Or do you want to call when we get to the house?" Jillian asked as they got back into the car. "What do you want to eat?"

"I'll call him when I get back to the lab. Can we just go through a drive-thru on the way to the house? You pick." Jamie was trying to be considerate of her sister's wishes—a new phase in their relationship.

Retracing their path, Jillian spotted a McDonald's and turned in. "I want some fries. The grease may help my hangover. Does that work for you?"

Jamie didn't want a burger, but Jillian had done her a huge favor, so it would have to do.

"That works," Jamie replied.

They idled in line for a few moments in silence.

"What you said earlier," Jamie said.

Jillian pushed her sunglasses up. "Do we have to talk about it now? What just happened made me feel better. We have all made decisions and had to learn to live with them. I'm in therapy—after I better understand my issues, we can talk about my sibling issues. I may even invite you to a session or two. You could use it," Jillian said.

"True. Are we OK? I will try to better consider your feelings in the future. I can be a little self-centered," Jamie said. Jillian snorted, which Jamie ignored and continued. "It's time for me to grow up. It's one of the reasons why I wasn't ready to get married four years ago. I'm not sure I'm ready for that type of relationship even now."

"Even with the pretty detective?" Jillian gave Jamie a small poke on the shoulder before continuing. "He *is* pretty, and you *were* making out with him last night. You're interested. Admit it." Before Jamie could answer, they had to place their orders for burgers, fries, and shakes. Jillian also ordered two Happy Meals® for her youngest sons, who'd be home with the nanny by the time she returned.

"What do you want me to say? He's cute, but I'm not there right now," Jamie finally replied after the break to place their orders.

Jillian snorted again but added, seriously, "Real talk. I think you also weren't ready to get married because you thought Eddie was boring. You like drama. You always have."

Before Jamie could reply, their father texted her again: *Where are you?*

"Tell him you're on your way back—we can get to the house before he sends another sad text looking for you. I have to go home to my children. You need to meet Dad and contact the police. I'm holding you to making that call. Don't make me embarrass you."

23
I Suck

When Jillian dropped Jamie off at their parents' house, she went inside to speak to her mother before taking the Camaro. She didn't think her mother would call the police if the car disappeared from the driveway—*good riddance*—but she didn't want her to be surprised.

"Mother!" she called from the foyer.

Olivia stuck her head over the banister upstairs. "Good afternoon, Ms. Jamie. Your mother went for a walk around the neighborhood. She just left. Do you want me to give her a message?"

Walking? Interesting. "Yes, Miss Olivia. Please, tell her I took my car."

Olivia nodded and returned to her work. The cleaning crew had not arrived yet, but Olivia was doing some prep work. Jamie ran upstairs to grab her iPad and then went outside. She walked around her car as if it were a long-lost friend. Sitting in the driver's seat, it felt like she had never been away. Since the car was a classic, it took some reworking to get it back to its former glory. She also had the black leather seats refinished when she purchased the car—the leather was so comfortable that she leaned back and sighed. The car started on the first try. She gripped the leather-wrapped steering wheel with one hand and the leather-covered gear stick with the other. The car leaped forward as she pressed on the gas—Jamie always found the roar of the refurbished original engine kind of hot. She roared out of the driveway, radio blasting, shifting to second gear as she passed her mother at the corner. Her mother was not pleased.

I'm going to pay for that one, she giggled to herself. The car drove well, and she started planning a nice long drive down the highway where she could open it up.

After an enjoyable first ride in her beloved car since returning home, Jamie drove into the lab's parking lot. She was so distracted by being in her car that she hadn't eaten her lunch. The sad, cold McDonald's bag rested in the seat next to her. Jamie grabbed it and used the access card to reenter the building. The security guard wasn't at his desk again. Annoyed by the entire lax security operation, she made a note of that and headed to the elevators. She saw the young security guard exit the bathroom while she waited.

"Hello, Dr. Scott. Do you need anything?" he asked, sliding into his chair.

"No, no. Thanks for offering. Just headed upstairs."

"I just went to the bathroom—I was only away from the desk for a minute. And I had the door locked so no one could get in," he stammered.

"Hey, I know you have to go to the bathroom sometimes. I hadn't planned to run upstairs and tell on you. Relax."

Jamie got on the elevator.

On the fourth floor, she knocked on her father's office door but made her way in when she got no response from inside. Gregory had ventured into the third-floor lab for a few moments, so he wasn't there. The office was quiet and imposing in its solitude. She searched the top of his desk for his calendar to see if there were any more meetings. There was a folder of expansion plans with her name on it. She picked it up and grabbed a seat to eat her unappetizing burger.

Looking at the plans, she had to admire her parents' drive. Even as they entered what should be their golden years, they were still pushing forward and trying to leave something significant for their children and grandchildren. They were financially prepared for retirement. The patents alone were worth millions. Money was not the motivator here.

It would be nice to be that sure about what you are doing with your life, Jamie thought as she tried to imagine herself in a leadership position. Would she be happy working as a manager? While she started practicing medicine in an unusual way, she loved the patient interactions and the ability to make someone feel better. Not every contact had a happy ending, but each had value. If she didn't see patients anymore, she would miss it. But working with her family could be cool, too. Maybe there was a way to do both.

The expansion plans were very detailed. Jamie took a few business classes in college, and while modeling as a teen, she got into the habit of reviewing her contracts with her agent. Nevertheless, she wasn't an expert, and she was quickly overwhelmed.

Her mind drifted to the conversation with her sister. *Jillian was really upset with me. Am I that oblivious to other people?* She didn't consider herself a completely selfish person, but some of her actions may have had an unpleasant effect on others.

Did she leave Jillian hanging when she left? She had been so focused after her fight with Mother. Jillian was involved in helping plan things—*oh shit*! *Hadn't Jillian been planning a bridal shower (or two) for her?* Jamie cringed. That *was* bad: she left her sister hanging! And she didn't call; she just sent messages through Jon, who was the only person she spoke to with any regularity.

I'm surprised she even speaks to me. I suck! Jamie thought.

By the time Gregory returned from his errand, Jamie had sunk into a mini funk.

"Hello, dear. I see you found the folder I left for you," he said, plopping down behind his desk. "Did you call the police?"

Jamie closed her eyes and dropped her head back. *My levels of suck are increasing by the minute.* "No, I got sidetracked by Jillian, but I will now. Aren't I almost done here for today?"

Gregory shook his head. "Jamison, I will not argue with you. You need to call Detective Marshall now." Jamie nodded her agreement—no need to piss off anyone else. Gregory leaned back in his seat. "Quickly, did you look at the plans? What do you think?"

"They're interesting, but I need to dig in more. What exactly would I do here? Am I even qualified for this job?" She frowned at the congealed remains of her burger, which she couldn't eat anymore.

"You would start at this office and move to the new one after we get that location built. You can help determine the location and take part in finalizing the plans. If you want to."

"I need some time. There are some practice opportunities that I have been considering. I don't know yet."

"Fortunately, you don't have to know yet. But I want you to think about it while you evaluate your options." He leaned forward. "Back to this morning. The security meeting didn't clarify any of my questions. I still don't know how the video disappeared. The security team needs some modifications because each one blamed the other. I didn't like how that went."

"I didn't like that either. It was a strike against this job!" Jamie joked.

They both cracked up for a moment.

"I think someone turned the video off," she continued, getting serious again. Gregory eyed her inquiringly, but she waved him off. "Something I heard last night suggests that. I think you need to have two guards on duty at a time—just from my short time here. The desk should never be unattended."

"That came up," her father said.

It pleased Jamie that her instincts weren't completely off. She changed the subject. "I saw David in the break room." She got a weird feeling about her conversation with David. He didn't seem to want her around. Given her sister's opinion of her, that may not be that uncommon a feeling.

"He likes to come in during off-hours and work on his research. He is applying for more grants since he needs to earn more money to help his family. Why? Did you talk to him?" Gregory asked.

"I tried. He didn't want to talk. That reminds me, can I go into the lab, or do I need to sign something first? Confidentiality issues."

"David not talking to you isn't a surprise. He's not very social." Gregory checked his watch. "Can we discuss your status later? I have a conference call coming up, and you *need* to talk to the police."

"True." She picked up all her trash and threw it away. "I'll do that now."

He held out his keys. "Don't you need my car?"

"Dad, Jillian took me home. I have my car back. Thanks, though."

"Good Lord!" This was the closest that Gregory ever came to swearing. "You still want that thing? Wouldn't you like a nice little convertible? My treat?"

"Nope. The only reason I would need another car is if I have children. Notice, I said children. A husband can ride in the Camaro, and one kid can, too."

"Fine. You can have your expensive muscle car, but please be safe. You like to speed. By the way, please keep it professional with the detective. I heard about your time at the gazebo last night," he said. "Why the face? I know that area's tempting. Your mother and I have spent private time out there before." He grinned mischievously at her astonished look.

It probably wasn't possible for Jamie to escape her father's office any faster. Reaching her car, Jamie took a few deep breaths and tried to erase from her mind the image of her mother and father making out on the gazebo bench. Brain bleach or sporking out her eyeballs wasn't enough. She wasn't sure who told him about her interlude with Nick, but Gregory, adding that comment about his history with Margaret in the gazebo, was simply cruel.

Speaking of Nick. She pulled out her cell. Both detectives gave her a business card, but only Nick wrote his cell number on the back of his card. Nick picked up the call after the third ring.

"Detective Marshall," he answered brusquely. Ron was talking with their lieutenant in the lieutenant's office.

"Hello, Detective Marshall. It's Jamison Scott."

There was an audible throat-clearing on the other end of the line. "Oh, hi. I didn't recognize the number. I rarely give my cell number out," he said.

"You gave it to *me*," she declared.

"You're different." His tone had shifted, and his voice had dropped with a suggestion of edge. Jamie felt a lurch in her abdomen and reminded herself to be professional.

Masking her feelings, she continued. "I wanted to reach out to you about the case. I found something this morning, and I think you need to know."

He didn't say anything, so she rambled on. "I know you wanted to check Rachel's work emails from the lab. I was digging around on my father's computer," she reported carefully, not wanting to throw her father under the bus. "The lab server stores all emails, no matter who sends them. I found a record of her emails."

Nick's ears perked up. He had spoken to the district attorney, who said they couldn't get a subpoena for all emails; the work product argument could drag this out for a while. This information might make that moot.

"That's great. Can I see those?" Nick asked before continuing. "This morning, we interviewed several other employees who worked with Rachel. Except for Tatiana," he told her.

"There's more," Jamie said. "There was an email that was sent to her on Friday evening at around six forty-five. It was the last one she opened. I tracked the sender's IP address."

Shit, this was getting better, he thought. "That's important. Can I meet you somewhere for you to show this to me? Should I come over to the lab?"

"I'm in my car and can meet you at the precinct if that's OK. I have the app and password, so I can pull the account up on my laptop."

"OK, that works," Nick said and tidied up his desk. He wanted to make a good impression. "Stop at the reception desk, and they will direct you." They both disconnected the call.

Jamie realized she hadn't told him about her journey to the address location and hoped it wouldn't piss him off. She headed out of the parking lot.

24
To Tell the Truth

Her phone rang while she was on the freeway—it was Jon. "Hey, what's up?" she answered, putting her phone on speaker.

"Still at the office with Dad?"

"No, I'm going to meet with the police. I found some information about Rachel's emails, and I'm going to hand it off as promised. What are you doing?"

"Working … I'm going to take Isabelle to Happy Hour, and then I'll come by the house this evening. Mother's repurposing some leftovers from the party by having a neighborhood gathering. Should I bring Isabelle or not?"

"I don't know. How did last night go for you two?"

"She's sweet and kind of hot. There might be something there. But I don't know. Besides, Rena has called twice."

"You aren't thinking of going back to her, are you? Jon!"

"No, no, *no*. While the package is wrapped nicely, the inside is like a bomb. Mother just called and said she called the house today. She's been calling my place and hanging up."

"Not a surprise. You manage to find the wild girls. Or is it you?" She checked her GPS. "I'm close to the police station. I'll see you tonight, OK?"

"Sounds good. Be careful," Jon said, ignoring that last comment, and hung up.

Jamie turned into the police station and parked in a spot labeled for visitors. She leaned back in the leather seat and reveled for a moment. She was so happy to be back in her car—she had missed it so much over the last four years. This wasn't a cheap car to maintain; at 40 years old, it needed regular, loving care. It took a nice chunk of her earnings to keep it running. Eddie had hated it. He wanted her to sell it and buy a suitable family vehicle. That was just another one of their issues. When she exited the car, she noticed several people eyeing it approvingly. She had never been a fan of car alarms—what were the chances someone would steal the car off the police lot?

Jamie walked into the front door of the precinct and looked for the front desk. The area in front of the desk was very crowded, with everyday citizens making stolen property reports, unruly neighbor reports, and other complaints. She made her way over to the right place and asked for Detective Nick Marshall at the front desk. The youngest of the two receptionists came over to help her and scanned her from head to toe with a semi-pleasant look on her face. Jamie knew that look—it said, "Checking out the competition." She wondered if the receptionist had an interest in Nick.

"Let me check," the woman picked up the phone to call upstairs.

Jamie plastered a smile on her face as she waited.

After making a quick phone call, the young woman said, "Detective Marshall is at his desk and said you could come up." Her tone was incredulous. "Humph," she added.

"What does that mean?" Jamie asked as she waited for the receptionist, Lindsey, to complete her visitor's identification tag.

Lindsey had the grace to blush. "I'm sorry. Nothing personal. I'm sure you've seen Detective Marshall—he's rather gorgeous. We have women of all types coming by with all kinds of sob stories trying to get back to his desk. They rarely get far. You getting an invitation threw me for a moment." She handed Jamie the clip-on badge. "His desk is on the third floor. Have a nice day."

Jamie clipped the badge on her jacket and walked to the elevator. She had to weave her way around a group of officers standing in front of the elevator in the lobby while talking about an upcoming sporting event. The precinct was bustling with both uniformed and plainclothes officers. There were also some civilian employees in the crowd as well. She could hear police radios chirping from their hips as officers passed by as she waited for the elevator.

The elevator opened right in front of the third-floor desk. The officer at the third-floor entrance desk waved her in after glancing at her visitor's badge. Jamie thanked him and asked where Nick's desk was located.

Through steepled fingers, the young officer replied, "He and his partner are located one row over and two desks back. He's at his desk, so you can't miss him if you've already met him."

Jamie entered the office. There were many desks grouped into sets of two or three spread throughout the room. Both uniformed officers and detectives occupied the seats, and there was a low-level din coming from the room. Scanning the area, she could feel eyes turning her way. Although she was used to being the focus of attention, she blushed. Spotting Nick and Ron, she made her way over. Ron saw her first and said something to Nick, who then turned around. Rising to meet her, he glanced at her appreciatively. His partner cleared his throat to remind him to remain professional.

Jamie worked to maintain her cool as well. *Keep it light*; she thought as she reached them.

"I hear you've been busy," Ron said. Unlike the first time Jamie met him, he looked different—shell-shocked.

The emergency room visit provided a surprise for Ron and his wife. Estelle was pregnant as well as sick with food poisoning. Ron hadn't told anyone yet—including Nick. He and Estelle tried unsuccessfully to get pregnant for years, which led to some strain and heartache. Ron was in his late forties, and Estelle was in her mid-forties. They had accepted that they would be childless and, while disappointing, adjusted their lives accordingly. Today, it was difficult to keep his mind on work. While Nick had noticed that Ron seemed tired, he knew to wait until his partner came clean.

Focusing on Jamie, Nick asked, "Do you have the information?" He sat down and motioned for her to sit in a chair at the side of his desk.

Jamie eased into the chair. "I can show you Rachel's non-confidential emails—my dad approved that," she said. "I also traced the origin of the last email's IP address and…" She paused. "But I also went by the location."

Nick put a hand to his forehead, and Ron stared at her. "You're not supposed to interfere with a police investigation. If you went to the place, the email writer's probably long gone," Nick said.

"You may have cost us valuable time," Ron added, hitting his desk. "If you cost us this case…"

This wasn't going well, she thought. "Wait, wait. I didn't ruin anything. The location was a coffee shop in Tucker. He wasn't still sitting there waiting for the police to appear."

That took some edge off the encounter. "A coffee shop?" Nick asked.

"And I saw the security film for that night around the time he sent that last email," Jamie added.

That added more heat—mixed with curiosity. "How did you manage that?" Ron asked.

"The women working commiserated with me looking for my sister's cheating boyfriend," Jamie mumbled. "I can tell you about everything I found." She pulled her laptop out of her crossbody bag. "I can log into the security app and let you use my laptop. That way, you can't log into the company server after I leave by having your computer folks pull the information out of the history or something." With a few clicks, she was in Rachel's account. She positioned herself so that neither of the men could see any passwords. Jamie handed the computer to Nick. He got up and went to the other side of the desk so he and Ron could read the screen.

"Your father didn't delete any emails, did he?" Ron asked.

Jamie pursed her lips and gave him a withering look. "I don't think so. He forgot the emails were on the main server until I asked him about it this morning."

The two detectives scanned the subject lines of the last three weeks of Rachel's life. Most were work-related, which made sense since this was a work account. Besides the "I KNOW" email, Nick noticed another one from Tatiana that seemed odd.

"We haven't spoken to Tatiana yet. She hasn't returned our calls. Didn't she know Rachel before she came here?" Nick asked. As he spoke, he emailed the computer techs with the IP address of the questionable email. He also wanted to download the non-confidential emails that Jamie agreed to—as long as she did the downloading to a flash drive.

"I don't know," Jamie added in response to his question as her phone vibrated. "I only met her in passing at the party," Jamie said as she checked her messages. Felice was texting her: *Dinner?* Jamie replied: *Yes, where?*

Ron frowned at Nick, who shrugged; he wasn't telling Jamie everything he knew. "Sounds plausible. Just shows the importance of speaking with her. There were also a couple of flash drives from Rachel's desk that Richard kept. Have you looked at them?" Ron asked.

"I didn't know about those. I can ask," Jamie said, returning her attention to the conversation. She fired a text message off to her father, who replied that she could check with Richard.

"That could be important. Hopefully, there won't be any work information on them," Nick said.

Jamie relayed Gregory's message. "Let me call Richard."

She dialed his cell phone and was surprised to get him on the first ring. He told her that most of the flash drives were blank except for one that held a few old pictures. He forgot to pass it on to Gregory the night before, but he could email them to her/the detectives now if it would help. Jamie repeated her email address to Richard and relayed the message to the detectives so they would give her an official email address for Richard as well.

"Thank you for bringing this information over to us. However, let me remind you, Dr. Scott, that you aren't part of this investigation," Ron started. Looking at Nick, he saw his partner wasn't backing his position, so he held his fire.

Jamie ignored Ron's comment and waited patiently for an email notification. A few moments later, Jamie opened her email account on her tablet and downloaded the two pictures from Richard.

One was a picture of several women. The officers recognized Rachel. Jamie recognized Tatiana, who, in Jamie's eyes, didn't look any different now. The other woman was a short, pretty woman of mixed ethnicity. They huddled together in what looked like a restaurant booth while someone else took the photo. There was very little background visible. The focus was on the faces of the women, who were young, vibrant, and joyous. A simple night out. The other picture included the three women, on a different night in different clothes, and a young, handsome man who had his arms around the shoulders of the unknown woman and Tatiana. The unknown woman was looking up at him while the other women focused on the camera. This picture appeared to be a party scene, and the other people in the background were blurry.

Jamie pointed out Tatiana in both pictures.

"Thanks," Nick said. "OK. So, Tatiana and Rachel *were* friends in an earlier life. She needs to identify the other people in this picture for us. But back to the emails--"

Ron's cell phone rang. "Alvarez? I'll meet you at your desk." To Nick and Jamie, Ron said, "I'm sorry. I'll be right back." He left the desk.

Jamie wanted to understand the line of questioning. "Why are you so interested in the email Tatiana sent to Rachel? We now know they were friends. Why is it strange that she emailed her?" she asked Nick.

"Why not a phone call? Why not go by her office?" Nick paused. "It just seemed like an awkwardly worded email between friends, asking to meet. Also, just scanning the account, I didn't see any other recent emails from Tatiana to Rachel. Joan told us they ate lunch together often. Why an email, then? It's tweaking my senses. There's more to that email. Now…" He smiled at her. "Tell me what you found when you went to that coffee shop."

She did. "Are you mad at me?"

"Not mad, annoyed." Nick closed his computer and stood up. "And not surprised. While I trust your computer skills, I sent the IP address to our tech folks, and they just confirmed your findings. Let's go."

"I'm invited?" Jamie asked.

"Only because I want you to reach out to Tatiana. I think she's avoiding the police. But you might get her to open the front door. You seem to be pretty inventive." Nick ushered her toward the door.

"I'm not sure I like that. Am I working on behalf of the police? Is that legal?" Jamie rattled off questions as he almost pushed her out the door.

"You aren't an agent of the police." Nick narrowed his eyes at her. "What? You now have scruples about lying to someone to get information? Didn't stop you before."

"I resent the implication here." Jamie was indignant; she hadn't lied. She'd only bent the truth a little.

He shook his head exasperatedly. She'd lied to those workers to get information. She'd said so. And she was extremely *hot* when she was annoyed. That he still felt such a powerful attraction at this moment pissed him off. "No implications here," Nick snapped back. "Based on what *you* said…"

Ron saw that the conversation between Nick and Jamie had escalated and hurried back over. They were glaring at each other.

"Looks like I'm just in time," Ron said, shaking his head at the pair. "Let me get my gun."

25
Born to Run

Outside, Jamie asked, "Can I meet you there?"

"Do you remember where you're going?" Nick said. "I still don't think this is a good idea," Ron said simultaneously, but it was a battle already lost before it started. "Do you have a car?"

"I have my car. I just got it back." She pointed it out, and both men made a beeline for it.

"This is your car?" Nick circled it, impressed. "How long have you had it?"

"I bought it in college, so I've had it for around fourteen years. It's a money pit. I love it, though, and wouldn't trade it for anything."

"It's a beauty. Just remember, no speeding. I would hate to give you a ticket," Ron said, tipping his head to her. "Come on, Nick. Got work to do." He started across the parking lot. "If you're coming, we'll see you there."

Nick affirmed quietly, "See you there."

Jamie smiled and got into her car. But once she got in the car, she took a moment to reflect. It surprised her that she was concerned with his opinion of her after that last exchange. She didn't want him to think she was a liar. Hopefully, he could see that she was resourceful and not prone to telling untruths. *He's kind of cute when he's angry*, she thought to herself. Since it would be best for the officers to complete their interview without her, she dialed her friend Felice's cell number as she pulled out of the parking lot. Felice answered on the second ring.

"So, we're doing dinner tonight?" Felice went directly into the conversation. She wasn't much for pleasantries. "Do you care where? I'm in the mood for vegetarian food. The Cafe Sunflower is summoning me."

"Sounds good. What time?" Jamie asked.

"I'll be available after I finish my dictations. Six forty-five, seven?"

"Six forty-five works. It'll be good to talk to you again. It's been a long time."

"True. I have a lot to tell you, and I still haven't yelled at you for leaving like you did. I won't make a scene, but you must feel some of my wrath, Trey." Felice paused. "Hold on; there's someone at my door." Jamie could hear her directing her office manager to reschedule some patients and thanking her for dealing with the inconvenience. "I'm back. Sorry about that. Internal medicine is insanity. I cut back on my clinic hours because I was tired and thought I would be married and have babies. I'm still crazy busy. Before I hang up, are you planning to go back into practice? I have room at my office, and we could split the space." Felice offered.

It was typical Atlanta traffic, so Jamie was driving below the speed limit. "I haven't decided yet. My parents suggested I work at the lab. Mother also introduced me to several directors at medical clinics," she replied.

"Of course, your mother would be in the middle of your business. I hope you'll have better luck managing her this time."

That stung a bit—the truth often did. "After four years, I have the will to try," Jamie said as she pulled off the freeway. "I have to go because I'm dealing with the police right now."

"Humph. Interesting. Till tonight." Felice hung up as Jamie tried to find an alternative route to the coffee shop that did not involve the crowded expressways—GPS was a godsend. Traffic in the Atlanta area was horrific, especially at rush hour. This was mid-afternoon, but it was nearing the holidays. People were leaving work early. She figured she was around ten minutes behind the officers. They also might have turned on their flashing lights—an option she didn't have. When she finally pulled up to the strip mall, she parked next to an empty Tahoe. Her phone started ringing back-to-back as she waited for the officers to return. She cringed at the volume because she had turned off the radio.

The first call was from a fellow doctor from the Doctors Overseas program. He and Jamie quickly exchanged pleasantries before he asked her about attending an upcoming recruitment event in New York City. She told him she would get back to him after checking her schedule.

The second call was from Margaret. "Hello, Jamison. I see you came home to retrieve that monstrous car. Why didn't you wait until I returned?"

"Hello, Mother. I was on a schedule and didn't know how long you would be out. Besides, you would have given me a hard time."

Her mother harrumphed. "Where are you now? Are you coming home for dinner? We are feasting on leftovers. Your brother and sister and her family are coming. Our neighbors may drop in as well. It should be nice."

"I have a dinner date with Felice at six forty-five, so I might catch the very end. We are going to Cafe Sunflower, so it likely won't be a late night," she replied.

"Is Felice bringing her girlfriend? She was alone last night," Margaret asked.

"I don't think so. I didn't know you knew about her girlfriend."

Margaret was evasive. "I keep up with my children's lives. Felice had an overt interest in you, as if you didn't know. I thought she was going to follow you to Africa. But she seemed to have been in a serious relationship while you were away."

Jamie's mouth was open, and her skin was burning. "Felice and I have been friends for years, through relationships on both sides. She isn't hanging out with me, hoping that I'll change my orientation." She saw Ron come out of the coffee shop but didn't get out of her car. "Have you been checking up on Felice?" she continued.

"Just a little. You didn't tell me where you were."

"Waiting on the detectives. Hey, Mother, I have to go." Jamie disconnected before her mother could reply. She saw Nick coming out of the shop. He checked the parking lot until he spotted Jamie's car and headed over. She rolled down her window.

"We've downloaded the files from that night. The owner was there this time, and he seemed keen to cooperate," he said as he neared her car. Leaning over the driver's side window, he added, "Now, I would like you to call Tatiana—here's her number—and see if you can get her to agree to meet you."

"What do I say to her? Why do *I* want to meet her?"

"I don't know. I think you should mention the picture of the three girls. She doesn't know that we have it. You can tell her you found the flash drive with pictures of her and Rachel on it and would like to speak with her before you turn them in. Pick a place to meet."

"How about I just show up at her house?" she suggested.

Nick shook his head and grinned; Jamie was a natural and likely had done something like this before. Jamie dialed the woman's number. It rang several times and went to voice mail. She shook her head at the detectives, but before they could speak, she lifted her finger to silence them.

The voicemail picked up, and Jamie, guessing that Tatiana was screening her calls, said, "Hi, Tatiana. This is Jamison Scott. You don't know me very well, but I found something at the lab—it involves you and Rachel. I'm unsure what to do with it, but I believe you might have some ideas. You should understand that I'm trying to minimize the scandal at my family's business, so I don't want this to get out. I'm coming to your house now. We need to talk. See you soon." She disconnected and looked over at the detectives.

"That sounded authentic," Ron chimed in. "No wonder people allow you to look at private security tapes."

"It doesn't just sound authentic; it *is* authentic. I want to minimize any scandals at the lab. That wasn't a lie." She fired up her engine. "I'll see you at her house," she said as she drove off.

Tatiana heard her phone ring but didn't recognize the number. After the episode with the valet, she was screening her calls. Her phone rang regularly from non-work numbers. After checking the first message, she realized the calls were from the police. They had made the connection between her and Rachel.

She didn't want to talk to them. There was no statute of limitations on murder, and they might construe the events in Wisconsin as murder or at least manslaughter. And the family was still angry about it. Tatiana had been running from this for a long time.

The newest voicemail was from Jamison Scott. After listening, her heart sank a tad more. She had found the picture and was going to take it to the police? *No, no, no!* Tatiana went into her bedroom and started throwing clothes into a small suitcase. *Wait*, maybe she could convince the doctor that there would be too much fallout for the lab. Wasn't there an expansion planned? Perhaps she could get her to keep quiet.

Tatiana zipped up her suitcase and put it in the closet. If this meeting went sideways, she was going to run. She had done it before. She washed her face and combed her hair. Trying to calm herself, she stopped to examine her face in the mirror.

She was very pale—even more than usual. Tatiana didn't know her father, and her mother didn't remember who he was, but Tatiana always assumed he was African American or Afro-Latino. She tanned quickly, had curly hair (outside of the straightening), full lips, and high cheekbones. Her mother spent the first decade of her life reminding her how much of a burden she was and treated her as one. Tatiana dreamed of a father who would come to save her, which, of course, never happened. She masked her misery by hiding in her books. Her mother was an angry drunk with no use for her daughter until she realized the girl was going to be a beauty. The best years with her mother were the four years of high school. Her mother treated her as a running buddy—her "road dog"—even though she was still a teenager. Partying, drinking, hookup sex—what her mother did, she did. She got on the pill at 14. By hanging with her mom, she finally received approval from her. However, it likely ruined every other relationship she would have in the future (without intensive therapy). Sex was a tool—to control, bribe, punish, and even kill time—but never for love. It had been years since that time, but she still operated in the same manner. It was a problem.

Steeling herself for Dr. Scott's visit, Tatiana had to refocus. She changed from her lavender sweats into a blue t-shirt and dark blue jeans. At least, she appeared presentable and not like her life was falling apart.

Jamie arrived and parked in front of a mid-sized house that had been remodeled into several apartments. Tatiana's apartment was on the second floor. The neighborhood was quiet, with shaded sidewalks and a few kids playing in various yards on the block. *Tatiana had been lucky to find this place*, Jamie thought.

The detectives were close behind and parked down the street. The house had a camera/buzzer combo, so residents on the second floor could let their visitors in without coming downstairs. Jamie got out of the car and hurried toward the door, stealing a look at the men who were headed her way. Hearing the bell ring, Tatiana checked the camera to make sure it was Jamie and granted her entrance. But when she opened her apartment door, two additional people were standing there.

Damn, she thought as she stood with her mouth open. Usually, she was smarter than this. Ron and Nick stood in front of her, displaying their badges, and Jamie stood behind them.

"Hello, Ms. Daniels. I'm Detective Nick Marshall, and this is Detective Ron Dixon. You know Jamison Scott," Nick said. "We've been trying to get in touch with you. May we come in?"

She played herself and figured she had no other good option. She stepped to the side so the three could enter her living room. Tatiana directed them to the loveseat, which functioned as her couch, and to the matching chair. The visitors grabbed the proffered chairs, but she continued to stand, inwardly panicking. To regain some control over her emotions, she decided she needed a drink. She offered her guests something as well—they all refused—and went into the kitchen to grab a beer.

Finding her voice, she called out, "I'm sorry I missed your calls. I've been preoccupied with what happened to Rachel. How can I help you, detectives?" She took a swig of beer and turned back to face them. "Unfortunately, you caught me off-guard. I expected to have a conversation with Dr. Scott alone, and I find detectives here." Her heart dropped a little. "Does this mean you've seen the photos Dr. Scott called me about?"

"Yes, we're familiar with the pictures of you and Rachel with some other woman. Would you care to explain those to us? Why are they so important?" Ron asked.

"I don't know." She went with a more benign explanation. "Perhaps because she may have fluffed my resume to get me hired. We didn't want it to be common knowledge that we knew each other before this job."

Nick smirked. "That's odd," he said.

"Why's that odd? I needed a job. Besides, I have some training in this area. I'm only a class or two from my degree." *A slight exaggeration*. She took another swig of her beer. "Rachel did me a favor. I don't want to ruin her good name now that she's dead."

"We have no interest in how you got your job. By all accounts, you've been a good worker," Ron said. "We won't rat you out, and I'm sure Dr. Scott feels the same way."

Jamie signaled her agreement to keep the conversation flowing, but she was now curious about her father's hiring practices. Why would he hire someone without scrutinizing their references? She knew it wasn't her mother's doing. *Something else to look into*, she thought.

"See? No one's trying to get you fired. We just want to know about your relationship with Rachel—in the past and the present. How long did you know her?" Nick leaned forward in his chair as he questioned her.

Tatiana exchanged glances with each person and sank onto the coffee table. "I met her in Madison. We hung out a while and went our separate ways. I heard through the grapevine that she was living in Atlanta, and I got in touch." Another swig of beer. "I wanted to live here."

"You just lost touch after college? Any reason?" Nick continued. He took over the questioning here, as was their practice. Ron and Nick found many women would answer harder questions coming from Nick. So, he took the lead.

"Of course not. Just people moving on. She was a year or two ahead of me, so she graduated and moved away. You know how it is." Tatiana paused and dropped her head to hide the fact that she was sweating. She swallowed and took a deep breath. "I'm not sure what you want from me."

"Do you know of anyone with whom Rachel had a problem? Either now or in the past?"

"No, I don't," Tatiana blurted.

Answered too quickly, Jamie thought.

Both detectives looked at each other. "Are you sure?" Ron asked skeptically.

Rattled, Tatiana continued, "She was into her education in Madison. We only went out a few times because everyone was studying hard. Down here, she had a boyfriend for a while, but they broke up. Well, he broke up with her. He was the only one that had a problem with her, but he wouldn't do something like this, would he?"

"You emailed Rachel a few weeks ago, asking to meet. What was that about? Why didn't you just go down to her office to chat? Your coworkers say that you two were in contact every day."

"I don't remember what that was about. Probably nothing important, and with what happened to her, it's escaped my mind."

"Well, we have her phone records, and she called you shortly before she died. Seems like she left a message."

"I had a missed call. That's it—no message."

"Before she called you, she spoke with a man who seemed to upset her. The valet said he was from Madison. He talked to her about a friend who died?" Nick watched her face and demeanor closely. "Do you know what that might mean?"

Tatiana swallowed and took a deep breath again. Nick read that as a tell—she was going to lie again.

"Don't know about that. I don't think anyone we knew died," she said.

Nick pulled out his phone; he saved a copy of the image of the man they knew as William from the security footage. "Do you recognize this man?"

An almost imperceptible gasp. All three visitors noticed the expression in Tatiana's eyes. She recognized him. A wave of fear washed over her, but she tried to maintain her composure.

"No, I don't recognize him. I'm really sorry." She stood up at that point. "I don't have anything else to tell you. I knew her, and she helped me. But nothing was going on."

Neither detective believed her, but Tatiana had put up a wall. There was a story here, and both detectives had ideas about how to fill in the blanks. The trio stood to leave.

"Thank you for your help today. We will need you to come down to the station to make a statement," Ron said, shaking her hand. "We're sorry for your loss."

Tatiana agreed but still seemed shaken. Jamie knew that look—she wore one exactly like it before—trapped and seeing no way out. Tatiana wasn't coming down to the station; she was going to run. Jamie suspected the detectives knew it, too.

She lingered behind for a moment—ostensibly to shake her hand—and impulsively whispered in Tatiana's ear, "Don't run. Maybe I can help. Will you meet me somewhere?"

Tatiana stared hard at her and murmured, "Maybe. I don't know what you can do. After this, I don't know if I can trust you."

Jamie glanced back at the detectives, who were eyeing her suspiciously. "I don't know either, but running's not the answer."

Tatiana bit her lip, knowing Jamie was probably right, but she didn't respond and pushed the taller woman out the door.

As she walked out of the apartment, Nick came over to Jamie. "What did you say to her?" he asked, standing close.

He was too close. "Nothing bad. I just told her not to run. I know that expression. Bet she's already packed and planning to disappear."

Jamie instinctively took a tiny step backward. The heat generated every time she stood near him was muddling her brain.

"I agree. We'll have a patrol car sit on her." He gazed into her eyes. "Where are you headed now?"

The first reply that popped into her head was too sassy for the situation. She said, "I have a date." Nick's ears perked up, and he listened with increased interest. Jamie blushed. "With one of my closest friends whom I didn't speak to while I was away. What are *you* doing next?" she tried to divert the conversation, and his intense gaze, from her.

"We're going back to the precinct to make some headway. As usual." Nick touched her arm. "Be safe tonight. I'll see you tomorrow." He went to his truck and started it. Ron was already inside.

She turned toward Tatiana's apartment for a moment. She could see Tatiana peeking out the window and talking on the phone, her expression unreadable. No telling if she was leaving or not.

26
Don't Go to Dinner Angry

After leaving Tatiana's house, Jamie checked the time. It was almost six, and she didn't have time to run home to change. It took forty-five minutes to get to the Cafe Sunflower restaurant in Buckhead.

At the restaurant, she stopped in the restroom and frowned in the mirror. *Geez, I looked like this in front of Nick?* Her hastily created ponytail from this morning had slowly loosened so that it was barely a ponytail at all. She hadn't reapplied her lip gloss all day. Four years ago, she would have primped before entering that police station—*oh, well.*

She pulled her hair out of the barrette and shook her head. That wouldn't work. There was an unattractive crimp in her hair after being in a barrette all day. Digging into her crossbody bag, Jamie found her comb. She raked it through her hair twice and re-clasped the barrette. She then applied some lip gloss and splashed some water on her face. *Better.* She checked the time again—it was almost seven. With no Felice in sight when she exited the restroom, Jamie went to the hostess station and asked for a table for two. She ate at that restaurant with Felice multiple times in the past. Felice wasn't a strict vegetarian, but dabbled periodically. Each time, she claimed she was going to convert. Then there would be a medical meeting at a lovely steak house, and all willpower immediately disappeared. It had happened several times. Even four years out, Jamie didn't expect anything different.

The restaurant wasn't crowded, and the hostess seated her at a rear booth. Jamie ordered a glass of tea (she was back in Atlanta, after all) and waited. After five minutes, just as the server brought Jamie's beverage, Felice rushed in full of apologies for being late. She wore a blue sweater dress with a pair of brown knee boots and a matching brown coat. Instantly, she plopped down into the seat opposite Jamie, put her coat on the seat next to her, and placed an order for whatever Jamie was drinking.

Typical, Jamie thought, smiling to herself. Dealing with Felice had always been like getting caught in a whirlwind.

"Trey! Have you been here long? My dictation ran longer than I thought it would, and then traffic was miserable. And my ex called moaning about some belongings she left behind. I told her to come to get them while I was out, of course. How was your day?"

Jamie relayed the broad strokes as the server returned with Felice's beverage and took their dinner orders: a Harvest Salad for Jamie and Mushroom Phyllo for Felice. After the server left to enter their orders, Felice leaned back and eyed Jamie curiously.

"Now that we got the pleasantries out of the way, how long have you been back?"

"Since Friday. It's been very busy. I'm trying to re-acclimate." Jamie took a sip of tea and directly jumped into her *mea culpa* speech. "I have had four years to think. In the past, I haven't been very considerate of anyone else because my problems were *so* important." Jamie made air quotes as she spoke. "I wouldn't be surprised if you were angry with me. You've always been there for me, and I just bailed on you," she uttered soberly.

"Yeah. That part was *not* cool. I figured you were embarrassed about the fact that I didn't think you should marry Eddie. You stopped speaking to me before you left town, anyway."

"Well. I wasn't worth talking to at that point! I was hanging out in Buckhead. There were some things I did I wasn't proud of and other things I can't remember."

"Were you unfaithful to Eddie?" Felice asked. "That was always your line in the sand. You were always so puritanical about that."

Jamie sipped more tea. "Well, yeah. There were indiscretions. One in a bar bathroom, another in an apartment." Jamie shook her head. "Not proud of that at all."

"I guess we all fall from our pedestals sometimes," Felice said. "It still doesn't explain why you stopped talking to me, of all people. I knew all your secrets, and I gave you your most famous nickname. And I've seen you drunk off your ass. I also witnessed your infamous make-out session with your supervising resident." Felice took a gulp of her tea.

Jamie smiled at the memory and took another sip of her tea. The resident in question was incredibly smart and incredibly gorgeous. He wasn't supervising Jamie when they made out. She'd just finished a rotation with him, where he'd ignored all her signals. After evening rounds one day, she'd manufactured a reason to run into him, to see if nature would take its course. Felice was her fail-safe, in case he didn't take the bait. But Jamie had forgotten to call, and Felice came searching for her and got an eyeful when she found them half-naked in a call room. From that point, the resident couldn't focus around them and avoided them until he graduated. It was OK with Jamie—he wasn't that great of a kisser.

"I was *so* angry when I heard you left the country without calling me. Maybe it was better that you waited a while to contact me; I had my own shit to deal with," Felice said, crossing her legs.

"Don't we all?" Jamie reclined in her seat. "I hadn't dealt with New York. Have another baby? I still feel guilty about the first one. I wonder where she is, how she's doing. Did my piss-poor prenatal care come back and bite her in the ass? Did my choice of a drug-addicted father do her any favors?"

"She's probably fine. You know she may come looking for you one day," Felice noted.

"I know. I've thought about that. My mother insists that I leave that part of my life behind." Jamie laughed bitterly. "At least, the messy parts."

"You have always been a mother-pleaser. Did you even want to be a model? I still find that difficult to believe."

"I thought it was fun, and I enjoyed making money." Jamie lowered her eyes. "I got to be an adult or, at least, pass for one. You know my mother had an iron grip on us during our childhoods. It was an opportunity to be free," she revealed.

The server brought their meals. Felice dug in immediately. "I didn't eat lunch," she said hungrily. "So basically, I was a victim of the sad-Jamison train that rolled over everyone in her path?"

Jamison lowered her gaze again, and Felice continued, "OK, I get it. But no contact in four years?"

Jamison had the good grace to blush. "I suck, OK? I just got comfortable. I didn't want to deal with anything or anyone I left behind. It was easier."

"The sad, chaotic Jamison train. I love you, but you can be exhausting," Felice said between mouthfuls. "And I had almost forgotten that."

"I'm sorry?"

"You love the chaos. It's why I knew Eddie was wrong for you. He's a nice guy, but he has no edge, no drama. You would have been bored to death. It's why you acted out." Felice leaned forward and tilted her head. "Real talk. You liked your photographer because he was forbidden for a variety of reasons, same as with the resident. After all, you just wanted to see if you could. Most of the guys you went through all had some edge. But Eddie, no. Your mother wanted you with him, which was a bad idea. Your tattoo is truly what you live by. I couldn't believe it when you emailed me about that—one of your rare emails. Does your mother know about it?"

"Nope. Do I look that foolish?" Jamie said sarcastically. "Now you have me thinking about my chaotic family."

"Hey, I'm not saying your family isn't a fat, burning pile of chaos, which I never understood. You all seem so normal." Jamie threw her dinner napkin across the table playfully. "I'm serious. Your mother lives for drama, your brother dates chaos whenever he can, your sister married into chaos, and you search it out. I should call you Trey Chaos," Felice joked.

"It can't be that bad. It's not all our fault."

Felice pursed her lips. "That's enough of that. You aren't ready to acknowledge the truth yet. So why are you back?"

Jamie took a bite of her salad before replying. She was trying to clear her head after all the knowledge Felice had dropped on her. "I saw people in dire straits—beyond anything I ever experienced." She furrowed her brow and continued. "For example, there was a woman whose village was destroyed, her husband killed, she and her daughters raped and beaten, and her young son kidnapped; nevertheless, she continued to carry on even as one of her daughters became pregnant. She was determined to, one day, find her son and help her daughter raise the baby. Amid all this, they still celebrated her other daughter's birthday. And I felt guilty for falling apart four years ago. An opportunity to come home arose. Then the murder happened. It's been bizarre."

"Whew! Your life may be messy, but speaking as a Jewish lesbian, we all got problems," Felice said, finishing the last of her meal.

"Do you want to yell at me? Jillian let me have it earlier today about my selfish ways." Jamie sucked on an ice cube and pondered her situation. "Why do any of you bother with me?"

"I don't know. I had written you off. Then I heard through your mother that you were coming back. I politely tried to blow her off, but she reminded me of how close we used to be. Maybe we can get that back. But you can't just disappear when things get tough." Felice got emotional. "I came out to you, Trey. We shared all our secrets. You knew that my mother still hadn't said the words 'My daughter's gay' after 10 years. Actually, that's still the case. *You* were the person who I could talk to." She pulled herself together. "So, we'll see how it goes, OK?"

The atmosphere became tense, so they sat quietly for a few moments. Jamie broke the silence. "What happened to…what was her name? Beverly…I thought she was your soulmate?" Jamie quizzed.

"That was over before you left the country!" Felice forced a smile. "Probably not good to remind me you weren't talking to me."

Jamie apologized again. "I'm going to listen; tell me what's been going on with you. Nothing about me. New leaf and all."

"Interesting. Let's see how long that lasts," Felice said sarcastically. But Jamie could see she was softening. "Beverly and I didn't want the same things. She wanted to live in Vermont and run a bed-and-breakfast, and I didn't. From what I hear, she's married and happy."

Wisely, Jamie changed the subject. "So, you almost tied the knot yourself? What happened?" she asked, sticking to her plan of focusing on her friend. Rebuilding a friendship—even a longstanding one—would take time.

"After Beverly and I broke up, I played the field for a while. There are some breathtaking women out there, you know?" She and Jamie giggled. "I even tried the online dating thing."

"How'd that work out?"

"For me, it made for good short-term relationships; sometimes, even only for one night. Nothing particularly long-term. And I was OK with that. But I'm in my thirties. I think I want kids," Felice stated in a conspiratorial whisper.

"Really? I thought that was the last thing you would ever want." Jamie recalled their conversations about child rearing and how it ruined your fun. Jamie was ambivalent on the topic, but Felice had been 100% sure. Felice had since changed her mind. *Interesting.* Jamie was still ambivalent.

"I thought so, too. But when I hit thirty-two, I started thinking about having a family. I want to be pregnant and give birth." Felice stopped speaking for a moment. "I hashed that out with my therapist to ensure it wasn't some midlife crisis. It wasn't. So, I had to rethink my relationship strategies—look beyond the outer beauty and get to know the woman better. I then met Susan through mutual friends. She had just moved here from Nevada for a job. We clicked immediately—we became exclusive, and she moved into my house after three months."

"That was fast," Jamie said.

"Yeah, I should have been more careful. We got engaged after twelve months. Hey, the wedding would have been this upcoming March. It was going to be small. We even started researching sperm banks; I was going to carry the first one, and we would decide if we wanted more kids after that. We wanted a black sperm donor, since we wanted our baby to resemble both of us. However, three months ago, I noticed Susan pulled back and didn't seem so sure about a kid. She was even wavering on the marriage. She said she still loved me but just needed more time. But one month ago, I received a phone call from a woman who had been spending time with Susan. Then I went through Susan's phone—I know it was bad—but I saw naked pictures from this woman and other women." Felice dropped her head. "I was humiliated, so I confronted her. Susan had only been in relationships with men before. I was her second sexual experience with a woman, but her first relationship with one. She wasn't ready to settle down."

"Didn't she tell you she hadn't been in many lesbian relationships before?"

"She lied. She exaggerated her time out as a lesbian. So, she was out on the scene while we were planning to have children. Therefore, I kicked her out." She tried hard to repress the gathering anger.

"That's too bad. You sound like you're doing OK now."

"I'm rebounding with every available woman that comes my way. I may just decide to have that baby alone. That way, I won't make any rash relationship decisions."

"When are you going to pull the trigger? I'm trying to imagine you pregnant," Jamie said as she finished her salad.

"Funny. I'm almost ready. I'm trying to eat better and get my body ready for the miracle of pregnancy. I've started charting my cycles. As expected, I am regular as clockwork. I figure in three to six months, I'll get inseminated."

Jamie was silent. That was such a tremendous step, and Felice was calm about it. The thought of having another baby made the butterflies in Jamie's stomach go wild. *To care for another human?* That would be a sign that she had indeed grown up.

"That's very cool. I would be glad to help you pick out a donor if you want my help," Jamie offered.

"Well, maybe. Since you know more about guys than I do," Felice joked. "This was a good start. Let's not let it fall apart again, OK?"

The server came by, and Felice offered her credit card for both meals. "I'm feeling generous tonight. Besides, don't you have a function with your mother to attend? I'll be nice to you now because that'll be painful."

Ha, ha. The two ladies burst out laughing.

27
Blocked In

Jamie left Cafe Sunflower in a better mood after her conversation with Felice. She was on track to arrive home at eight forty-five. That should leave plenty of time to visit with the neighbors. The gated community was friendly and often had open houses where everyone would just drop in, and today, the Scotts' home was the gathering spot. The neighborhood contained a close group of friends, so impromptu gatherings of this nature were common.

When she arrived at her parents' house, she could see her brother's car and Jillian's SUV in the drive. There were also other cars she didn't recognize, so she assumed they belonged to their neighbors. There was also a Tahoe at the end of the driveway. It seemed familiar but did not have any markings, so she thought it was a neighbor's, too. There was barely any room on the circular driveway; when she parked, she blocked everyone in.

Poor parking planning, she thought. She would have to come back out to move her car when each person left.

Two small boys met Jamie at the front door. Anthony was chasing Jacob, who had grabbed the phone from his older brother.

"Give me that phone! I was winning. You're going to mess up my game!" Anthony yelled. Jacob just gurgled and continued to run until his uncle, Jon, scooped him up.

Once in the foyer, she watched Jon pick the smaller boy up and turn him upside down. While Jacob yelled and giggled with his uncle, Anthony grabbed the phone from his hand.

"Hi, Aunt Jamie. Everyone's in the kitchen," Anthony said while trying to salvage his position in the video game.

Jamie acknowledged him and the wrestling pair as she passed them to the kitchen. Margaret and Gregory were talking with an older white couple she recognized as the Bentons, Miriam and Lawrence. They had lived in the neighborhood for as long as the Scotts, but they spent six months at their condo in Paris and frequent weekends in Colorado during ski season. Aaron sat on Margaret's lap. Jillian sat next to an older man named Dr. Arturo Andretti—if Jamie remembered correctly. He was a surgeon in his early sixties who lived two houses down. He had a wife—or at least he'd had one when Jamie left—but she wasn't present tonight. Joining the pair were Kumar and Sumitra Singh, an Indian couple who were both physicians. Standing by the bar were more neighbors: a man that Jamie didn't know with a wife who looked ready to deliver, and an African American man who was pouring beverages for the trio. She vaguely remembered that Jon mentioned him when they spoke before her return. There were several other people in the kitchen she didn't recognize.

Margaret glanced up when Jamie walked into the room. Like an excellent hostess, she excused herself from her conversation and made her way to her daughter as she stood in the kitchen doorway.

"It's about time. Did Felice come with you?" she asked, giving her a perfunctory kiss on the cheek.

"No. But we had a nice dinner."

"Good. Let me introduce you to everyone."

Margaret started at the bar and introduced Jamie to almost every person in the kitchen, breakfast room, and living room. Jamie made small talk with several guests. After several chats, she felt the need to escape. Politely, Jamie excused herself and sat quietly, eyes closed, in a small sitting room next to the living room. This room probably served as a place for her younger siblings to study while she had been in New York. It still had the small cherry table, chairs, and bookshelf from their teens, along with a whiteboard and projection screen. It wasn't that quiet, but she was alone for a moment. There were too many people in the house. It felt a little claustrophobic, like four years ago.

She could feel a shadow in front of her. Opening her eyes, she saw Nick.

Nick? What is he doing here? She had missed him during the introductions. The Tahoe she parked behind was his. Before they could say anything, Margaret appeared in the doorway of the small room; she was keeping tabs on them.

"Detective Marshall came to tell us about Tatiana and Rachel, so I invited him to stay." Margaret looked intently at both. Uncomfortable, Jamie fiddled with her hair, pushing a few loose strands behind her ear, and Nick tucked his hands in his pockets.

The older woman rolled her eyes. *Like she didn't know what they were up to.* "Don't be antisocial. Come mingle." Margaret directed them back to the kitchen.

Eyeing both women, Nick thought it best to go on ahead.

Jamie walked alongside Margaret and asked, "What else did he tell you about the case?"

Nick took a seat next to Dr. Andretti, but Jamie saw him peek in her direction when she entered the kitchen.

"He said that Rachel and Tatiana knew each other before they came here. I had no idea. Neither did your father."

"That's unbelievable. Did you do any background on her before you hired her?" At the look on her mother's face, Jamie changed tactics. "Tatiana does her job well, right? So, there shouldn't be any story there. Don't worry." She then turned to walk toward her sister.

"Wait, Jamison. Let's talk to the Bentons." Margaret stopped her before she had gotten away and walked Jamie toward Gregory and the Bentons, steering her away from the detective. Jamie kept glancing over at Nick, trying not to be obvious. The Bentons wanted to know more about her time in Africa. They were interested in taking that trip themselves.

Jamie appreciated their interest but didn't want to go into details right then. Fortunately, Gregory stood up to address the gathering at that moment.

"Good evening!" He saluted everyone. "Margaret, I, and the entire Scott family are so glad our neighbors could come by this evening—on such short notice! It's a tremendous opportunity for neighborhood building and to enjoy the holiday season." He paused for a moment and scanned the room with a smile. "We need to do this more often, but I know life gets in the way." He lifted his glass in a toast. "To happy neighbors!" he called out, a bit more audibly.

Everyone lifted their glasses. Margaret jumped up to add, "Most of us know each other. However, we would also like to extend a welcome to our detective friend, who is investigating the unfortunate events at the lab over the past few days." She smiled at Nick, which surprised him. "Make him feel welcome!"

This gesture also surprised Jamie, but she knew not to read too much into it. Margaret was the queen of pleasantries, doled out icily. She didn't even use his name.

When she turned to lift her glass to Nick, she saw he had excused himself from the room. Jamie got up to follow, but changed her mind. To avoid any comments from her family, instead of sitting back down, she stopped at the table where her brother and sister sat, watching the weird dynamics. Jillian quickly started a conversation.

"I just wanted to apologize again for unloading on you earlier today. I don't take back what I said, but I could have said it better. A lot is going on, and I really shouldn't dump all over you because I'm frustrated."

"I should apologize to you," Jamie replied to her sister. Jon was making a face while continuing to eat his appetizers. "What are you looking at, Jon-Jon?"

Jon smirked. He had been in this position, between his sisters, over clothes and toys when they were children and cars and political views as they got older. It was best to stay out of it, if possible, although he enjoyed listening to the back and forth. "Nothing, Jamie Jay," he snickered. "Your guy just went out. You'd better go catch him."

Jamie made a face at him, and Jillian smirked, turning her head toward the door Nick had just gone through.

With a wink, Jamie got up and left the room. She could feel the glare of Margaret—real or imagined—on her back. She found Nick standing in the foyer and speaking excitedly into his phone. He disconnected as she neared him, but he appeared upset.

"What's wrong? Is it about Rachel's case?"

Nick eyed her briefly before answering. "We have a car patrolling Tatiana's neighborhood because we couldn't sit anyone specifically on her." He exhaled deeply. "She just left, as you said she would. Our officer spotted and followed her. She drove to a cheap hotel and met with someone. The officer couldn't ID him. When they left, he lost them completely. I'll have to check the video cameras in the area. There's more going on here than meets the eye."

Nick checked the messages on his phone while he related those facts to Jamie. He then focused his full attention on her. The din from the other visitors in the house faded away—it was just the two of them now. "How was your dinner? You went out with your friend, right?"

She smiled—his blue eyes warmed her soul and other places she tried to ignore.

"Yeah, my friend Felice, from med school. It was nice. Thanks for asking." Jamie could feel her mother staring at them from the doorway. It was like a sixth sense. The waves of disapproval burned a hole in her back. "So, you're leaving now?" she quickly asked.

"Work—it never ends." The corner of his eyes crinkled up as he smiled. "It's the job. But I feel like we're close to some answers. In my gut, I believe Tatiana holds the key to this case." He leaned in. "Your mother's coming, so I'll maintain decorum. I'm on the job and all. However, I promise you and I will get dinner and see what happens when we get this solved."

"See what happens," she repeated in a whisper. He smiled mischievously. It sounded like a sexy promise.

"Do you think *you* can handle it?" Jamie asked softly as she maintained eye contact. She could see the hard glint in his eyes—he *could* handle it… her imagination started to drift.

Margaret cleared her throat loudly.

The sound brought Jamie rudely back to the present situation. Nick straightened himself and bowed his head politely to Margaret. "I have to go take care of something. Thank you very much for your hospitality, Mrs. Scott, and extend my gratitude to your husband." As he left, he added, "I'll be in touch." Jamie blushed, which Margaret noticed.

"Keep your clothes on," she hissed at Jamie as she reached her side. "I can't believe you are throwing yourself at the first man in your vicinity. Have you learned nothing from New York?"

Anger overtook the original blush. Jamie took a deep breath to steady herself. *We are not going to do this again,* she thought. "I can't *believe* you're throwing New York in my face again! I'm not throwing myself at anyone now, and I didn't throw myself at anyone in New York. Yes, I made some stupid decisions, but I'm trying to make better ones. If you plan to keep throwing NY at me, this visit is going to be very difficult—and short," she hissed back.

This made Margaret angry, but before she could retort, Nick reappeared in the front doorway. "I'm blocked in," he stated.

That reminded her of her car location. "Sorry, I need to move my car!" she said to her mother while actively trying to regain her cool; Jamie then followed him outside. Her mother furiously turned away and bumped into her son.

"Where's Jamie going, Mother?"

"She had to move her car for that detective. She's probably propositioning him as we speak. That girl makes so many wrong decisions about men. I don't know what I'm going to do." She headed back to the kitchen in a huff.

"Wait, Mother! You seem furious for no real reason. Hold on. Mother, wait," Jon started after her, but his cell phone rang again. He checked the display and shook his head. Rena was still calling him. If this continued, he would need a new number. He joined the others in the kitchen, the phone call unanswered.

By the time Jamie got to her car, Nick was leaning against his truck. Fortunately, she had calmed down a little, but the sight of him made her heart speed up.

"Sorry, there was nowhere to park inside the gate," she said, as she prepared to walk by him. He reached out and gently grabbed her arm, pulling her toward him.

"You asked me if I could handle it," he stated in a low voice as she neared him. He ran his fingers along her jawline and was gratified to hear her gasp softly. "The question is, can *you*?" he said as he leaned in for a kiss. She was into it—*so into it*. It would be so easy to get pulled in here—and then she remembered where she was. She quickly pulled back and eyed the house.

"Sorry," Nick said, noticing her discomfort. "I lost my head for a moment." He took a deep breath. "Anyway, I need to focus. To solve the case." He exhaled and closed his eyes for a moment.

"Will I talk to you tomorrow?" She backed away toward her car.

He flashed a heart-shattering smile. "Probably. Have a good night," he said quietly and climbed into his car.

Jamie moved her car and allowed the Tahoe out. Once he left, she could pull her Camaro onto the circular portion of the driveway toward the garage and not block anyone else in. She took a second or two to collect her thoughts about the gorgeous cop she was trying to work with while unsuccessfully fighting an attraction to and about her mother, who seemed to have picked up where she left off four years ago. One circumstance, exciting and confusing, the other infuriating. Realizing that her mother would assume the worst if she didn't get back to the gathering, she got out of her car to avoid any extra drama.

She entered the house to riotous peals of laughter. Gregory must be telling a story from the early years. Jamie had to admit that the stories from her parents' courtship and marriage before kids were quite hilarious. Her mother seemed like a different person. *What happened to her?* At the door of the kitchen, Jamie ran into Jillian, who was holding a sleeping Aaron.

"We're crashing here tonight," Jillian said. "I'm still recovering from last night's stupidity and the fact that someone—who will remain nameless—didn't let me sleep this afternoon. I need to put this one down. Could you help me by ushering the other boys upstairs?" She made her way to one of the guest bedrooms with the sleeping boy draped over her arm. When she had her children with her, she typically slept in one of the guest rooms, which were larger than her old childhood room.

After a few minutes of joyfully chasing the evasive boys through the delighted partygoers, Jamie finally corralled all three boys. As she tried to wrangle the boys upstairs, the rest of the gathering dispersed. Jon caught up with her halfway up the stairs—Jacob was holding her hand dutifully, but Ricky and Anthony were making minimal progress up the stairs. They had resumed an earlier argument about the phone. Jon scooped up Anthony and sprinted the rest of the way upstairs. Since Anthony was holding the phone, Ricky raced around the slower-moving Jamie and Jacob to catch up with his younger brother.

After Jamie and her charge made it to the bedroom suite, she noticed that there was a suitcase at the foot of the bed and that Aaron was sleeping in a portable playpen. Jillian handed pajamas to the older two boys, who carried them and their bickering into the adjoining bathroom. Jillian took Jacob's hand and deftly swapped his jeans and a long-sleeved t-shirt for a clean overnight diaper and a pair of footie pajamas. She then directed him to brush his teeth with his brothers in the bathroom.

Once Jacob reached the bathroom, there was more good-natured chatter between the boys, and Jillian closed the door behind them. Jon melted into the recliner on the other side of the bed, and Jamie perched next to Jillian after she returned to her spot on the bed.

Jamie pointed to the suitcase. "What's that about? Is something wrong?"

Jillian squinted wistfully at the bathroom door. "Richard and I had a huge fight about having another baby, and I just needed some space to think. I love my boys—I do. But I miss having something else to do. Am I supposed to rely on babies forever to keep busy? What happens when Aaron goes to school all day?"

"Didn't you and Richard discuss this before you got married?" Jamie asked, grabbing her sister's hand. Jon listened to the conversation intently.

"We did. At first, I was good at being a stay-at-home parent. I loved Richard so much! But now… I still love him, but this can't be all there is to my life, can it?" Jillian regarded her older siblings plaintively. "I have researched law programs—I want to go back to school, part-time, when Aaron goes to preschool."

"You could do that," Jon said. "I take it Richard isn't OK with that."

"Richard doesn't want to change the status quo. His first wife worked a lot, and they grew apart. He thinks this would end the same way. So, we fight. And he still wants to have a girl." Her eyes welled up.

Jon leaned forward and patted Jillian on the knee, and Jamie put her arm around her. The family had always worried that this day might come because Jillian had wanted to work in the legal field for as long as they could all remember. Then there was Richard, and suddenly she was adamant that she wanted to get married and have kids. It was a tough place for the couple to be—neither was completely wrong. And another kid? The odds were that it would be another boy, anyway.

Trying to lighten the mood somewhat, Jamie joked, "Well, if you had another baby, it's very unlikely he would have a girl this go-round. He already has six boys. Or you could try some of the old wives' suggestions." Jon snickered uncomfortably at the TMI portion of the conversation. Over the past two days, he learned too much about his sisters. He shuddered inwardly. *TMI.*

Jillian smiled weakly through her tears. "Funny. That's not the issue. I don't want *any* more kids. I have four. He travels for his clients. I'm at home all the time. I'm *done* having babies."

"Have you told Mother about this?" Jamie asked.

"Yeah. But you know what she said. 'You wanted to marry him and skip law school.' 'You made that decision.' 'It's not those babies' fault that you are now rethinking your decision.' As expected," Jillian mimicked their mother's strident tone.

"That's pretty harsh." Jon frowned.

"Well, she also said I need to work it out with Richard. She remembers how we got together and how it would look if we ever got a divorce."

Jamie considered Jillian thoughtfully. "He's not cheating, is he? You would tell us if that's what's happening, right?"

"No, he's not." Jillian swallowed. "But I worry sometimes. He has a history of cheating. And my reputation in that area isn't stellar, for that matter. I pay attention to any pretty interns at their office, which frustrates him because he says I don't trust him." She got up and paced in a circle. "I think I have too much time on my hands to think about this stuff. I believe he also worries that I'll leave him if I go to school. Younger options, you know?"

"So, this," Jamie waved her hand at the suitcase, "visit is just for tonight?"

"Yeah, Richard's out of town for a few days. He left this evening. Mother wanted us to come over here anyway, because she has plans with Aaron and Jacob tomorrow."

"Is that why you were ready to chop my head off this morning? I was another person demanding stuff from you?"

"I sometimes forget that you took psych in medical school," she said, exhaling. "That may have been part of it. But I stand by what I said. You do take over." She stopped by the bathroom door and listened. "You boys have been in there for a long time. Are you jokers still alive in there?" she asked, throwing the door open.

The boys had spent five minutes getting toothpaste all over the mirror and each other, as well as on their toothbrushes. Jacob was standing in the tub as his older brothers feigned jousting with their toothbrushes.

They came out of the bathroom just as loudly as they went in. Jillian directed the two older boys to Uncle Jon's room across the hall. They were excited because there was a TV and no mother in there. She tucked Jacob into her bed—he protested he wasn't sleepy yet.

Jamie gave Jillian another hug. "It'll be all right. You'll figure it out." She stepped back as Jon hugged her as well. "No matter what, we'll support you," he added.

"I don't know about 'both of you'. Our big sister will not have time because she is going to be very busy. That detective's always around—I don't think he came to talk to Mother and Dad. He was pretty disappointed when he arrived." Jillian smiled as she wiped the remaining tears from her face. "Go for it. I need someone to remind me how to go for what you want!"

Jamie shook her head. "Don't worry about me," she advised.

"I don't know, Jamie-Jay. What was going on with Mother downstairs?" Jon said. "Both of you were angry."

"Please, don't tell me you two are arguing again?" Jillian said with concern. "You just got home."

Jamie narrowed her eyes and shifted her weight restlessly. "Just Mother being Mother. She seems to have a bug up her rear about Nick. It didn't sit well with me." She didn't want to get too deep into the details, as she realized that Jillian probably didn't know *all* the facts. *One day, I'll tell her, but it has to be the right time.*

"Was that all it was?"

"Essentially." Jamie tried to downplay the situation with minor success—her siblings were eyeing her suspiciously—so she changed the subject. "OK, we need to go so Jacob can get to sleep. Goodnight, everyone. See you in the morning." Jon added his goodnights and followed Jamie out. Jillian watched Jamie leave with a questioning look but decided to leave it alone for now. She had to make sure the boys were all settled so she could get some rest herself.

By the time Jon and Jamie arrived downstairs, the kitchen was a ghost town. Margaret and Gregory had retired to their suite, and Olivia was putting away the remaining food. There was almost nothing left. Jamie snagged a dessert and walked Jon to the door.

"I'm worried about Jillian," she said.

"Me, too. But she always figures it out. I think she'll go back to school, and Richard will accept it. He loves her way too much to let this tear them apart."

"I hope you're right," Jamie said. Olivia walked by them to go home for a few hours. She was always welcome to stay at the house on late nights, but she had a husband at home that she wanted to see and she lived 10 minutes away.

After Jon left, Jamie locked the house and turned on the alarm. While getting ready for bed in her room, she thought about her sister and her choices. *I've made some choices that I regret now, too*. She was determined to make better ones from here on out.

28
A Little Diversion

It was dark, a bit before sunrise.

Tatiana couldn't sleep and lay in bed thinking. As the detectives and Dr. Scott left her apartment yesterday, Tatiana's cell phone rang. It was her fling from the office, Marcus. He was 'Christmas shopping,' meaning he had some free time and wanted to spend the time having sex with someone other than his wife. He also wanted to tell her that someone came by the lab searching for her during the afternoon—and tried to get her address. Marcus spoke to the older gentleman for a few minutes. He wouldn't describe the man any further unless she agreed to meet, but she thought she knew who the man was. William. He was getting closer.

To be sure, she agreed to meet Marcus at a cheap motel for an hour or two. He was a fun lay, so it wasn't a distasteful way to waste time—anything to postpone running again. She hadn't saved up enough money from this job, and she'd found that effective disappearing required planning and a significant stash. Right now, she had neither. She had a little, but not enough.

Tatiana knew the detectives had left an officer to watch her, but the young officer mistakenly believed she was unaware of his presence. She waved to him as she left the house, and he slumped down in his car.

Must be new, she thought.

At least with the police tailing her, it was unlikely that William would pop up out of nowhere. It wasn't until she got to the motel that she considered that he might have followed Marcus. She could see the police officer across the street as she entered the building, but he couldn't see her destination from his vantage point.

Marcus was waiting in the room, naked. There was no conversation until afterward. She rolled over, grabbed Marcus' shirt from beside the bed, and pulled his lighter and one cigarette from the pack in the pocket. He always had a pack of cigarettes in his chest shirt pocket. He had tried to stop smoking without success, and she only smoked after sex. Taking a deep drag, she asked him about William, being careful not to mention his name.

Marcus took the lit cigarette from her and took a drag before answering. "He seemed eager to find you. I think he knew you from college, but he seemed too old for that. He said you had common friends and wanted to take you out for coffee." The security guard took another drag. "He said he couldn't find your phone number or your address. I looked it up, and I couldn't find it either. That's a cool trick."

Tatiana took the cigarette from Marcus and propped herself up. "I like my privacy. I know who this guy is, and I don't want to have coffee with him. So, if he comes back around, do your security thing, and make him go away—and stay away." She started to retrieve her clothes.

"Where are you going? I still have an hour before my wife expects me back," Marcus said, reaching for her.

She jerked her arm away. "Sorry. I would love to stay, but I have stuff to do. You need to do some actual shopping, so she won't be suspicious." Tatiana paused in the middle of putting on her pants. "Doesn't this make you feel weird? Don't you regret being unfaithful to your wife?"

Marcus swung his legs over the edge of the bed. "My wife? We've been together since we were teenagers. She's my best friend. After a couple of kids, we live together as best friends—mostly."

Tatiana howled. "That's what I like about you—you're so full of shit. I know better than that. But if you like it, I love it." She finished getting dressed while Marcus used the bathroom. She stood by the bathroom door, waiting for him to come out. When he did, she kissed him and said, "Thanks for this. I needed it. I'll see you at work. Have a good one."

The police officer tried to pick up her trail as she pulled out of the motel parking lot, but she lost him in traffic. When she got home, however, the officer had just parked his cruiser across the street. She waved again—no need to be impolite, right?

Tatiana entered the house and ran into her landlady outside her apartment. They exchanged pleasantries, but the young woman was eager to get away. The lady seemed chatty this evening, which was unusual. She usually only asked about the rent. As Tatiana turned to head up the stairs, she had a sense of apprehension. She turned back to her landlady, who was standing giddily at the foot of the staircase. "Did someone come to see me?" she asked.

The lady blushed but was excited to tell the secret. "He wanted it to be a surprise. Oh, there he is—it's your uncle. Isn't this sweet?" William heard Tatiana's entrance into the house, exited her apartment, and was now standing behind her. There was no escape—she had to make the best of it.

29
Studying the Past

Small boys bouncing on her bed again awoke Jamie the next morning. Before falling asleep, she spent some time considering her career options, so she wasn't happy to be awake so early. These boys were roaming around at six in the morning—what kind of household was her sister running?

"Where's your mother? Why are you bouncing on my bed and not hers?" she groaned.

Anthony and Jacob continued to bounce. "Good morning! Good morning!" they repeated. Jamie grabbed a bouncing Jacob and gave him a tickle, which caused a cascade of laughter. Anthony continued to bounce while speaking between landings. "Grandpa sent us upstairs to see if you were going to work with him today."

"We're here to wake you up!" Jacob said, giggling.

"Nope. I've got things to do this morning." She leaned forward in the bed. "Aren't you going to school?"

"Yep. I already had breakfast—Grandpa made me some oatmeal and toast," Anthony continued. "Mother has to get up so she can take me to school. We're having a spelling test and a reading party."

Jillian stuck her head in the door, Aaron on her hip. "I'm awake, and Ricky's getting dressed. I'm going to take the boys to school and come back here to take a nap because I'm so tired. Our nanny will be here today." To Jacob: "Grandma has something planned for you and Aaron while your brothers are at school." Jealous, the older boys started complaining as Jillian shooed all of them out of Jamie's room.

"Did I hear you say you're not going in with Dad? What are you doing today?" Jillian asked, switching Aaron to the other hip.

"I want to do some digging on one employee from the lab, Tatiana. She knew Rachel before they got here, and the police believe there may be a connection to the murder. They went to school together in Wisconsin," Jamie said, lying back down. "Wake me up when you get back, please."

Jillian nodded and closed the door. Jamie rolled over to take a brief nap and plunged into a dream.

She slowly climbed into the jacuzzi where the blue-eyed detective sat waiting. She straddled him, and they kissed. He deftly took off her bikini top and leaned down...

Jamie snuggled down deeper into her blankets, preparing to ride her fantasy to its completion. The sense that someone was standing at the foot of her bed jarred her out of her dream. Opening her eyes, she saw Jillian, who looked wearier than before.

"Hey, you asked me to wake you after I dropped off the boys. So, wake up." With Jamie's groan, Jillian turned to leave.

"I said that, didn't I? Ugh—you are interrupting a nice dream." Jillian made a face at her sister and asked, "Where are you headed?"

"Back to bed. Come get me in a couple of hours. Maybe I can help you with your research."

Jamie watched her go and tried to catch a couple more minutes of sleep. She wanted to see if she could get back to her dream. But no such luck. After five minutes, she got up, put on a pair of jeans and a royal blue tunic, and went to get a cup of coffee and some breakfast. It was still early—around eight—and in the kitchen, her mother, Olivia, and her two nephews were sitting at the table. The boys were eating smiley-face pancakes Margaret had made for them. She was cutting up Aaron's food. Whipped cream and syrup covered his face.

"Good morning!" Jamie said, pouring herself a cup of Jamaican coffee. Seeing her mother playing in whipped cream and syrup with her youngest grandson was weird, but she seemed quite adept at managing him. Margaret had already helped Jacob cut up his pancakes. He then drowned them in whipped cream, chocolate chips, and strawberries and needed no help getting his food into his mouth. Jamie glanced around the kitchen and asked, "Are there pancakes for the adults?"

Margaret jumped up. "Sorry, Jamison. I left the batter over there. The grown-ups can make their pancakes. There's bacon, sausage, and hash browns over there if you want some. Eggs are in the refrigerator."

As Jamie made herself pancakes, Margaret said, "So you didn't want to go into the office this morning? Have you decided about your next plans? Do you want to work at the lab?" Aaron splashed some whipped cream on Margaret's cheek, causing her to snicker along with him.

“I’ve been thinking about it. The expansion seems intriguing. Felice also mentioned going into practice with her, and I can’t forget about the people you introduced me to. It’s a lot to process.” Jamie internally crossed her fingers. She’d blown Felice off when she’d mentioned it, and now she might have to go back and reevaluate that offer. She didn’t think she could work at the hospital dermatology clinic, given the way she left four years ago.

“That’s fine, dear. There’s no rush about the expansion. After that poor woman’s death, your father and I have discussed the wisdom of building right now. We don’t know how this will affect business. Perhaps next year.”

Jamie finished cooking her pancakes and placed them on a plate. She poured some maple syrup and took a bite. The pancakes had a hint of vanilla flavor and were warm and fluffy. She added some bacon to her plate. “Mother, can I use Dad’s computer in the study?” she asked, with a mouth full of pancakes.

“Mind your manners, Jamison; your nephews are watching. Do you know the password?”

“Has he changed it from four years ago?”

“Sadly, no. Just let me know if you have a problem logging in.”

Aaron finished his pancake and held his arms up for help getting out of his highchair. As Margaret lifted him, she asked, “Jacob, are you finished? Hurry! Grandma’s going to take you two to the museum and the aquarium today. We’re going to get lunch while we’re out. Let’s get cleaned up, though. Thanks to Aaron, I need to clean up, too!”

While Margaret playfully wrestled the boys out of the kitchen, Jamie quickly downed her pancakes, grabbed another slice of bacon and more coffee, and went into the study. She always liked her father’s study—it had an open design with many wood shelves on two walls. In the corner opposite the desk was a spiral metal staircase leading to a second story filled with more books. Next to the staircase was a wall of windows. The desk wasn't oversized; her father didn't work in this room much. She stretched out behind the desk and fired up the computer. Google was a good starting point—she suspected that her father and mother hadn't done any background research when they hired Tatiana. They probably relied only on Rachel's advice.

The articles that came up with a search for 'Tatiana Daniels' were from all over the country, and most weren't about the same woman. She added the search term 'Wisconsin' to see if she could narrow down the results. Jamie clicked through a page of links and scanned through the articles. Nothing. On the second page, she hit an interesting possibility—a story about the death of a coed around the time Rachel and Tatiana were in Madison. Jamie then added Rachel's name to the search parameters.

Another story about the same coed, but it mentioned that Rachel testified in court.

Shit, she thought. That sounded tough. She read through a couple of articles that gave an overview—a woman Rachel knew had died after being roofied. The young man—a football player—was on trial for her death. It didn't go well for him. It was difficult to determine how Tatiana was involved.

Jamie leaned back in the desk chair and checked the time on the computer. She had been searching for almost two hours; it was now mid-morning. She didn't hear her mother or the boys anymore, but before she could get up to see where everyone was, Jillian appeared at the door.

"I thought you were going to wake me up, PJ," Jillian said with mock indignation while carrying a cup of coffee and finishing a piece of sausage. She had changed into a gray, long-sleeved maxi dress and black boots. "I feel better than I did last night," she said, settling into the chair opposite the desk and taking a sip of her coffee.

"I lost track of time. I thought you needed the rest." Jamie picked up her coffee cup, but it was cold. "Is Mother still here?" she asked.

"Nope. My nanny came by and scooped them all up to go on their adventure." At the expression on Jamie's face, Jillian momentarily lost it. "Don't look so shocked. They do this every month. Mother is very interested in how her grandchildren are doing. She takes the older boys to concerts, local games, and other events. She watches them play little league baseball!"

"Really? That never happened when we were kids. We played sports, but she never watched us—she had work to do." The new Margaret sounded interesting to Jamie, though.

"Truth. But maybe old age is softening her up a bit." Changing the subject, Jillian leaned forward. "What did you find?"

"Searching for articles about Rachel and Tatiana. Nick believes that there's a connection between Madison and what happened to Rachel. Tatiana's not talking," Jamie said. She stood up. "I need more coffee. Want some?"

Jillian jumped up and followed her out. "So, what did you find?" she asked again as they walked to the kitchen. Olivia paused in her tasks and greeted them when they entered. She was cooking a pot roast and cutting up some vegetables for dinner. Jamie refreshed her coffee and found another piece of bacon to nibble on.

"Rachel was a witness in some trial a few years ago. A young woman died after being roofied, and Rachel testified that the young man in question gave her the drink."

Jillian scratched her head and asked, "What was the charge?"

"I think they convicted him of involuntary manslaughter. Why?"

"Well, the guy could be out of jail now. I wonder if he wanted to hurt Rachel for testifying against him. What other details were there?"

"Not much. The man's story was that he never put anything in the drink. He said *he* was the intended victim. There were no details in the story about how he explained that." The pair headed back into the study.

"Well, I can see if I can track down the trial transcript."

Jamie smiled at her. "You've been waiting to ask that, haven't you?"

Jillian smiled back at her sister. "You know it! I'm more than just a lady who lunches."

Jamie left that alone for now. "If I give you a link to an article about the case, will that help?" She asked. "Please and thank you."

Her sister smiled again. "I'll see what I can do. It's nice to do something that has nothing to do with diapers, fruit snacks, or potty training. Give me a few hours—I still have a few contacts. Some even in Richard's office."

Jamie thanked her again and added, "I'm going to make a few phone calls myself. I would love to get the story from a Wisconsin resident." She stopped speaking and held up her hand. "Do you hear that ringing?"

There was a faint ringing in the distance, coming from Jamie's room.

Jillian paused, listening. “Yeah, I do. Jesus, girl, you have that ringer set to stun. How can you be in the same room with it without blasting out your ears?” she yelled at Jamie’s already retreating form. “Worse than a flashbang,” she mumbled as she sat down to start her search.

Even with a small burst of speed, Jamie couldn’t quite get to her room before the ringing stopped. The display showed her brother’s number, so she hit redial.

“Hi, Jon. What’s up?” she said lightly when he answered.

“I’m trying not to call the police,” Jon said.

“What’s wrong?”

“Rena happened. To my *car*. Could you come talk me off the ledge?” Jon told her where he was and asked her again to come.

Rena happened? Jamie shook her head as she grabbed her purse and car keys. The breakup curse strikes Jon again.

30
One Bad Idea

As the sun rose on Tuesday morning, Tatiana squatted on the edge of a chair, staring at William as he slept on her couch. He was angry with her—from before—but she told him what he wanted to hear. She didn't have his money but lied and told him she could get it. After years of practice, the lies came much easier.

She didn't want to go to jail or die. William didn't want to go to jail, either. He had paid her and Rachel each a substantial sum out of his retirement fund to make sure they testified at his daughter's murder trial. William wasn't rich, and it almost cleaned him out. But Tatiana didn't hold up her end of the deal, and he wanted his money back. It just took him a while to track her down.

What a mess! she thought.

After William followed her back into her apartment (the oblivious landlady was still cooing about the beautiful reunion), Tatiana waited for the inevitable blow or shot with her eyes closed. She figured he was planning to kill her immediately. When nothing happened after a minute, she opened her eyes. He had moved around the room and was rifling through her desk. He, too, looked tired as he stooped over her papers and peered through his glasses.

Emboldened, Tatiana asked, "Why did you kill Rachel?"

William whirled around. "You think I did that? Oh, no. I'm the least of your worries. That was another one of your victims. He's out of jail and very angry."

Tatiana's blood ran cold, but she tried to maintain an air of calm. "I know he got released. I saw him on Sunday night. Besides, he wouldn't have killed her. He didn't know what we did." Sweat collected on her forehead as she flashed back.

Playing around in the lab—creating something like Rohypnol. A moment of poor judgment—spiking a young man's drink. The horror of finding out that he handed it to their friend, Bianca, as the pair went into another room to make out. Then, the whirlwind of Bianca's death, the accusations against the young man who'd given her the drink. The fear that the authorities would find out what Rachel and Tatiana did. In his grief, William tried to make sure they testified against the young man. He even paid them to make sure they showed up. Rachel showed but was ineffective on the stand. Her backtracking and confusion made it impossible to piece together a straightforward story of what happened that night. Tatiana just took the money William offered and ran. She spent a little and then lived off the grid with the rest. Until she got this job…

William was out of his mind if he thought she still had that money.

After her naïve statement, William answered sarcastically.

"Yeah, he should be in Wisconsin. But he might have a specific reason to look for the people who sent him to jail—the one who lied on the stand and the one who refused to testify to clear his name. I'm your best bet right now. Get my money, and I'll turn him in for you." He sat down, taking off his glasses and wiping them on his shirt.

"If I give you some money?"

"*All* my money. 50 grand. You didn't earn it. And I want it back."

"You would let him kill me? Why would I still have tens of thousands of dollars left after all this time?"

William leaned forward. "Doesn't matter, it's *my* money. You'll get it for me, or I will just get out of the old boy's way."

Tatiana exhaled shakily and replied in a panic. "I have an idea about how to get some money. Let me think a bit." She stood up, hoping he would take the hint that this meeting was over.

"Oh, you didn't think I was going to allow you to run away, did you? No, I'll stay here with you until you give me my cash." He leaned back again. "However long it takes."

With that, he made himself comfortable. All night, Tatiana thought of running, but she couldn't think of a plan to get rid of him that wouldn't shine an unwanted light on her. How could she get money? Who did she know that had that kind of money? She knew only one person–one family. Thus, a stupid, evil plan formed in her head.

By morning, she had an outline of that plan. Now she had to sell it to William. It was risky and involved a kidnapping, but hey, she could be very convincing.

31
Birds of Chaos

Jamie gave Jillian an overview of the Jon situation, then got in her car to meet him at his office. Jillian just rolled her eyes. This was not the first time a young woman played out her adolescent revenge fantasy after a breakup with Jon. Jillian remembered when a twenty-year-old jilted girlfriend broke a window and set off his house alarm. She had been throwing rocks with love messages taped to them at his house, while wailing about her eternal love. The neighbors called the police. The young woman agreed to pay for the broken glass to avoid being arrested. That event didn't keep Jon from chasing women who lacked maturity, though.

Jon's office was in a small business complex in Decatur. It was a relatively new, up-and-coming firm where Jon had a genuine opportunity to succeed if the woman issue didn't trip him up. Finding a parking space was a challenge this morning. After circling the block twice, Jamie slid into a spot across the street from the office parking lot when a minivan finally pulled away from the curb.

She had to dodge traffic to cross the street. Her brother stood huddled by his car in the small parking lot; she could see his fury from a distance. He was so angry that he couldn't say anything except point at his slashed left rear tire. Someone had also slashed the left front tire. Jamie wished she could say that she was surprised.

"Are you sure she did this?"

"Damn it, I know Rena did it!"

"What? Did you see her?" Jamie walked around the car. "Are you sure?"

"I'm sure," Jon said, pacing. The tow truck was on its way, and he had called Jamie after that. His third call was to his client to reschedule his meeting, using car trouble as an excuse. He didn't want his colleagues to know the entire nature of his problem; he hoped that no one from his firm would see him.

"She's been calling me non-stop this morning."

"Have you called her back?"

"No," he said. "And when she called Mother, I became less interested in closure and more in avoidance."

"That's becoming less of an option here." Jamie shivered—she had neglected to put on her coat today. "Can we stand inside the lobby?"

Jon agreed and led her into the building. The young, uniformed desk attendant cocked his head quizzically. "Mr. Scott, are you back from your meeting already?"

Jon turned to him and said, "Someone slashed my tires. My car's right there." He pointed out the front window to his car, two rows over. "Hey, did you see a pretty African American girl with reddish-brown hair hanging around here today?"

The attendant responded enthusiastically. "Yes, sir. She said she was your girlfriend. She left something for you here at the podium. The young lady asked me to give it to you when you returned from your meeting."

The attendant stooped behind his desk and brought up a box about the size of a shirt box. "I thought it was a nice gesture." After scanning Jon's and Jamie's faces, he asked, "Should I call the bomb squad?" He dropped the box on the desktop.

Jon leaned over and put his ear to the box. "It's not ticking."

"What the hell, Jon?" Jamie said. "This isn't a TV show! Bombs don't have to tick. And she could send you any number of horrible things. What does she do for a living again?"

"She's a student-teacher," Jon said.

"Of what? What did she major in?"

"Biology? Some science subject?" Jon seemed unsure of his supposed love's history.

Jamie exhaled, exasperated. "Yeah, you were truly committed there." A chilling thought hit her and caused her to take a step back. "You don't have any pets, do you?"

They exchanged glances. "Pierre the parrot," Jon said.

"Was Pierre healthy and happy this morning?" Jamie asked, her heart sinking.

Jon touched the box haltingly. "He was fine," he replied. He took another step back. "I don't want to open it."

"Does she have a key to your place?" Jamie pressed. She leaned closer to the box, and on further inspection, there appeared to be a feather poking out.

Jon was sheepish. "I haven't had time to change my locks yet."

Jamie poked his arm. "Geez. For a player, you don't know the rules of the game. Why do you give keys out?"

"I thought she was the one."

"After a few weeks?" she said, quite astonished at his foolishness.

Even the attendant gave him the evil eye. "Nah, sir. You don't give out keys until you give her a ring. And maybe not then." He shook his head and chuckled at his joke.

Jamie side-eyed the attendant. "I wouldn't go that far. But he's not completely wrong. We're calling the locksmith right now and getting your locks changed." Jamie pulled out her phone. "Next time, this girl may come into your house and hurt you."

"Hey, Google. Locksmiths in Decatur, Georgia," Jamie spoke into her phone. Many business names popped up.

The tow truck arrived. "I'll call the locksmith while I'm in the truck," Jon said. "Hey, how did you get away from the house?" He was significantly calmer. "Doesn't Mother have the boys today? I figured you would be helping."

Jamie waved her keys. "She took the boys to the museum. Don't change the subject. This is a mess."

"What's new? Thank you for coming by and calming me down. I'll call you from the repair shop—can you pick me up?" Jon hugged her and started toward the door.

"Excuse me, sir." The attendant gestured toward the box. "You need to take that with you or call someone to come get it." He shook his head. "I don't get paid enough to deal with bombs or dead animals."

Jon gave Jamie the most pitiful face.

"Damn," she said. "You can't be serious."

"You're my older sister. We've always had each other's backs." He pointed at the tow truck driver, who was tapping his foot impatiently. "I have to go."

"All right, fine, go." She held her arms out for the box. "If I blow up, this will be on you, and I will haunt your ass until the end of time."

Jon kissed her on the cheek and sprinted out.

The attendant chimed in. "I wouldn't accept that if I were you. Don't you have any police friends or bomb types who could ensure this thing is OK?"

"I doubt this is a bomb," Jamie replied.

"Ma'am, call the police. Or I will."

He had a point. Her mind raced to one specific officer. Perhaps a tall, handsome detective? Should she call him? She figured he wouldn't want her to blow up, right? His job was to protect and serve, right?

"I think I have a friend who can do this without making a mega-deal out of it." Sheepishly, she realized Nick's number was already on her phone–she just needed to add his name. She couldn't be too mad at her brother about this inconvenience. She had to admit she wanted to see Nick, anyway.

Nick was waiting for a call from Madison, Wisconsin, when his cell phone rang. He checked the number—local—and didn't recognize it, as he had always been bad at remembering numbers. He motioned to Ron as he stepped away to take the call.

"Marshall."

Jamie hesitated for a second, but quickly plunged in. "Hello, this is Jamison Scott. I have a situation that I hope you can help with."

Nick perked up and stood straighter. "Situation? Does this involve the murder case?"

"Actually, no. It involves my brother and his poor choices in women." She gave him a quick rundown of the problem. "I don't think there's anything dangerous, and we don't want to call the police on the young lady in question if we can avoid it." Jamie paused—he *was* the police. The doorman motioned for her to hurry it up as building tenants in the lobby were noticing. Jamie plunged on. "I hate to impose, but I wasn't sure what to do."

Nick hesitated before replying. This was not something he wanted to be involved in, but he understood the sentiment. *What could it hurt?*

"Tell me where you are. I will have to involve the bomb squad if this is an explosive device."

Jamie gave him the address.

"I'll be there soon," Nick said, disconnecting the call and standing up to leave.

Ron didn't even have to ask who it was. After only a couple of days, his partner seemed to be taken with this woman. Not typical. Women hung around them all the time, and Nick ignored most of them. Any dates he went on usually ended in a horror show of misunderstandings and Houdini-like escapes. At least, this one appeared not to be too unstable. Besides, he thought, he had enough to worry about with the surprise pregnancy and all.

"What did she want?" Ron asked.

"Who's *she*?" He grinned at Ron's expression. "How did you know?"

"That woman is the only thing that has your attention. You got it bad. I think we've met the next Mrs. Marshall." Ron winked at him.

"What? Man, you are exaggerating." He got his gun out of the safe in his bottom desk drawer. "I just think she's interesting."

"And beautiful. Look, I've been your partner for over a year, and I've seen your dates. Some of them would not have been able to get you to change your schedule if they were dying. This one… is *different*. Will you be gone long?"

"No. I'm going to handle a situation, and I'll be back. Hopefully, Madison will have called by then. When I get back, we can visit Tatiana again."

It took him 20 minutes to get to Jon's office building. Jon was still in the lot next to a tow truck driver who was having some trouble getting the sports car hooked up. Nick almost asked Jon for the name of the suspected slasher—he could have a quick talk with her. *Hold on*, he stopped in his mental tracks. That's something he would do for *family*—maybe he needed to slow down.

The attendant continued assisting clients as they entered the building, steering them away from the podium. Jamie was standing by the elevators, talking on the phone to Jillian, when Nick entered the building. He flashed his badge at the attendant, who walked over and tapped Jamie on the shoulder. As Jamie turned around, the attendant hurriedly declared he was going on his break. Nick eyed her appreciatively—even in casual mode, she was stunning. To avoid getting distracted, he focused on the matter at hand.

"Where's the box?" Nick asked cautiously, looking around. "I probably should have called for backup here. Even the doorman's running away."

"It's not an explosive device. There's no ticking." She mentally slapped herself as the words left her mouth. *That sounded so dumb.* "This woman—alleged sender, I should say—is a biology teacher and Jon's ex. It may be a dead parrot. The attendant had already dropped it, and part of the box popped open. No explosion, but I saw feathers."

"Feathers?" Nick leaned over and peered at the box, which was still on the desk.

"Jon has—had—a parrot." Nick lifted his eyebrow questioningly. "Don't look at me," she continued. "He likes birds—he had one when we were kids and taught it to talk. He had one before I left. I assume this is the same one. It's possible a bird may be in that box." Jamie paused and began to fidget when regret and embarrassment washed over her. *This was stupid….* "I didn't mean to waste your time. I'm sorry."

"Not a problem. I protect and serve, right?" Nick noticed the wing poking out of the corner of the box. "We have to decide what to do with this now. I might be able to take it to the medical examiner without opening an incident report." He straightened up. "Or you could just take it to a vet."

"That seems cruel. I guess we can't bury it in the backyard?"

"Not really legal… if this was a crime," Nick said, lifting the damaged edge of the box slowly. "It's a bird. There's a note here as well." Grabbing a pen from the attendant's workspace, Nick tried to slide the paper out of the box without disturbing the brightly colored dead bird. He stopped mid-process and reached in to pull the bird out.

Jamie said, "What are you…" but Nick interrupted.

"This is a stuffed bird. Here's a receipt."

"Really?" Jamie came over to examine the creature more closely. After hearing the word 'stuffed,' the attendant magically reappeared and came over to have a peek.

"Now, I'm incredibly embarrassed," Jamie said. "I'm sure you have important work to do." Nick grinned at her. He was relieved this wasn't an actual threat. And it would be nice to have a chit to call in with her. Royal blue was an exceptional color on her, and she was still *hot*. Seeing her relax in relief seemed like the perfect opportunity to give her a hard time.

"This may seem like an insignificant crime. But it isn't. I'm going to take this evidence back to the station house. Can I get a statement from you? And where's Jon? I need his side of the story."

Jamie probably hadn't blushed so much in her life. Jon would kill her—she was supposed to handle things—not get Jon's name on the news and Rena on the police blotter. Her mother would be horrified.

"Couldn't we keep this to ourselves? No harm, no foul?" she asked, pacing again.

It was all Nick could do to avoid bursting into explosive laughter. The attendant smiled as he figured out what was going on and went over to greet another client who'd just entered the building. "Hello, sir. Where are you headed? Do you need any assistance?"

Jamie turned around, prepared to strike a deal to avoid familial humiliation, but the expression on Nick's face tipped her off he was only kidding. Before she could respond, her phone rang. It was Jon.

"Where are you? Are you ready for me to pick you up?" She was a smidgen flustered, speaking with her brother, with Nick standing right there. The detective handed her the stuffed bird, which she took gingerly.

"Well, I finally got towed to the tire store. I'm angry again." He paused and exhaled audibly. "Since you answered the phone, I guess you didn't blow up?"

"No bombs, no dead animals, either. It was a stuffed parrot," Jamie told him. "She left us the receipt."

"Really? Was it on a credit card?" Jon sounded panicked.

"I don't know. Let me check." She motioned for the receipt from Nick. "I'm reading it now. It says credit sale."

"Damn! I need to call and cancel my credit cards!"

"What? Why?"

"Rena doesn't have a credit card. But," he added sheepishly, "I gave her my credit card. She used it once or twice."

Jamie put her hand to her head. This was indeed a comedy of errors. "Jon, you might not want to tell Mother about this," she said while trying not to cackle in his ear.

"Tell me about it. But this raises another issue. I need to cancel all my credit cards, but I was going to use one to buy my tires."

"Pitiful. Lucky you, I didn't spend all my money in Europe. Store location?" Jamie asked.

He told her.

Jamie hung up and turned to Nick to relay the latest developments in the story.

Nick said, "This woman's venturing into criminal territory now. Tell him to cancel his cards, but if this continues, we can pay her a friendly visit."

"You would do that?" Jamie asked, incredulously.

The detective shrugged and looked into her eyes. "Maybe I would. Maybe I'm hoping you'll find me very nice and kind and would consider having dinner with me when everything's over."

She blushed. He continued blindly. "I wasn't planning on saying that aloud again since you didn't say yes the last time. Think about it." He smiled. "I need to get back to work. Go help your brother. See you later." To her surprise, he leaned over, kissed her on the cheek, and walked out of the building.

Her insides melted.

The attendant, who had returned to the desk, smiled. “Dang, you got him hooked! You just need to reel him in.” He leaned over and picked up the remains of the box to hand to Jamie. “Here you go. Mr. Scott’s always full of excitement. A barrel of fun, huh?”

“He’s a barrel of something,” Jamie said. Looking at the attendant, she accepted the battered box and stuffed the bird back in it.

32
Research

Jamie met Jon at the tire store and let him borrow her credit card to purchase four new tires for his Mercedes.

"I'll pay you back as soon as I get my finances straightened out. I just called to cancel my credit cards, and I have to go to the bank to get a new debit card," he assured his sister.

"Why did you give your short-term girlfriend your financial information?" Jamie asked as she took her credit card back. "Remember, I don't have a job right now, so I need this money back. I've been carrying a zero balance for the past four years."

"As soon as possible. I would write you a check, but my checking account may also be at risk."

"You suck," Jamie said lovingly. While she waited for him to complete the purchase, she bought a snack out of the vending machine—she missed lunch fooling with Jon's drama. "I've got to make a few phone calls. Do you want to wait for your car, or do you want a ride?"

"I'll wait," Jon said. "I have things to do before everything gets further out of hand."

Jamie's phone rang. It was Margaret. "Hello, Mother. What's up?" she said, putting her finger to her mouth in a shushing motion for Jon.

"Your brother's not picking up. Jillian told me that something was wrong. Do you know if he's OK?"

Out of the corner of her eye, Jamie could see Jon shaking his head wildly. "He's fine, Mother. He just had to get his car fixed. I'm sure he will call you back soon." She wasn't going to get into details with Margaret—Jon could have that honor. "What are you doing right now?" she said, changing the subject.

Margaret exhaled loudly. "I was enjoying myself with my grandbabies, but now I'm worried about my children. Everyone's being rather evasive today." She changed the subject. "The boys will be home by dinnertime. Jillian's still at the house, so if you're not busy, go spend some time with her—she's having issues right now. It would also be nice if you would spend some time with me, too, or figure out your plans or something. It's so hard watching you flail about." Another quick, under-the-radar shot. Margaret plowed on as if she hadn't said anything. "OK, I need to go. The boys and I are going into an exhibit now. I'll see you tonight."

Jamie shook her head. It wasn't uncommon to hear that type of comment from her mother, but she had forgotten how jarring they were. While she was away, she told herself she wouldn't let them get to her. *Easier said than done.* As she disconnected, she tried to get her brother's attention before she left. He waved her off. She went to her car and, once inside, tried a Google search for phone numbers in Wisconsin to call while driving back to her parents' home.

Who was the author of the article she read? That might be a good place to start. Luckily, she quickly found the article again and committed the author's name to memory.

She tried to track the author back to the newspaper that had published the article but couldn't determine if the writer still worked there. Since many newspapers had reduced their reporting staff, the writer might not be at that paper anymore. Speaking into her phone, she searched for the author's name to find more recent articles. Nothing from the author in the paper or web over the past year and a half. She tried to perform a deep dive for the author's name to find the contact information. Luckily, she found a phone number on a White Pages site and jotted it down.

As she finally pulled out of the lot, she dialed the number for the author, Franklin Biermann. A female voice answered after four rings. Jamie offered a greeting, and the voice became surly and suspicious. "Who's this?"

Jamie asked to speak with the journalist about an article she found on the Internet. She pretended to be a potential employer of Rachel's and crossed her fingers that he didn't have a Google alert set up for all former article subjects.

"Hi, my name is Brittany… Marshall." She had to think quickly to find a name and blushed when she realized she had used Nick's last name. Keeping her eyes on the road, she continued her inquiry. "A young woman, Rachel Thorne, applied to work for our company. My background check on the Internet led me to an article by Mr. Biermann about her and a trial. I wanted to get more information before the interview."

The voice lost some of its edge. "Well, he wrote a lot of articles. He's not doing that anymore. He's sick and bedbound. Besides, why would he remember any details?"

Jamie recognized that this was his caregiver and that she needed a reason to let Jamie speak to him. "Well, I understand that. I just wanted to ask a few questions. I'm worried about allowing her to work with kids and babies." Jamie was winging it. "There's nothing on her record, but I saw this article. I don't want to make a mistake. The children…"

Mentioning children in danger softened the caregiver's disposition significantly. "Well, I don't know. He says he's bored. So, maybe talking with someone about his work might help him. Hold on."

Jamie heard muffled voices, and then someone picked up. "This is Franklin Biermann," a man stated in a weak voice.

Jamie quickly jumped into the reason for the call. "Good afternoon, Mr. Biermann. I'm Brittany Marshall. I'm calling about an article you wrote about a case a few years back. One woman you wrote about is interviewing for a position with my company. There doesn't seem to be anything on her record, but I performed an Internet search on her name and came up with your article. It was a case about a murder."

Franklin's voice got stronger. "So, you wanted to see what I knew about her and what her role in the case might have been?"

"I know it's been a while. If you can remember anything, it would be helpful." She'd hit traffic on the freeway and hoped he could tell her something she didn't need to write down. Her timing wasn't very good.

"My wife said that you were looking for information on Rachel Thorne. She believes that since I got sick, I'm too fragile to even think on my own. I still remember some cases I covered. I remember that case because it was weird."

"Well, I saw Rachel was a witness in a manslaughter trial."

"She was. She was supposed to testify about a young man giving a girl a drugged drink and going to make out. The girl died because of the drugs, so they charged him with her death."

"Well, that seems pretty straightforward," Jamie said.

"But…" Franklin injected.

"But, what?"

"They found the young man guilty; however, he was a football star and had an excellent shot at getting drafted by the NFL. It always seemed odd that *this* guy would drug a girl at a party. He had a spotless history before that and was *squeaky* clean. He insisted that someone gave him the drink, and the young woman took it from him. There were no witnesses to that, so it was his words against witnesses who saw him give her the cup." The man stopped to catch his breath. Jamie heard his wife make disapproving noises; she must have been hovering nearby.

"What did Rachel testify to?" Jamie didn't want to push, but it seemed like the man wanted to talk.

"She was a woman who said she saw him give the victim the cup. There was another woman too who didn't show up—disappeared or something—but there was some thought that her story would have proven intent. She got eliminated from the witness list or something." Franklin was warming up to his topic. "But no one saw him put the drug in the drink, which may be why he just got released from prison. He had weak representation and no character witnesses, so really, he got off better than you would expect with those circumstances."

Jamie sensed something else behind his words. "There seems to be something else to what you are saying," she said. "Like you think there might be more to the story. Oh yeah, do you remember the name of the other woman? I might be able to use her as a reference." Jamie thought she knew who it was, but she didn't want to give him any suggestions.

"I always thought there might be something to his story. No one ever found any trace of drugs in his car or dorm room. The police couldn't find anyone who admitted to selling it to him. So how did he get it? He was a good kid, and there were no drug contacts, phone calls, or visits that anyone knew of. Does he just manufacture it out of nowhere? He wasn't a chemist." He coughed, and she heard him take a sip of something, probably water.

"However," Jamie continued. "Was there someone who had access to a chemistry lab in that scenario?"

"Yeah, I think you get my meaning. Rachel was a scientist. Her testimony was weird, but the prosecutor had tunnel vision. That other girl was a science person as well—her name began with a T. I can't remember what it was. She also had a vague history with the football player, but that investigation didn't go anywhere. As I said, the police were aiming for the player."

Jamie gasped as the implications washed over her. "Thank you—you have been very helpful. I have one more question—you said the man just got out. What was his name?"

"Let me think. Omar. Omar Atkins. I had heard that his prison time was horrifying—that probably also helped him get released sooner." The man paused for breath. "I'm getting tired, young lady. That's all I have. Hope I was helpful."

"Thank you for your help. I hope I haven't tired you out too much."

"No, it's fine. I want to work, but since I developed stage four cancer, I spend a lot of time in bed. I've finished my chemo and radiation and just waiting for the inevitable. It was nice to chat with you and exercise my brain a bit. I hope it helped you with your interview."

"It did. Well, I'm not sure what to say. I hope you find peace." She wasn't sure how to end the conversation since the man was dying. She wanted to avoid being crude.

"Thank you. I appreciate that. It's better than saying goodbye, huh? Have a good one." He hung up.

Traffic had finally started moving. As she neared her home, Jamie dialed her sister's cell number. Jillian picked up on the second ring. Jamie could hear boys squawking in the background.

"Hi, Jamie. Hey, boys, quiet! Aunt Jamie's on the phone."

"What are you doing?" Jamie asked. "Are you at the house?"

"Not right now. The boys needed cupcakes for their holiday parties, and Mother decided she wanted some cupcakes for dessert. I just picked Anthony and Ricky up, and they rode with me to the cupcake shop. Do you have a request?"

"Lemon, strawberry, or chocolate would be ideal. Where are you going?"

"Atlanta Cupcake Factory this time, but there are several good cupcake places in town." She reprimanded her sons again. "Sorry about that. I'll check and see if any of those flavors are on the menu. By the way, I got an electronic copy of the transcript you asked for. I'll get it to you this evening."

"Thanks, sis. I found out some information myself; we can compare notes." Jamie quickly rolled through what she learned from the reporter.

"Interesting. That seems to fit what I learned, too. Hey, how is Jon? Mother told me he wouldn't tell her what was going on."

"Yeah, slashed tires and an angry woman."

"So, nothing new?"

"Same old, same old." Jamie was nearing her exit but noticed that she was almost out of gas. "I have to stop and get some gas. On second thought, buy something with salted caramel at the cupcake place."

Jillian broke into a grin. "You're always difficult, aren't you?"

33
Another Bad Decision

She hadn't filled up her car in a while. The Camaro was an old gas guzzler, so she wasn't surprised that she only got a couple of days out of the full tank Jon bought. Luckily, there was a gas station with a mini mart at the exit nearest to home.

There were few patrons when she arrived, and she immediately pulled up to a pump. Getting out of the car, she grabbed her cell phone to call Nick to give him a heads-up about her call with the reporter. Right before swiping her card, she remembered the tank was in the back, so she jumped in to adjust the car's position. After she exited the vehicle again, Jamie leaned against her car as the tank filled, dialing Nick's number. His phone went to voicemail, and she left a quick message: "Hello, it's Jamison Scott. I just wanted to update you on what I learned today about Rachel. Call me when you have a moment. Thanks." As she hung up, the gas nozzle clicked to let her know the tank was full. She finished the transaction, got back in the car, started the ignition, and changed the radio station.

Too much Christmas music, she thought. As she pulled forward, her phone rang.

Thinking it was Nick returning her call, she snatched it up from the passenger's seat, where she tossed it. But it wasn't Nick; instead, it was Tatiana.

"How did you get my number?" Jamie asked. A green Honda trying to pull up to the pump honked to get her to move. Jamie pulled up to the front of the convenience store to finish the call.

"I'm sorry to bother you. It's true, I feel better talking to you—you aren't police. I have more information, but..." Tatiana paused for effect. "You asked if I wanted to meet somewhere to talk?"

Jamie cursed herself when she remembered that tidbit. "Yeah, I said that. You can come to our house."

"*NO!* I'm so ashamed right now that I can't look your family in the eye—after all they have done for me." She paused again. She wasn't sure how much Jamie knew or suspected or how well her begging was working. "You said you wanted to help me."

Jamie thought quickly. She hadn't yet worked out all the information she had. Did she think Tatiana killed Rachel? *No*. Did she think Tatiana was involved in that drugging in Wisconsin? *Yes*. So, if she was careful, she should be fine. Besides, she was taller and stronger than Tatiana and didn't think Tatiana was suspicious.

"Since you don't want to come to my house, I can meet you in the morning. Where are you? Are you at home?"

"No. I'm sitting in the parking lot of a fast-food restaurant down the street from my house. I went for a drive to think after you and the detectives left. Are you sure you can't meet me now? It shouldn't take too long. I know you have things to do," she persisted.

Jamie exhaled but didn't back down. She wanted more time to plan before she met with her.

"I can't. The family's waiting for me. We have plans I can't miss." Lying through her teeth to avoid alienating the young woman. "First thing in the morning. We will have enough time to figure out what to do with no rush. Besides, I'll spring for breakfast."

Tatiana heard the resolve in Jamie's voice and mentally started reworking her kidnap plans. Since she had no choice, she gave the woman the name of a restaurant near her house and bare-bones directions.

"Please, don't tell anyone that you spoke to me or that we're meeting in the morning," she added, trying to sound frightened—no reason not to try to change Jamie's mind.

But it was to no avail. Jamie confirmed the time and date and disconnected. She pulled out of the gas station to get back on the road, and her sister called back.

Jillian launched into a conversation. "I got some lemon cupcakes for dessert. Mother has ice cream and sorbet. The combo sounds delicious. Are you almost home?" The boys were yelling hellos to Jamie through the phone.

"Hi, guys! That sounds wonderful. On my way," Jamie yelled back at them. "I'll wrestle you boys for a cupcake!"

The boys cheered.

Stress was getting to Tatiana. The restructuring of her already-risky plan made her movements even more difficult.

William wouldn't like the delay, either. He was sitting in the other room, waiting for her to confirm. Hopefully, he wouldn't kill her in anger. On the bright side, the delay gave her more time to come up with something with more chance of being successful. And she already had the beginnings of a plan that could do just that, but she'd need to visit the lab tonight to make it happen.

Tatiana walked into the other room to tell William about her idea but found him hanging up his cell phone. "Who are you talking to?" she asked.

William put his phone down next to him. "Are we a go with the doctor?" he asked, ignoring her question.

She sank into a chair by the door. "Well, we are a go—just in the morning."

William raised his hands and shook his head. "In the morning? How does that work?" he roared.

Tatiana winced. "It was unavoidable. But I do have an idea that might help us get this done." When William got up angrily, Tatiana internally flinched, but remained upright in the chair. She would have to play this cool if she wanted to survive. "Hear me out. This plan's risky anyway, but I may give us a way to improve our odds."

"*Why* am I listening to you? You're just stalling here. You don't have my money, and you're trying to set me up to get arrested or killed." He stood over her menacingly. She could see a vein pulsating on his forehead—she had seen that before in some of the deviant boyfriends her mother had dated when she was in high school. Tatiana realized she was a lot like her mother—self-destructive and reckless. That thought chilled her to her core, but perhaps those tendencies would help right now.

Tatiana quickly stood up but held her ground. He was almost a foot taller than she, so if he became physical, she had no recourse. Her best weapon was her mouth—she would have to talk fast.

"Why would I do that? That would get me arrested, too. Hey, you coming here has forced me to run again. I can't stay here anymore. So, just hear me out. I have just as much on the line as you do."

William relaxed and slowly returned to his seat. "Yeah, sure, why not? What's the new plan?"

Tatiana recounted the new plan. William was silent. "I have to go to the lab tonight," she continued.

"Actually, *we* have to go to the lab. Do you think I'm letting you go anywhere alone?" William asserted, then gave her a sinister look. "I also invited someone else who wants to see you. He's going to take part in our project—since it involves him as well."

Tatiana recoiled. "Who?" although she already knew.

"You'll see when we get to the lab. Excuse me." He went into the bathroom. "Don't go far," he yelled.

Fear washed over her. *Please, not him.* She grabbed her cell phone and called Marcus, praying he would answer. If William were calling in an angry, vengeful colleague, she would also have to call in backup.

Marcus answered his burner phone in a hushed tone. "Who is this?"

"It's me, Marcus. How many women have this number, huh?" she tried to joke with him to cover her discomfort.

"Aw, Tati, you know better. So, what's up? You know I'm at home, right? My wife's here."

"I know. I shouldn't call you, but I'm in a bit of trouble. Can you meet me at the lab in an hour? Tell your wife that you got called in to cover." When he didn't immediately answer, she threw in some enticement. “I’ll make it worth your while.”

“I think I can manage that. One hour, huh? You sound weird. Are you OK?”

“Just a bit wound up. You’ll help with that. See you in an hour.” She hung up quickly when William came out of the bathroom. He saw her disconnect and asked her who she was talking to.

“If you have someone coming, I will, too,” she retorted.

34
Heart-to-Heart

After the trip to the office building, Nick returned to the precinct to touch base with his partner. When the detective arrived, he found Ron seated at his desk.

"Hey, man," Nick stated as he slid into his desk chair. Ron gave him a sly glance.

"Did you see her?" he asked. "Do we need to file a report?"

"No, it ended up being a prank by someone with borderline criminal tendencies. It sounds like her brother has girl problems, but nothing to report officially to us yet," Nick answered. As he got comfortable in his seat, he checked his messages, which included a new one from Jamie. He could feel Ron looking at him; he could tell that something was weighing on the older man. Nick carefully studied Ron. "Is there something on your mind? Is Estelle OK? You never said how she was after the ER. I should have asked."

Ron shook his head. "She spent the night in the ER—she's back home now."

"Is she OK?" Nick asked again.

"Yes, and no. I've been trying to wrap my mind around it."

"Around what? Is something wrong?" Nick leaned forward in his seat.

"Nothing will ever be the same. Nick, she had been nauseous and was just not quite right for a couple of days. She didn't mention it at first because she thought it was food poisoning, but it wasn't. She's *pregnant*, Nick. We're going to have a *baby*!"

Nick put down his phone and gave him an astonished grin. "Really? I thought you two had stopped trying—"

"We had. Which is why this is a surprise," Ron smiled. "Due in June. My carefree days are over… you will have to give me some tips."

"Congratulations! I know how much you two wanted this."

"Yeah. We're excited. However, we're not spreading the news yet—Estelle's 44. We're scheduled for some testing to make sure the baby is OK. So, you're the only person we're telling for now."

"OK, I respect that. I'm so happy for you."

"Thank you. I'm worried—with our ages and all. But otherwise, it *is* exciting." Ron paused. "Back to you. Have you asked Dr. Scott out yet?"

"Hey, that relationship's strictly business."

"Uh, *no*. You've been devouring her with your eyes since you first saw her…" Alvarez and his partner, Xavier Davis, entered the squad room; the partners redirected their attention to them as they approached Ron and Nick's desks. The pawnbroker was again being difficult after almost being killed a couple of nights before. He retracted some of the information he initially provided and refused to cooperate further without witness protection. The detectives had already arranged a rotation of officers as the protection detail for the pawnbroker; however, it wasn't enough for him. Alvarez and Davis were going to follow up on a tip they received about the potential killer(s). The detectives stopped by Nick and Ron's desks on their way out.

"Buenos Tardes!" Alvarez greeted the seated detectives while Davis offered a chin tilt. Alvarez wore his customary leather jacket and a big grin. It was difficult to believe that this detective went undercover in gang territory—and blended right in. He was rather friendly.

"Isn't it time for you old heads to go home?" Davis added, giving Ron a hand dap. Davis and Ron were related to each other, although no one was clear about how.

"Hey, didn't your victim in the lab case have Wisconsin ties?" Alvarez sat on Ron's desk again. He waved a piece of paper at Ron.

"Dude, stop putting your ass on my desk!" Ron snapped grumpily and shooed him off.

"Yeah, our victim went to college there. Why?" Nick replied, ignoring the drama and standing to grab the paper from Álvarez.

"It's a small world. A bulletin just came out about a parole jumper from Wisconsin. He allegedly has relatives in the area, so an alert went out. He went to college in Madison, too," Davis noted. "Is Atlanta the new endpoint from Wisconsin?"

"Let me see that." Nick scanned the document. "I missed this alert. Who is this guy?" He hunkered down and started searching the database for information on the parole violator.

"Anyway, we came by to tell you about your friend, the pawnbroker. I *hate* him," Alvarez said. "He probably cheats at solitaire. He's been barely helpful and downright confusing. I think he believes he's worth relocation to a midwestern paradise."

"Well, I would love never to see him again. He cursed out the maid at the hotel for knocking on the door," Davis added. "We have to solve this quickly, so I won't catch a case of my own."

"We warned you…" Nick reminded them as he turned back into the computer.

Davis shook his head. "That you did." To his partner, "Let's talk to the fence again—he should be on his corner by now. Catch you later."

The men walked out.

Nick barely acknowledged their departure as he found an internet posting on the parole jumper. "Former football player from Wisconsin who was there at the same time as our victim. I wonder if they knew each other?" Nick mumbled.

"That's an incredible coincidence," Ron remarked, looking over his shoulder and then at his watch. His thought drifted back to his current situation. "I'm a father-to-be and an 'old head' now. Who would have thought?"

Nick did not reply to his partner's comments and continued mulling the information on his computer screen. "I don't know—there's something here." He leaned back in his chair. "Just weird that these people were in Wisconsin at school at the same time and all end up here in our faces," Nick added.

"Are we going to dig into this now? Is this your gut talking again?" Ron asked his partner.

"It won't take long, I promise. I can't keep the old man out too late."

35
Invitation for Chaos

Jillian arrived at her parents' house 45 minutes after she spoke to Jamie. The boys trooped out of the car, whooping and running, leaving Jillian to manage over 60 cupcakes: 24 chocolate, 24 vanilla, and 18 lemon cakes. Before she could safely arrange everything to carry it inside, Margaret came out to help. The two youngest boys came out with their grandmother and started dancing around the two women's legs.

"Thank you, Mother. My boys aren't helping! I should keep the school cupcakes, since they aren't willing to carry them!" Jillian griped.

Margaret took two boxes from her daughter. "You know you didn't want them holding those cupcakes because they would make a mess of everything!" she stated as she walked away.

Inside the front door, there was a scene of controlled mayhem. Jillian's nanny, Garcelle, was still there and was helping get the boys ready for dinner using the kitchen sink.

She had started with the younger boys, but they had just come back inside and needed to rewash their hands and faces. It was a tough chore for Garcelle because the boys were excited about the prospect of cupcakes. The two older boys decided they didn't need the nanny's help and tried to assist her and their brothers, who didn't want any help, either. The younger boys loudly protested everyone's interference.

Barely controlled mayhem.

Putting the boxes on the island in the kitchen, Jillian wearily slid into a seat at the kitchen table. Leaning back, she asked her two youngest sons about their day with their grandmother. Jacob told her about the Georgia Aquarium while Ricky tried to wash his face and Garcelle tried to referee. Water went everywhere, and Aaron climbed into his mother's lap to escape. After putting her cargo down on the island, Margaret ignored the chaos, gave Olivia some quick suggestions about dessert, and came over to the table.

"Jon just called. He's going to stay home because he said it'd been a trying day. Where is Jamie?" she asked.

Jillian stopped watching the preparations for a moment. "She should be here any minute. She told me she had one more errand to run. I don't think we should wait for her to get home before we eat, though. The boys need to eat their dinner."

The front door opened, and Gregory walked into the foyer to his grandsons' cheers; three ran to meet him at the door.

"Hello, young men! How are you?" he asked.

Each boy clamored to tell him about their days while climbing over him. With three boys attached to him, Gregory stuck his head into the kitchen, gave his wife a quick kiss, and issued a general greeting to everyone in the room. He asked, “Where is Jamison? Let me know when she gets in. I need to speak with her,” and walked into his bedroom with the three boys trailing him.

Olivia placed the dinner of pot roast, potatoes, vegetables, salad, and rolls on the island. She also placed the lemon cupcakes on a platter—the ice cream remained in the freezer—and quickly set the kitchen table. Margaret checked her watch and summoned everyone into the kitchen. Since the dining room was very formal, they only ate there on special occasions.

Gregory and the boys came in after being called; Margaret and the nanny inspected the boys’ hands again before seating them at the table. After a prayer from Gregory, Olivia transferred everything to the table, and everyone dug in. Gregory entertained the boys, and Margaret tried to get Jillian to clarify how long she was planning to stay at the Scotts’ place. Jillian adeptly avoided a commitment—only that they were staying tonight since Richard wasn’t coming back into town for another day or so. Of course, Margaret pressed the question, but Jillian shifted the discussion to Jamie to avoid the subject.

“I’ll call her. She should have been here by now.” Jillian pulled her phone out and hit redial.

Jamie answered the phone as she entered the front door. “Traffic was a beast. The cupcakes better still be there!” She quickly washed her hands, slid into an empty seat at the table, and joined her family for the meal.

The lemon cupcakes were divine.

So divine that Jamie forgot what Olivia served for dinner. And so divine she moaned when she bit into the lemony little cake, which was a little embarrassing. So divine she wanted to tackle her oldest nephew when he grabbed the last one after dinner. She needed to ask Jillian again which bakery these came from—this would be one of her go-to treats!

A stuffed Jillian leaned back in her chair and closed her eyes. The nanny rounded up the boys to get them ready for the last day of school before the holidays. Olivia started cleaning the dishes.

Gregory used that moment to speak to his eldest daughter. "I know it's only been a few days, but have you made any plans? Since you didn't come into the office today, I wanted to see where your head was."

"Really, Dad, no decisions. I've been digging into Rachel's death. But I've considered doing some half clinic days with Felice—could I split my time for a while?"

Margaret lifted an eyebrow, but before she could chime in, Gregory smiled and said, "That might be something we could work out, Jamison." He turned to Jillian. "As for you, is there a problem with your husband?"

Jillian shook her head. "Nothing serious, Dad. Richard's away, and Jamie's here. I didn't want to be at home alone."

Gregory looked as if he wanted to push the subject, but he got up and kissed her on the cheek instead. "If there's a problem, you know you can talk to us, right?" he noted. Margaret agreed grimly. There was no way Jillian would admit to a problem with her mother's opinionated eye there. The elder Scotts looked at each other and left the room together. Jamie was sure they were going to discuss their daughters and their choices.

Jamie turned her focus back to the case and asked Jillian about the trial transcript.

"Oh, my..." she groaned. "I'm so full; right now, I don't even want to think about it. I printed out parts of it for you. Can we talk about it tomorrow?" Looking at Jamie's expectant face, Jillian groaned again and got up to get the document and her laptop. Returning to the table, she gave Jamie the chief points.

"Rachel testified at the young man Omar's trial. She muddied the waters somewhat, but her overall gist was that Omar gave the dead girl the drink. *He* said that Rachel and another woman—who seemed to be Tatiana—made the drink and gave it to him *for* him to drink. He was hitting on the deceased woman at the party, so his story was that he had the drink in his hand, and she took it and drank it all. This was at a party in an apartment, so everyone was milling around and focused on themselves. No witnesses to his story, and the two women against him. The prosecutor was gunning for him."

"OK—so the story seems fishy. Anything solid deep in the transcript that lends credence to his story? Besides the obvious?"

"In one of the pretrial hearings that Tatiana appeared at, she admitted she had a relationship with Omar in the past. That should have been submitted into evidence at the trial—his defense attorney was sleeping at the wheel. And they could never determine where he got the drugs from. The two witnesses were chemistry geeks, and one had probable bad blood with the defendant. That's reasonable doubt."

"So, are we saying that the girls drugged the guy's drink, and the wrong person drank it by accident?" Jamie shook her head incredulously.

"Think about it. It's a common story—a popular football player, or any guy, hooks up with a girl. Gets bored. Wants to move on. Dumps the first girl and starts hooking up with other girls. The first girl doesn't take that well and decides that she wants to get back at him. This is the less common part—she tries to drug him at a party—perhaps to take some embarrassing pictures. Maybe she thought she could get him back in bed with her. Who knows what she was thinking?"

"But the friend drank it. She probably was significantly smaller in mass than the football player, so it's more likely an overdose. Instead of admitting what they did, they let him take the fall. In some ways, they try to give him a shove," Jamie added. "He's probably angry about that. He was a possible NFL prospect and ended up in jail."

"I would be angry about that."

"Also, the writer told me that the defendant's time in jail was difficult… but this still doesn't explain the man at the bar who spoke to Rachel. Where does he fit in?" Jamie stated, then paused, leaning forward. "On another note. I spoke to Tatiana this afternoon," she revealed, shifting the topic. "She wants to meet me in the morning to tell me her side of the story and tell me who killed Rachel. She says she knows."

Jillian shook her head. "You can't meet her by yourself. We now believe she's guilty of at least involuntary manslaughter, perjury, possibly fraud, assault—the list goes on. I don't think she wants to have a friendly chat with you."

"Look, I'm not going to drink anything around her. I'll take some pepper spray…"

"A gun," Jillian injected.

"No guns. Not fond of guns. Had them shoved in my face in Africa. No guns."

"She may try to hurt you."

"What good would that do her? Besides, we're meeting in public. And you know, I'll tell you where the meeting is. If anything happens, you can alert the authorities."

Jillian didn't like the plan because it wasn't much of one. But Jamie was sold on her idea, as she often was. Jamie had trouble standing up to their mother, but sometimes, their mother had a point about Jamie's decisions. Jillian could only hope that her sister's plan went smoothly and was not as stupid as it sounded.

36
Face-to-Face with a Ghost

Tatiana and William drove to the lab in her car. It was a silent, tense ride. Tatiana felt like someone had wrapped a vise around her chest, but as she glanced at William during the drive, he seemed perfectly calm. She couldn't understand that at all. Her apprehension only increased as they pulled into the lab's parking lot. Since it was after hours, there were few cars in the lot. However, she recognized Marcus's car and the young man in it.

Marcus exited his car as Tatiana and William exited her car. William purposefully directed her to park out of range of the security cameras. Marcus met them halfway.

"Who's this?" Both men asked at the same time.

Marcus added, "I'm not down for this kind of action. He's a bit old, don't you think?"

William glared at Marcus. Quickly, Tatiana corrected him. "This is a friend from out-of-town. I thought it would be better if I brought a security guard with me to hang out with my friend." *She knew that didn't make sense*, but thankfully, no one pushed her on it. "I need a few minutes in the lab. Do you want to stay outside or come inside with me?"

Marcus stated, "You already know the answer to that. He can't come in. I'll wait outside with him as a favor for you." He leaned over to whisper in her ear, "You tricked me into coming here. I don't know what you're into now. But you owe me!"

She would willingly repay him if they survived… Tatiana smiled at him and kissed him on the cheek. *If only it were that easy.*

She had stopped at a drugstore on the way and picked up a few items, like a bottle of water. But all the chemicals she needed were in the lab—even the heavily regulated gamma-butyrolactone. She was going to use the quicker chemical recipe for GHB because she was short on time, but as a chemist, she always enjoyed the cook. *Oh well, I just need to get the job done.*

Letting herself into the lab's front door, Tatiana waved at the security guard on duty. It was a part-timer that she didn't know by name; again, the security guard did not do their job with the sign-in sheet. "I'm going upstairs. I won't be long." He nodded at her as she walked to the elevators.

At her lab bench, she set about making a small batch of GHB using only the bare minimum of safety equipment. She had done it several times as a student and sold her concoction to some shadier classmates when her funds were low. She hadn't been proud of it, but she was a damn good chemist; things just hadn't gone her way to use that skill properly. With what happened to Bianca, she should have felt guilty mixing any more of this stuff up. And she did—a little. But not enough to stop.

The process didn't take that long, so she put the mixture in a jar and screwed the top. To cover her tracks, she also set up some glassware for a different experiment, so there would be an explanation for her presence after her shift if anyone asked. Tatiana placed the used glassware into the sterilizer, which would destroy any evidence of her work. Placing the jar in her purse, she exited the building approximately 30 minutes after she entered.

Marcus was checking his watch when she exited the building; William had directed him to wait by Tatiana's car—out of camera range. The current events continued to get more confusing to the guard. He wasn't sure about the level of danger yet, but he didn't want to do anything that might get Tatiana in trouble. He knew he wasn't enjoying himself. But the annoyance on his face wasn't what got her attention. It was the other man standing with the pair—Omar!

Dread washed over her, followed by panic. Tatiana knew Omar was who William had called, but she was surprised by how frightened she was when she saw him. She had once been crazy about this man, but his treatment of her had made her angry. She did something stupid, which ended one life, altered the course of two others, and essentially destroyed Omar's. He wasn't in football shape anymore, but he was still way larger than she was. He could rip her into shreds—and he probably wanted to—not that he wasn't justified in those feelings. Tatiana could feel the sweat running down her back under her coat. She couldn't think of anything to say since nothing would ever be enough. Having no place to run, Tatiana ambled to the group of men. She would have to face him.

Omar had spent years imagining what he would do if he ever saw Tatiana—Tati—again. It was different with her. Rachel was just someone who wronged him; he had no relationship with her before that fateful night. But he had thought Tati was cool. Not a love match, but cool. They had fun, but it wasn't going to last, and she had to have known that. And for her to throw him, wholesale, under the bus hurt a lot. Bianca probably wouldn't have lasted, either. But it was her dead face that popped up in his dreams in prison—his 'dream girl'. In addition, jail was terrible. He had tried to keep his head down, but one or two of the lifers decided he thought he was better than everyone else because he was a college boy and an NFL prospect. It was misery. Suicide was an option, but revenge had been more important. At one point, he snapped and started getting angry, fighting, taking out his rage about the shambles his life had become through no fault of his own. All of this swirled around in this mind as he prepared to see her again. He thought he might feel some compassion for the girl he once cared about. But seeing her coming out of the building, Omar felt a rush of rage. It crowded all the other feelings out.

"Hello, Tatiana. Frame anybody recently?" the former football player asked as she stopped in front of him.

Tatiana froze. She remembered how gorgeous he was just a few years ago. She thought she might have been able to slow down with him; they hooked up one weekend and then extended it for almost a month. When she thought about it now, she knew he hadn't been serious; they rarely left the bed, and he only fed her delivery pizza. But he treated her better than any of her previous conquests, so she was in love. And when he started sniffing around other women, including Bianca, she got mad. Such a beautiful man—she couldn't believe this was the same guy. Besides looking like he had lived a hard life, he looked *vacant*—like if he broke her neck like Rachel's, it wouldn't register with him.

Omar patted his front pocket. Tatiana could see the butt of a revolver sticking out. She felt her knees almost give out on her, and it was getting a little difficult to breathe. *Bad time for her first panic attack*, she thought as she tried to gather herself.

Marcus frowned at Tatiana, confusedly, and William grinned at her discomfort. "It looks like everyone doesn't know each other. Let's fix that. Get in the car." William pulled a small-caliber weapon out of his pocket and aimed it at Tatiana and Marcus.

It wasn't the first time Marcus had a gun pointed at him. But today, he was unarmed because he had been expecting a different type of encounter. *Shit.* Then he thought of his wife and kids—they did not need this kind of drama in their lives. *Stupid…* He looked over at Tatiana, who looked like a deer in headlights. She led him into this mess! *Shit—she didn't even give him a heads up… Fuck, fuck, fuck.*

Tatiana mouthed an "I'm sorry" to Marcus as he got in the car.

This was not going to plan at all.

37
For Those Who Seek Chaos

Jamie got up early to make her meeting with Tatiana. While she wasn't afraid, Jillian's comments ate at her. *Maybe she should call the detectives to tell them what she was doing.* While contemplating this decision, she could hear the boys getting ready for their last day of school before the holiday break. They sounded so happy!

Optimism for the future—she needed that. She jumped into the shower and hurriedly got dressed in a pair of jeans and a green pullover sweater. When Jamie got to her hair, she exhaled in frustration. She had barely wrapped her hair the night before, so it was in shambles. *Oh well.* She raked a comb through it and placed a clasp at her nape. She wanted to catch the boys before they left.

Her sister had gotten up while it was still dark to take some time to think about her situation before she had to deal with her sons. After getting them dressed, Jillian tried to keep the boys focused on their breakfasts and not the cupcakes they would eat at their class parties. The two younger boys kept walking over to the labeled cupcake boxes (ingredient lists for those with allergies) to peek. This was dangerous, as the cupcakes almost became casualties of small curious fingers several times.

Olivia had made biscuits, bacon, eggs, and grits, a nice Southern breakfast Jamie couldn't turn down. While her sister was eating, Jillian asked her to contact the detectives to either support her plan or talk her out of it. Sensing potential drama, Jamie agreed to make that call before she left the grounds.

Jillian continued to protest as Jamie left the house. *Why was her sister so difficult to deal with sometimes?* she thought with frustration. But she couldn't follow her out the door as there was a minor cupcake catastrophe looming and a school uniform shirt disaster occurring with the boys.

Jamison left a message for Nick as she got in her car around 7:30 am. However, she didn't wait for a reply.

Sometimes, listen to your little sister.

Given Atlanta traffic, she made good time using the side streets and pulled into the parking lot of the designated area less than 30 minutes later. The location was a store that was closed for business.

Shit, I should have looked this up, she thought. There was no one else around. *Stupid!*

The isolation of the location forced her hand. She dialed Nick's number again and left another message. Unease washed over her, her heart started to race, and her mouth got dry. She remembered this feeling—she had experienced it many times in Africa. The slow-rising panic, the heightened senses, the regret about her choices... she felt it whenever soldiers had threatened the healthcare workers for helping the wrong person. She had survived each of those encounters, but each one always felt like it would be her last one.

Why am I doing this? She thought to herself. Jamie restarted her car to retreat and reconsider her options, but then she noticed another car in the lot. The driver parked it on the side of the building and the car resembled the one that was parked outside of Tatiana's apartment the last time she was there; she also saw one person in the driver's seat. Looking around, Jamie didn't see anyone else. Sitting in her idling car, curiosity got the better of her; she parked her car and cautiously walked over, knocking on the driver's side window. Tatiana slowly lowered her window.

"Why did you pick this place? I..." Jamie asked.

However, before she could finish the thought, a man came up behind her from the back of the building and shoved a gun into her ribs.

"Don't move," he hissed in her ear as he pressed her against the car. She could feel his hot breath on her neck. She recoiled instinctively, which made him angrier. He then wrapped his arm around her neck, pulling her back toward him.

Jamie kicked herself for not checking the perimeter more carefully. Shock, regret, and fear washed across her. When she left the country four years ago, she had promised herself that she would make better decisions, and here she was again, flying by the seat of her pants into a flaming dumpster fire. But above all of that, Jamie was angry at herself and Tatiana. If she didn't get out of this, she was going to haunt Tatiana's ass until the end of time.

Jamie struggled against him—not to get free, but to get a better shot at Tatiana. She was not a fighter, but if she could have reached Tatiana at that moment, she would have done some damage. Jamie took a few wild swings that didn't reach their target.

"Stand still, bitch," William grunted. They were about the same height, and Jamie was likely in better physical shape. She was giving him a workout as he tried to keep her under control. "Stop moving, or I'll shoot," he threatened her.

Jamie ignored him in her fury, but she realized the futility of trying to reach the younger woman at that moment. But if she got a chance…

Taking a deep breath, she vented some of her anger and frustration at Tatiana. "What the hell! Did you set me up? I was just trying to help you." Her face was red, spittle flying, and she had more to say. "Just because you made a mess of your life doesn't mean you have to drag me into it! What the hell do you want from me? I am going to kick your ass!" William pulled back on her throat, causing Jamie to stop talking and struggling. However, she didn't calm down.

Tatiana refused to look at her throughout the verbal barrage and refused to respond. Exasperated, the man with the gun took over.

William said, "You can take up your issues with Miss Tatiana at another time. However, right now, we need your help. Let's talk." He pushed the gun a little harder into her ribs when she didn't immediately respond. "Get in the car," he snarled.

Finally, the fear overtook the anger, and Jamie considered how much trouble she was in. She didn't trust this man's intentions; he was disheveled, sweaty, and rattled—not good odds for her. At least she had seen guns aimed at her before. "And if I don't?" she asked, trying to sound braver than she felt. The building was deserted, and anyone passing by probably thought they were looking at an illicit sex or drug transaction. No help there. She wasn't going to escape right now, so she would have to cooperate for the time being. But if there were an opening, she would have to take it.

"I'll shoot you where you stand," William stated. "I've got nothing to lose."

"But…" she started. However, William positioned the gun at the nape of her neck, and she flinched. *Time to stop playing chicken here,* she thought.

"OK, Ooo-K. I'll get in—just be careful with that," she said in a shaky voice. William opened the driver's side rear door and directed her into the back seat. He slid in next to her, keeping the gun trained on her, and zip-tied her wrists.

William glanced at Tatiana, waiting for any response. While this was Tatiana's plan, she didn't appear happy with its execution. She seemed downright ashamed. "Damn it, Tatiana, don't wimp out on me now!" he yelled.

Jamie realized this might be an opening and tried to rein in her anger at the woman in the front seat. "Tatiana," she started. No response. "Tatiana, you don't have to do this. We can talk about this." She forced herself to keep talking, although she felt like the top of her head was going to blow off. She was seeing red.

The constant chatter only angered William. The entire situation angered him, but it was too late now. Annoyed with both women, William shouted, "Just shut up!" and hit Jamie on the back of the head with the butt of the gun. She slumped over as everything went black.

When Jamie woke up, she was no longer in the car. She was lying on an unmade bed, but she couldn't tell where the bed was. Whatever she was in was moving—*or was that her head?* She was groggy, and her head ached. The flexicuffs still cinched her hands in front of her, but now she was also blindfolded, and her ankles were bound, too. The bed smelled like sweat and booze. She could also detect a hint of marijuana in the sheets and air. She wasn't sure if it was because of her head injury or the mixture of unpleasant smells, but she was feeling kind of nauseous as she lay there.

As Jamie slowly regained her wits, she heard voices nearby—not right next to her, but in the vicinity. She couldn't tell how much time had passed. However, she realized her situation was way worse than she thought it was.

In one area, Jamie was right—they were moving. While she was unconscious, Tatiana and William met up with Marcus and Omar. With that number of people, they used Omar's RV as their getaway vehicle. Marcus and Omar transferred Jamie to the RV. William squeezed into the booth dinette table in the mobile home; Marcus slouched across from him. Omar was driving, and Tatiana followed in William's rental car.

When Tatiana devised a plan to kidnap Jamie, William included the previously incarcerated Omar. Partly to harass Tatiana, partly as muscle. Omar also had a mobile home they could use as a hiding spot until the family paid the ransom. Of course, Omar wanted a cut of the money, and Tatiana agreed to the split since she didn't want to end up dead as Rachel did. Marcus was just along for the ride as Tatiana's back-up or wingman—against his will, of course.

Omar pulled the RV into the Twin Lakes RV Park in Cummings, GA outside of metro Atlanta, and found a spot.

He had used this location as a rest stop before because they took cash payments.

At least it was out of the way, William thought.

Tatiana pulled in, located a parking space, and got out of the car, clutching her lightweight jacket close to her body. Maybe it could shield her from her poor decisions. To be honest, she had to admit she was scared. She flirted with the criminal element in the past—selling GHB, a little shoplifting, pick-pocketing—but this was moving into the big time. She didn't consider what she did to William a real crime since he bribed Rachel and Tatiana to testify and, thus, was breaking the law, too. Reluctantly, she walked over to the RV to join William in making the ransom call. Her current course of action filled her with regret; there had to have been some other way to deal with William, but she couldn't find it. She especially regretted dragging Marcus into this mess; hopefully, she could keep him from getting hurt because of her stupidity.

The three men looked up when Tatiana entered the RV.

Jamie could hear their conversation, which scared her more. The nausea had subsided a little, and she tried to focus on what their plans were. Knowing what they would do was the only way she could escape from this mess, but she knew some of them. An icy chill went up her spine at that thought.

The lead kidnappers, Tatiana and William, agreed to make the call/text at 1 P.M. to give the Scotts time to get to the bank to get the ransom (they thought). But that was as far as the plan went. Jamie shuddered to herself—this 'plan' did not bode well for her. It was nerve-wracking that these kidnappers were not attempting to hide their identities from their victim. It made it less likely that she would get out alive.

She kicked herself again for not listening to her sister or even thinking before she acted. Jamie thought back to when she first met Zach, the photographer, when she was 15, in New York City. She went to his apartment with him the first night they met, which was foolish since he was twice her age. That night, she got drunk, smoked some weed, and hopped into bed without a care in the world and with no protection. She rectified that situation soon enough, but it still amazed her to think of how reckless she was then. But then, she thought, she still exhibited reckless tendencies today.

If I get out of this, I have to do better.

As the men expected her to advise them on the plan, Tatiana clarified the fact that she was winging it. "I'm not sure this is a good idea anymore. I welcome any suggestions," she stated, sitting down heavily.

William replied incredulously, "This was your idea and your plan. I'll repeat–I'm not going to jail."

Marcus shook his head in amazement. First, he couldn't believe how half-cocked these 'masterminds' were. They completed the kidnapping portion of the program and did not know what to do next. Second, he couldn't believe he was stuck in the middle of their dangerous ridiculousness—all in the name of sex. *Perhaps cheating wasn't a good thing.* Third, he had been so easily duped by the easy sex that he missed Tatiana was *nutty.* Finally, he was sure that his wife was frantic by now. He had called last night to tell her that there was an emergency at work, so he wouldn't be home overnight. She was probably calling his phone—which William had discarded—and getting worried. *This needed to end soon.*

Omar scoffed. "Odd how that's a concern now. It was no shit when it was my ass going to jail!"

William stood behind Omar and gingerly put his hand on his shoulder. "I've apologized for that mistake. Hopefully, this money will help you get over the wrong that was done to both of us." William pointed at Tatiana. "Has she apologized to you?"

Tatiana swallowed hard. Of course, he would try to make this as uncomfortable as possible. "I would like to apologize..." she started timidly at Omar's back.

Omar whirled around. "Apologies?" he roared. "Four years gone. I'm a felon, football career gone, body destroyed... Yeah, that apology would be *OH-SO* helpful." He took a deep breath, and a sinister grin inched across his face as he reached out and grabbed her arm. "It didn't help your friend. She tried to apologize, too."

Tatiana gulped but tried not to show her fear. "I'm going to get you that money. Let me think about this." Snatching her arm away, she swiftly moved out of range. She had always been impulsive, but smart enough to think her way out of most situations. This time, she might be able to make that happen. She just needed to *think*.

Omar, however, was still angry about the lies that sent him to jail, killed his chance to play professional football, and set him up for some atrocities in prison. Atrocities he had told no one the full extent of. This bitch—both actually—lied on him when it was their ridiculous "prank" that started everything. They had been trying to drug him because he had hooked up with Tatiana at one point but then moved on to other women. Rachel and Tatiana got even with him and shit just spiraled from there. He had hit on Bianca—partly to make Tatiana angry and partly because she was pretty. Every day, he wished he had drunk that cup of punch. He was being chivalrous that night, and it cost that girl her life.

He listened as Tatiana and William debated the ransom amount—between $1 to $2 million. They figured the number should be an amount the family could raise quickly; while the Scotts were worth more, the pair was sure that most of their wealth was inaccessible quickly. However, no amount of money would make up for all that Omar had lost. In reality, the money wasn't important, but he liked the fact that Tatiana would have to appease him. Rachel offered him some money the night of her death, but he lost control when she started talking and shifting the blame for what happened to him. After his release, his psychiatrist told him he had anger management issues from being in prison. He didn't like his medications and didn't like his doctor. In a guilt-filled panic, he reached out to Bianca's father, William, to clear the air about his daughter's death when he first got out of prison.

Hearing the full story enraged William—both women extracted money from him for their testimony; William had wanted to send Omar up for the rest of his life. Bianca was his only child, and while she had insisted on being independent, William spoke to her every Sunday on the phone. But after one careless night, it was all over. He wanted revenge… that's where Rachel and Tatiana came in. He was easily suckered, filled with numbness, anger, and weariness from caring for his ailing mother. She died one month after the trial, and William believed that sorrow over her beloved granddaughter's death sped her own along.

He took money from his retirement savings to ensure those liars got on the stand. It was illegal and stupid, and he didn't even get his money's worth. He paid for lies and avoidance. After Omar contacted him and told him the full story, he felt duped. It didn't take him long to track down Rachel—she was active on social media. Tatiana was harder to find—she had lived cash-only for the last five years. To his surprise, after shadowing Rachel for a few months, he found Tatiana working with Rachel, and both were living as if nothing had happened. Like they hadn't caused a girl's death, sent someone else to jail for it, and took his money to boot. To help in his quest, once he moved to Atlanta, William contacted Omar to update him. Omar had reached out to him when he got out of prison, so they had formed an uneasy alliance. William had also played a part in ruining the young man's life—even if it was by accident. Omar then skipped parole and traveled to Atlanta to help.

Tatiana could feel the resentment and hate oozing off both men. After the ransom debate with William, Tatiana curled up on the small couch across from the dinette. She avoided eye contact with the other people in the RV, since everyone hated her guts right now. Tatiana used the time to map out a workable plan--a proper plan that allowed her to get away. Hopefully, this ransom would get everyone off her back, so she could disappear again—this time to some island. Looking back at their victim lying quietly on the bed in the back of the RV, Tatiana now regretted involving her; she seemed like a nice enough person. Unfortunately for her, Jamison was the only person Tatiana could think of that could generate some quick cash that would make everyone happy. Another sad fact: she didn't think these trigger-happy men would let Jamie live. Tatiana was also walking a tightrope to see if she would survive. She glanced at Marcus, who was an unwilling participant—*more guilt*—he had kids!

At this point, everyone had retreated to their own thoughts; it was tense and silent in the RV while everyone waited for the 1 P.M. call/text. Thirty minutes before the call, the duo left Omar and Marcus with Jamie during the ransom call. Leaving Omar with anyone was risky, but Marcus might buffer Omar's anger issues. Tatiana couldn't be left alone with Omar. Omar was too angry.

In her gut, Tatiana knew this plan would not go well.

38
Incommunicado

Margaret came out of her suite to find Jillian sitting alone at the kitchen table mid-morning. Her daughter was lost in thought and sipping a cup of coffee. With Jillian's extended visit, Margaret suspected there was an issue with her daughter's marriage. Jillian wasn't ready to talk about it yet, but Margaret planned to nag it out of her. She slid into a chair across from her youngest daughter.

"Good morning, dear—are all the boys off to school already?" she asked as she settled in.

Jillian jumped when she heard her mother's voice. She had intended to retreat to her room before her mother could catch her and ask more questions. But it was so nice and quiet that she lost track of time.

Damn, too late...

"Hi, Mother. Yes, the boys are gone, but they'll be back by lunchtime—school for everyone is only half-day today." She took a last sip of her coffee and tried to stand up to escape. "I have a few things to take care of before they come home…" she said, turning to leave.

Margaret expected that move and nipped it in the bud. "Before you go, what's going on with you? I know you said that your husband's out of town, and that's why you are here. But I know something else is going on. I expect you to tell me now."

Jillian exhaled noisily. "Mother, there's nothing wrong!"

"Are you getting a divorce? You know that's unacceptable."

Jillian shook her head. "No, Mother. We are *not* getting a divorce. If you must know, since my kids are getting older, I'm planning for my future. I am finished having babies, so I want to find out what's next. Richard and I may not agree on that…"

Margaret's mouth dropped open. "You want to go to law school, don't you?" she asked incredulously. After no response from Jillian, the older woman shook her head sadly. "I told you to finish school first… I love my grandbabies, but I knew this was going to happen," she stated mournfully.

Jillian sighed. She didn't want to get into this right now. Her mother would browbeat her about her choices, and she didn't want to hear it. Trying to change the subject, she interjected, "I need to call Jamie to see if she called the cute detective this morning."

Margaret was not to be deterred from her original task, but the mention of Jamie and that detective piqued her interest. "Why is Jamison calling him?" she asked archly.

"Jamie set up a meeting with Tatiana this morning. She thinks Tatiana's in trouble, so she wants to help. I told her to call the detectives before she went, but I don't know if she did…"

"Why did you let her go?" Margaret complained. "I never liked that woman—carrying on with the security guard… He's married. She should have more pride!"

Jillian smirked at her mother. "Tatiana's having an affair? How do you know this?" she asked.

"Dear, there's little that I don't know about in that building. It's my job. But that's not important right now. Where did Jamie meet this woman? What time?" Margaret, who rarely showed vulnerability, felt a knot form in the pit of her stomach. This had only happened to her once or twice in her life—the most recent was when she lost her first baby 35 years ago. She needed to find Jamison… *now*. As Margaret grilled her other daughter about Jamie's whereabouts, she pulled her cell phone out of her pocket to call her. "I can't believe you let her go," Margaret mumbled again as she dialed. Bad things were happening, especially if Tatiana was involved!

The phone rang and went to voice mail. Margaret dialed again.

With no answer, she then called Jonathan. After multiple rings, Jonathan answered, sounding a bit out of breath.

"Hi, son. I hate to bother you," Margaret started, while trying to maintain her calm. "Hey, why are you still at home?"

Jon stammered and answered, "Just… um… took a personal… uh… day."

Margaret rolled her eyes but continued, "Have you spoken to Jamison this morning? Do you know where she went? Jillian says she had a meeting."

"Uh, no. She didn't… uh… have any plans that I know of. Hold… on." Margaret could hear some rustling and a female voice. "Sorry about that, Mother. I'm not sure where she is. Do you need me to come over?"

Margaret was incredulous. This boy has no sense at all. She pounced on her son. "That better not be that girl that has been calling this house! The one messing with you?" The silence at the other end proved Margaret's assumption. "Boy, have you not learned yet? If you want her to go away, you need to stay away from her." She tsked-tsked and exhaled angrily. "Shouldn't you be at work?" she asked.

"I have a late meeting…" he mumbled.

"Typical…" Margaret fussed.

Jillian heard her mother's side of the conversation and shook her head. Jonathan was a sucker—all a woman had to do was to flash a thong, and he would forgive many sins. Hopefully, that wouldn't come back to bite him one day.

"You'll learn one day," Margaret continued. "Back to your sister. I'm going to call a few people to see if anyone has heard from her. I'll call you back." She paused. "And please, be careful." She disconnected, worried about her son's weakness for sexy, dangerous women and her older daughter's lack of foresight. *These children…*

"Had he heard anything?" Jillian asked. Margaret's attitude caused some reconsideration of her previous behavior toward her sister. *I should have made her call before she left,* she thought.

"No, he hasn't heard from her, but he's been busy."

Jillian raised an eyebrow at her mother's expression. "I'll bet. Please, say it was Isabella," she pleaded with her mother.

Margaret shook her head. "He spent the night with that girl, Rena…"

"Rena? After she sl…" Jillian caught herself. "After all the unnecessary phone calls?" she finished lamely.

"You can't fool me. I know this girl did something to his car yesterday. Whatever that was did not supersede her charms." Margaret crossed her arms. "I'm not sure what happened with him. He's a good man, but any pretty woman can distract him, and he has shown that he's unable to make reasonable choices for companionship. I worry that he's going to end up in a fatal attraction scenario."

Jillian sank back down next to her mother, silent because she had the same concerns for her brother as much as she would love to deny it. "Can't worry about him right now. He'll be OK. One day, he'll grow up. But Jamie…"

"I have a bad feeling, Jillian. We need to find your sister."

Starting the search required a few phone calls to Jamie's friends in town that she had contacted since her return. That was a small group—only one, Felice—at this point.

"Let me call Felice," Margaret noted. After a quick conversation with the woman, Margaret hung up. "She hasn't spoken to Jamie since Monday night."

"Who else has Jamie spoken to since she returned? Eddie?" Jillian asked.

"I can call him, but I don't think she talked to him outside of the party. He's married with a kid now. She seems to have another fish on the hook," Margaret stated, meaning Nick.

"Well, call that other fish. She was supposed to call him about this meeting. And if not, at least he's police," Jillian noted.

Gregory came into the room at that moment. While he had already dressed for work, he didn't appear to be planning to leave yet. He was already late for the office. "Have you found Jamison?" he asked.

It surprised the two women that Gregory was aware of their concerns.

"Stop treating me like a dim old man. I know when something's wrong. Please, keep me in the loop. I want to know upfront if there's something I should be worried about." There was a tinge of anger in his voice, which usually only appeared when he felt that his headstrong wife was hiding something from him.

Margaret heard the tone and acknowledged his comment. She and Gregory didn't fight often; most times, Gregory allowed her to have her way. However, occasionally, she hid something about his kids from him—like when Jamie got pregnant or when Jillian was having an affair with Richard. Those occasions didn't bode well for their relationship; the one with Jamison almost caused an irreparable rift that took time to resolve. While Margaret was strong-willed, she was careful not to destroy her marriage: she loved Gregory after all. "I will, dear," Margaret replied with a wee smile.

Gregory tipped his head to them and returned to his study to make a few work-related calls.

Margaret scrolled through her phone history to find the detective's phone number and placed the device on speaker. As she dialed, Jillian called Jamie's phone again, which continued to go to voice mail. Nick, however, answered on the first ring. "Marshall here," he stated.

"Hello, Detective Marshall. This is Margaret Scott. I'm sorry to bother you—and this might be presumptuous—but have you heard from my daughter recently?"

"She called me earlier, but I missed her calls. I called her back, and she never answered. Do you know what she wanted?" Nick asked.

Jillian bit her lip to prevent the obvious silly retort that rose to her lips, since her mother looked like she was having a mild stroke. It unsettled Jillian to see her mother scared. To help her mother, she took the lead in the conversation.

"Hi, Detective Marshall. This is Jillian. Jamie probably called you to tell you what we learned about Rachel and Tatiana." She wheeled through what Jamie told her—some of which the detective already knew—and added that she got the trial transcripts herself. Jillian also added that Jamie went to chat with Tatiana.

Margaret struggled to control her rising panic. She rose from the chair and stood uncertainly behind it. As Jillian relayed the info to Nick, she watched as her mother changed into a different woman. Margaret's hands were trembling, and she was on the verge of tears. Jillian was stunned but had to pull herself back to the phone call.

Nick listened to Jillian's story. "Nice work. However, before you get too smug, you and your sister should have called me. I'm the one investigating this case! We had pieced together some details, but you have filled in the gaps. I hope this doesn't bite us all in the ass. Excuse my language, Mrs. Scott." Nick paused. "Perhaps you two should be private detectives."

Jillian exhaled. "Sorry. This just came together in the past day or so…"

Nick continued over her, "We'll deal with that later. OK, so Rachel and Tatiana were involved in this old court case. You said that the young man just got out of jail. Perhaps he's who we're looking for, and maybe why Tatiana doesn't want to talk. Have you called Tatiana? She and Jamie seemed to have some camaraderie yesterday. Do you have her number?" With her negative response, he added that phone call to his queue. "I would love to read that transcript. Do you mind if I come over now? Also, I can't officially search for Jamie yet, but I can go through a few unofficial channels, like the hunt for her car."

"That would be great!" Jillian said gratefully.

"I'm on my way."

After the phone call with no fresh news of Jamie's whereabouts, Margaret started pacing around the kitchen, wringing her hands. She was having a flashback to the loss of her firstborn son. I*t was too much…* Her voice rose an octave, and a tear or two rolled down her cheek. "You two were digging into things you did *not* understand. I hope this *felon* didn't find your sister."

"Mother, don't worry. She's probably fine. She's driving that old decrepit car, so she's probably on the side of the road with a dead phone." Jillian tried to calm her mother down, to no avail.

As she got more agitated and her imagination started working overtime, Margaret called out for Gregory. Surprisingly, he heard her—or maybe he sensed her—and entered the kitchen, wrapping his wife into his arms without a word.

39
Clues from the Past

When Nick pulled up to the front of the house 30 minutes later, he ran into Jonathan walking up the driveway. Before he arrived, Nick put out an unofficial BOLO for Jamie's car; he pulled the information from the Department of Motor Vehicles database and was still waiting to hear some news. He also called Tatiana's number, but there was no response or GPS location.

"I didn't know you were coming by," Nick noted as he and Jonathan shook hands. Jonathan was self-conscious, which Nick recognized as the male version of the 'walk of shame'. While curious, Nick wasn't going to inquire without encouragement.

"I wasn't planning to, but my mother called me about Jamie. She sounded upset, so here I am," Jonathan replied, pushing his hands into his pockets. "Besides, I needed to get out of the house. Nothing good happens when you impulsively call in sick."

"Girl troubles?" Nick grinned, then gave Jon the side-eye. "Not the same one that sent you the stuffed bird?"

Jon hung his head. "I don't know. I mean, I know better, but she came over to apologize—in only a trench coat—and there it was."

"Well. As a police officer, I suggest you don't encourage someone who seems unstable. Slashed tires, threatening your pets? The sex can't be that good," Nick stated as they hit the front door.

Jonathan gave him a smirk and said, "It is."

Nick snorted and shook his head. "It's *your* ass. I'll pick her up when she burns down your house or takes a shot at you. Take my advice because I've seen this before: walk away," he finished as Jillian met them in the foyer. She was more stressed because there was still no answer from Jamie; Jonathan hugged her.

She whispered in his ear, "I see you pried yourself away from Rena. It's not going to end well."

Jonathan dropped his head again. "It's stupid, I know. She came over to apologize for fucking up my tires. I don't know what happened—it's so hard to say no. I'm done for real now. Promise," he replied plaintively.

Jillian disengaged from her brother and acknowledged Nick's presence. "Steel yourself. Mother has turned into a crying, angry bear or something that should be soft and cuddly but can slash your face off," she warned them as they entered the living room. "Mind what you say."

By the time the two men arrived at the house, Margaret was a pissed-off, wired bundle of nerves, and Gregory was a stoic mess. Gregory looked like he had aged 10 years during the morning, but Margaret looked like she could bite everyone's head off—with tears running down her face. She was angry at Jamison for going, Jillian and the police for letting her go (even if they didn't know about the meeting), Jonathan for entertaining that girl, and Tatiana for who knows what. When angry and upset, Margaret was not to be toyed with. Jillian worked to keep both her parents calm while managing her own rising sense of terror. They had all moved to the living room, with each person calling Jamie's phone repeatedly—even if it seemed futile.

Nick walked straight over to Gregory and Margaret while Jillian continued into the kitchen. Margaret's weary appearance was a surprise to him. Typically, she was very regal and composed, and to Nick, she seemed worried before there was any reason to be. Before he could ask, Jillian returned with the transcript information in hand. Jonathan joined the pair to hear what was going on.

"This is impressive," Nick replied as he flipped through a few pages. "It would have taken me more than one day to get this. I had been digging into Tatiana's and Rachel's past lives and ran across a mention of Omar and his parole jumping, but I hadn't quite put all the pieces together."

"It pays to have connections in the legal world. This trial was a horror show. If I were the defendant, I might have been angry upon my release, too," Jillian told him. When she skimmed the case's transcripts, as a future lawyer, she found the evolution of the trial worrisome. There were definite holes in the prosecution's case that any competent defense attorney should have been able to highlight. Everyone was operating under the assumption that the young man was guilty, including his attorney. She saw a mention of a relative of the victim: an older man who testified but seemed to have nothing to add because he had no knowledge about the case. *The defense attorney should have objected to his testimony*, Jillian thought. It was only prejudicial.

Jillian parked herself on the living room couch and gestured for Nick to join her; Jonathan sat on the arm of the couch to listen. Margaret and Gregory remained where they were and murmured comforting words to each other.

"Let me show you something before my kids return," she said, taking the transcript and flipping to a specific section. It was a passage of testimony from a preliminary hearing; she showed him the area he needed to read. In the text, Rachel noted she made the drink in question for the young man. She backtracked in her next statements, but the truth was right there on the page.

She made the drink that the girl drank and OD'ed on? How the hell did that get overlooked? Nick raised his eyebrows and cast a glance at Jillian. She understood what he was thinking and pointed to another section. Quickly scanning through the pages, Nick saw Tatiana's name, but she hadn't testified at the trial. She was a participant in the entire shenanigans, and there had been a subpoena, then a bench warrant out for her at the time to compel her testimony. She didn't testify, so the warrant could still be active somewhere.

After seeing Jillian and Nick's in-depth conversation, Margaret and Gregory came to stand in front of them. They were figuring out something important—maybe even her daughter's whereabouts. But they weren't sharing. The woman began tapping her toe impatiently, then turned to her husband and looked at him plaintively. Gregory tried to calm her by holding up his hand, but Margaret had had enough.

"What do you see? *What*?" Margaret shrieked, watching the pair intently.

Jonathan, Jillian, and Gregory's heads all turned incredulously to Margaret. *Shrieked?*

No one had ever heard Margaret make such a sound before. Realizing what she had done, Margaret covered her mouth with her hands, shoulders heaving. Gregory enfolded her in his arms.

Her children were in shock. Neither had ever seen their mother cry.

Nick could sense Margaret crying in the background, but he refused to acknowledge it. He and Jillian were on the verge of some type of breakthrough, and he didn't want to stop the flow. "How did Tatiana avoid testifying?" Nick asked. Nick's question pulled her back to the transcript and the questions about the long-ago trial.

"And how did she get hired at the lab with an outstanding warrant—no matter how old?" Jillian replied.

"We'll have to figure that out," Nick added. Jonathan had been watching his mother, who was still in her husband's arms; he wanted the answer to Jillian's question, too, but he didn't want to upset his mother further. Once her tears had decreased to sniffles, Jonathan held his hand out for the transcript to read through it for himself.

To the room at large, Nick asked, "Jamie hasn't called anyone back yet?"

Everyone shook their heads. Piecing together what he had just learned, and the planned meeting between Jamie and Tatiana, he felt trouble in his gut. He pulled out his cell and called his partner.

"Hey, Ron. I'm over at the Scott House. Hilarious. I have a bad feeling about the status of Dr. Jamison Scott. She had a meeting with Tatiana Daniels this morning and hasn't checked back in yet." Margaret whimpered a bit in the background as she paced again. The weeping also restarted at this point.

On that note, Nick walked out of the living room and into the foyer to give Ron a quick rundown of the previous court case. "*Shit*. Why would Tatiana hurt Dr. Scott? If we suspect that this Omar character killed Rachel—why would Tatiana even be dealing with him? He might kill her, too," Ron asked as he slid his gun into his holster and started toward his lieutenant's office.

"We're still missing some pieces, but I'm sure Dr. Scott stumbled into an old mess. Send a squad car over to Tatiana's home and tear it up. There's an old bench warrant out for her in Madison, Wisconsin. Find it and use it. Track her phone." Nick instructed his partner.

Ron could hear the intensity in his voice. "Got it. I will also get the lieutenant to contact the FBI. We can't legally track Jamison's phone yet—she's not officially missing, and we have no actual evidence that something is wrong. Just hunches. Never will get a warrant. Does she have a GPS locator service on her phone? Her parents can log into that."

Nick leaned back into the room and relayed that question to the family. Gregory and Margaret did not know but seemed hopeful at the suggestion. However, Jonathan shook his head.

"She probably hasn't yet. She purposely had all GPS services disabled because she didn't want anyone to locate her. I thought she should register while she was in Africa, but remember, she was trying to get away from everyone," he added.

"Doesn't have it, Ron. Let's check the BOLO on her car." He walked back out of the room.

At that moment, a gaggle of boys arrived at the front door. Jillian panicked because she had been so preoccupied with her mother, father, and sister that she didn't make a lunch plan for the boys. Jonathan jumped up and opened the door for the nanny and the loud boys; he shepherded them to the game room upstairs. They didn't have to come into the living room and get scared by the gloomy mood of their grandparents.

Jillian excused herself from the living room and raced to the kitchen. Fortunately for Jillian, Olivia had already started making sandwiches. Jillian thanked her for her quick thinking. The housekeeper, who had been listening to the conversations in the next room, told her to take care of her mother. She and Garcelle would manage the boys until they found Jamie. Jillian hugged her to say thanks and headed back toward the living room.

She ran into Nick, who was also returning to the living room. Both could hear the signal for a text message on someone's phone. When they reached the doorway, Margaret had stopped crying but was wordlessly looking at her husband's phone over his shoulder. There was a text message on Gregory's phone:

Two million dollars for your daughter. Will call in sixty minutes with drop details. Do not contact the police, the message read.

40
Hapless Criminal Elements

The kidnapping trio (and Marcus) kept Jamie on the hard bed in the RV. It felt like it had stilts instead of mattress springs. She finally rolled over onto her side after several painful attempts. The springs had little give and were almost poking through the thin mattress, making it incredibly uncomfortable. Plus, the rocking motion she used to generate the force to roll made her head hurt more. She couldn't tell who was still in the vehicle with her. Whoever remained in the trailer was listening to music; she could faintly hear the beat. She tried to get her captor's attention.

"Hello?!? Hello?!?" Jamie yelled with a minimal response from the person or persons in the trailer.

Omar had remained in the driver's seat once William and Tatiana left to make the ransom text. He tried to focus his attention on his music—he didn't want to acknowledge the kidnapped woman at all. Music had been a distraction in prison: soothing arias, peaceful concertos, music to calm the soul. Although he was currently listening to calming music, he kept his gun nearby. Marcus sat quietly and watched the pair's actions, trying not to draw Omar's attention since he seemed to have a hair trigger.

Jamie tried again. "Hello? Why are you doing this? Please, talk to me."

Omar exhaled loudly and turned his music up to drown her out. Her whining was interfering with his solace. Hearing the increased volume, Jamie realized he was trying to ignore her.

"Hey, sir. I'm sure that my family will pay. What do you want?" Jamie asked again.

So many words… Omar thought. She kept talking, and Omar didn't want to physically gag her, but he might have to. "Please, shut up!" he growled and turned back to his music.

Talking to this captor wasn't working. Jamie then tried to maneuver herself into a sitting position. However, she was too close to the edge of the small mattress, so she ended up on the floor, face down, with a thump. The floor was covered with a rough shag material that smelled like urine, which was nauseating. She was wedged between the bed and an internal wall and couldn't get back up alone.

"Help!" she begged, lifting her head weakly. "I'm stuck!"

Marcus and Omar heard the thump and thrashing around as Jamie tried to get up with her hands and feet bound. Omar paused his music and looked back exasperatedly at the woman. On the other hand, Marcus got up and worked his way down the trailer to stand over her. Jamie could sense someone's presence, but she couldn't see who it was: was it Omar? Hopeful, she lifted her head in his direction as far as she could.

"Let me help you up." Marcus stepped over her, placed his feet on either side of her legs, and hooked his hands under her armpits, pulling her up to her knees. With another lift, he pulled her to her feet. She could tell whoever was helping her was shorter than her and strong enough to pull her up into a standing position from the floor. He turned her slightly and pushed her backward on the bed. She ended up closer to a sitting position, leaning against the headboard. To her surprise, the man huddled beside her and leaned in to whisper in her ear.

"Dr. Scott, it's me, Marcus, from the lab. I would take your blindfold off, but he's got a gun," Marcus whispered in a hurry.

"Marcus, the security guard? Why are you here?" Jamie whispered back at him, getting angry again. *How dare he be involved?* she thought.

"Hey. I got forced into this." He shook his head and watched Omar, who was monitoring their conversation with interest. "I was just going to hook up with Tatiana, and here I am."

"Hey! Stop talking! This is not a dating service," Omar growled, spinning the driver's seat around and taking his headphones off. "I have no problems using my gun because I don't care about either of you. I already killed Rachel—what's one more?" He stood up. "Man, get your ass back up here!" he added menacingly, holding up his gun.

Marcus jumped up, leaving Jamie alone on the mattress.

Jamie took several deep breaths to calm herself. After the fall, her arms were sore, and she had scraped one of her knees. Although she was near tears again, she promised herself she wasn't going to cry. Crying made it too difficult to keep her ears open so she could find a way out of this dilemma. At least Marcus sounded almost as frightened as she felt. Perhaps he could help her get free at some point? But how he got involved was more worrying: *the kidnappers were so disorganized that they just brought anyone along?* Didn't bode well for either of them.

William and Tatiana sent the initial ransom text from a burner phone about 20 minutes away from the location of the trailer. Tatiana had parked herself quietly at his side during the process itself. Once William finished and handed the phone to her, Tatiana removed the battery from the burner and noted, "Cash is easier to trace. We'll get caught. I have an account where we can have the ransom wired. But we can leave the country and meet up after the heat has gone down."

William scoffed. "Cash only. Do you think I would allow the money to be wired into your account and have you vanish with the money? We need to come up with a plan that'll keep us all out of jail." He turned to consider her. "At least, me and you out of jail. I think jail might be the best place for our friend. He's furious," he added.

Tatiana got defensive. "I thought he was your friend, too. You brought him along," she retorted.

William swallowed hard. He knew he had established a deal with Omar, but—hey, he didn't owe him anything. "I wanted him punished when I thought he killed my daughter. Now, I feel sorry for him since he didn't do anything wrong," he glowered pointedly at Tatiana, who, to her credit, blushed. "However, prison wasn't kind to him, and I wouldn't put it past him to kill both of us afterward, keep the money, and disappear."

That sent a chill up her spine. "I can't be alone with him, you know. He hates me," she moaned.

"Well, do you blame him? Your actions and lies ruined his life… and mine."

"I know that. I would change it if I could." Tears welled up in her eyes, but she tamped them down. "But I can't. All I can do is try to get this money for you. I don't want to end up like Rachel," Tatiana added.

"Understood. But I can't control him."

Recognizing that to be true, Tatiana changed the subject. "It would be easier to have the ransom wired to an account." She paused. "My account is in a non-extradition country under a different name opened by an attorney. I used it when you gave me that money—before," she ended haltingly. William surveyed her from head to toe; she wilted under his glare but continued. "If we must get cash, we will need to use someone else to pick up the money. Can we use Omar? Can we trust him?"

"Bad idea. I'm sure they've found out about your history and that of Rachel's by now and have uncovered your association with Omar. I'm sure they have a mugshot of him. Besides, I said he would take the money."

"Oh, I didn't think they would have figured that out by now," Tatiana stated meekly.

"You planned a meeting with this woman before we kidnapped her. They are probably tearing your apartment apart." William kept his voice even, but inside, he knew how stupid their current situation was. If he didn't know better, he would have guessed that Tatiana had set him up so he could take the fall. She couldn't know he was just as scared.

She put her head in her hands. "I need to think. I still think we need to get the ransom electronically," she repeated.

William started reiterating his refusal, and Tatiana interrupted him. "OK. How about diamonds? Bonds?" She was waving her hands anxiously as she spoke. "Either way, we don't have anyone to collect the ransom."

The idea of diamonds piqued William's interest. "Do you think we can get diamonds that quickly?" he asked.

"Perhaps."

"That wouldn't be too bad. But we must get out of here by tomorrow—on to our new lives. They don't know about me, so my vanishing won't be so hard." He picked the burner phone up again. "We'll have to do something with our hostage back there."

"Yeah, we let her go," she stated.

"Not so fast. She can ID all of us. We need to get rid of her as well. Omar would do that for us. It might work out some of his aggression until you can get away. It's something to consider," William uttered, to the astonishment of Tatiana.

Kill the hostage? Of a myriad of bad ideas, that was the worst. "This entire thing was a bad idea," Tatiana moaned, closing her eyes with regret for all her recent life choices. "We can't get the money without getting caught. Omar wants to kill me. Hell, you probably want to kill me, too," she said.

William ignored her.

That's not a good sign, she thought. "Maybe we should call this off?" she suggested.

William shook his head. "This was *your* idea," he stated. "Let's just set up a drop, use Omar as a decoy, and see what happens."

41
Manhunt

After rereading the ransom message, Gregory threw his phone down in disgust. Margaret's eyes welled up as she willed herself not to break down again. Jillian ran over to her father and hugged him.

Nick walked over and picked up the discarded phone while dialing the precinct on his phone. Jonathan grabbed his mother's hand as Margaret tried to maintain control. She had just gotten her daughter back home, and now she may have lost her for *good*?

"Daddy, what's happening? Is Jamie going to be alright?" Jillian asked with tears in her eyes. This amount and range of emotion from both parents was frightening, since they were typically very stoic.

"We received a ransom text," Gregory stated weakly, knocking a couple of books off an end table. "I can't believe I was so wrong about that woman…"

Margaret sniffled. "Not just you. I knew she was up to no good. I should have fired her then." In desperation, she tried to call Jamie's phone again, to no avail.

After calling his lieutenant to update him, Nick looped his partner Ron in again—Ron was already on his way over. He had also passed the phone number from the text from the kidnappers on to Ron. He also called the computer technicians at the police station to track Jamie's phone.

"This text probably came from a burner phone," Nick noted to the family. "However, Ron's going to have one guy in the department do a trace on the number anyway and the cell towers it bounced from. Also, I'm going to suggest you download this app to your phone to allow someone to monitor any phone calls from the kidnapper. We can legally set up a trace with this ransom text, but this app is faster." Gregory and Margaret agreed as they both downloaded the spy app to their phones.

Time ticked away as the Scott family stood by helplessly as police detectives and CSU technicians set up equipment before the actual ransom call. Two detectives asked Margaret which room was Jamie's and went through it. Ron arrived with one of the computer techs 30 minutes after the initial contact; the computer tech took over the technical aspects of managing the phones. The other computer tech joined the detectives in Jamie's room to get any computers or tablets in her room. Several FBI agents had arrived to coordinate with the Atlanta detectives.

Ron updated all the detectives on the search for Jamie's car, which the police spotted in an abandoned restaurant parking lot near Tatiana's home. Upon hearing this news, Gregory dropped his head in agony, and Margaret muffled a gasp. Ron also had news about the location of

Jamie's phone; the technicians found her phone near her car, unfortunately. They dispatched a squad car to that location to secure the car and get the actual location of the phone, and a CSU team searched the car for clues.

"Tatiana's involved in this kidnapping," Ron added as he ended his report. "The officers are tearing her apartment up. There's a suitcase packed, but otherwise, there's nothing that points out what the plan was. Nothing on email, and we are waiting for her phone logs. They are still looking."

Nick continued that train of thought. "How long has she been planning this? And who is she working with?" he asked.

Gregory piped in. "How do you know she's working with someone?"

Ron chimed in, "Sir, it's unlikely one woman who's significantly shorter and smaller could easily take your daughter alone. Tatiana probably had help." Ron thought about adding that a weapon would have made capturing Jamie much easier, but he didn't want to panic her mother any further at this point.

"It may be that parolee," Jillian added, to the shock of Gregory and Margaret.

Parolee? Margaret mouthed.

Jillian continued. "I believe that this is all associated with that court case. Hang on, let me get the transcript." Jonathan handed it to her.

As she flipped through the document, Nick said to the room, "We need to get the picture of the recently released man—we saw the bulletin about him—what was his name? I need to get a fresh APB on him. Let's find his parole officer."

"If he's down here, it's obvious that his parole officer's not watching his/her charge closely," one of the other detectives chimed in ironically.

"True. But we need to notify his PO that we're interested in him and see if there's anything else we should know about the man. Where does he live? What does he drive? The original APB didn't include much, except that he had a relative in the area. Talk to the relative again—make sure there hasn't been any recent contact."

Ron called Marco and his partner and sent them over to Tatiana's home to question the landlord and any neighbors; they were glad to help because it took them away from their whining witness. The lieutenant also had approved the extra help. Ron added he would send over a recent photo to their phones.

Jillian found the information she was hunting for. "His name was Omar Atkins," she said.

"That's the guy!" With a quick phone call, Nick had the Omar mug shot on his phone, which he forwarded to Marco and the other detectives, who were heading over to the suspect's home.

"What else can we do?" Margaret asked. Patience was not a virtue she was familiar with.

"We have to wait," Nick replied solemnly. "While we wait, we need to discuss what you will say on the ransom call…"

"We will pay whatever they want!" Gregory said vehemently.

"Great. But you don't need to tell them that upfront." Ron nodded as Nick spoke. "We have handled a few kidnappings and taken classes on negotiating in these situations."

"OK. What do we need to do?"

Nick quickly listed some guidelines: don't accept the first offer, counter with a lower offer, and demand proof of life. If possible, get them to put Jamie on the phone. "You need to put the call on speaker, but we're going to remain silent, so they won't know we're here. I need a sheet of paper," he added.

The lead FBI agent agreed with Nick's plans.

While someone hurried to grab a sheet of paper, Gregory's phone rang. The officer in charge of the trace held Gregory off for an extra ring to ensure they had set everything up correctly, and then he waved him on. Nick and Ron stood nearby for support.

"Hello?" Gregory said.

"We have your daughter. We want two million dollars in diamonds by the end of the day," William said, speaking through a cloth placed over the phone's mouthpiece.

Nick motioned 'lower' to Gregory and scribbled 'one million' on the paper. "Two million in diamonds? I don't know if I can get that quickly. How about 1 million in cash?"

Negotiating? The ploy surprised William. "No, $2 million in diamonds, or you won't see your daughter again," he threatened.

Emboldened, Gregory repeated his counter. "I don't have access to diamonds. It would take me several days to get that. I don't want this to go on that long. Let me speak to my daughter…" Nick wrote "proof of life," and Gregory repeated the phrase.

William clenched the phone tightly and bowed his head. This was not going as he planned; Tatiana, who was listening to the call, frowned because she didn't know how to counter now. "She's at another location. We'll send you a picture. Get the money. We'll call you with a location for the drop." He disconnected and took the battery out of the phone. On TV, that seemed to keep the police from tracking a call, but what did he know? He and Tatiana drove back to the trailer.

Gregory exhaled shakily. Nick was impressed; the older man kept his cool and bravely negotiated the ransom down. He patted the man on the back encouragingly. Gregory nodded at the detective and sank to sit on the arm of the nearest chair. Margaret walked over and pulled him into a hug. Gregory relaxed against her for a moment and noted, "I have to contact our banker." One of the FBI agents accompanied him to a quieter corner of the room to make money arrangements.

The officer doing the trace got a cell tower but could not localize it further. The department dispatched several patrol cars to the area serving the cell tower to do a grid search looking for Omar, Tatiana, or Jamie. Using one of the screens the computer tech set up, Ron directed the grid search along with the sergeant on the scene. Unfortunately, there wasn't anything positive to relay back right away. Marco checked in with Ron with one interesting tidbit.

"Hey, we talked to the landlord over here. Last night, Tatiana's 'uncle' came to visit. It was a surprise," he said, walking towards his car.

Ron raised his eyebrows and gestured to Nick, putting the phone on speaker. "An uncle last night? Did we get a description?"

"It was rather generic—older white guy, graying hair, glasses, average build. What struck the landlord was the decided lack of happiness when Tatiana saw her uncle. And they both left early this morning."

A light bulb went off for Nick. "Are you still at the building, Marco?"

"Yeah, we just got in the car. We looked in Tatiana's apartment. There's nothing there. Why?"

"Go back to the landlord. I'm texting you a photo. See if this is the uncle." He pulled up the picture of William on his phone and sent it over. Marco acknowledged receipt and disconnected the call while he went to speak with the landlord again.

Ron looked at the picture Nick had sent and nodded. "The accomplice?" he asked.

Nick shrugged his shoulders. "Maybe. We knew he wanted to talk with Rachel. Tatiana probably knows him, too. This guy might be a part of the case they were involved in Wisconsin. He was from there, according to the valet's statement," he stated as they waited for Marco to return.

The phone rang with a breathless Marco on the other end. "Ok, I showed the photo to her. It's the same guy. Does that help?" He caught his breath. "I need to work out more," he added.

Nick and Ron thanked him, promised full details when things calmed down, and sent the image of William to the officers on the grid search.

Who is this? Where does he fit in this mess? Nick thought.

Jillian wished she smoked or something because she needed something to do with her hands. She walked over to Nick. "You seem to be awfully calm about this. I thought you were interested in my sister." She exhaled to gather herself.

Nick smiled and avoided her intention. “I’m doing my job. Emotions have no place in this type of situation.”

“Hmmm,” Jillian replied skeptically. “If you say so.”

42
Plot Implosion

With all the drama, the police tasked Jillian and Jonathan with keeping their mother sane, which was an unpleasant task. Margaret had turned into a woman her kids did not recognize. They had walked Margaret back to the elder Scotts' bedroom suite to lie down while the police and FBI worked to find Jamie. Standing out amid all the noise and activity seemed to increase Margaret's stress levels. She jumped at each beep or call, hoping that one would be the one that found Jamie. Her kids didn't think she could handle much more, but she refused any sedatives. She settled for a shot of bourbon.

Jillian had always liked the atmosphere of their parents' suite. Most people probably thought it would have been a tastefully decorated space with expensive furnishings and artwork. Refined and somewhat aloof—like the rest of the house. But the suite was very cozy and a shrine to their children. There was a section for trophies and certificates. But what Jillian loved most was the section of framed family pictures and a bookcase filled with photo albums. She never knew where her mother got some of the athletic pictures—she hadn't been at the games—but somehow, she had pictures of all their activities.

Probably paid someone, a little evil voice said in her ear as she settled her mother in her bed. But, at least, she had them, right? And there was an album with most of Jamie's modeling campaigns. Jamie didn't talk about its existence, but she knew their mother had it. Jonathan grabbed it from the shelf to look through it. As Margaret dozed off, Jillian and Jonathan looked at some of their older sister's famous photos. Hopefully, these memories would not be all they had left.

The proof of life glimpse was just that because Jamie was not allowed to speak; the kidnappers just texted a short video of her to Gregory's cell phone. Immediately, the computer tech and CSU team attempted to extract information from the video.

The kidnappers then texted the drop information. Nick and Ron coordinated with Gregory and the other officers on the location and safety measures.

The ransom drop itself was confusing to the officers. Nick had been involved with other kidnappings, but all of those seemed to be better thought out than this. The drop itself was in an awkward location that did not seem to offer hope of escape for the kidnappers—a parking lot at a mall. It just didn't seem logical at all. But that's the information he received, and they were running with it.

The kidnapping put research on hold, but Nick wanted to continue reading the files Jillian had gotten. He suspected that the answers to his questions might be in the transcripts.

Jamie attempted to communicate with Omar with no success. She was still perched awkwardly on the small bed where Marcus had left her. She hoped she might talk to Tatiana—at least she knew her, and hopefully, she wouldn't be as eager to kill her. *But she had seen their faces.*

The door to the trailer opened, and both Tatiana and William re-entered.

"We made the call, Omar. We requested diamonds, but that didn't work. Instead, we ended up with one million in cash. Someone needs to pick the money up," Tatiana cautiously noted as she parked herself down at the table. Omar eyed her and slowly rotated his chair to face her, pulling his earpieces out to better hear what she was saying.

"Could you repeat that? You asked for diamonds?" He tossed down his earbuds angrily. "Stupid! Glad you settled for actual money." He stood up and began walking in a tight circle next to the driver's seat. "I bet you want me to go retrieve the ransom—no, I bet I'm going to be the distraction, right?" He reached out and grabbed the woman by her arm; she mistakenly had not seated herself out of his reach this time. *Poor her.*

Tatiana stared at him wide-eyed. Omar could feel everyone else's eyes (minus Jamie) on him, so he backed off a bit. He let her go and took out his frustration on the side of the trailer; everyone inside jumped. William and Tatiana eyed each other anxiously, and Marcus slowly stood up.

Omar shook his head vehemently, pointing at Willian and Tatiana. "No, no, Uh-uh. I don't trust you two. I'm gonna leave now cuz I can't see this working out well. I'm not your fall guy! I'm out!" He threw the door open to stomp out of the trailer, as Tatiana and William watched him in amazement. However, he retrieved the keys from the ignition.

"Can't have you leave me in the park," he said, pocketing the keys. "Now, why don't you folks get your stuff together and get out of my trailer? I don't care what you do with her," he pointed back to Jamie, who was listening to the drama from her perch on the bed. Everyone looked back in her direction as if on cue.

Jamie had been trying to get her hands free but had no success. She could feel everyone staring at her and tried to adopt an innocent expression.

"This is a huge clusterfuck. I agree," William stated, trying to refocus the discussion. "But we need to get something out of it, right?" He glanced at Tatiana. "Hasn't he been punished enough?"

Tatiana nodded hopefully.

Looking back and forth at the incompetent kidnappers, Omar scoffed. "Fuck this! As I said, I *am out*. Get out of my trailer and take her with you."

Once outside the RV, he lit a cigarette—a habit he picked up in prison, sadly.

Tatiana watched him leave, and her heart dropped. "I know this was a spur-of-the-moment plan, but without him, it doesn't work," she murmured.

William agreed, placing his hand on her shoulder. "Let me talk to him," he replied and followed Omar out for a few minutes. Tatiana was left in the trailer with a confused Marcus and a trussed-up Jamie, who used this time to plead her case. She could see that things weren't going well for her here, as the plan to get money for her appeared to be collapsing. They might just kill her and leave her out in the woods. She cleared her throat.

"Tatiana? Are you still here?" Jamie asked tentatively.

Tatiana turned back toward her. Reluctantly, she answered, "Yeah, I'm here."

"Could I have some water? I'm so thirsty," she asked quietly. She briefly thought about Tatiana's penchant for dosing drinks, but desperate times, right? It couldn't get any worse.

Tatiana briefly considered her request. *Seems reasonable*, she thought. Tatiana searched in the small kitchen area of the RV for a bottle of water or a clean cup. The clean cup seemed like a distant hope, so she settled for a small water bottle. Without untying Jamie's hands, Tatiana opened the bottle and held it up to her lips so she could get a sip or two. After a few swallows, Jamie nodded and offered her thanks.

Tatiana brusquely ducked her head and stepped back a foot.

Jamie tried to assess her situation. "If he doesn't stay in, what's your plan?" she asked Tatiana softly before she could walk away. Marcus remained at the front of the bus; he couldn't hear the women's conversation.

Tatiana gave a thin, uncomfortable smile—which Jamie could not see—and stated simply, "I don't know."

"Why are you doing this?"

Tatiana lowered her eyes. "It's nothing personal," she noted. "I needed money quickly, and you're the only person I knew that could get it."

"What did you ask for? I have money myself—from my modeling days. Can I buy my way out?"

Tatiana paused and thought about that for a moment. That might not be bad—then a more sinister plan surfaced. Taking money from Jamie, letting her go, and getting out of the country could eliminate her problems. Thinking quickly, she considered her other options and contemplated cutting the men out of the money. That probably wouldn't work either. As she considered her options, she could hear the other two coming back in and arguing. She said quickly, "I'll think about it. Keep it between us." Tatiana hurried back to her original seat.

Jamie heard the ruckus, too. She appreciated Tatiana's answer but realized she couldn't completely trust her. *What were her options?* She thought as she tried to find a better position on the uncomfortable bed. She couldn't think of any other choices, so she would have to let this play out for now and stay alert.

Omar and William had almost come to blows before re-entering the small trailer. Fortunately, there were no RVs near them to hear the specifics of the argument. The other occupants in the park seemed used to this type of disturbance, so no one seemed to care.

"I brought you into this! It's an opportunity to make some money so you can live a better life! My way of apologizing for everything!" William shouted.

Omar had had enough and dismissed his co-conspirators. "This plan's stupid and just a poor plan and ridiculous. You don't even know how you're going to pick up the ransom! You expect me to trot out there and get clicked—like bait or something?" He plopped back into the driver's seat. "Not happening! I have enough on my soul already," he added, swallowing deeply. "Not adding her to my list of sins. If I go back to jail, it'll be on you." He pointed at Tatiana. "She hasn't never done nothing to me."

"We're almost there!" William shouted. He tried to grab Omar's arm, but he shook him off and started the ignition.

"Not my concern. I'm officially not in this anymore, and I want each of you to get out of my vehicle. Where am I dropping you?" Omar asked.

William added quietly, "I'll turn you in."

The young man whirled around and glared at him. There were a few moments of angry staring that Tatiana and Marcus watched uncomfortably. Omar broke eye contact first and said sadly, "You do that. It would be the first time I served time for something I did." He put the RV into reverse. "Where you wanna go?"

Jillian found Nick in the study, sitting with her father and another agent at the wooden desk in the corner. The Scott family banker was working to fulfill their request and would call back. Her mother was resting quietly in her bedroom. Jon was watching the agents in the living room, and she wanted an update on the situation. When she entered and bent down to kiss her father on the cheek, his cell phone rang, and he excused himself. For Nick, her appearance was perfect timing; he had questions for Jillian since she had already looked at the court transcripts.

Nick had a brainstorm while flipping through the transcript again. There was mention of the dead woman's father in the transcript, and a light bulb went off. Bianca's father…

.

"So, the older man that came to see Tatiana according to her landlady—do you think he might be the guy from the trial? Bianca's father?" Nick asked. "I'm not sure if you know, but he also spoke with Rachel before her death."

"I think he might be. William. I tried to google him, but I couldn't find anything specific. His name is William Wade—per the transcript."

"Well, with a name, I can find out who he is. Hang on…"

Nick got up and stuck his head out of the study to get Ron's attention. He updated Ron on the potential identity of the William character. Both detectives agreed to take separate avenues to track the man down. Nick would use the police and state computer systems to find him. To further investigate, Ron would make a few phone calls—his wife had spent some time working as an investigator for the district attorney's office. She had contacts in the DA offices in other cities that might help dig into the weeds of the previous case. He stepped away from the crowd.

While Ron spoke to his wife, Gregory completed the call from his banker. The same FBI agent sank into the chair across from the enormous desk. "We have a million dollars coming," the agent said to the room.

It wasn't a particularly comforting statement.

After 30 minutes of uncertainty, Ron ran back into the room. "Shit!" he exclaimed. "I didn't think you were right there. As you thought, his name is William, and he is Bianca's father. He was active during the trial and very outspoken about what should befall the young man. He also was close to Rachel and Tatiana, pushing the DA's office to put them on the stand." Ron also relayed a rumor about payments for testimony.

"If he gave them money, he didn't get his money's worth. Tatiana didn't testify, and Rachel was ineffective," Jillian noted.

"So, he probably wants his money," Nick suggested.

"Oh, one more thing," Ron added. "My contact says that despite the conviction, there was a significant contingent around the courthouse that believed the young man was innocent."

Everyone in the room gaped at him incredulously. "What?" Gregory repeated. "Innocent?"

"He had always said that someone gave him the drink," Ron continued. "The DA was focused on him, and, with William's persistence, the young man didn't stand a chance. But keep in mind, Rachel and Tatiana were biochemistry students."

Jillian let the words wash over her. She and her sister were right. This man spent time in jail for something he didn't do. *Not a happy man.* Then she became more frightened for her sister—these were a bunch of questionable people with shaky moral compasses. Jamie might end up in a dumpster.

Jillian's eyes teared up, and her heart fell into her shoes. She struggled to keep a calm demeanor because her father was in the room. She couldn't fall apart; he was just hanging on himself.

Nick could read her face. "She's going to be OK. We'll find her," he said in a low voice. But they both knew he was only being optimistic.

Jamie was silent as the kidnapping plot crumbled right in front of her blindfolded eyes. If it weren't so frightening, it would have been funny. Perhaps she would laugh about it with her family one day.

Her family. She had only been home for a few days. There were many things she wanted to say and do, and she was just getting started—working with her father, repairing her relationship with her mother. Then, she flashed to her daughter. She didn't hold her after she was born, but she got a quick peek.

Small, pale face with a shock of reddish-brown hair. She remembered the hair because she thought her daughter would be incredibly distinctive if she kept that coloring as she grew up. She wondered what her daughter looked like now and if she would even get the chance to find out.

This situation sucked.

I'm not going down without a fight, she thought fiercely.

The Scotts' banker rushed one million dollars in cash over to the house, and the police and FBI discussed strategies with the Scotts about the drop. That money request and delivery to the house took less than an hour—Nick was always surprised, in these types of cases, what money could do. The officers also planned to dispatch plainclothes officers to the area so they could apprehend the bagman—whomever it might be. Gregory insisted on being the one to drop the ransom. The rest of the Scott family remained at home. Nick and Ron remained behind as Tatiana would recognize them.

Gregory drove his car to the mall's parking lot and arrived a few minutes before the handoff time. But no one came to pick up the ransom. The officers searched the mall area and found no one suspicious or fitting any of the descriptions of the criminals. Gregory called home to relay the sad and scary news. Nick told him to return to the house to wait for further contact.

"Why haven't they called back?" Margaret asked when Jonathan came into the suite to update her on the situation. She had remained in bed for the time being. Jon couldn't give her an answer. No one could.

After two hours with no contact, the Scotts feared the worst.

The police officers believed the worst as well. They looked for rental cars and credit card activity linked to William Wade. But that had been unsuccessful, and otherwise, they had no leads.

At first, there was silence in the trailer after Omar's declaration. William then stood up and roughly pulled Tatiana toward the back of the trailer. She angrily jerked her arm away and glared at him. Then, the recriminations began.

"Now, what are we going to do?" Tatiana asked William quietly.

"How the hell should I know?" William snarled at her. "This was your idea."

"I didn't invite *him*; that was all you," she snapped back. "Besides, I suggested a wire transfer. But noooooo," she wagged her finger at him. "You didn't want to trust me, so here we are. Stuck with a kidnapee, but no way to get the ransom."

William looked away a little sheepishly. Maybe she had been right. At this point, it was moot. Now, the plan was to get clear and get out of town. Omar still played a large role in their immediate futures. Omar yelled again from the front of the RV, "*Where. Do. You. Want. To. Go*?"

"Well, since this has turned into a colossal fuck-up, we need to get out of here," William stated to the young woman. "Let me talk to Omar."

Tatiana warily watched William walk back to the front. While she couldn't hear them, the conversation seemed surprisingly low-key, considering the animosity that was rampant just a few minutes before. She cut her eyes back to Jamie, wishing she could ask the woman for some advice. *That* wasn't happening. Marcus refused to look at Tatiana. She was on her own.

William convinced Omar to take him to his rental home, with Tatiana following in the car. William could see her watching them and gestured for her to return to the front. Once she got there, William quickly relayed the new plan. Tatiana didn't like it, but what could she do? She left the RV and got into the car.

Omar drove the RV out of the lot without a word. William lowered himself across from Marcus without acknowledging Jamie's presence. With Omar driving and William across from him, Marcus was just hoping to get home—sex outside of marriage had lost all its appeal. The newly faithful man tried to be inconspicuous.

William hoped he could just grab his stuff at his home and go; Omar could go his own way, and Tatiana could figure out what to do with the hostage. With Omar's refusal to participate further, everything was truly fucked now.

Poor planning indeed...

As Omar drove, William fumed silently at the table. He didn't care about the others. He finally glanced back at Jamie, who was still sitting quietly on the bed. She was way more trouble than she was worth.

He couldn't wait to get away from this mess.

43

Evading Responsibility

On the other hand, Tatiana wanted this car ride to last forever. She slammed a baseball cap on her head to offer a small level of disguise as she trailed the motor home. She frequently checked the rear-view mirror for flashing lights. William dumped the mess—and a small-caliber revolver—into her lap, and she did not know what she was going to do next. She didn't want to kill Jamie. Perhaps she could just drop her off somewhere to buy some time.

Most of all, Tatiana was disappointed. She was going to have to leave Atlanta and this job. Her social life was minimal, with only her married boyfriend, who she would miss only because he was brilliant in the sack. But she had hoped that this city might be her last stop. She realized her cheeks were wet because she was blubbering about how she had destroyed a good thing.

She noticed the RV was leaving the freeway and had to scramble to get to the exit. A couple of drivers honked at her as she tried to reach the far right. Traffic was backing up as it neared rush hour; however, she made it across the lanes without causing an accident.

This was an unfamiliar part of town for Tatiana. After driving into an older neighborhood, the RV stopped in front of a small bungalow with a small Mini parked in front. Tatiana had to turn around at the end of the street to pull into the driveway. The three men were standing in front of the trailer, with William and Omar arguing again as she walked up.

"I don't care what you do—I'm leaving and forgetting that I even knew either of you. I advise both of you to get out of town," Omar said. "Don't call me. And make sure to delete my number."

William opened his mouth to reply and decided against it. He turned on his heel to enter the bungalow he rented under a false name and paid for in cash with the last of his retirement savings. The Mini was not in his name either. He could get out clean here.

That left Tatiana, Marcus, and Omar standing together.

Marcus recoiled from the other two. Tatiana reached for his hand, but he avoided her grasp.

Backing away from her, he stated, "I'm sure there's a convenience store somewhere. I didn't see *anything,* and I don't know *anything*." He took a deep breath and added, "Dealing with you has made me see how wrong cheating is."

Tatiana took a step toward Marcus but stopped short. The guilt was overwhelming, but any apology would ring hollow. This was supposed to be just fun.

"I don't know you anymore, either." Looking into her eyes, he remembered why he got sucked into this relationship. But looking around, he knew why he was out. "From now on, I'm a one-woman man," he added as he broke into a jog toward the street corner at the entrance of the neighborhood. It was a humbling and mind-resetting experience for him. He had learned his lesson, albeit the hard way.

Tatiana and Omar watched him go. She didn't believe he would be faithful, but she believed he would be *quiet*; she made no move to stop him. Omar considered his options, decided it would take too much effort to do something, and let Marcus escape.

Tatiana turned back to Omar, who gave her a withering glance.

"I don't know what to say," she started, but Omar cut her off.

"You are hell on any man who deals with you. I don't care what you have to say. Just get the girl out of my RV, and I'll disappear," he stated.

Tatiana looked around nervously. "I don't know what to do with her. She's going to tell the cops," she said timidly. "I hate to ask you…"

"Then don't ask. You're just a bad person—I already did time for your shit." He turned his back and walked back to his RV. "Get *away* from me."

She reluctantly followed him into the vehicle and stood in front of Jamie, removing her blindfold. Jamie kept her eyes straight ahead and refused to show any emotion. *If she's going to kill me, I'm not going to show any fear*, she thought.

Seeing no answers in Jamie's eyes, Tatiana reached over and struggled to help the taller woman stand on her feet. Jamie's hands and ankles were still tied.

"Do you expect her to walk like that?" Omar snarled. "I want you folks gone before the police figure out where we are!" He tapped his right toe in frustration.

Tatiana bent down to untie Jamie's legs, who, to her credit, stifled her inclination to kick the woman in the face. Once Jamie's legs were free, Tatiana nudged her toward the door, past Omar, and down the steps of the RV.

As she stood outside of the RV, Jamie considered the odds of success if she started running right now. Before she could act on that thought, Omar had already backed the RV up—they were barely out of the vehicle. Within moments, William came out of the bungalow's front door carrying a duffel bag.

"Why the hell are you still here?" William asked Tatiana, tossing his bag into the Mini. "I advise you to dump her somewhere and get out of the country. Like I said, I don't know you, and you don't know me."

While William was snapping at the two women, Omar turned the RV around to pull out of the neighborhood, barely missing the mailbox. William shook his fist at him while not ceasing his tirade; it would have been difficult to fix the mailbox on the fly. Fortunately, Omar missed, so he was out of here.

Tatiana tried lamely to get some help from him with the hostage, but William brusquely brushed her off, hopped into his car, and drove away from the house.

44
Play Stupid Games

Tatiana watched his retreating car for a moment and then turned back to Jamie, who was inching toward the corner of the house. Tatiana exhaled angrily and rushed over to Jamie, grabbing her arm, and a minor wrestling match ensued. Jamie tried to wrench her arm free, losing her balance. Tatiana pushed her back against the house. The jolt knocked the wind out of her; Jamie leaned over to catch her breath. Tatiana was winded as well, but she had extra courage—she lifted her shirt to show the gun tucked in her waistband. Jamie's eyes widened, and she obediently followed her captor back to the car. Opening the passenger door, Tatiana guided Jamie in.

"You see, I have a weapon, and I'll use it if you give me a hard time. I don't want to hurt you. Just work with me, and we'll get along just fine," she hissed before closing the door.

Jamie listened silently, trying to catch her breath. Tatiana entered the driver's side. As she started the ignition, Jamie quietly exhaled, which didn't go unnoticed by the driver.

"Sorry to involve you in this mess," Tatiana attempted to apologize as the car started moving.

She sounded sorry, but Jamie wasn't in the mood to let her off the hook. She needed to confront her kidnapper about this shitstorm, but she was incredibly thirsty. The stress of the last few minutes caused her to hyperventilate, making her dry mouth worse. Glancing around the car, she didn't see any unopened water bottles. *Damn!*

"Why did you do this?" Jamie croaked out. *Thirsty, thirsty, thirsty.*

Tatiana kept her eyes straight ahead. No answer would suffice.

Jamie tried again. "I'm thirsty. Do you have anything unopened to drink in this car?" Tatiana reached under her seat, pulled out a full bottle of water, and tossed it in Jamie's lap. After checking the cap seal—there was a nice pop as she turned the sealed cap—Jamie opened it with effort as her hands were still zip-tied and downed half of the bottle at one time.

"Thank you," she continued gratefully but still winded, then changed the subject. "What are you going to do with me now?" All the while, Jamie monitored the gun sitting on Tatiana's lap.

Tatiana headed back the way she came to get back on the freeway. "I was in trouble. I was desperate," she noted without looking at Jamie. "You were convenient."

Jamie didn't want to provoke her captor but couldn't help but note, "Speaking as a neophyte to kidnapping, this didn't seem well-planned."

Having her failings so pointedly identified by her hostage caused Tatiana's cheeks to redden. "I'm not a hardened criminal. This is *not* what I do. William asked for money, or he would send Omar after me. You know *he* killed Rachel. I was next. I had to do *something*." She got annoyed—*shouldn't Jamie be afraid of her?* Her tone changed slightly. "I'm a better planner than this," she stated as they headed out of Atlanta.

Jamie noticed the almost imperceptible change but tried to play along. "I would imagine you're a smart woman. I would still like to help you because some of this was self-defense," she said. She was still hoarse, but her mouth didn't feel like a desert anymore.

"Yeah, it was. But the initial incident wasn't," Tatiana tried to explain further. It was the least she could do. "Omar was the star football player and left a trail of broken hearts all over campus—mine included. It was a one- or two-month fling for him. But I guess I developed a thing for him. Following him around campus and stuff. Afterward, he acted as if he had never met me. Rachel and I—and Bianca—banded together because we were taking the same classes. We were the science chicks. We had breakfast together every week and scheduled our labs together. It was a fun time." The woman paused to get her bearings as she drove.

Tatiana's voice seemed to drift far away from Jamie during her explanation. Jamie struggled to concentrate and stay awake—*FUCK!* The damn water, she thought, pissed at herself. She drank a lot, but maybe if she fought hard, she could remain awake.

Tatiana continued to talk. "Rachel was always more adventurous in the chem lab and wanted to help me make Omar pay for dissing me. It was supposed to be a joke. We whipped up some GHB in the lab and dosed his drink at a house party. But we didn't tell Bianca because she wouldn't have approved. And she thought Omar was cute… we gave him the drink… and he immediately hit on Bianca and gave her his drink—being chivalrous and all…"

Jamie pinched her leg to force herself to stay awake.

"Bianca drank it all. He took her to the bedroom in the apartment for some private time. Omar passed out drunk as she lay dying." She paused and swallowed audibly. "We were scared. We didn't want to go to jail. I didn't think they would convict him. He was a *star*," she finished pitifully.

Jamie forced herself to speak. "But you were going to testify?"

Tatiana shook her head vehemently. "Not me! I took William's money, planning to rip him off. Rachel wanted to get out of it, but she kept her deal with William. She gave shit testimony, though—he didn't get his money's worth. But they convicted Omar. I had already dropped out of school and left town. I laid low for a few years—using some of the money he gave me—I still have some of it now. Then I saw Rachel had a job in Atlanta at a lab. I had hoped William wouldn't find me… I was wrong." Tatiana looked over at Jamie, who was struggling to stay focused. "Sorry about that. Just stop fighting. Everything'll be OK," she added.

Fully doubting Tatiana's last statement, Jamie allowed her to think that she had passed out by being quiet. She used the silence to search for an escape. Nothing particularly useful came to mind.

45
Win Stupid Prizes

After 30 minutes of tense driving, they pulled off the road next to a secluded wooded area just south of the city limits; it was getting dark. Tatiana turned the ignition off, looked over at the woman pretending to sleep in the passenger seat, and repeated, "As I said before, I'm a good planner. I made that GHB concoction myself. Sadly, since you didn't drink a lot of the water, this isn't going to be as easy as it could be."

"What do you mean?" Jamie asked innocently, opening her eyes. The tone of Tatiana's voice made her hair stand on end. The charade of being passed out was unnecessary now—time was of the essence now. She had been suspicious since Tatiana began spilling her guts that the woman was planning to kill her. She was woozy, but the churning adrenaline kept her from falling completely apart.

Tatiana pointed the gun at her and nudged her shoulder with it. "Get out. I have places to go." She had been aware that Jamie was still conscious.

Jamie weighed her options as well as she could. There was only one choice she could see.

Running. Into the woods. Blindly.

She would need a distraction to avoid being shot instantly; she wasn't sure about Tatiana's skills with a gun. *This is one time that flying by the seat of your pants might be of benefit,* she thought. Jamie carefully placed the water bottle on the console between them with the top loosened. "OK. Give me a minute—I'm loopy right now." She made a show of opening the door and struggling to get out, knocking the rest of the water onto Tatiana. At the same time, she jumped out of the car and ran.

The water bottle landed and spilled on Tatiana's lap, and she reacted as Jamie made her break. Tatiana silently cursed and scrambled to get out of the car. The area was dark and undeveloped. Jamie headed into the woods with her hands still tied in front of her. She was also fighting to keep her wits about her. The branches of the trees were catching her clothing and scratching her face; with her hands tied, she couldn't do much to protect herself from any of them. She didn't know where she was going but knew she had to get away.

Tatiana got to the edge of the wooded area and stopped, considering her options. *What the fuck was this?* she thought. For a moment, she allowed despair to creep in. She gave herself a mental head slap. She knew Jamie was smart and dogged, and she wasn't going to just allow herself to be killed without a fight. Now, what? What were her choices?

To search for Jamie in the woods in the dark, or just leave her out there? They were in an undeveloped area. It was dark, Tatiana did not have a flashlight suitable for this work, and the woman she was chasing was disoriented. Jamie might die out here with no help from her. It sounded like a better option and less messy from her point of view. Tatiana turned and went back to her car. She could still hear some rustling in the trees, but she couldn't identify where Jamie might be or how far she might have gotten. Leaving now was probably the best move.

Jamie stopped running and crouched behind a tree. She couldn't tell if Tatiana followed her—at least, she didn't see any flashlights or muzzle flashes. From where she was located, she couldn't see the car and couldn't tell if it was still there, either. Jamie leaned against the tree, closed her eyes, and took a few deep breaths. She was still fuzzy headed, but even she realized she couldn't stay out there for long. It was December, even if it wasn't ridiculously cold right now.

Tatiana might get her wish without any effort, Jamie thought. *I could die from exposure out here.* After a couple of deep breaths, she forced herself to stand up, using the tree as a brace. She could hear a few cars in the distance, but it was difficult to tell directions. She felt a wave of nausea mixed in with a wave of dizziness. Something slithered across her foot, which strengthened her resolve to get out of the woods.

Using her hands, she made her way toward the direction she assumed the vehicles' noise came from. The underbrush was dense, causing cuts and scratches through her jeans and shirt. After 10 steps, she almost fell on her face but caught a tree branch as she went down, cutting her palm. Pressing her injured hand against her thigh, she couldn't hear any more cars, as she disoriented regarding direction. Her fingers were also going numb from still being bound. Jamie paused and changed directions, hoping she would reach a road. Finally, she got closer to the edge of the forest; she saw headlights—*two* sets.

Shit, Jamie thought and stopped in her tracks. She crouched down to make herself inconspicuous in the underbrush and trees.

To her surprise, William and Tatiana were standing by William's car in the middle of an argument, but his car was further away from her than Tatiana's. They didn't see or hear her.

Jamie watched the scene from her place of cover. William must have followed them in his car and caught up with Tatiana before she could drive away. He appeared livid and wouldn't let Tatiana walk away. Both people raised their voices, but Jamie couldn't quite figure out what they were saying.

Jamie bit her lip as tears welled up in her eyes. Maybe they were going to come to find her in the woods. She was too tired, scared, dizzy, and nauseous to run again or even to put up much of a fight right now. This sucked… she was kind of missing the clinics in Africa right now… All she could do now was watch the scene unfold and keep her teeth from chattering too loudly.

Suddenly, Tatiana pulled her gun. William produced his own gun.

Lovely—maybe they'll shoot each other... Jamie thought.

William hadn't trusted Tatiana to do what was needed. After he drove away, he pulled over at the corner of the main street—out of sight from the house but with a good view of the cars entering and leaving the neighborhood. He then followed Tatiana and Jamie on the highway to their destination and pulled up just in time to see Jamie bolt for the woods and to see Tatiana make no effort to find her. After he leaped from his car to berate the surprised woman, Tatiana made excuses that simply made him irate. She—probably irrationally—walked over toward him and his car to plead her case.

As Tatiana neared William's car, she mentally prepared herself for the fight—possibly to the death—she knew was coming. She would not hunt Jamie down in the woods like a dog, and she knew William would insist. Only one of them could get their way. She intended it to be her, although she had never actually shot anyone before. But she had spent time in a gun range as part of her misspent childhood with her mother.

The pair bickered back and forth about who had fucked this situation up the most.

William wasn't backing down. If Tatiana wasn't going to find Jamie, he was. And Tatiana was going to pay for his effort.

"If I have to find her tonight, I am going to have two bodies to dispose of," William stated menacingly.

Tatiana gave him a look of barely suppressed disgust. She realized she was the only one of the two who had taken part in someone's death—albeit unintentionally. He didn't know how that felt. She had already been that irresponsible; William had only talked about it. She had had enough of him talking recklessly to her like she was some meek, stupid woman. Taking charge of the situation, Tatiana pulled her gun first, but he followed suit. They eyed each other warily.

"I am tired of your silliness. You are a mind-mannered father who worked in an office until he retired. You don't know me like that." She released the safety. "I am sorry about everything. I am. But I am not murdering a woman who has done nothing to you or me. Neither are you. We can get out clean *NOW*. But if you want to try me… You don't know me…" She hoped she sounded tougher than she felt.

Not wanting to be in the middle of two angry gun-toting folks, Jamie started sweating as she watched the situation escalate. She was steadily getting colder, and it was harder to keep her chattering teeth quiet—soon, it wouldn't matter much who won the argument. Tatiana's car was closest to her—about 15 yards away and was still running. The driver's side door was still open, too. If she crept over to it, she had a chance of getting in and driving away from this hellscape.

Her head was still slightly woozy, and her legs were getting numb from crouching. Adrenaline would have to be her friend. Moving almost at a crawl, she crept through the cover of the woods and underbrush. If either of the kidnappers had turned around, they would have seen her, as she was in the open. After a tense minute of inching along, with her muscles screaming and sweat beading on her forehead, she reached the trunk of the vehicle. Leaning against the trunk, she took several deep breaths, ecstatic that she had made it that far without being seen. The only good thing about her current situation was that she felt more alert. *Amazing what soul-crushing fear can do for you.*

Peeking around the trunk, Jamie could see the pair were still arguing with their guns drawn. Moving around to the driver's side could bring her into view of the people with guns, but the open door offered a little cover.

It's now or never! Jamie took a deep breath and slid along the side of the car. As fast as she could, she got into the seat, put the car in reverse, and put her foot on the gas. Jamie tried to close the door with her elbow as the car sped up. William and Tatiana both jumped when the car started moving. William got off a shot that hit the windshield on the passenger's side. Jamie backed onto the road and tried to get the car turned around in a three-point turn. Slowly. A big slow target.

I'm a sitting duck, she thought.

William landed a second shot into the rear passenger window. Jamie heard the third shot as she attempted to get the car back on the road. Looking in her rear-view mirror, she saw William crumple to the ground. Tatiana was standing behind the man with her arm extended. Jamie felt a jolt of gratitude, which was weird, and looked over her shoulder. She locked eyes with Tatiana at that moment, and the woman nodded at her to keep going. Jamie then turned her attention back to maintaining control of the car.

Accelerating away, Jamie frantically tried to find help. She glanced around inside the car to see if Tatiana had left her cellphone. There was a purse strap under the driver's side seat; she slid it out with her foot. Fortunately, the area was deserted at this hour because she wasn't staying steadily in one lane. *Being pulled over by the police would be a relief,* she thought as she tried to stay in her lane.

Her next challenge was getting the bag off the floor and into her lap; using her foot, she tried to get it up to one knee where she could hopefully grab it with both hands, which would mean they weren't on the steering wheel. It took a couple of tries, but she got it.

Placing the bag on her lap, she started pulling things out. A wig. A wallet. A case that she suspected held a diaphragm. *Ugh, what has my life come to?*

Tossing those items aside, Jamie tried unsuccessfully to dump the whole thing into her lap. She was about to stop the car reluctantly when she heard a beep (text message) from the bag's outside pocket. *Thank God!* Digging into the zipped section, she located a burner phone. Hands against the steering wheel, she shakily dialed her brother's number. She felt a little proud of her success—her hands were still bound.

Back at the house, Jon's phone rang. He had separated himself from the rest of the family and hid in his room because the mood downstairs varied from hysterical to almost morose. It was too painful to sit through. And watching his mother, who had finally taken something to calm her nerves, come back into the living room still wired was more than he could bear. Although he didn't recognize the number, he hoped it wasn't Rena. *If Jamie comes back, I swear I will do right by women*, he thought.

"Hello?" he stated absently.

"Jon? Jon!" Jamie yelled into the phone.

"Shit! Jamie? Are you OK? Where are you?" He jumped up, putting his phone on speaker and racing down the stairs. He almost became a casualty himself as he yelled at Jillian (the first person he saw), "It's Jamie! On the phone!"

Jillian ran out of the kitchen to the study to alert their parents and the police. Nick had been working the phones, but he quickly took control of the situation with Jillian's message.

Jamie still didn't know exactly where she was, but she was glad to hear her brother's voice. Jamie probably garbled whatever she had initially said to Jonathan. She located a street sign that could ID her location and babbled something about William getting shot.

Nick took over the conversation at that point and got patrol cars en route to her vicinity. Jamie didn't care—she just wanted to get home.

46
Gratitude

The phone woke Jamie up the next afternoon. It was Nick calling to tell her they found William dead a few miles from where they picked her up.

"We've run his prints. He was the father of the girl killed in Madison. Since then, he had been drifting from place to place until one year ago when he moved to Atlanta," he added. "He probably had been searching for Rachel and Tatiana with all the moves."

"Did you find Tatiana?" Jamie asked tentatively. While the woman helped her in the end, she figured she would be looking over her shoulder for some time to come.

"No, she left William's body and took his car. Unfortunately, we have little information on that car except for your vague description of it. There's no record of him renting or owning a Mini, so there's not much to go on. We have a BOLO out and are searching for the neighborhood where he lived before his death, but we don't have any solid information on that. We're also searching for the aliases he used for his house and car. If you remember anything new about the neighborhood, please let me know. No sign of Omar, either. We brought Marcus in for questioning, too." He paused and shifted his tone. "How are you? That was a lot of information all at once. Maybe I shouldn't have called you yet. Have you gotten any rest?"

She yawned and stretched without sitting up. "I haven't gotten out of bed yet. I could hear my family hovering around the door, though. They have been checking on me every couple of hours because of my concussion. What about you? Have you been to bed?" Jamie asked.

He smiled, which she could feel through the phone. "Nope! We still have work to do—with both Tatiana and Omar in the wind. Omar might be easier to find, and we have gotten some tips based on the description you gave of the RV. It shouldn't be too long. But Tatiana…"

Jamie eased herself upright in bed. "She'll be more difficult, right?" Without waiting for an answer, she changed the subject. "I can't believe I said anything of use last night. I only remember bits after the car ride out there."

"You were weird by the time we saw you. There were still some effects of the drugs Tatiana had given you in the water, but you were still helpful with information. You also had amnesia. When we found you, you were so desperate to talk, we just took notes. Some were gibberish, and some weren't. What can you do?" She could tell he was still smiling on the other end. "I also wanted to warn you about the press. The kidnapping plot leaked out; they want details, but you don't have to talk to them," he added.

"Thanks for the heads up." Jamie was curious. She suspected all this information had already been given to her family earlier in the morning. "Is that the only reason you called?"

He replied hesitantly. "That obvious? I just wanted to say hello. I'm really glad you're OK and back home."

"Me, too." She paused. "I distinctly remember that you offered me a meal of some type once this case was closed." Difficult to flirt with after a botched kidnapping, but she was willing to try it.

"That may be a possibility… I must get some sleep first, and you need to recover. We have time."

"That sounds good. By the way, do you know where my car is?"

Nick chuckled at the mention of her car. "It got towed in and is being evaluated by the lab. It was a crime scene. You can get it back in a few days. In fact, I'll drive it over to you. Does that work?"

Jamie smiled—her flirt game was still working despite almost dying. "Yes, that works. I'll treat you to a cup of coffee or a sandwich to thank you."

"It's a date. I'll reach out to you later," he concluded and ended the call.

Jamie laid back down. She hadn't planned to get up yet, but once she woke up, she couldn't fall back asleep—her head was throbbing, and she was mildly nauseous. Her mind was racing with the events of the previous day and night. She snuggled under the blankets and recounted what she could remember of the last 12 hours.

During her garbled call to Jon, she passed a small gas station and pulled into the parking lot, hitting a pole on the way in. She stumbled into the attached store and collapsed; the clerk was angry about the pole, but with one look at her, he helpfully took over from there. With his help, the police located her, and an ambulance loaded her in. They took her to a hospital for a check-up and forensic gathering and released her to her family. The doctors wanted to hold her for a day, but her parents made such a fuss and promised to look in on her, and the doctors gave in. Jamie didn't wake up when her family members came into her room during the night, but she sensed people were coming in and looking at her as she slept.

Apparently, she provided a statement about her ordeal and the shooting. Jamie had no memory of that or getting home. She vaguely remembered seeing her father and mother, then everything was blank until the phone woke her up. She was naked under the covers, and her arms, legs, and body had multiple scratches and cuts from her time in the woods. There was a large dressing on the hand that was cut by a branch. Did she get stitches? Why was she naked? Did she take a shower?

Impressive! she thought.

Getting out of bed, she located her clothing from yesterday in a pile in front of the shower stall. *Showering while half-alert—I must have been desperate to get the stench of yesterday off me.* As she passed the mirror, she noticed she had skipped her shower cap—she had gotten her hair wet. It had started to revert to its natural state. Pulling her hair into a messy ponytail, she pulled on a pair of jeans and a long-sleeved shirt and wandered downstairs to get something to settle her stomach.

Since Jillian's boys were still at the house, it was important to maintain a semblance of normalcy. Garcelle had gotten three of Jillian's boys up and dressed to go visit their friends; the youngest stayed with her. Jillian, while upset with Richard before the kidnapping, had called her husband in a panic while Jamie was missing. He returned to Atlanta on a redeye flight to support his wife. When Jamie got downstairs, the couple was sitting in the kitchen deep in conversation; Aaron was playing with a toy at their feet. Olivia had made a large batch of oatmeal for breakfast and warmed up some chili for the family members who wanted lunch. Gregory and Margaret went to the office to manage some details; they also thought Jamie wouldn't be awake before they returned. Jonathan checked in with his job, successfully ignoring several calls from Rena on the way. *A promise is a promise, right?*

Jamie greeted the couple at the table and started rifling through the cabinets for something gentle, like ginger tea. Her sister and brother-in-law stopped talking when she entered.

"Don't stop on my account," Jamie stated. Aaron toddled over to her and grabbed her legs as he tried to show her his toy. She scooped him up and made a show of examining the item intently for Aaron's considerable enjoyment.

Jillian said, "I can't believe you're up already. Do you want me to get you something to eat? Sit down—you have been through a horrific experience." She stood up to help her sister.

"Aha!" Still holding Aaron, Jamie pulled a box of ginger tea of indeterminate age out of the back of one cabinet. "I would love to still be asleep, but my stomach's upset. This," she held up the tea, "might help. Are Mother and Dad still here? I heard that the press is on the trail."

"No. Mother and Dad went to the lab today to play defense. Who told you about the press? They've called and parked outside already. They want to talk to you if you are up to it." Before Jamie could reply, Olivia appeared, took Aaron, directed Jamie to a chair, and started making the tea. Olivia also refilled Jillian's and Richard's coffee cups.

Richard chimed in. “It’s probably a bad idea to speak with the press. We don’t have to do anything yet. Just rest.”

“Since you are awake, are you interested in going to the lab with me? We can help Mother and Dad out,” Jillian asked.

Richard frowned at his wife. He mouthed to her under his breath: *didn’t I just tell Jamie to skip the press and rest?*

Jillian shrugged and mouthed back: *she’s going to say no.*

Jamie rolled her eyes. These two weren’t very stealthy at all.

She nestled into a chair across from Jillian. “I might as well. I need to understand what just happened to me. If they are investigating, I need to be there,” she said as she took a tentative sip from the ginger tea; hopefully, this would work for her tummy.

Jillian’s face fell as Richard leaned back triumphantly. Of course, he was right. “Sounds like a plan, I guess. So, how are you dealing?” he asked.

“I’m sure I am going to have to get into the details at some point, but right now, I feel like it was a dream. I know I should be traumatized—and that’s coming—but now I am just *happy* to be alive. You know, I spent four years trying to find myself. Not that my time was wasted, but I can’t do that anymore.”

“It sounds like you did some soul-searching. What did you come up with?” Jillian was curious.

“I have done lots of soul-searching in my life, but yesterday was probably the deepest I ever got. I figured out some things—I’ll tell you about ‘em later,” Jamie smiled and got up to go to her room, taking her tea with her. “What time are we leaving?”

Jillian frowned—she had hoped that her sister would have forgotten. “As soon as you get dressed.”

“Give me a few minutes!” she yelled from the stairs.

Richard shook his head. “You know your sister. Don’t give her the option.”

Jillian sipped her coffee and defeatedly replied, “Alright, alright. Don’t rub it in.”

47
A Final Note

Outside the gate of the house, there were a few members of the press hoping to get a soundbite or an actual photo. Gregory Scott was a well-known wealthy business owner in the community. A reported kidnapping of his physician daughter was big news in Atlanta. Jillian zipped right by them while shielding Jamie, causing a few to hurriedly get out of the way.

Jillian was correct about the press staking out the lab. When they drove up, the press was idling around the parking lot. The security guards were at their posts, and the lab itself was functioning at full strength, although the police were roaming around on the third floor. The guards kept the front doors locked to prevent any eager photographers from sneaking in. However, they couldn't—or didn't—chase them off the property completely. Once Jillian hit the parking lot, people yelling questions and snapping photos swarmed the car. After parking, Jillian and Jamie got out, smiled pleasantly, and entered the front door, refusing to answer questions or stop for pictures.

After a couple of stops to speak with employees and security, the women met up with their father, who was watching the police essentially dismantle Tatiana's desk on the third floor. He didn't look pleased to see his eldest, but he didn't comment. As they waited, Jamie leaned against the wall and logged into her email account on her tablet; she had transferred her tea to a travel cup before they left the house and continued to sip the warm liquid slowly to calm her stomach. There were several emails from both yesterday and today since she hadn't checked her account in over 24 hours; however, one, in particular, caught her attention—sent early this morning from a free Gmail address—with a title line of "Dr. Jamison Scott".

"Hey, look at this. This is weird," Jamie called over to her father and sister as she clicked on the email. After reading a few words, her mouth dropped open, which caused both to walk over to her. As they reached her side, she whispered, "I think it's from Tatiana."

Jillian gently took the tablet from her and read the message aloud to Jamie and their father.

"*Dear Dr. Scott,*

If you're reading this, you made it back home, and I'm back on the run. I have done some stupid things in my time, but this kidnap plan was the stupidest. After some thought, I recognized my error and sincerely offer my apologies. Things got incredibly out of control. The decisions I made were out of necessity, including shooting William. What is it—everyone's got a plan until they get hit?

But don't worry about me. I'll always keep moving forward—at least until they catch me. Take care of yourself and tell your father and mother thanks for giving me a chance.

I am sorry.
Tatiana."

Gregory read the email over his daughter's shoulder, and, with every word, he barely concealed his anger. *How could he have been so wrong about an employee?* However, before he could utter a word, a CSU investigator interrupted them and held out her hand for the tablet.

"Did I hear you right? Did you just receive an email from your kidnapper?" the investigator asked as Jillian handed her the phone; she started scrolling down the screen. "Thank you. I will take this to our computer experts. Dr. Scott, I hope you don't need this right now. Excuse me, Dr. Scott, are you ok?"

Jamie was still leaning against the wall, feeling herself being pulled back to yesterday. *Blindfolded on a smelly bed in an RV. A gun pressed into her side. Running through the woods.* She closed her eyes and took several deep breaths, trying to regain control. Her father gently nudged her, which jolted her back into the present, and the tech repeated her question. Jamie absently nodded; the woman placed the tablet in an evidence bag and walked back to the other investigators.

Gregory looked at his daughter, who still looked a little dazed. "Where are you, Jamison? Do you want some water?" he asked.

"No, Dad, I'm fine. My mind wandered for a bit, is all. I'm OK." *Lies...*

Gregory shook his head. Jillian tried to change the subject.

"Maybe they can use this to figure out where Tatiana is," Jillian said. Jamie wasn't sure it would be that easy to find Tatiana. She seemed to protect herself quite well.

Before Jamie could express her doubts, there was another flurry of activity with the photographers outside the lab's front door. The detectives, Nick and Ron, had returned to the building to check on the progress of the investigation. They also refused to speak to the press and came straight to the third floor. Nick's eyebrows raised when he saw Jamie—she looked great considering what had happened; she wore a fitted long-sleeved t-shirt, blue jeans, and a winter jacket. Jamie gave him a little smile, which made him a little weak in the knees, given what had happened the day before. He didn't have time to chat as the tech brought the tablet over to him immediately. Reluctantly, he broke eye contact and followed the tech over to the remains of Tatiana's desk.

Although it surprised Ron to see all three Scotts at the lab, he didn't follow his partner, as he had some news for the family. He walked over to the family.

"I was going to call you to let you know, but you're here. The Florida state police caught Omar in North Florida. He tried to dump the RV and steal another car and was caught by the state police," Ron stated as a technician came over to ask him a question. After answering, he continued, "We would like to extradite him back here, but it might be difficult. The car's owner was still in it—sleeping in the backseat when he drove away. Carjacking..."

Gregory exhaled. "At least one of those criminals is in custody!" he stated forcefully. Jillian and Jamie, again, looked at their soft-spoken father in shock and then at each other. Jillian shrugged and gave a slight head shake to prevent her from commenting, but Gregory saw it. "I see you two looking surprised. Can't a father get angry when someone kidnaps his daughter?" Gregory was still a little heated.

Silence from his daughters—with these responses, they didn't know what to say exactly. Ron wisely remained silent.

Nick had come back over to the group during Gregory's outburst and caught the last part of the comment. "Of course, it's understandable that you would be angry." To Ron, he continued, "You were telling them about Omar's capture? It's going to be complicated—now he has a carjacking charge in Florida, and the feds might want a piece of that. We believe he committed murder here in Atlanta. Now we only have to connect him to the crime," Nick added and addressed Jamie. "We know he was also a part of your kidnapping, but it may take a while to sort it out."

Jamie nodded. "I get it. It's OK." She smiled at him—more broadly this time, and Ron groaned as Nick blushed. Jamie frowned at Ron and continued, "Will I have to testify?"

"Unknown. So, don't worry," Nick added hastily. "One of the techs over there had a quick look at this email. There's not much there. It doesn't give us any clues to her location or her 'plans'."

Ron suggested thoughtfully, "Perhaps we can get something from the IP address where she sent it, or at least guess the general direction of her travels. You ended up with her car, so hopefully, there're some clues there. We have little information on the car William had."

"Now she has it," Jillian noted.

"I suspect she's going to be in disguise now. She had a wig in the purse that she left in her car. I think it'll be a while before you find her. She has some money and is good at living under the radar," Jamie replied.

Everyone agreed; Tatiana seemed to be a survivor.

48
Mom and Me

After two hours at the lab, Jamie had almost fallen asleep on her father's office table. The police finally left after giving a brief statement to the press with Gregory, who then chased the press off the property. Gregory then shooed his daughters out of the lab. By the time they arrived at their parents' home that evening, both women were goofy from lack of sleep.

The boys had returned to their grandparents' home and were all hyped up from their Christmas activities over the past two days. They hadn't gotten to tell Aunt Jamie about their fun yet, so they were disappointed to be put off for a while longer so they would not overwhelm their aunt. They didn't understand what had happened to Jamie, but they knew they needed to be nice to her and not jump all over her for a few days.

Richard was running an errand but planned to spend the night at the Scott house with his wife and sons.

Somehow, Jamie wandered into the house through the melee and into her bed with little memory of doing so.

Jamie slept soundly for three hours. She only woke up when her mother brought a tray of dinner to her.

"Good evening, dear," Margaret whispered. "I brought you a light dinner since it is so late. You need to keep up your strength. We have some grilled chicken, salad, rolls, and iced tea."

Jamie opened one eye. She was no longer nauseous, and the smell was enticing. She sat up, and Margaret placed the tray on her lap and perched tentatively at the end of the bed. Jamie dug into the meal with one eye on her mother.

"What's going on, Mother? Do you have something on your mind?" she asked in between bites.

Margaret took a deep breath. "I almost lost my eldest daughter yesterday. This highlighted the fact that you had been gone for a long time, and I was furious about how you left," she stated calmly.

"You wanted me to marry Eddie and have kids. He wasn't the right person for me. He's perfectly happy with his wife." Jamie stopped chewing and sat back against the headboard.

"That's not what that was about. You were—are—still angry about giving up your daughter. I don't understand it." Margaret fiddled with her hands. Jamie was stunned. Her mother was nervous! Margaret continued. "In New York, you were a mess—couldn't eat without being forced or looking for a toilet. You were pregnant by a drug-addicted photographer who ODed before you even knew you were pregnant. I had to save you!" she finished insistently.

"Perhaps I didn't need to keep the baby, but it should have been my choice," Jamie conceded quietly. "You walked in and found an adoptive family. I didn't get to have a say. Then you bribed me into going to college." Margaret opened her mouth to protest, but Jamie rolled on. This was the most honest they had ever been—they needed to finish it. "I went to med school because I was ashamed that I made such a mess of things in your eyes."

Margaret frowned at that. "What? I thought you enjoyed being a doctor?" she asked. "Is that why you quit? Because I made you go?" Margaret was indignant.

"Not like that, Mother. I do like being a doctor, but I found the noblest profession I could—outside of being a nun—to make you respect me again. Everything I did from age 17 until age 30 was to regain your respect—it was obvious I didn't have it anymore."

"What do you mean? Your siblings believe you are the favorite child. We have issues with both because they feel dwarfed by our relationship," Margaret dropped her head. "We must be a mess if all three children feel like no one loves them."

"I didn't say you didn't love me—I said you didn't respect me. There's a difference. You think I make poor decisions…and I do, too, but not how you think. From 17 to 30, I made decisions based on what I thought you would want. And since you were always second-guessing my choices, I just tried harder to please you. Things that I probably wouldn't have done on my own. I didn't want to do my residency in Atlanta—I wanted to go to Seattle. I knew you would hate that I let my perm grow out, and if I had been in Atlanta, you would have berated me until I put the perm back in. I woke up at age 30 with a guy I kind of loved who wanted me to stay at home with a gaggle of kids. Another decision I didn't want…"

"You can't blame me for the poor decisions you made," Margaret cut in, taking a deep breath. "But I realize that I may have continually brought up your mistakes. I guess I hadn't forgiven you for destroying the trust we had when we sent you to NY. It broke my heart to see what happened to you. You were broken, and I didn't want you to get broken again. I didn't think you could manage your own life—I didn't allow you to get past the original mistake." Margaret swallowed and clasped her hands together tightly. "Maybe I caused you to continue to make mistakes when I wouldn't let them go. I am sorry if I made you feel unable to do what you wanted. I am pretty pushy, aren't I?"

Jamie shrugged. "We needed to have this conversation before. I know my complaining about you not trusting me seems ironic considering the stupid decision I just survived through no actions of my own. Trust me; I learned my lesson there: stay out of other folks' business and leave it to the police. But really, I can take care of myself without falling flat on my face most of the time. I am almost 34. You didn't raise a complete fool, you know?"

"I know. But NY, I still don't get how… you were a level-headed girl," Margaret started.

"You just said it; I was a *girl*. I fell in love and had a lot of money. Things happen, unfortunate things, but not world-ending things."

"I was right about the baby," Margaret said with her arms crossed.

"Probably so. But I had to come to terms with that myself. I hadn't done the work for that until now. Besides, even if you were right, I shouldn't have done it just to please you. I needed to be sure I didn't want to raise her myself:

wrongheaded as it may have been. You have to accept that I may do things you don't like." Jamie took a sip of tea. "And I have to be OK with *my* choices."

"All of you do things I don't like. Jillian skipped law school to get married. Jon refuses to settle down and continually dates immature girls, and you go live in a war zone for four years." Margaret exhaled. "Only your father listens to me, and I *am* right most of the time."

"You might be," Jillian said from the doorway. "Maybe I should have gone on to law school. I think I'm going to fix that now." She came in and huddled down next to her mother. "You raised headstrong children. We have to find our way—even if you disapprove."

Margaret sighed. "Whatever. Don't expect me to hold my tongue. If I don't like something, I'm going to say so. Like that damn detective sniffing around you, Jamison. You need to steer clear."

Jamie snorted, and Jillian shook her head. "I think that's a long shot, Mother. Let's just see what happens," Jillian stated. Jon heard their voices from his room and entered Jamie's room.

"What am I missing? Is this only for girls?" he asked.

"Mother's trying to run our lives again," Jillian chimed in.

"Oh, is that all? Is she trying to fix someone up again? Remember Adrianne? She was so shy she couldn't even tell me her name?" he added, hugging his mother.

"None of you have the common sense that the good Lord gave a goose," Margaret laughed at herself for once.

"And if you think the detective is going to stay away, you're in for a tough ride, Mother," Jon grinned. The mood was almost giddy—a definite reaction to the stress and horror of yesterday.

Jamie felt she needed to defend herself against the (true) allegations. "This conversation started about me—what were you saying? It's not that deep—he thinks I'm attractive. But he's not that into me—not like *that*," Jamie protested weakly as her comments sounded stupid, even to her ears.

The other three Scotts said in unison, "Yes, he is."

At that moment, Gregory stuck his head in the door, followed by four little boys who poured into the room and jumped on their aunt's bed. Jillian had gotten them ready for bed before she entered Jamie's room; Gregory had read them a bedtime story, but everyone got sidetracked by the conversation and laughter coming out of Aunt Jamie's room.

"Boys, boys, don't be so rowdy. Auntie Jamison had a rough day yesterday," he said.

"That's OK, Dad. It sounds fine to me," she said, hugging her nephews. While she had not decided what she would do for a living yet, she knew she was exactly where she needed to be. During a time of hard decisions, she made the most important one—she was back home.

D. W. Brooks

Author, Physician, Kidney Transplant Survivor

I have always been an enthusiastic reader. Breakfast in my childhood home was a slow process, as I would read any object on the table—newspapers, cereal boxes, milk cartons, anything with inscriptions. Taking away my books was an effective punishment.

As part of this interest, my cousins and I created a neighborhood of preteen and teenage characters who had adventures and solved mysteries. We drew out this neighborhood, identified where everyone lived, and created character profiles for each one. We were well ahead of our time and wrote many unfinished stories, which ended up in the attic as we got older. After this failed experiment, I still nurtured thoughts of writing my own stories one day.

Becoming an author was an early dream pushed aside by practical thoughts and fears. Hence, I decided to take a more surefire route of going to medical school and residency. While I didn't write my own stories, I spent time writing in a medical and educational capacity.

A health crisis awakened the desire to write again. And with the ability to self-publish, I could see a path to getting my words and stories out of my head and into a bound book others could read and hopefully enjoy.

The author lives in Texas with her husband and children. She enjoys trying to stay in shape, sporadically cooking, reading (still), writing, and working on her blog. She is eternally grateful to the woman who donated a kidney to her over 5 years ago and continues to advocate for organ donation as much as she can.

To learn more about D. W. Brooks and future publications and events, visit https://authordwbrooks.com.

D. W. Brooks

Made in the USA
Monee, IL
17 October 2023

44693060R00261